REVENGE
OF THE
SCAPEGOAT

Other books by Arthur D. Colman

THE REVENGE, INC. SERIES

Cloud of Terns

NONFICTION

Up from Scapegoating:
Awakening Consciousness in Groups

REVENGE
OF THE
SCAPEGOAT

ARTHUR D. COLMAN

A novel in the psycho-thriller series
REVENGE, INC.

Colman House Publishing
Sausalito, California

Cover design by Jon W. Greenleaf
Book design by Dennis Gallagher/VisDesign.com
Book production by Bayside Bookworks
Editing by Elissa Rabellino/StyleInSites.com
Author photograph by Pilar Montero
Marketing and website by Karen Peterson/TheWordBiz.com

Revenge, Inc. is a division of Colman House Publishing.

Colman House Publishing
412 Napa Street
Sausalito, California 94965
www.revengeincthrillers.com

First printing, 2013
Printed in the United States of America
ISBN 978-0-9888055-0-7

Seven social sins:

Politics without principles
Wealth without work
Pleasure without conscience
Knowledge without character
Commerce without morality
Science without humanity
Worship without sacrifice

> —Mohandas K. Gandhi
> *Young India*
> October 22, 1925

Contents

CHAPTER 1

Darling, He's All Yours

HARVARD YARD, SUMMER 1990

DJ is 17, so self-conscious that she can almost see herself: cute white shorts and a tight crimson T-shirt, strolling seductively from Widener Library toward the steps of the university chapel. A year from now, she'll be packing her bags for here, or Yale, or her sure-thing backup, the University of Chicago. A year ago, she was just a kid playing lifeguard on a raised chair by the pool of her parents' tennis and swim club in Akron. But right now, she is doing just what she wants to do, which is stalking Harvard men on a lazy summer afternoon, and it doesn't get any better than this. She has her eye on one really cute guy, and he has to be at least a junior. She has been watching him for a week as he chats up girls in coffeehouses on the Square or at Lamont Library, and if he is not the absolute coolest guy on campus, he comes pretty close.

He keeps glancing her way; guys are always looking her over, but it doesn't mean a thing. She looks like a high school kid, so there's more looks than action, but she's feeling especially hot this afternoon, and maybe she is. Anyway, she is trying to act sexy, just like her mother, who never has to act at all. DJ is trying hard. Like she won't be lured away by the odd glance of a male on the prowl. She's trying to keep her focus on her current prey, who is especially delectable; something about his blond hair cut short, square face, and stocky body turns her on.

She is one of many high school juniors whose parents hope they can leverage college credit courses from Harvard Summer School to their college applications. Not that her parents' hopes matter. What matters is that they come up with the $7,500 for tuition, room, and board that

1

a summer semester here costs. DJ desperately needs to leave home in a year, and she is also passionate about getting a great education. Her mom, who envies her ambition, would like to stop her. But DJ knows she can't, because DJ has the grades and extracurriculars to go anywhere, and her junior SATs were off the scale. She's planning to win first prize at the Ohio Science Fair and maybe go all the way at the Intel fair, and then she'll get to shake hands with President Bush, and that will ensure her place at any school she wants.

These are good thoughts, but she determinedly puts them aside to stay focused on this particular Harvard guy, who isn't a wannabe like her and her classmates in summer school but someone who has already made the cut. And right now *he* is watching her from his comfortable perch, propped up on one shoulder on the grass near the old iron statue of John Harvard. The guy is totally self-assured, reminding her of a lazy lizard ready to unroll his tongue and catch the next delicate, moist fly coming his way. She is ready to be caught, well coached in the game of pretty coed, trying out her young wares in the '90s market of summer students, who definitely wants to date a bona fide Harvard man.

Sex is a given at 17, and it's no big deal if that's what he wants, and he will. She's done it with high school classmates—with mixed results, as far as she's concerned. She hopes it will get better, more like her fantasies of the way it's supposed to be. She'd like to tell her friends back in Akron that she's slept with an upperclassman at Harvard. But what really matters to her is getting romantic e-mails in the fall to pine over when she is feeling stifled in her senior year of high school. Or being invited for a house party or Harvard football game. Or, in her wildest daydreams yet, being visited over Thanksgiving or Christmas by a college guy. Sure, she wants him to look good—her lizard up ahead is just right—but mostly she wants to feel more like a woman in a family that treats her like a child. With the kind of mother she has, she knows that will take a guy of her own.

She halts her walk at his feet and looks down. "You were watching me," she says. She eyes him with what she hopes is an alluring look.

"You wanted to be watched. I could tell."

"Still, you were watching me."

"Why not? You're adorable. My name's Carl, by the way."

2

"DJ."

He unwinds from his lazy pose and sits up on the grass. "Well, how about some iced tea, DJ? Then we can watch each other."

He takes her to a place on the Square that's perfect and orders both of them iced tea. He talks about himself. That's fine; she's a little nervous. Anyway, she's been taught how important it is to listen to guys.

He has just finished his junior year. He lives in Adams House. He is planning to go to business school when he graduates, probably Harvard Business School for the contacts and convenience. He wants to make a lot of money when he gets out. He grew up in New Paltz, a small town in upstate New York where his dad owns the local dry cleaners. He likes Harvard, but it's not like he was real eager to get in. Colgate or Syracuse would have done just fine, but his parents wanted the status they would get from having a son at Harvard. There wasn't enough money without a scholarship, so he applied just in case. What with being smart enough, senior class president, and a quarterback at Kingston High, he filled one of those rural public high school niches that Admissions wanted for breadth in the class of '88. He got a big athletic scholarship. He put in time playing JV football his first year, but he didn't make the varsity cut and now plays first doubles on the tennis team, which he likes a lot better. To make do financially, he works half-time for a big perfume company during the school year. His territory is women's schools around Boston, and he likes selling to coeds for obvious reasons. He is full time over the summer but already way over his quota, and so he is taking an afternoon off, which is why he is here with her today.

He pauses and looks embarrassed. She nods happily. "So, how do you like Harvard Summer High?" he asks, suddenly aware of his extended monologue.

She leans close and looks into his eyes. "So you think I'm a high school student?" She drawls the question in her best Harvardian.

"DJ. C'mon. I *know* you're a high school student," he drawls back. "How old are you, anyway?"

"Seventeen," she admits. "I'll be a senior when I go back home."

"Well, that makes you dangerous. I'm 20. Three years' difference means no Romeo-Juliet clause for me if we, well, get it on."

She is trying to imitate his mood. "My father might be a bigger danger

3

than the law. He's very possessive and worries a lot about his little girl."

"Your mother doesn't care?"

DJ frowns. She doesn't answer but continues to look into his eyes.

He nods. "Your mother's a problem, DJ?"

"Yes," she admits. "Sometimes."

"But she's not here, is she?" He laughs. "At least not at our table." He smiles and cocks his head, obviously happy with his comment. "So tell me—why does she worry you?"

She badly wants to tell him the whole horrible story about Mom's men. She's already more at home with him than with other guys she's met this summer, the ones who talk about radical politics, the joys of mind-expanding drugs, and the wild parties she *must* try out with them. She feels he might understand and doubts that there's any danger of making trouble for her family. She appraises Carl through the lens of her parents and their wealthy suburban culture, and he comes off well. They are arriving in a week to see her and take her home by way of Bermuda. She'd love to have a boyfriend whom she could invite to dinner. It would make their visit more bearable. But he has to know the scene.

She takes a deep breath. "See, Mom is always angry—sometimes at me but mostly at Dad. He's very successful and is away a lot. I guess she has lots of reasons for being pissed off." She stops, gathering courage. "I don't blame her, except what she does when he's away really bothers me."

"Which is?"

She feels a catch in her throat and a knot in her stomach. "This is hard." A blush rises up her chest and across her face. She crosses her legs and doggedly continues. "She invites men over. There. I've never said that out loud. You're the first, Carl."

He nods his appreciation and waits.

"It can be anybody—a deliveryman, a neighbor, and sometimes even Daddy's best friends. I go upstairs when they begin drinking and put in earplugs. They get pretty loud, and it's horrible to hear their sex noises. At least the guys never bother me, and they always leave before I'm up the next morning. I guess Mom thinks it's the least she can do."

"That sucks." He puts his hand over hers.

His hand feels nice. "It's like any man who comes to the house when

Daddy is away is fair game. This may seem stupid and unrelated to you, but I don't feel comfortable bringing guys home after a date." Her voice catches again, and she dabs at the tears running down her cheeks. He moves toward her, and she breaks down completely. She wants to flee, but he's holding her hand and shoulders tightly, and she can see that he's concerned. She puts her head on the table and sobs. When she calms down, he's still there holding her hand, with another arm laid gently across her back.

He pays the bill. She gets up quickly, feeling like a fool. "So I'll see you around."

He reaches for her. "It's OK, DJ. Let's take a walk."

He puts his arm around her, and they wend their way through the small streets between the Lowell, Winthrop, and Leverett houses and across Memorial Drive to the Charles River. The sunlight on the water shows the ripples of an occasional scull and a few sailboats taking in the light breeze. The grassy banks along the river are filled with joggers and strolling couples. Carl is with her all the way to MIT and back. The tears helped, and she talks easily—tells him about wanting to be a musician or scientist and how hard it is to be smart and also attract boys. He chuckles and says he doesn't know about that. When she laughs, he turns serious and says he can already see that she's a lot smarter than he. Then he confesses that many of his women classmates won't even go out with him because he talks about business and finance rather than medicine or law and isn't an intellectual like them.

They sit on a bench near where they started. The sun is setting on the water. "I like you, DJ." She waits for him to kiss her, but he just holds her close. She swallows hard and asks to see his room at Adams. He looks at her and frowns. "My roommates are away for the summer. You'll be alone with me, and you know where that could lead."

She feels wet between her legs and looks down at her shorts for blood, though she knows it's not time for her period. His pants are tented, and she wonders if he will look like her father. Surely not like the guys she's been with so far. Their eyes meet, and he takes a deep breath and lets it out with a little shiver.

She kisses his ear, hoping he will not be disappointed by her body and lack of experience.

By the end of the semester, they are seeing each other every day, and they spend hours making love in his room. Surprisingly, she loves the sex and amazes herself with what she is willing to give and take. When after a particularly long and gymnastic night in bed he calls her a great lover and "sexually voracious," she tells him that it's because of him, but he puts his hands on her thighs and slowly caresses her body all the way to her face. Then he gives her a thumbs-up. She knows he's right; it's like finding a new hidden part of herself with a high IQ all its own. She tells him she's in love, and he doesn't laugh.

When her parents come to drive her home, she does the unimaginable and invites Carl to dinner at the Parker House the day they arrive. She stays with him every moment, waiting for her mother's call. She hears the sharp intake of breath on the other end of the line when she mentions bringing a boyfriend along, and all of a sudden she is afraid. The dinner goes well, but her fear continues when Carl brings her back to his room afterward. For the first time, she is sure that her lovemaking bores him.

The next day, she leaves on vacation with her folks. She and Carl exchange a few e-mails but don't correspond regularly, as she had hoped, so she's surprised when two months later he accepts her invitation to Akron for Thanksgiving.

* * *

Carl rings the doorbell at the Case mansion. DJ's mother greets him at the door.

"It's good to see you again. DJ is really excited about your coming for Thanksgiving, and so am I." She stands back, sizing him up, before giving him a long, close hug. "You're going to like it here."

Carl untangles himself from her embrace and waits, feeling disoriented and aroused by the unexpected intimacy.

She smiles at his disquiet and again looks him over from head to foot with a knowing smile. "Don't worry," she tells him. "DJ will be back in just a few hours. She was planning to meet you, but just this morning she got it into her head to do a little shopping. I think she wanted to surprise you with some new clothes that fit her figure better." She smiles again. "She's quite grown-up. You know what I mean because you were part of it. She's more woman ever since Cambridge, and now she wants to look the part. She said you'd understand."

He doesn't. "Why would she do that, Mrs. Case?"

"Please call me Veronica, Carl." She stands closer and gently touches his forearm. "DJ can be difficult with her boyfriends, particularly those she's sleeping with." She pauses to give her words emphasis. "I'll show you around. Leave your bag at the door. Then we'll get you settled in your room. After that, some lunch." She takes his hand. "My afternoon's free until DJ gets back, and then I'm off to the club. Mr. Case is away for the weekend, so you two will have the house to yourselves this evening." She looks up at him. "In the meantime, I'm your hostess. Maybe she's already told you that I love to get to know her friends."

The rooms on the bottom floor are richly decorated; the kitchen is the best equipped he has ever seen.

"Grab your bag," she tells Carl when they finish the downstairs tour. He follows her up the circular staircase, which looks as if it has been re-assembled from a French castle. She is wearing a short tennis skirt and a white T-shirt. It is impossible to ignore what her tiny panties reveal.

"I'm giving you our best guest room. DJ's is directly across the hall."

She takes his hand as they enter a small suite with a bedroom, bathroom, and sitting room. "Come look at the view." She walks him through to the bedroom. They stand at the window, which overlooks several acres of gardens that front on a river.

"Does the land belong to you, Mrs. Case?" he asks.

"Veronica! Yes, it's all ours."

"DJ told me she lives in a suburb."

"I'm afraid DJ takes all this for granted." She tosses her head in displeasure. "No matter what I say, I can't get her to see that she is a spoiled princess."

"She wasn't that way this summer, Mrs. Case."

"Please, Carl. Veronica. 'Mrs. Case' makes me feel like I belong to someone else." She moves closer to his side until their bodies touch. "My daughter is extremely smart and can fool people."

He moves away.

"Don't be afraid of me, Carl," she said with a little smile. "I'm not going to hurt you." She goes on talking. "Anyway, I was born relatively poor, but I had what it took to marry Hamilton Case." She twists her body toward him to show off her figure.

"You met him back in Boston, so you got the picture. He's what we in Akron call a Midwestern blueblood. The Cases have owned rubber factories here for several generations. They made a fortune in World War II, and it's grown ever since. Hamilton is clever and has continued to do very well, even after his father died."

"I never thought of Akron as a wealthy place, Veronica," Carl says her name shyly.

"It is for a lucky few. There's a good deal of poverty here and a large black population, although they're mostly working class, union people. The bottom of the barrel is what Hamilton calls white trash. My parents qualified, by the way. Hamilton sees himself and his friends as their benefactors. He gives them 'charity' at holidays. There are a lot of mothers on welfare, and unemployment is high. There's also the new Latino population coming in from Mexico. Good people. They keep the gardens in very good shape, don't you think?"

"I guess so. It looks like a public park."

"What a nice way to put it, Carl," she says wryly. "I'd rather you said Versailles, but I know what you mean."

She moves away, showing him around the room. "This is a walk-in closet. There's a king-size bed under all the comforters. Fun to sleep in." She points to a polished oak armoire. "That holds a TV and great sound system. In the sitting room there's a duplicate of this one and also a word processor if you need one. The new password is 'Carl.' Spelled with a 'C.' I think that's right."

All he can do is stare and nod.

"We change it for each of our guests. And we've had some very special ones right here. Hamilton is a big contributor to state and national politicians and the local arts. Musicians often stay here when they perform at the Cleveland Orchestra. We are big supporters. Hamilton's the president of its board."

She opens the door to the bathroom, twice as large as his room in Adams, and shows him how to work the huge whirlpool and eight-nozzle spa-style shower. He can barely contain his body as she leans over the tub.

"This is great," he says, sounding idiotic to himself. "This is far more than I expected." He tries to change where this seems to be heading. "I'm from a working-class family myself and live pretty simply at college."

"But you don't plan to do that forever."

"No," Carl says, "but I have a way to go."

"I don't think it will be as long as you think. Anyway, you might as well learn how the rich live. It didn't take me long to learn to love it."

She brushes past him as they leave the bathroom and walk to the front door of the suite. "Get unpacked and take a shower," she orders, hands on hips. "Wash away the travel."

She lets a moment pass, watching him. "Do you jog? DJ says you're quite an athlete, and you certainly look it."

"Thanks," he mumbles.

"I'm planning to take a run before lunch. As you could see from the window, our land is adjacent to the Akron River, which has quite a beautiful running path."

"Will DJ be back before we finish? I want to be here when she gets home."

"Yes, of course, and you will. I know my daughter. Once she gets into shopping, she'll do it until the stores close at about five. Please don't blame her. I told you that she's nervous at seeing you again, and she wants to look good for you, and … well, even I can understand that."

"Will I be able to keep up with you, Veronica?" Carl says, trying for a casual irony.

She laughs. "Oh, I hope so, Carl. I dearly hope so. I'll just slip on my running shorts and wait for you downstairs."

They run together for an hour. When they return, she makes him lunch, which includes sharing a bottle of red wine. "A very good Burgundy," she says. Then she points him to the living room and a large sofa. There is a Steinway grand in the middle of the room.

"I usually play for my guests after I feed them. The Romantics: Shubert, Rachmaninoff, Brahms, Liszt. Piano is my great love; it's where DJ got her musical talent. She's a pretty good clarinetist, you know. Her As at school come from Hamilton, but he is tone-deaf."

She sits and slowly finishes her glass of wine, and then settles herself at the piano. Carl lies back on the sofa and listens. Her playing is exquisite. He closes his eyes. The wine, the music, the opulence of the setting, all blend together. When the music ends, he is completely relaxed. He feels her sit beside him, touching his knee, but doesn't open his eyes or move. He feels her breath, and when he opens his eyes, her face is very close. She leans over and kisses his lips. He can't help kissing her back.

"DJ?" he moans as she brushes his lips over and over with her tongue.

"Easy. I'm certain she won't be back for a while."

She kisses him again, harder, and with lots more tongue and teeth, and then, wasting no time, has him out of his jogging shorts and underpants before he can resist. She holds them up like trophies and brings them to her chest. "Still wet from the run. Good—I like the smell of a healthy man." There is no stopping her from getting what she wants. Which is everything he has.

Much later, he lies next to her in an incapacitating post-sexual haze, but his eyes snap open at the sound of the outside door closing. Before he can move, he sees DJ enter the room, laden with packages. She looks at them naked on the sofa and freezes.

Veronica eyes her daughter and then leans down and lazily kisses the blond hair on the ridges of Carl's lower belly. Still watching DJ, she burrows deeper into his groin and then smiles up at her. "Don't worry. If you still want him, darling, he's all yours."

CHAPTER 2

An Accomplished Woman

Dave stood on the deck of the barge that housed Revenge, Inc., and watched the new client shakily approach on the worn floating pier. She was an attractive brunette, dressed expensively in leather pants and jacket. She looked to be in her mid-30s but could have been younger. She was clearly ill at ease—no sea legs on the movable dock or just plain anxiety, he couldn't tell. With the precision and grace of a gymnast, he grasped the rail and vaulted to the pier 15 feet below, and then walked out to meet her.

"Dave Blue at your service." He offered his hand, and she shook it timidly.

"That was quite a move," she said. "May I ask how tall you are?"

"Six feet five inches plus sneakers."

"And you work for Revenge, Inc.?"

"A partner, actually. You here to see Wiley?"

"Wiley Stone. Yes. My name is Debra Jean Lieberman."

"We've been expecting you. Follow me." He walked back the way he had come. "Our office is dead ahead," he said over his shoulder. She was already walking with more confidence. "It's the last boat, that bright yellow one." He stopped and admired it. "What do you think?"

"Lovely, especially in this wonderful setting. All these different boats—I'll bet 50 years of history are represented here."

"The culture of Sausalito," Dave exclaimed, appreciating her enthusiasm. As he led the way, he pointed out the old sailboats and small yachts to their left and right with a running commentary.

"These are mostly live-ins: old hippies, boat people, and divorcées

11

looking for their next partner. The farther out we go, the better the view and the more expensive the boat." He pointed 100 yards ahead. "Look at that yacht at the end of the dock next to where our barge is moored. Huge, isn't she? But very high-tech and seaworthy. We're getting a lot of these docking in Sausalito. That one's from Singapore. It comes equipped with a helicopter."

"And I'll bet they're horrified by your quaint yellow barge sitting among them."

"You're quite right about that. The Asian mogul who owns this particular boat actually tried to hassle us a bit. Sent two of his deckhands over to our barge. Wiley caught them smoking on our deck. One guy had a knife, so Wiley put an elbow in his ear. Hard. When the other tried to help his mate … well, they're both still recovering in Marin General. I didn't see the fight, but I wish I had. Wiley rarely needs to do much more than stand up. You'll understand when you meet him."

"Am I in danger?" she asked with mock apprehension.

"Wiley's tame."

"What about the Asian mogul?"

"No problem. He came over to apologize, but Wiley wouldn't let him on board."

"And doesn't he want revenge?" Debra Jean said with a smile.

Dave laughed. "Touché." She was getting more interesting.

"And if someone like that came to you … for help?"

"We're not thugs or hit men, if that's what you mean."

"I wonder if you'll take me on," Debra Jean said thoughtfully as they stood staring up at the barge. "What a beautiful office," she said in frank admiration. "It's really quite homey—it hardly looks like a structure connected to revenge."

"Would you feel more comfortable in a sleek black vessel with a mermaid on the prow holding a long bloody spear?" Dave switched to a slow poetic drawl. "But then what is the shape of revenge? What are her vital statistics? Revenge can be sinister, ugly, or outrageously beautiful. She can provide the release of violence or the balm of hope."

He returned to his matter-of-fact voice. "The office is a barge. The hull sits on a giant rectangle of concrete. Did you know that most concrete can float?"

"Of course." Her voice took on an air of authority. "The infusion of air into the chemical mix makes it lighter than water. That's why it's such a good building material."

"I forgot you're a scientist. Most people don't understand that about concrete."

"And where did you learn, Dave?"

"Wiley and I are both trained as engineers, and I've studied a little architecture. We like to think of Revenge, Inc., as an organization that helps build structures to focus emotions."

"Am I supposed to understand that?" Debra Jean said.

"No. But are you ready to try?"

"Yes." She smiled again.

"Then welcome aboard," Dave said and held out his hand to lead her across the small bridge to the barge.

Wiley was waiting on the top deck, watching his favorite blue heron hunt from its perch on the edge of the pier. He held out his hand to Debra Jean. "Wiley Stone."

"Debra Jean Lieberman," she said, peering up at him and watching her hand disappear in his. "Damn, how tall are you?"

"Six-foot-seven."

"And still growing," Dave added with a malicious grin. "What can I get you—coffee, soda, water?"

"Nothing right now, but thanks."

The three sat at a deck table in a semicircle facing the water. Wiley placed Debra Jean in a comfortable seat with the best view.

"How was your trip from Walnut Creek?"

"Traffic and freeways! But now I am here, and here is beautiful. I love your barge."

"I'm glad you feel that way."

"We see it as a cross between a stage set for Agatha Christie and a location for Dashiell Hammett," Dave added.

She sat back in her chair and turned from the water to look at Wiley. He was huge and perfectly proportioned, with Midwestern good looks. Almost reflexively, she smoothed her hair down on her shoulders and lowered her eyes. "Why did you choose this place?"

"It chose me. I bought it right after I came out here. After growing up in the Midwest, Sausalito felt like living a vacation. I live on this boat now. I like the idea of sleeping on a mattress of saltwater and working where I live. It's a good location for what Dave and I do."

"Is being out here instead of in San Francisco good for business?" Debra Jean asked.

"It's served us well so far. Sausalito's location is conducive to private projects and confidentiality. Being on the water makes it harder to approach us without our knowing. Sometimes people don't like what we do."

"Dave made it sound more poetic," she remarked.

"Then you're getting to know the difference between us," Wiley said. "I'm the pragmatist; he's the artiste. And together we like to think we get the job done with style."

"Well said, Wiley," Dave murmured. "We are like that duet in Bizet's *The Pearl Fishers*—two men serving the Great Mother of Revenge."

"He's not a showoff, Debra Jean. Just knows about everything," Wiley said.

"Impressive." She turned to Dave with a grin. "I like literate men and I love opera."

"You'll like Dave," Wiley said. Then, his tone becoming more businesslike, he said, "So you are looking for help. Right now, we need to know what kind of help you want."

She looked down at the table. "I'm not sure."

"Take your time," Wiley offered. "If it were easy, you'd have handled it without us."

She sat straight up in the chair. "Before telling you my story, I'd like to have some assurance that you will take me on."

Wiley appraised his prospective client. Pretty and poised, he thought, but her eyes showed strain, and her facial muscles were almost rigid. He could feel the tension in her body. "You know that's impossible."

"Wiley means that without information, we can't give you assurances," Dave said, looking to the dark clouds coming in from the western headlands. "We'll have to hear enough to make up our minds."

Wiley nodded toward Dave and then turned back to her and shrugged. "Look. Everyone is nervous when they first come here. But you've gotten through the hard part, which is showing up. Here's an idea: We stay on the deck and watch the clouds come in, and we tell you about our fee structure and general policies. Then, as it begins to rain, we all retire to the living room and you tell us why you're here."

She looked at the blue heron, beginning to stir now and staring intently at the blue-green water. "That bird. No indecision there."

"Especially when he's hungry," Wiley said. "Otherwise, he takes his time. I take that as a yes to our compromise. We charge $3,000 a day plus expenses and travel. There's a sliding scale if you need it."

"My father was a rich man, and when he died six months ago, he left half of his assets to me and the other half to my mother. I've got the financial resources to afford you for as long as it takes."

"Not as shy about your money, are you?" Dave said.

"I loved him," she said angrily. "And I never wanted Daddy's money. I've always been on my own, and he liked that. … So I bare my soul, and you leave me dangling until you decide."

"That's the deal."

She looked out at the water for a few moments. "Some of it is embarrassing."

"But embarrassment isn't the whole problem, is it?" Dave ventured. "Something else is bothering you."

"Yes. There's trusting you guys."

"Take your time, Debra Jean," Wiley said gently. "The rain is still in the sky."

"Giving you a breather," Dave echoed. "Once you begin, it's hard to stop." Wiley was right. Pushing too hard wasn't going to help.

She nodded abstractedly, looking up at the sky and then at the water again, anywhere but their eyes.

"Look, Debra Jean," Wiley said, leaning back in his chair, "not every situation requires revenge. Just coming here and deciding not to go ahead can be enough. I think it's better to tell your story and let Dave and me chew on it a little. We'll give you something back even if we decide it's not for us: whether we think what happened to you justifies revenge and whether our involvement in your revenge would help. And we can give you some ideas about what is possible and how it might proceed."

"At least tell me how you decide to accept a client."

Dave said, "My intuition and Wiley's good sense."

Wiley took over again. "Once we accept, we will need your continued commitment at each stage. Revenge has its own rhythms. I assume that you've tried a lawyer and the police, if that was appropriate. We try to be extra-legal but not 'illegal.'"

"Nothing that happened was clearly illegal, Wiley," Debra Jean confessed. "I thought there was nothing I could do, but the cost to me has been growing: my life's work, relationships, self-respect, all in shambles. So now, I want something bad to happen to them. Otherwise, I wouldn't be here."

"'Them'?" Dave looked at the overcast sky. Then he turned to Wiley and Debra Jean. "This feels too much like adolescent foreplay, and we're all supposed to be adults."

"If you're so intuitive, then you must know that I'm afraid."

Dave said, "It's just a matter of deciding how far you want to go."

"Getting me into bed would be a lot easier than my telling you the story." Debra Jean chuckled and smoothed her hair again. The image of being in bed with these two hunks was both daunting and exciting.

"Every once in a while, I really like your style," Dave said.

She thought of Xavier, her referral to Revenge, Inc., who emphasized that she could trust them both.

"How do you know Xavier Le Grand?" she asked, conscious of stalling.

"I first met him on a vacation in Seychelles," Wiley replied. "We also worked on a case together."

"How did you meet him, Debra Jean?" Dave asked.

"I took a long vacation after Dad died that included Seychelles. His death on top of what I was going through was incredibly painful. I thought a warm ocean and exotic islands would help ... everything. But I couldn't enjoy all the beauty. I went through the motions of going to the beach, having drinks at the cabana, and looking at the stars through crystal-clear skies. When men came on to me, I'd turn them down. I'd say I was mourning my father. It also got me past some of the difficulties of a single woman traveling alone."

"Especially an attractive one, grieving or not," Dave said.

"I wasn't feeling very attractive. I rarely do."

"Another hint. Go on."

"Seychelles seemed like a good place to hide. I had the fantasy of buying property there, becoming a recluse." She turned and stared out at the water.

"And?" Dave prodded.

"I had trouble being a tourist and enjoying the beauty. So one morning I decided to learn about the island culture. There was a political rally for the upcoming presidential election. Rallies in Seychelles mean lots of dancing and singing, with very occasional speeches. But Xavier made a speech about what he wanted to do as president that moved me to tears."

"You understood his language?" Wiley asked.

"I learned French as one of the languages toward my PhD."

"Learning French for a PhD exam and understanding Seychelles's patois seem far apart to me," Dave said.

"I'm lucky—I learn languages quickly. The rules of grammar and a few hundred words is all I need to speak and understand. It's a knack: languages, music, chemical interactions—they all feel of a piece. Memory too. People think I'm smarter for it, but it seems like a bunch of tricks to me. So yes, I understood most of it. After the speech, I stood in line to shake his hand. I asked him about one of the comments he had made. He said he had suffered and succeeded. It was a strange line for a man trying to get elected."

"But why did Xavier mention us?" Dave asked.

"I was one of the only white people there, and I imagine he was curious why I had taken the time away from the beach and casino. He asked me why I had come to the islands. I told him the truth, about trying to give up my need for revenge. He looked at me for a long time and then asked me if I would have a drink with him after he was finished at the rally. I assumed it was a high-level pickup, but how could I say no? I was being asked out by the next president of the country. And I've always been interested in strong men."

"Like the scientists you choose to work with?" Dave cut in.

She stared at him intently. "Yes. Exactly. Did I say anything about that?"

"No. I'm just on a roll."

"Anyway, Xavier took me to an elegant restaurant," she continued. "We small-talked and drank some wine. It could've been romantic, but he kept coming back to the issue of revenge. Eventually I told him just a little of what had happened, and he immediately mentioned you, Wiley. He said I should meet with you when I went back to the Bay Area. He quoted you: 'Running away won't work. Revenge needs action; otherwise, the regrets will never end.' He said that kind of thing several times during the next hour, and I began to think he really knew something about it."

Wiley said, "I guess you didn't expect that kind of psychological sensitivity from a politician."

"No. I've known some powerful people. None of them had ever talked to me the way he did. It felt good."

"You trusted him," Wiley said.

"Yes, but my judgment about trust is one of the things that's been shaken."

"You're right about Xavier, Debra Jean," Wiley said. "He is powerful and he's also trustworthy." Wiley looked up at the dark, billowing clouds surging down from the headlands. The surface of the water was speckled with drops. "The rain is coming. You can see the dark line moving on the water toward us. It's just under the bridge. Another five minutes and we'll need to go inside, and you'll have to figure out whether you want to continue."

"Something Xavier said must have connected," Dave remarked. "I think he challenged your victim status."

"And he didn't make a pass."

"Not unrelated," Dave said softly. "So what happened to make you so angry and afraid, Debra Jean?" He held her eyes. "Why are you here?"

She tried to ignore him, but he leaned forward and spoke directly to her. "I think your confidence and your femininity were undermined together. That's the key, isn't it?"

"Yes," she grudgingly agreed. "But neither has ever been my strong suit."

"And yet you're very successful."

"It may look that way."

"But you don't know anymore because of what happened to you.

And you think getting even will help." Dave leaned closer. "You may be right. But Debra Jean, revenge is a passionate and unpredictable process; it can't just be turned off once you take a few steps forward. It will take guts to pursue, and there can be unintended consequences." A few drops fell on the glass table with a delicate splash.

"I think I understand that," Debra Jean said, feeling more frightened.

"We want to know and help," Wiley told her, "but as Dave implied, once you begin, everything will change."

"That's part of my fear about starting," Debra Jean said. "Once I get into this, I know it will take me over. Experiments do that to me ..."

A light rain was now peppering the surface of the water. She felt more alive than she had for a while. Wiley made her feel secure, while Dave pushed at the uncomfortable edges of her fear. Xavier had told her that they had been All-American football players and teammates ten years ago and had started Revenge, Inc., soon afterward. They must have been a great duo, like Joe and Paul, the men who had hurt her so badly, the reason she was here.

"I'd like to see the inside of your boat," she said, blushing.

"Well, at least we'll be dry there," Wiley said, shaking drops of rain from his shirt.

"In our business, going inside is the best way to begin," Dave added.

19

CHAPTER 3

Truth and Action

The barge's upstairs interior was a small museum. There were miniature paintings, sculptures of various sizes, religious icons, old bones, stones, paleoliths, and deer and elk antlers, some gold-leafed, others painted. There were musical instruments too: drums, cymbals, gongs, and tambourines to complement an electronic piano and a large acoustic bass in the corner. But above all, it was a place of light; even with the rain clouds blotting out the sun, the reflections from the water and the expanse of sky through each window made the entire room and each object in it luminescent.

Wiley directed Debra Jean to a well-upholstered sofa, and the two men sat opposite her on leather chairs. She saw Wiley press a button near his phone and watched a tiny light on the wall high above her change to red.

"You're recording this, Wiley?"

"Is that all right?"

"You should have told me before you started the camera."

"I am now. It will help us and any consultants we decide to use."

She nodded, sighing. "Where should I begin?"

The silence from both men spoke for itself.

"My work history is the easiest. I entered the University of Chicago when I was 18; I was in one of the last groups to go through the Hutchins program for gifted students. I never felt like I belonged, but I did OK, and my grades were excellent as always—all that glibness I mentioned earlier. I graduated directly into Chicago Medical School after three years and went to UC San Diego as a joint medical and PhD student. My thesis was on the synthesis of the molecular structure of photosensitive biological substances. The work I did there led to a paper in *Nature* and some local notoriety in the scientific community. Around the same time, I married Richard Lieberman, a medical resident. He's still working in the Department of Medicine at UCSD. We're separated now."

"What was your maiden name?" Dave asked.

"Case. My father's name was Hamilton Case."

Dave said, "It's a good Midwestern name. Any relation to Case Rubber?"

"My father was the president; my grandfather founded the company."

"Quite a background," Wiley said. "And you lived up to it. An MD, a PhD, and a published scientist—in *Nature*, no less—before you were 30. You're obviously a very accomplished woman."

"The lady thinks overachiever. Right?" Dave said.

"I'm not a genius. I have academic skills, I'm glib, and I'm a good observer of nature."

"Do you include people in your definition of nature?" Dave asked.

His accuracy was disconcerting. "No. That made medical school much harder. I don't relate easily to people, so I had trouble in my clinical years. There were times when I didn't get vital information in a medical history because I couldn't make enough personal contact to get the trust of my patients. But the science of medicine is what counts these days, so I got through it." She hesitated. She could feel her pulse rise. It was getting very close.

"Please go on," Wiley said.

"I applied for a postdoc. The most interesting position came from two scientists who had just begun a boutique research institute connected to the new research campus of the UCSF medical school. They were studying photosensitive molecules; I had based my experiments on their work …"

"What about your husband?" Wiley asked. "Did he plan to join you in the Bay Area?"

"At the beginning, yes, but there was no energy for that, and now our separation is permanent. He's already opened a small practice in La Jolla, along with his university appointment at UCSD. He's dating other people. Eventually we'll get divorced. Is this important?"

"Maybe."

"Why?

21

Dave cut in. "Well, for example, you seem pretty cool about losing your marriage, which doesn't sound like a person who's obsessed with revenge."

"I'm not mad at my husband. What he did hasn't changed my life," she added angrily.

Wiley placed a warning hand on Dave's shoulder. "How long does a postdoc take in your field?"

"It can last years and years, but having an MD is a big help with getting grants, and that's the coin of the realm. Joe and Paul thought that with their help it would be two years to finish. They all but promised help in getting me tenure."

"Joe and Paul," Dave said. "The names remind me of a Yiddish song I knew as a kid."

"Never heard it mentioned," Debra Jean said. "So you're Jewish?" She eyed his lanky six-foot-five frame. "You don't look Jewish—not Richard's kind of Jew, anyway. ... Don't worry. I have nothing against Jews. Richard was just a guy with curly hair and a lot of brains."

Dave was silent.

Wiley pushed on. "So you took the job and then came here to San Francisco."

"Yes."

"And?"

She didn't answer him. This is it, she thought.

"The tape is running," Dave said.

"Take the leap, Debra Jean," Wiley advised. "In my experience, it gets better once you do."

She took a deep breath and then continued. "My work at the lab was pretty intense, right from the start. Joe and Paul were interested in my work. I got some good results."

"Do these guys have last names?" Dave queried.

"Joe Diamond and Paul Stokes. They'd worked as a team at UC on Parnassus and then founded their own place, Molecular Institute, at the new biotech research complex at Mission Bay. MI and its founders soon became legendary. They got big grants and infusions of venture capital. They hold several patents in common with the university, which have really paid off financially. Joe and Paul maneuvered to stay on the

22

faculty at UC, and they had their pick of hardworking postdocs like me. They are on the short list for a Nobel Prize. Most people in the scientific community feel they deserve it."

"Sounds intense," Wiley said.

"It was … it's why I went to work with them. I love being close to good science."

"Why is science so important to you, Debra Jean?" Dave asked.

"It is my life. It is more important than anything else. Much more important than my marriage or the possibility of children."

"Are those things mutually exclusive?" Wiley said.

"You don't know science or scientists, Wiley. Science is a religion for its practitioners. It makes everything else seem unimportant. In the religion of science, there's truth without fantasy, fact without little stories that you have to buy on someone else's authority. Everything can be tested objectively without emotion." She was talking rapidly. "I want you to understand how important it is to me, especially now. Without it, I would become a negation: without competence, without expectations of the future. A nonperson. No chance of redeeming DJ."

"DJ? Who's DJ?" Dave repeated. "Ah, I get it. DJ was you when—"

"When I was a kid. And DJ is gone now, I'm afraid. A casualty of growing up in my family." She shifted on the cushion self-consciously. "And now Joe and Paul have taken what's left away from me. I think about getting even all the time."

"So you *are* obsessed," Dave noted.

"But I'm a coward. I've thought endlessly about how to get even and be safe, but I can't figure it out. I get frightened."

"We'll work on the 'how' later, if we take your case," Wiley said.

"Understood." She turned in her chair to face him. She glanced over at Dave, and then turned back to Wiley. "If it were just you, Wiley, maybe all this would be easier. But Dave—his sarcastic comments remind me of …"

"Of what, or whom, Debra Jean?" Dave asked quietly. He stood and walked over to the sofa where she sat and put his face in front of hers. "Of truth? Of action? Of Joe or Paul?"

"Of all of them. It feels like you're against me. I've got to believe that you're not, that you're like my best consultants on the medical wards, the ones who were tough to make me a better doctor even when it felt like they were tormenting me."

Dave walked the few steps up to the kitchen. "Anyone ready for some coffee?"

"Sure." She pitched her voice to follow his movements.

"You too, Wiley?" Dave called.

"Why not."

Dave spoke as he poured the coffee. "You're obviously an accomplished person, Debra Jean. But you've stopped believing in yourself, if you ever really did." He balanced the three coffee cups as he took the stairs down two at a time. When he passed her a cup, it shook in her hands.

"I don't want to be all alone with this anymore."

"Then you're ready," Wiley said, and gave her a welcoming smile.

CHAPTER 4

Mafia Science

ebra Jean sat on the extra-long couch in Revenge, Inc.'s downstairs office, and Wiley and Dave each took one of the corner chairs. Half the size of the upstairs living room, it had the feeling of a submarine: small windows looking out over water now sprinkled with raindrops, spare furnishings, and a few artifacts—trophies and pictures from football days and some family snapshots of Wiley in the half-empty bookshelf. A large oak desk dominated the room. On it was a simply framed portrait of a handsome man. He looked like Wiley but was at least a decade older—probably his father, Debra Jean thought.

When Dave had shown her around the barge and then asked her what would be the easiest place for her to tell her story, she immediately picked this quiet room with its great music system. She popped the first of Bach's Unaccompanied Cello Suites into the player, arranged a pillow under her head, and closed her eyes, concentrating on the sound of the bow crossing the cello's thick strings, relishing each vibration and overtone. As a child, she had spent endless hours listening to her parents' classical music, calming herself when she couldn't escape her anxious thoughts.

She began by visualizing a neutral image that could trigger the memory; then she worked on relaxing as the imagery unfolded. She knew the principle from a psychiatry course in medical school. Visualize, relax, visualize, speak, and then just relax and speak. Eventually the memory sequence flowed easily from her mind and mouth.

She focused on the sign—*Jardinière*—for an elegant restaurant that served the guests and performers at Symphony Hall and the Opera House, where her nightmare had begun. At first she saw the letters through the mist of her anxiety, dark blues and indigo. Gradually the colors brightened as she focused on the elegant door, which a handsome valet opened for her. She had been there before, sitting at the bar or lounge after concerts, enjoying the nearness of orchestra members from the opera and symphony, and assorted soloists and divas.

A week before, she had presented her research findings to a conference in Lisbon and received kudos from several interested scientists. When she returned home, her bosses came to her lab bench.

"Join us for dinner at Jardinière," Joe had said. "We want to celebrate your success." Paul stood behind him, nodding as he spoke.

Now, remembering the invitation, she was flooded with anxiety. Darkness obscured her inner vision and she stopped speaking. She forced herself to open her eyes just enough to see the two very tall men listening intently in the corners of the room. She tried to relax again, feeling the slight rocking of the barge and hearing the sound of rain and wind against the large windows, focusing on the calming sounds of the weather and the resonance of the cello.

She opened the door of Jardinière and pushed through the crowd of couples. A spiral staircase dominated the room, the spine of a nautilus, probably inspired by the 20th-century iconic structure of DNA. The helical motif was everywhere in the room. She thought of the great scientist James Watson and his intuitive leap to the double helical structure of all genetic material. She had been told that he was an incorrigible womanizer. In the past, that seemed to go with being a creative scientist. There were so many more women in science now than in the '60s, she thought, and education about abuse and committees backed that up. Even the great Watson would have been called on the carpet for his behavior. Or would he?

"Can we help you?" The attractive Asian woman standing at the reception podium sounded cool.

"I'm looking for Joe Diamond and Paul Stokes."

She acknowledged the request. "I'll have someone take you to their table."

Debra Jean followed another hostess to the open second floor and then along the wide circular balcony that ringed the room. They stopped at a booth set back from the tables that overlooked the horseshoe bar below. Joe and Paul both smiled warmly at her and she smiled back.

They were gracious and relaxed, so different from their brusque vitality at work.

"Come sit between us," Joe said, helping her to the center seat on the plush sofa that hugged the wall. He was the smaller of the two men. His hair was gray-brown and cut short, and he sported a small mustache. He wore dark slacks and a dark blue cashmere sweater with a zipper open down the front, revealing a black shirt with a Mao collar. She had never found him physically attractive, but his dominating energy was hard to ignore. He sat on her right, edging very close to her so that their thighs touched. Paul, waiting for his colleague to find a place, then eased himself into the booth on the other side of her, leaving a sliver of air between them. Tall, thin, and wiry, he was a strikingly handsome man. His face was clean-shaven, and he had a full head of raven black hair, light blue eyes, and long, languid features. He wore a blue silk jacket over a tan turtleneck sweater that matched loose suede pants. She had never seen him out of jeans before, even for formal speeches at scientific meetings and dinners.

A young man in a white shirt, black tie, and black pants handed each of them a menu. He gave Joe the leather-bound wine list. An older man in the same dress joined them immediately and began chatting with Joe. Paul whispered to Debra Jean that the man was a renowned sommelier tasked with helping knowledgeable guests choose wine for the coming meal. Debra Jean knew the routine—but from the intensity of the conversation now, she could see that Joe was a true wine aficionado. Or was it just that he did everything with uncanny focus?

Having picked the wine for them, Joe suggested that they all order a prix-fixe meal. She readily agreed, and they made small talk as they enjoyed the food and wine. But after the dessert and espresso, the mood changed abruptly.

"Some of your data doesn't work for us," Joe said without preamble.

Debra Jean could not help flushing with surprise and anger.

"We'll have to do something about it," he continued.

She summoned up the courage to respond. "The data is accurate and important. I've replicated it several times, as you well know."

"We are not saying you're wrong, just out of step with our work."

Paul turned to her, his face very close, his manner conciliatory. "Try

27

to understand, Debra Jean. It's not that we don't trust your work. You've done good science. It's our larger research program we're worried about, and your analysis includes information we'd like to keep under wraps."

"You're saying I should hold my work up for your research program?"

"Yes. Just for a while," Paul quickly added. "A year at most. Don't worry. You'll get the chance later on."

"Or not!" Joe barked. "It's not what our lab is emphasizing. It's our own fault. We wanted you to follow your ideas, but we should have insisted that you begin by working more programmatically, contributing directly to our research program and then adding your own work later on."

"You're a good researcher, Debra Jean," Paul said quietly. "We're very proud of you. Don't worry. Eventually your work will find its place in our program."

"Wait a second. This doesn't make sense," she began.

Joe cut her off. "In return, we'll talk with the dean of the medical school to get you on that tenure track as soon as possible."

"As early as next year," Paul said.

"This isn't fair," Debra Jean said, feeling like a child. "I can't believe you're taking my work away from me." She was furious as she watched her future spinning out of control. "With all due respect," she said tightly, "what you're suggesting is clinically and scientifically unethical." She paused, acutely aware that she was challenging the men who were the preeminent leaders in her field and the key to her success in the future.

Before they could speak, she changed her tack. "Look, we're scientists. I know your work. It's founded in real curiosity about the workings of the natural universe. I admire that. In the short run, my work may screw up a few drug trials, but it also suggests new directions for understanding photosensitive molecules. Eventually that's bound to be of great use to patients and to science."

"You're too self-centered, Debra Jean," Joe said calmly. "When you're more fully integrated into our research program, you'll see that your findings, though interesting, are at right angles to our line of work. Your data will definitely hold up the whole program."

She was shaking with anger. "You both know that science should not be manipulated this way."

"Yes, yes, but save it for first-year ethics lectures," Joe chided, lowering his voice slightly. "This is not an argument, Debra Jean. It's a fait accompli."

She tried to ignore his tone. "You hired me. You encouraged me." Her voice was quivering. "You funded me. You've introduced me to your colleagues. You've been great." Her eyes began to tear up, and she dabbed them with a napkin determinedly. "Now you're ruining everything."

Paul put a hand on her shoulder. She tried to shrug it off but was too wedged between them to move. "All we require is your agreement to hold up on your current work," he insisted.

"Everyone who heard about my work at Lisbon will want to know why I've stopped. Besides, I've already submitted a preliminary version of further work to *Nature*."

"You will withdraw it," Joe said angrily. "You could say you need to reconfirm your results. It happens all the time."

She was conscious of Joe's eyes boring into hers and the heat of the men's thighs next to hers. "I have my own plans, and some of them depend on what you promised when I took the job," she said. "That was part of the deal when I came to work with you in the first place."

"You're acting like a child," Joe said contemptuously. "Your were hired to be part of our team. No one is independent in the scientific community anymore. Certainly not a postdoc."

"Look, we don't want to lose you," Paul said softly, as he leaned his body slightly toward her. "We want you to become even more involved with us, Debra Jean."

"I wish I could believe that."

"I've been too harsh with you." Joe sipped some wine and looked into her eyes. "Paul's right. We don't want to lose you. But we also don't need you as much as you need us."

It was then that she felt a hand move slowly up between her legs. It rested briefly on the inside of her thighs and then slowly slid along her groin, spreading her legs slightly apart. It pressed gently into the cleft of her panties, caressing the silken cloth as if it were skin. Neither man had moved or given any sign of what was happening under the table. Neither man's hands were visible on the table. With horror, she realized that she'd have to lift the tablecloth to find out whose it was.

"We want you to work more closely with us," Paul was saying with his usual smoothness. "We all came to science with a great deal of idealism, but things have changed. There's a new commercial context that rules the way we all must work. There's more financial responsibility now at universities, and different management rules apply."

"I'm sure you know that in many labs, postdocs don't get to work on projects of their own for years," Joe added, still staring directly at her. "Some of your classmates are just cannon fodder. With luck, they get a bench in someone else's lab and eventually a teaching job in a community college. Help us with this, and we'll help you bypass all that."

Debra Jean was frozen to the seat, unable to speak or move. She felt numbness spread through her thighs and groin as fingers pressed deeper, moving aside the cloth of her panties, touching her flesh.

"We gave you everything you wanted, and we expect some loyalty, Debra Jean," Joe continued.

His words coincided with a finger forcing its way into her vagina. She tightened her thigh muscles, which were beginning to tremble, but that didn't stop its progress. She felt it slowly caress her insides.

With a sudden effort, she forced her body upward against the heavy table and pushed hard, rising to her feet. The table teetered and then fell with a resounding crash, sending utensils, china, and glasses smashing to the floor. Wine, water, and bits of food flew everywhere.

"What the hell!" Paul exclaimed, as he moved away from the landslide of food and drink.

Debra Jean stood in the middle of the trauma zone as waiters hurried to deal with the catastrophe. "You won't get away with this!" she stammered, breaking into tears. "I won't let you take away what's mine!" She burst out of the dining alcove, and dodging the overturned table, the shards of broken glass and dishes, and the mess on the rug, she bolted down the circular staircase, past the reception station and waiting patrons, and out the door.

CHAPTER 5

Abuse

Debra Jean opened her eyes. She was standing in the center of Wiley's office, the strains of the cello concerto still playing in the background. Wiley and Dave sat quietly on the corner chairs. She walked slowly to the window, trying to quiet the rage and fear coursing through her. The rain had stopped and the sky was clearing. For a moment, a sliver of rainbow showed through the window, coloring parts of the beige rug with blues and indigos. Then the clouds moved to cover the beauty. She waited in silence until her pulse return to normal.

"That was intense, Debra Jean," Dave said, when she finally turned toward them. "It's quite a gift to be able to re-create a scene, even the nightmare you described, with such vividness through words."

"It wasn't just words to me. It was all too real."

Both men were silent.

"It was so bizarre, and … and they're so famous. They didn't need to do that."

"Meaning?" Dave questioned.

"To be blunt, if either of them had come on to me, I might just have gone with it. I mean, why not? They're both incredibly attractive in different ways. Paul is gorgeous, and I was really attracted to him, but Joe has a crackling energy that makes you think about sex. The man's mind is a turn-on. If asked, I might have gone to bed with either of them."

Dave said thoughtfully, "It doesn't make sense."

"I know. Bringing a complaint to the abuse committee at UC would have hurt them, certainly diminished their chance for a Nobel Prize." She turned away from Wiley and Dave and stared at the floor. "But as I said, I didn't do anything."

"Why?" Wiley asked gently.

"I'm used to having things taken away from me and doing nothing." Her anxiety peaked again, and she began pacing the room until some of it subsided. She slowly returned to the sofa and sat straight-backed on the edge of the cushion. "I could use some water or soda."

Dave went up to the kitchen and came back with three cans of Pepsi, which he passed around. "You want to continue the story?"

She nodded. "I don't stick up for myself very well. That's been true as long as I can remember."

"What do you mean?" Dave asked.

"It's my pattern. You wouldn't know it from all my academic success, but it's true. So no complaint, no committee. I was in shock for weeks. The way both of them continued to talk while one of their hands was deep in my crotch was, as Wiley said, a nightmare. I couldn't get over it. Somehow, not knowing whose hand it was made it even more horrible. Not to mention deciding how to handle their threats about my research findings and paper."

"Come back to the scene at Jardinière," Dave said. "You could have forcefully taken that hand away while making a nasty remark, couldn't you? It's pretty common for women to be pawed when they are jammed into tight quarters. Think of the trains in Japan or concerts at the Fillmore."

"Easy, Dave," Wiley said.

"You don't have to protect me, Wiley. He's right," Debra Jean admitted. "In retrospect, I could have done something at Jardinière, or later at the lab, and certainly through a UCSF committee. But I didn't. I couldn't."

"Your pattern? Their status? Fear of reprisals? What?" Dave questioned.

"All of the above and more. Men in powerful roles think they can do what they want and get away with it. Superstars in medicine are like that."

"Marauding men in the hallowed halls of medicine. I've heard lots of stories. It's the theme of so many TV shows."

Despite herself she laughed. "I'm just one of the stereotypes—is that what you're saying?"

"Maybe," Dave said. "What do you think?"

"Sure, and it begins early. There's a lot of sexist joking around cadavers. Then there are endless hassles around the physical exams with women physicians. Male patients are always getting erections. They're usually embarrassed, and most of the time I felt sorry for them. But every once in a while, there is some guy who thinks his genitals are God's gift to women, and you have to put up with a lot. Not that women don't play similar games. There've been a lot of cute guys in my office who've tempted me to play around."

Dave smiled and sat back in his chair. "I'll remember that the next time I have a woman physician. But we're talking about something very different here. So let's get back to you that night. You said you became obsessed. You couldn't stop thinking about it."

"Right. Exactly. Of course I knew that what happened at Jardinière wasn't objectively that terrible, but that's not the way it felt to me."

"But all that time you didn't tell anybody?" Wiley asked.

"No. Of course I thought about it, but I just couldn't act. I knew they would deny it and I would be humiliated. No one would believe me. Remember, these guys are becoming legends. They're probably going to win a Nobel Prize, for God's sake. And how could I prove it?"

"Nevertheless, it was sexual abuse," Wiley said.

"I know. And there's a medical school committee set up to investigate complaints. But there is always a lot to lose when you go that route. I was afraid of the consequences. Once I made a complaint like that, my career could be all but over, or so I imagined. It's happened to others." She sighed deeply. "I kept putting it off, and then it felt too late. A month after what happened at the restaurant, they told me there was a problem with funding and they would have to take one of my graduate students out of my lab, along with a quarter of my budget. When I complained, Joe said that it was only a temporary response to a small cut in their budget, and I'd get that and more back in a few months. It was within their right. Postdocs are like slave labor.

"They kept me in limbo. Maybe it was deliberate; it made it even more difficult for me to act against them. After a couple of months, they pulled another student and his training money from my grant. That really bothered me, but again I didn't complain. By then, I had let it go too long."

Dave frowned. "Hardball strategies are one thing. They had a lot of leverage: money, bench space, computer time, control of students. But why sexual harassment, and why so childishly conceived? What did they know about you to make it worth the risk? How did they know it would paralyze you?"

"I'm not sure what you're saying. I'd never been harassed that way before, if that's what you're driving at."

Debra Jean closed her eyes and leaned back against the sofa cushion. "Look, I wasn't sexually abused in childhood. But I know the signs of sexual trauma, and I don't have them—not the bad ones, anyway." She finished the soda, placed the empty can on the table, and rested against the cushions again. "I've been through my family's dysfunctions with my therapist and gotten nowhere."

"Give us a sense of what you're talking about," Dave said. "With your family, I mean."

"Is it really necessary?"

"Frankly, I don't know, Debra Jean, but you're being very defensive. Did you ever talk about your family with Joe or Paul or any of the MI employees?"

"No."

"Anything at all they might have heard that would make more sense of this?"

She shrugged. "I don't see how. My family had problems like all families. My dad was very handsome and a lady's man. As a Case son, he had old-family status and made a lot of money besides what he inherited from the tire business. He was away a lot. Maybe he had affairs, I don't know, but he was a great father to me. Mom started off poor but was the town beauty. After she married Dad, she made the most of her new resources—clothes, travel, leisure. She was much too interested in the men that came around the house. My boyfriends said she made them feel uncomfortable, anyway. She never apologized when I asked her about it. She'd say things like 'I'm friendly with everyone' or 'How could an old lady compete with you, dear?' She didn't much like my academic interests. My therapist thinks she was jealous of me, and that made sense, but I sure didn't feel it. I wasn't beautiful like her and knew it, so I did what I did best."

"And Joe and Paul knew nothing of this history?" Wiley asked.

"I don't think so. Anyway, why is that so important? What difference would it make?"

"It depends," Dave said. "Those kinds of patterns—some people know how to use them as a weapon. What happened to you after the restaurant experience?"

"A downhill slide. I stayed at MI, but I stopped functioning. I couldn't sleep. I lost weight. I was anxious and suspicious, unsure of myself, numb. I was miserable in every way."

"That's almost a clinical description of … ," Dave ventured.

"Yes. PTSD. Depression. Paranoid reaction. All of the above," Debra Jean declared.

Wiley said, "In laymen's terms, you were having a breakdown."

"Totally. And I'm never like that, Wiley—not that I can remember, anyway. I'm a control freak. This felt like it was coming from a place that I didn't recognize in me. It was alien, the kind of thing I'd seen as a fourth-year student in psychiatric emergency wards."

"Were you able to work?"

"Not really. I went through the motions. I'd come into my lab and stare at my screen. I stopped reading the journals I needed to read to keep up on things. I felt no pleasure in what I was doing. My reputation pulled me through for a while; the lab assistants and other postdocs gave me a break. But that didn't last long in the high-competition, high-stakes research environment."

"And Joe and Paul?"

"They were always civil, but when the time came for new funding for equipment or personnel, the money wasn't there. Hell, who could blame them? I wasn't pulling my weight. I was no longer their star. Other people were filling my role and vying for my space—and their attention."

"And then they came to you and suggested that you seek some kind of therapy, right?" Dave asked.

"Yes, as a matter of fact, that is exactly what they did. Joe and Paul called me in one day and said my work was no longer up to their standards. They couldn't recommend me for the tenure-track position. They said I should get some psychological help, and then they'd revisit all options. They mentioned the name of a psychiatrist they thought was good. They also said they would help me find somewhere else to work that was less demanding, if things didn't work out. No rush, but they needed the lab space.

"I got very upset. I just broke down crying, but I still couldn't confront them. It was like another moment in the restaurant."

"Like everything was being taken away from you?" Dave said soothingly.

She looked up. "Exactly the feeling. ... I remember Paul reaching out his hand toward me and feeling panic. I just ran out of the office. And the building." She sat up suddenly. "I never went back."

"Did you go to the psychiatrist?" Dave asked.

"Yes."

"The one they recommended?"

Debra Jean nodded her head dejectedly. "Dr. Potter, the very one."

"Why would you have trusted their referral after what they did to you?" Wiley asked.

"His office was in 400 Parnassus, the prestigious building near the medical school. I checked him out with friends and on the Internet. He had a good reputation and he was good: supportive, and he acted as if he believed my story. And I liked feeling understood and taken care of. But soon all that dependency began to work against me. I actually got worse. I began to fall apart in a way that was visible to my friends."

"So you quit," Dave said.

"No."

"Why not?" Wiley asked.

"Because she was starting to fall apart. Why else?" Dave interjected.

"I didn't know it then, Dave, but I think you're right. I actually increased the number of appointments. I began to call his home at night and try to find him on his vacations. It was pretty humiliating."

"You became obsessed with the process," Dave said. "Isn't that what's called a negative therapeutic reaction?"

"How did you know that?" Debra Jean asked.

Dave ignored her question. "So you didn't want to let go of him even when it was hurting and humiliating you. I imagine you also wanted to know what was happening. Curiosity can be a killer—it's also why you are a gifted researcher."

Debra Jean stared at Dave for a long time. "Eventually I just couldn't take it, and I quit—against his advice, by the way. I let go of everything. I gave up all my links with the university. I got a part-time job doing outpatient general medicine at a hospital in Walnut Creek. Then my father died, and I had to deal with that." She paused. "That was two years ago. So now you've got the whole story."

"The rain has stopped." Wiley walked to the window and looked out. "If you don't mind a wet deck, let's take a look. There's fresh coffee. And we all might need a bathroom break."

Debra Jean stood and stretched. Her relief was apparent. "What next?"

"Feedback. First impressions, Debra Jean," Wiley said. "But first our break."

* * *

Ten minutes later, Debra Jean found Wiley standing at the deck railing. The clouds were still thick and a few raindrops were still falling, but a dim circle of sun brought slanting rays of silvery light to the water's surface. A full rainbow rose over Angel Island. A fresh wind was blowing in from the Golden Gate, and the barge was rocking with the waves.

Dave came up the stairs from the kitchen carrying rain gear and snacks. "I'm about to apologize for all my meanness," he said happily.

Debra Jean smiled in spite of herself. "Dave, you remind me of some colleagues, hot-shot scientists, so good that they don't need to get along with anyone."

He helped her with a rainproof slicker and moved to stand on the other side of Wiley. "Maybe you'd like to be more like me."

Wiley stretched an arm around each of them. "Try a few minutes of silence. Enjoy the rainbow. Watch the clouds. Listen to the wind."

They were silent for a long time. Then Wiley began to speak. "The link between sexual harassment and curtailing your scientific work seems pretty direct to me. You knew that, yet you didn't take care of yourself."

She took that in. "Would you have suggested going to a committee, Wiley?"

37

"Yes. But I can see some practical problems. Number one: Postdocs don't always continue to be stars; they might have a big success and then fall apart; they blame their mentors like all-star college athletes blame their professional coaches. The ethics committee is full of mentors! They've seen angry mentees waiting for a shot at their teachers. Second: What happened in the restaurant can never be proved; you must've looked pretty crazy to the restaurant staff, and they'd likely be on the side of their famous customers. Third: Going the route of complaining to a sexual harassment committee has at least one obvious problem—you don't know which man to accuse."

"That covers a lot of it, Wiley."

"So I understand your decision, but there were major psychological consequences for taking them on directly. Your scientific work went badly and you became depressed. You resigned. They probably gave you good recommendations, right?" Debra Jean nodded in acknowledgment. "Case closed. You become an ordinary doctor. You help people get well. So sorry, but it's what you were trained to do. Next case."

"Yes. I've been over that scenario a thousand times." She tilted her face upward to meet his eyes. "But they could have accomplished all that without Jardinière."

Wiley continued, "Right. Why risk your accusations and their huge potential losses?"

"For fun," Dave suggested.

"You can't be serious," Debra Jean said.

"Perfectly. Fun with a capital F. Whatever 'Fun' means to them. Scientists like Joe and Paul are superstars. Pretty young scientists are fair game. Maybe they just wanted to prove they could get away with something shocking. Maybe it's how they get off."

Debra Jean shook her head. "What they did was just plain mean." She grabbed the railing tightly as a gust of wind struck the barge.

"To you," Dave said. "But how did it feel to them?"

Wiley frowned at Dave. "It doesn't hold together."

Dave nodded. "Just think of it as trying out some crazy ideas. Because what Debra Jean is describing is pretty crazy. Says something about the maturity of renowned scientists, doesn't it?"

She colored. "You're too cynical, Dave. It may sound corny to you, but I still believe most scientists are devoted to their work and to truth. That's why I got into the field, and I'm not alone. Sure there are bad apples around. That happens in any profession. But on the whole, scientists are more committed and honest than most."

Dave interjected, "Despite what happened to you, you still believe in the Gods of Science, even if they abused you at the altar."

"You can be so mean," she said sarcastically. "Are you saying you won't take the case?"

Wiley held up his arms to stop them. "What Dave is saying, Debra Jean, is very much about taking this case. But suppose you're an episode in a bigger and dirtier picture that has little to do with you? Remember your negative therapeutic reaction? Revenge can be like that. You may find yourself a passenger on a powerful train going somewhere you don't want to be."

"I'll be OK," she said. "I'm pretty strong."

"Are you?" Dave asked. "You told us you've had trouble fighting back in your family and other social situations."

"Yes. You're right. And now it's happened again. That exactly why I'm here—to do something about it. Even if, as you suggest, I was just a pawn in some big rotten fun game that I know nothing about, I'd still want to get those bastards. The larger game, their 'fun,' is now personal to me." The wind had died down, but her hands were gripping the railing as if there were a hurricane. "Revenge is the name of your company. It's what I want."

"Revenge may not get you your career back, Debra Jean," Dave said.

She planted her feet firmly on the deck and leaned against the railing. "I know that."

"You're very determined," Wiley said.

"And scared. But if you're worried about my following through, don't be."

Dave appraised her carefully. "First steps on a long road?"

"Thanks for that, Dave. Yes. But what do I ... we do now?"

Dave smiled reassuringly. "Just sit tight. We'll do some background checks on Joe and Paul and start poking around their laboratory and neighborhoods, investigate previous problems with hires, that kind of thing." He turned to Wiley. "I haven't had a good look at science since

I left Purdue. Remember those labs we aced, Wiley? I used to like being around all those test tubes and retorts."

"There aren't many of those left," Debra Jean said, amused. "Mostly screens of different sizes."

"Are we that old?" Dave said mischievously.

"No," she laughed, looking up at his extra-tall body. "No, you're just right. And I'll be sitting by my phone, just like a teenager, waiting for your call."

CHAPTER 6

Counterphobia

The next day, Wiley and Dave sat at an outside table at Poggio, a restaurant occupying the bottom floor of the Casa Madrona hotel, located across from Sausalito's central plaza. The food was billed as rustic Italian and was excellent. Wiley ordered the veal meatballs with fresh pasta and a beer; Dave ordered the fried artichokes and a plate of bucatini with a glass of well-aged Barolo.

"She's smart and obviously hardworking," Dave began. "I've checked her background: she was a rising star in graduate school as a postdoc." He paused. "But achievements aside, my impression is that there's something two-dimensional about her. And I'd bet anything the missing dimension is about something in her past. That comment about the mother being interested in her boyfriends woke me up."

"Me too," Wiley said, looking up from his food. "But we don't know much about its impact. So let's move on. Play expert shrink for a moment."

"I called some of my professional women friends," Dave began.

"What did they think of the situation?" Wiley asked.

Dave sighed. "You mean being groped in the middle of a fancy dinner party by one of your bosses, who happens to be high on the list of famous and influential scientists in the world? They all thought it was pretty extreme behavior but were surprised that Debra Jean would fall apart. Hurt and angry, for sure. Nonetheless, I was told, women in high-stress and high-status positions experience all kinds of sexual taunts. They pride themselves on not falling apart.

"Here's a twist. Sexual turn-ons aside, a few of my friends wondered if her bosses got what they wanted."

"Meaning?"

"They got rid of her without a fight. Apparently, firing a postdoc at UC can be a problem."

The waiter came with a bottle of sparkling water, bread, and their beers.

"Still, everyone agreed that there's a bit of madness here," Dave said after sampling the beer with great satisfaction. "These are extremely prominent scientists, yet what happened under the table was more like an adolescent's fantasy."

"Or an adolescent female fantasizing about a teacher," Wiley noted. "It could have been all made up."

Dave buttered a roll. "Unlikely, Wiley. Absolutely no motive. Look, on the surface, she's tough, smart, and competitive. There aren't that many women who get both a PhD and an MD and land a great research position and do top-level work. She lost her marriage in the process, but nowadays that almost goes with the territory."

"All of which speaks to lots of experience dealing with brilliant peers, not to mention men in authority," Wiley said.

"Right. Women who are that successful use everything they can muster, including their sexuality, to compete with male peers."

"Do you think she was coming on to them and one or the other responded in a dumb way? I doubt if it's politically correct to sleep with your boss in today's world, but she did talk about her attraction to both of them. I mean, it's a way of getting ahead in cultures dominated by men."

"Titillation and the promise of more does sometimes work wonders in any culture. Acting on it is a different matter."

"But men can misinterpret flirtation," Wiley said softly.

"Or men with reputations and power like Joe Diamond and Paul Stokes might feel they have the right to do anything they want to women in their labs. Everyone agreed that what happened at the restaurant was off the wall, but her response, particularly after that episode, was definitely, shall we say, nonadaptive. She panicked and then couldn't fight back. My guess is that there is trauma in her childhood that mirrored this situation."

"Physical abuse?" Wiley asked.

"Not necessarily physical, but surely connected to her sexuality."

The waiter brought their entrees. Dave continued, "Let's try out Debra Jean as a counterphobic personality that has been structured to defend against a deep fear. For example, as a child she's afraid of not living up to the demands of her parents for success. She forces herself to work against that fear. She becomes an intrepid scientific superhero, capable of surviving in a cutthroat high-octane environment. But it's all built on a deep vulnerability. It's a common enough scenario for many big achievers. Not all of them, of course. The very best are personally secure and deeply confident about their abilities."

"So a CEO could be either counterphobic or the real item," Wiley mused, popping a meatball into his mouth.

"Both are real, but they react differently to certain stressors, the ones that touch potential weakness," Dave commented. "And it's hard to tell the difference until the test."

Wiley was alert. "A lot of the successful linemen on our football team might have been counterphobics. They were always proving themselves at extreme risk, but when they got injured, which they inevitably did, they were crybabies. They had a hard time getting back into the game. Some of them never did."

"That's the MO, all right." Dave finished his food and leaned back in his chair. "Great meal. Poggio always delivers. ... My own opinion is that lots of successful women in Debra Jean's generation are like your linemen. They spend extra energy working against their fear. It doesn't get them into trouble as long as they actively keep up the aggression. If they are forced back into a helpless and passive role, they often fall apart.

"Debra Jean could fit that picture too. Remember what she said about her super-seductive mother being interested in her teenage boyfriends? That and more could have been frightening to little DJ, now re-created as Debra Jean Lieberman, PhD, MD, published scientist and sophisticated temptress at a fancy restaurant, where she dines with her famous bosses. The armor she built is pretty fragile. She knows it could turn to sand at a moment's notice."

"And you're saying the passivity time bomb could be set off by something like what happened under the table," Wiley suggested. "A single event that touches a ready nerve and ignites a firestorm."

43

Dave nodded.

Wiley mopped up the sauce on his empty plate with half a roll. "Debra Jean's vulnerability is one thing; real helplessness in the face of malevolence is another."

"Right," Dave said. "The factors that shaped Debra Jean are one thing. The strange behavior of her bosses in Jardinière is another. The mix was certainly volatile. It led to her becoming a victim, which she no longer accepts. If we do our job, that stage in her life could be over."

"I think she came to the right place. We give traumatized people who've been victimized the means to get revenge for themselves," Wiley declared. "Any more ideas, Dave?"

"The great mystery is Joe and Paul—specifically, their motivation," Dave replied. "We don't understand it. Wiley, you used the word 'malevolence.' We could be facing quite a lot of that if we take her on."

"So here's our critical question," Wiley said. "Would Debra Jean be better off staying in Walnut Creek treating ear infections and minor depressions? Joe and Paul are formidable and probably more than that. If you're correct and she's been badly hurt before, will she disintegrate if she takes them on?"

"Good question," Dave said. "All that talent and ambition went belly up very quickly. Still, I think she deserves a chance."

"So do I," Wiley said. "We'll start by concentrating on Joe and Paul and see how she reacts to what we find."

"One more thing," Dave said quietly. "People like Debra Jean and me need genuine heroes nearby. It's part of our defenses. And sometimes we don't look closely enough at whom we worship. That's not my problem, but it sure is Debra Jean's."

"Wait a second. You're the best athlete I've ever known, not to mention having an endless array of other talents I can't touch. It's I who should be dependent on the likes of you."

"But you're not. And guys like you don't really need anyone. Heroes never understand how they affect people, Wiley. I'm just one more victim of your charms."

CHAPTER 7

Upstairs, Downstairs

Joe Diamond and Paul Stokes had almost symmetrical offices on the top floor of the Molecular Institute in the heart of the new Mission Bay Campus of UCSF, south of Market Street in San Francisco. The view was of the Bay Bridge surrounded by blue water, the AT&T ballpark, and the new marina. It was a comedown from their former digs on the tenth floor at UCSF overlooking the Golden Gate and Marin Headlands. But MI and their independence were ample compensation for lost vistas.

They had designed most of their own space, including the large conference room where they and their colleagues usually met. It combined a select paper library with high-speed Internet access to scientific and medical libraries and labs all over the world. Counters of teak and maple were crammed with published and unpublished papers and the detritus of ongoing experiments and trials. In the middle of the room stood a long, narrow weathered oak refectory table. A large window framed the side of the room with the bridge view. The other three walls were filled with chalkboards, computer and conferencing screens, and bookshelves.

The room was accessed only through their personal offices. That was one of Gloria Garcia's ideas when she had arrived as head of security. Security was critical in high-risk cutting-edge scientific ventures: a stolen molecular formula could be worth millions of dollars in the marketplace and ten times that much in potential stock equities. Gloria had added multiple cameras, sensors, and security software to Joe and Paul's dyadic sanctum. A Latina was good politics in the liberal scientific community, but that was only the beginning of her manifold talents.

This morning, Gloria, Joe, and Paul sat together sipping coffee in the conference room. Gloria had a pile of files in front of her. She had asked for the meeting.

"I'll come right to the point," she said, with a Spanish cadence. She was dressed in a stylish dark business suit cut medium length at the knee and a white scooped-neck blouse. She wore a gold cross around her neck. Her skin was dark like the color of brown olives, and her features were elegant and strong, reflecting the Indian side of her forebears. She sat facing them across the conference table.

"In the past few days, there have been several attempts to gain access to all MI's computer files. Looks like their interest is in both unpublished scientific research and personnel files. None of these attempts have succeeded. Nevertheless, the presence of such probes is unusual and concerns me."

"Can you be more specific about what they were after?" Paul asked.

"We have no idea. We're investigating, but nothing has turned up yet."

"We're close to the end of the drug trials," Joe said. "Could that data be a target?"

"Unlikely. Remember, the probes were also directed at personnel files."

"Sounds like *People* magazine is after us," Joe said with a laugh.

"Not a bad guess," Gloria responded. "Personal data requests often come from journalists or public-interest groups. You're well known and Nobel Prize nominees. Newspapers and magazines want up-to-date profiles on file when the announcement is made, and they could be looking for dirt."

"Any other theories, Gloria?" Paul asked.

"Not yet," she said, eyeing both of them with suspicion. "I assume that you've kept me well informed about any activities you're interested in suppressing."

Joe said, "Obviously, there's a lot going on scientifically that you wouldn't understand, but you've been apprised of everything relevant. I assume precautions are in place."

"State-of-the-art. It's part of why we picked up these intrusions."

"What about former employees?" Joe asked. "There are people with grudges."

"They are an obvious concern. I brought some names. I'd like to run them by both of you." Gloria picked up a thin file from the pile on the table and opened it. "In the past few years there have been three people who have resigned or been let go under unusual or hostile conditions. Naturally, we keep tabs on all of them, if just to make sure they comply with termination agreements. They're legally bound not to use any data generated while they were at MI for five years, but of course many try to bend the rules. It's difficult to monitor that kind of thing unless they publish something that gives them away, so we keep them under personal surveillance as much as possible."

She thumbed through the file and then dropped it on the table. "Richardson and Cohen are still at startups in Menlo Park and Santa Barbara. They could be trouble later on, but we have good liaisons with their employers, and for now there's nothing suspicious. Lieberman works as an emergency physician in Walnut Creek. To our knowledge, she's stopped doing science. One of the reasons I called this meeting was to ask if you've heard personally from any of the three."

"No," Joe said immediately.

"Now that's strange," Paul mused, suddenly interested. "I've seen Debra Jean twice at the Opera House lately—*Macbeth* and *Carmen*—but we didn't speak."

Gloria said, "She was always listening to some kind of classical music in her lab. And she told me once that she loved opera."

"Before she left, I often saw her at music events," Paul said. "We seemed to have the same tastes. Back then, she'd have come over and said hello." He recalled, "This time she didn't say hello but did make eye contact. I kept my distance."

Joe stared at Paul. "What did you make of it?"

Paul looked away. "When she left two years ago, she was in pretty bad shape. Maybe she's better now and getting on with her life. Concert going would be a good beginning."

"It's quite a coincidence, given the break-in attempts," Gloria remarked.

Paul shrugged his shoulders. "Of all the people we let go, she knew the most about our programs. She's certainly smart enough to understand where we're going in our work."

Gloria nodded. "I'll check out Debra Jean more carefully. You both keep me informed of anything new. I count on that to do my work."

"Of course," Paul said.

She stood, gathered her material, and left the room. Both men silently watched until they heard the door click behind her.

"Do you think Gloria has access to the conversations we have in this room?" Joe asked his partner.

"I'm sure she tries. She's not happy about being kept out of anything."

Joe leaned back and looked at the ceiling, smiling at his own secret relationship with Gloria. "I couldn't help think about what she'd be like in bed. Controlling but insatiable is my guess."

"Joe!"

"Unfortunately, the fashions she chooses keep her body well hidden. She's tall and sexy with just enough Mesoamerican earthiness to give me a jolt of the primitive."

Paul reluctantly joined in. "She once told me she was from the mountains in El Salvador."

"She definitely has some Spanish landowner's blood in her." Joe chuckled. "Does she attract you, Paul?"

"You're being tiresome. You know I'm a committed husband."

"Sure, except when you're not."

"Sharon and I are fine. It's science that really turns me on."

"That's where I come in," Joe said wryly.

"Yes."

"Don't forget that I rely on you too," Joe said. "Which brings me to my point. Why didn't you tell me about seeing Debra Jean at the Opera House?"

"Why should I?"

"Don't be cute."

"To be honest, I didn't give her presence a second thought until Gloria asked about her."

"You weren't suspicious of the way she behaved?"

Paul countered, "I'm not as paranoid as you, Joe. I assumed she was having trouble facing an ex-boss who had helped get rid of her. Made sense to me. Still does. I never wanted to get rid of her, remember?" Paul said, annoyed.

"She got rid of herself," Joe said.

"I guess. With all her successes, it was odd the way she came apart so suddenly."

Joe laughed. "Her scientific ability was always irrelevant. Our post-docs should be lab rats, not peers. I have enough ideas for all of us."

Paul frowned. "Anyway, she's been back watching operas. So what do I do if she asks for her old job back?"

"Let it pass. That's not in the cards." Joe stared at Paul. "If and when you see her again, please don't lead her on."

Paul nodded. "Suppose she is part of the break-in? What could she be after, Joe? Is there something I don't know?"

"You're in on everything. There are always vultures looking for left-over morsels from the gods."

Paul laughed nervously. "Joe, you make me wonder about your inflated analogies."

"Why? Our work is important, and great scientists are modern deities. We deserve all the perks that come to us, including worship."

"OK, Joe. Don't start. We've been successful, and I know it's mostly because of you," Paul said. "I have limitations, and one of them is anxiety."

Joe waved him off. "You're just fine, Paul. Maybe a little troubled about flying too high, but we need to protect ourselves from mediocrity, which includes the Debra Jeans of the world. It's Gloria's job to find out. Thankfully she's good at what she does." He walked to the bookcase that held their unfinished work and leaned his back against it. "But if Debra Jean is part of the break-in, we do have a problem. She isn't stupid, and she's very manipulative. She used her husband to get status at UCSD and then ditched him when she found something better. Meaning us. Who knows what evil our Debra Jean is planning for us …"

"If my Achilles' heel is anxiety, yours is paranoia."

"Think of Wagner and Napoleon. The great ones usually worry about everything," Joe said. "It's the lesser mortals that call it paranoia."

"Joe …"

"I'm just kidding. But let's not underestimate Debra Jean. Two years ago, she was dead in the water; she won't be that way forever. We may need to deal with her."

"Just remember that I have limits on 'dealing' with people," Paul said uncertainly.

"I know your boundaries," Joe said carefully. "I rely on you and them every step of the way." He walked to the open cabinet marked "New Experiments." "Now let's use our time together to plan our next step. I have some ideas about transforming the molecule you synthesized downstairs, but I'm not sure what is technically possible."

"Almost everything."

"Right," Joe said with a broad smile. "But only if we stick together!"

* * *

After leaving the meeting, Gloria walked down the stairs to her first-floor office to think. Corporate espionage could be as ruthless as spying, especially on a hot property like MI. She had presented important data, and this time they had treated her with respect. Understandable, given that they needed her help.

She refocused on the break-in attempt. She had to figure out the big picture. She didn't know all that was going on at MI, but she had some ideas.

Money was important to them, of course. But MI was not primarily about money. Joe and Paul were more concerned with a successful and daring experiment than a private jet or lucrative stock options. They were most ruthless when it came to science. And that seemed to have been Debra Jean's downfall. Debra Jean was a privileged white girl with brains, but she had no survival skills.

Gloria took out the earpiece that monitored the small microphone she'd placed under the table in their conference room. Nothing. They knew she was bugging them, and they were clever about dealing with it.

She entered her office and closed the door. She mentally compared what she saw with their conference room. Their disorder was the fallout of complexity. She compared its apparent chaos with the organization of her own office. Everything here was brutally functional. Even her small

50

window looked out on the high-tech construction housing the many biotech labs mushrooming next to UCSF's Mission Bay campus. She could see right into some of the buildings, where white-coated men and women manipulated complicated instruments in tiny spaces. It made her wonder how Joe and Paul could work together so well—and share a conference room, no less. That wouldn't work for her. She loved being alone in her own space, even if it had an ordinary view and was filled with conventional furniture. She housed her two assistants in small cubicles strategically placed near the front and back entrances on the first floor. She held morning and evening briefings in her office; otherwise, she used e-mail to communicate with them. She made a point of going to their cubicles when she supervised their work. It was a good management strategy, but that wasn't why she did it.

Her office was austere. The walls were bare except for two framed pictures from her past. The first was a black-and-white picture of her mother and father with a little child in between them. Soon after it was taken, her parents were killed by guerrillas who had overrun her village looking for food. She had brought it with her to the orphanage in San Salvador where she was placed.

The second picture was located a few feet away from the first. It was a professional color photograph of her taken at a recent conference with her staff and bosses at MI. She was dressed smartly in a dark business suit with a splash of turquoise in a scarf at her neck, contrasting with her coral blouse. High heels emphasized her long legs. She loved the blend of competence and femininity that the picture displayed. And she particularly loved the way the photographer had caught admiring glances in the faces of the men and women around her.

Gloria turned her chair away from the wall. The pictures of her birthplace and little family were reminders of her heritage; the picture of her current workplace was a symbol of what she had accomplished. It was the space in between that still woke her up at night with terror in her heart.

CHAPTER 8

Green Eyes

After two days of hacking into the databases and e-mails at MI, Dave had learned little. As expected, security was first-rate. But he deliberately did not disguise his attempts; he wanted them to know that he was looking.

In the meantime, standard search engines confirmed Debra Jean's narrative of her former bosses. Drs. Diamond and Stokes were brilliant and respected scientists. MI, which they had founded together, had an excellent scientific reputation. Prestigious colleagues in their field had nominated them for the Nobel Prize in chemistry. Security at MI was top of the line and included strong electronic and human systems. Dave was up against a pro in the field.

So far, he had been unable to land an appointment with either Joe or Paul. On the phone, secretaries refused to speak to him without vetted referrals. A personal visit was a total bust. The receptionist was closed-mouthed, and two burly security men wandered the halls. He was given a card listing Gloria Garcia as director of security, with her phone number. She was as hard to make an appointment with as Joe and Paul. Checkmate for now!

Which was why he was two beers down at Borstal's, a new South of Market Irish-Latino watering hole serving the Mission, Potrero Hill, the AT&T ballpark, and the scientific community brought by the new campus. It was a great mirror of the diversity of its clientele: Guinness on tap, decent music, and poetry readings on Monday nights. Once a year they held a pre-Christmas concert by a local chorus featuring the last movement of Beethoven's Ninth.

Now he was waiting for Gloria Garcia, whom he had observed going into Borstal's after work the night before.

Dave wasn't a regular drinker, and he rarely went to bars. When he was with Wiley, people deferred to them, but when he was alone, his eccentric looks often got him into trouble. Despite his intimidating height, he looked vulnerable—thin face with a dusky complexion and features set in permanent curiosity, a prominent nose, a long chin, and clean-shaven. His hair was long, brown, and burnished with an unlikely reddish hue. He moved with an elegance that was almost feminine, and his body was in continual motion.

Friday nights were freewheeling in the South of Market area. If a conflict brewed in Borstal's, experience told him that he would be a natural target. Dave was very good at fighting and took pleasure in his adversaries' surprise at his unorthodox moves. But tonight, if it came to that, he had every intention of losing.

At 6:45, Gloria walked into Borstal's and took a seat at the far end of the bar near the door. She ordered a beer and sat back like a star. There were a few other single women scattered around the dark room, but she stood out. She was both elegant and sensuous. The combination attracted Dave and everybody else in the room. He was positioned well to watch for her, but it was she who first caught his eye. So after a decent interval, he grabbed his mostly empty glass, walked toward her place at the bar, and stood next to her.

"Want to meet someone new?" he asked.

Gloria glanced up at him. "Not tonight." She swiveled away from him.

"It could be interesting," he countered softly over her shoulder.

She turned back toward him. "You don't belong here, and you'll make trouble for me. Anyway, I'm not interested." She turned away again.

Dave said gently, "But I like it here. Cut me some slack. All that poetry and music advertised on the door. It's an interesting place. Maybe you're interesting."

"And you think I'll go for that line?" she smirked.

"By the way, my name is Dave." He extended his hand. She took it briefly.

"Gloria," she said. "But please don't sit down. I'm still talking to my friend Manuel here." She pointed to the stocky man sitting on the stool on the other side of her.

"We do need to talk," Dave said, moving closer.

She shrugged and turned back toward Manuel.

"I've been trying to find a way to speak with you," he persisted. "This is the best I've come up with."

"Find another way," Gloria said and turned to Manuel. "I could use some help here."

Manuel stood on cue. The dirt and sweat on his T-shirt were those of a laborer. "Gloria here is off-limits. Leave while you're ahead." He spoke bluntly, obviously expecting results.

"I wasn't talking to you. I was talking to Gloria."

"Not as far as I'm concerned," Gloria said, with an insinuating nod to Manuel.

Dave turned toward the tense man with a friendly smile. "Manuel, give me a break. I really need to talk to Gloria. Let's exchange seats for just ten minutes. I'll buy you a beer to go with it; then I promise I'll take off if she wants."

"Get lost," Manuel said and turned back to Gloria.

Dave put a hand on his shoulder. Manuel shrugged it off. "Look, man, I don't mind a fight, but Gloria here's a real lady who needs our respect. You're tall, but you don't look so tough. And I've got buddies."

"I just want to talk to Gloria."

Without looking back, Manuel jabbed an elbow hard into Dave's gut. "Get lost!"

Dave lurched backward with the force of the blow and found himself entangled in the arms of several men poised to help their friend. He shook himself free, rapidly dropped to a crouch on one knee, and swept his other leg very hard against the sea of feet. Two men went down, and two others tottered backward. One of them steadied himself by putting his foot against Dave's chest. Dave reached past it and grabbed the man's wrist with both hands; leaning back, he brought his hands up, propelling the man over his shoulder. The man landed hard against Manuel. With a loud curse, Manuel leaped out of his seat and dived toward Dave.

Gloria grabbed him by his shirt to stop his progress. Then she put two fingers in her mouth and whistled loudly. "Stop it! All of you!"

Manuel gave her a brief look and reinstituted his charge. Dave ducked to one side and slapped him hard across the face as he careened past. Dave moved back into a crouch and circled slowly, defending himself against a potential rain of kicks and blows from the hostile group.

Gloria let out another piercing whistle. The bartender produced a bat and waved it in the air. Everybody stopped for a moment, and Gloria whistled for a third time; then she stepped down from her barstool as she held out her hand to Dave. "You're going to end up hurting them, Dave," she said under her breath.

"Probably," he said, wiping some blood off his forehead. "But how can you tell? I'm still playing around."

"Your moves are dangerous. You're a pro. I'm trained to recognize the real thing." She held on to his hand, and Dave let her pull him up to a standing position. "Save the seat, Manuel." The men hesitantly parted for her, and she led Dave to a small booth across the floor.

She took a seat against the wall, and Dave sat next to her, facing the crowd of men eying them warily.

"It's Friday night, and we work hard for a little recreation. Fights are part of the fun, but not with guys like you." She settled back in the booth, watching the men as they re-formed in their drinking groups. "OK. Here I am. You got your wish. Say what you have to say and then get out of here. They're not going to give us much time."

"I hoped you would rescue me before it got out of control. And you did."

"So you're clever too. Big deal. I don't want any violence. Manuel is like a brother, and this place is all about bonding with our own kind."

"I know. And that's not why I'm here."

"That's obvious. So talk and then get out of here."

"I'm checking out Debra Jean Lieberman."

Gloria glared at him. "I don't talk work, especially on Friday night. Besides, my work is confidential. Does that help?"

He ignored her angry gaze. "It's about what happened to her at MI. She's been a basket case ever since being let go. I'm trying to help her."

"You're a lawyer? A detective? You know I'm not going to talk about her even if I could. And if you're right, I'm part of the company that let her go."

"I'm not a lawyer or a detective."

Gloria turned toward the men, who were looking at them with increasing hostility. "We need to finish this. I'm not saying I even know her. But if I did, why should I listen to you?"

"Look, I know you work at MI. I know you were there when she left." Dave leaned toward Gloria, his palms on the table. "You obviously know her; I bet you didn't like what happened to her."

"Even so, why should I help her? I like my job; it took a lot to get it because I'm not white, rich, and connected like her." She met his eyes. "Or you."

"There're reasons that might make you interested. Maybe we need to find a place without all these guys staring at us."

Gloria liked his eyes. Then she realized she needed to hear what he had to say. Security at MI was her job, after all. Maybe he was the one involved in the recent data break-in attempts.

"OK, I'll listen and answer what I can, but not here, and only if you leave without hurting my friends."

"Might be difficult if they come after me."

"That's the bargain, Dave. I don't want to be the cause of a fight. I want to come back here and still have my friends."

He smiled amiably. "These guys are just being nice because of you. That won't last. Your bargain is more like a trial by fire."

Gloria was enjoying his dilemma. It was the most interesting thing that had happened her entire week. "You're right about that, and I am curious about how you're going to handle it. These men are just being polite, but the moment I get up from this table, you'll be fair game. Macho pride is what it's about on Friday nights, especially in an Irish bar half-filled with Latinos, most of whom want to show their Irish buddies how tough they are."

"An interesting challenge," Dave mused. "OK, you're on." He pulled out a cell phone, dialed Wiley's number, and spoke briefly. Then he turned to Gloria. "My partner, Wiley, will be here in ten minutes."

"So what? What makes you think I want to meet your partner?"

"Because you're going to like him. I can tell."

"You're thinking he'll help you get out of here without too much blood on the floor."

"No doubt about that."

She looked at her watch. "Ten minutes. Then you leave and we'll meet. That is, if you don't hurt them."

Dave glanced over her shoulder. "OK. Let's say the Empress on Union Square. The upstairs restaurant, half an hour after we leave. The reservation will be under my name, Dave Blue."

"I know the place." Gloria shook her head to help dismiss unpleasant memories. "Blue, huh? Can't place that one." She looked at her watch. "Seven more minutes."

They waited in silence. Gloria was feeling happy. A late-night adventure with two new guys was more promising than another boring night drinking with guys who treated her like a sister. "Remember, no bloodbath or I don't show up. That's the deal."

"Fine," Dave said more jauntily than he felt. He hoped Wiley was nearby. Taking on the whole room nonviolently would be a real challenge without him.

"You've got five more minutes," she said offhandedly. "Say, who made you so tall?"

"I hear my family came from Ukraine a hundred years ago. It's a tough country that breeds survivors. But if you think I'm tall, wait till you see who's coming to help."

"And your job?"

"I—Wiley and I—help people who are in trouble. People who need revenge and can't get it the legal way."

"Your clients should include most of us," she said ruefully. "But what do you actually do? Do you talk to people, try to get them to forget? That doesn't work with some of the people I know. Anyway, you don't look like a therapist."

"I'm not, and we don't just talk. We're more like Robin Hood or his Latin equivalent ..."

"Zorro. He was in California before this was a state."

Dave handed Gloria a white business card. "OK, a modern Zorro, then."

She read it and then put it in her purse. "Revenge, Inc., and a Sausalito houseboat address? You've got to be kidding."

"I'll be glad to show you our office, Gloria."

"Probably isn't going to happen. Your time is about up."

Dave was getting worried. "Still got two more minutes. Use it to tell me about yourself."

"Me in two minutes?" she said, continuing to feel pleased with herself. She liked controlling him; it was an interesting situation.

"Give me something personal and new. I checked MI, so I know the basics."

"Gotcha," she said. "You're the naughty boy who's been poking around where he shouldn't. I've been waiting for you to show up."

"I've told you I'm checking out MI's bosses for Debra Jean. The security you've set up is pretty effective. So you're the logical next step."

"Time's up," she said, rising to her feet. "Unless your friend arrives in the next 30 seconds, it's going to be you against the wolves."

Suddenly she was staring at the opening door. "Oh my," she said, with a sharp intake of breath. "I think he's here." She continued staring, her mouth hanging open. The man was stunning, at least six-foot-seven and perfectly proportioned. His features were clean cut, his hair sandy blond, and his skin the color of pearls. He stood perfectly still and scanned the group until he saw Dave. He smiled and waved his arm toward them. The men in the bar gradually turned to face him, and they parted to give him a great swath of space as he headed toward their table.

Dave grinned. "Yep, that's my friend. Name's Wiley."

Gloria felt her cheeks redden and breath quicken. "He's imposing—I'll give you that." She tried to regain her composure. "Well, it's all yours, Dave. I'll watch the melee from the bar."

"See you at the Empress, Gloria."

She looked again at Wiley. Even taller than his friend and much broader, he walked with the ease of a man who wouldn't and couldn't be threatened by anyone. She felt the twinge of a challenge grow inside her. He was like one of those Caucasian gods that probably doomed her Mayan ancestors to servitude for centuries. She walked quickly to the bar and sat next to Manuel. A new cold beer was waiting for her. She took a sip.

"Finally," Manuel said, loud enough for everyone to hear. "Making a date, Gloria?"

"It's really none of your business, Manuel," she said sarcastically. "For the record, he's definitely not a boyfriend. He wanted to talk to me about work. I told him to get lost."

"You took your time," Manuel mumbled, but Gloria ignored him. Wiley was striding toward Dave, his head floating a foot above the men surging toward him and Dave.

Gloria draped an arm over Manuel's shoulder, holding him back. He tried to shrug it off, adding his angry energy to a heavy-drinking mob ready for a fight, but she held on. Some of the men watched her.

A few men were crowding Dave's table as Wiley arrived. One threw a hard punch at him. He stayed perfectly still, letting it bounce off his chest. More kicks and punches followed, and Dave tried to stand up to help his friend, who was now weaving and bobbing to keep the blows from hitting his face. Wiley continued to shake off blows but motioned Dave to sit down.

He stepped into the melee, clearing a space in front of him. Then he took a deep breath and began to sing, quietly at first and then louder, his voice gradually filling the room with a high sweet tenor. The song was familiar, "Green Eyes," and he sang it with great feeling.

Gloria watched from the bar with amazement as the confused men gradually become quiet. A hush fell over the room. Most of them knew the song, although some had not heard it since childhood in their homelands. A few men began to hum along, and some drummed on the tables. She could see their eyes glistening, tension leaving their bodies, the room suddenly alive with the Spanish words and rhythm.

Gloria felt something melt inside of her, and from the deepest part of her soul she began to sing, too. She hadn't heard the song for such a long time. Her father's voice came to her. Her throat filled with emotion as tears rolled down her cheeks.

Aquellos ojos verdes
de mirada serena,
dejaron en mi alma
eterna sed de amar.

Those green eyes
with their serene gaze,

they left in my soul
eternal thirst to love.

The tall man never looked her way, but Gloria felt as if he was singing it to her, just as her dad would have done in the village square at night around a fire. It was the sound of her ancient home.

Her singing was the catalyst for others, and soon the room was filled with men's and women's voices. The fight that had never begun was over.

No saben las tristezas
que en mi alma han dejado,
aquellos ojos verdes,
que yo nunca olvidaré.

They do not know the sadness
that in my soul they have left,
those green eyes,
that I never will forget.

As the song ended, Wiley and Dave moved slowly toward the bar, and Wiley held two $100 bills in the air. "The drinks are on us." He placed them on the bar with a sharp rap, and he and Dave moved to the door and through it.

"Just in time," Dave said, once they gained the street and walked quickly away from the bar along Mission. "Your singing was great."

"It was Gloria's adding her voice that really rescued us."

"No, Wiley, it was you. But how did you recognize her?" Dave asked.

"It was her green eyes. It had to be her. Didn't you mention her eyes? That's why I chose the song."

"No, Wiley. I didn't mention her eyes."

"Well, I guessed. Do you think she'll meet us at the Empress?"

"Yes. Gloria agreed, but only if no one was to get hurt. But you're right. I wasn't really sure what would happen until she came in on your song. I think she's hooked on you. Her body started shaking when she first saw you. Pretty voice, nice body, long legs too. She wants you ..."

"C'mon." Wiley cut him off. "Is she worth all this trouble—for our case, I mean?"

"Absolutely. She's our only decent lead."

"There must have been some other way to contact her. You risked a bad night, my friend."

Dave slowed their rapid pace. "I think she was secretly glad this all happened. All those adopted brothers keep her on a tight leash. It got a bit rough before you arrived."

Wiley appraised his friend. "Or maybe you just felt like some action."

"She made me promise that I wouldn't hurt them or she wouldn't talk. I was lucky that you made it here so fast. How did you do it?"

"Fortunately, I was already in the city when you called. I'm glad that I rescued you for lots of reasons. The whole scene was like being in the middle of a great big family: you were making trouble, stealing their little sister."

"You're such a romantic, Wiley. And that song! I'd bet it moved the guys in the bar because you reminded them of how they missed their mothers rather than their current girlfriends. It's you who once told me that bar drinkers are usually mama's boys." Dave rolled his eyes. "The way you looked at her had nothing to do with the maternal. Watch out for Gloria. She's tough, she's trouble, she's after you, and right now you're a pushover."

CHAPTER 9

Men Are Like That

The Empress Hotel, on Union Square, was an easy 20-minute walk, and Wiley and Dave relaxed from their Borstal's encounters by ambling up Fifth Street toward Market and watching the last of the happy-hour revelers gearing up for the bridge commutes to their suburban homes in Marin and the South and East Bay.

They had to wait a long time for a pedestrian signal to cross Market and head up Powell Street to Union Square.

"Now tell me what you learned at the bar before I saved your ass," Wiley said. "And *por favor*, more about Gloria before we meet."

Dave smiled knowingly. "Gloria is diverting, isn't she, so we'll start with the obvious. She's a beautiful and sexy woman. She's savvy with lots of street smarts. Example: When I first made contact with her in Borstal's, there was a little altercation with some of her men friends. Nothing serious, but Gloria spotted my martial talents. She agreed to talk with me so that I wouldn't hurt them. Very counterintuitive—the whole bar was against me, but of course she was right."

"What else, Dave?"

"She's very loyal. She went out of her way not to get her friends hurt. But she's also needy. She values her community."

"You said before that she wanted to get free of them."

"She's like a sister to those guys and feels smothered. She wants some other kind of action, and she was clearly having fun with me, but she's serious about her work as head of MI security. She connected me to the data break-in from the start. She gave me a hard time, but she knew that we had to talk."

"You like her."

"Yes."

"Do you want her?"

Dave stopped at a crosswalk. "Wiley. What's going on? You didn't even talk to her and you're interested?"

"She's very good-looking. I could feel her energy across the room."

"So I was right. That nice tenor vibrato that wowed the group—it was all for her, and she knew it."

"I guess."

"'Green Eyes' indeed. No wonder you chose a love song. Not exactly the best idea if you didn't want to make them jealous."

"For these guys, it was a memory of better days," Wiley said.

"You touched something deep," Dave said, nodding. "Sometimes when I hear a Yiddish song, I feel something both alien and dear, and I end up sad and a little lost. But also more alive."

"Gloria was crying," Wiley said.

"I know," Dave said quietly. "You obviously hit a nerve in her. But her singing reflected more than nostalgia. She sang because she wanted to help you and her brothers. She was hoping there would be no fight so that we all could meet tonight."

"Just doing her job?" Wiley questioned.

They both spontaneously picked up the pace and were soon a half-block from the square. "That and more," Dave said. "But I'll bet we'll learn a lot about MI and its bosses in the process."

Wiley nodded. "Gloria is at the hub of the organization."

They dodged a few homeless men pushing shopping carts loaded with clothes and blankets. "You know, when I mentioned Debra Jean, Gloria's eyes lit up," Dave said.

The green-and-white awning of the Empress was just in view a block ahead on the right. Wiley leaned toward his friend. "You did good to connect with her, Dave. And I'll do my best to make sure that she's well motivated to give us what we want."

CHAPTER 10

Extreme Pleasures

T onight will be one helluva night!" Joe Diamond shouted exuberantly to the darkening sky as he walked out of MI to the waiting limo.

The work session with Paul had exceeded his expectations. He only wished their work collaboration could include tonight's plans as well. What would Paul be doing? Probably reading alone, waiting for his wife to return from a lover's bedroom. If that was the extent of his colleague's eccentricities, so be it. Paul's practical brilliance was still indispensable for MI's success.

He asked the chauffeur to stop in North Beach to pick up an espresso for him at Trieste and then walked up the short, steep hill to his penthouse at the top of Green Street. He headed directly for the outside entrance to his home office, a room he had crafted himself with the help of a pricey designer. He opted for a décor of 19th-century Victorian: lampshades of colored smoked-glass mosaics from the Netherlands, and plush silk and velvet divans in shades of red, purple, and indigo with matching pillows and wall coverings. The floor was strewn with expensive Oriental rugs. Only the walls violated the authenticity of the décor, with an eclectic mix of Dali, Eakins, Velázquez, and Hockney, all original and colorful enough to blend together without jarring the senses too much. It exactly expressed his eccentric, sybaritic tastes.

A switch at the door turned on the floor lamps, and he added to the atmosphere by lighting sandalwood candles throughout the room. Then he opened an elegant humidor, from which he took out a pinch of cocaine, some marijuana buds, and a small amount of tobacco. He filled a cigarette paper with a connoisseur's mixture of all three ingredients and then rolled a small joint, which he lit from one of the candles.

Smoke streaming from his nostrils, he walked to the old-fashioned desk at one end of the room and sat in a black and gold padded chair with Harvard's motto, "VERITAS," embossed on its back. A large computer monitor framed in ornate oak took up half of the desk. At the touch of a button, a computer keyboard, simulating an old-fashioned typewriter, slid out from a hidden recess at the front of the desktop. Joe activated access to the Internet and videoconferencing. A few touches connected him to his favorite site, the encrypted virtual world of Sons of Mozart.

The organization he had founded in adolescence was his first and best iteration of an endless need for an alternative social universe, a self-sculptured family. It had fulfilled his best hopes, a place where he could feel at home with a group of individuals who matched his perverse genius.

His original family had been desperately ambitious. When his father discovered that his only child was a prodigy, he decided to concentrate all his energies on exploiting his son's multiple talents. Newspaper and magazine articles featuring their child-rearing practices sold particularly well in the child-oriented culture. But little Joe was as prodigious at understanding the dynamics of his parents' financial exploitation as he was about everything else. At nine, he began turning the tables on them, persuading a newspaper reporter who covered his first prize at a state science fair to exclude his mother and father from the photographs. Two years later, he refused to turn over royalties from his best-selling collection of poems about the death of a girl in his class from leukemia. Seeing their life plan slipping away, his father challenged his son aggressively, first over the kitchen table and later in the courts. Lawyers and child advocates rushed to fill the void left by a warring family. In a well-publicized settlement, Joe eventually gave his father a lump sum of money in return for his parents' relinquishing all future rights to their son's earnings.

Joe found his mother's manipulative love a tougher challenge than his father's avarice. He needed her attention and love, and she knew and used that need to control him. When Joe was 12, adolescence hit, and by 14, he grew tired of the increasingly petty battles over his freedom. At 15, he was admitted to Harvard, which freed him from any further guardianship.

He had high hopes of finding intellectual and social stimulation from his classmates. Unfortunately, there was little respect among the other students for a child genius, so he set about designing the proto-group that would eventually morph into Sons of Mozart.

Secret societies had been a part of scholarly life for thousands of years, he reasoned, and Harvard students were bound to be particularly susceptible to their allure. He began to search for others who shared his particular interests, which he gradually understood were all about the pleasures of control.

He began by sending letters to all the undergrads, advertising his group. His first attempts met with failure. Even at Harvard, there were few extraordinary students, and none who were immediately interested in joining a group with a 15-year-old student as its leader. So Joe broadened his target population to include students in elite universities worldwide. The response was still meager. Undaunted, he focused his appeals on young prodigies who might share a special psychology derived initially from their battles with greedy parents. That seemed to work, and so Sons of Mozart was born, named after the great prodigy and composer whose difficult relationship with his father spoke so poignantly to its members. He liked the double-entendre of the initials of the group's name, for he had already grasped that the pleasures of control went to the heart and soul of most prodigies' psychologies. Now, 30 years later, Sons of Mozart claimed a carefully vetted membership of 300, with another 300 junior and associate members waiting for "full privileges," a euphemism for access to some of SM's more licentious activities.

Joe finished his smoke and turned his full attention to the SM website. He clicked the events portal of the San Francisco bulletin board. It showed a party in the 29th floor suite at the Empress, a superb hotel on Union Square. The posted details suggested a midnight discussion of the influence of Schopenhauer's philosophy on Richard Wagner's personal history and habits. Translation: ultra-sex, possibly snuff potential, and other high-risk pleasure games. That gave him time to post a video of some of the new developments in his research for his scientific peers in the group and also to post a description of the recent attempts to breach MI's database, as well as a little history of potential suspects. Helping each other's progress in their rarefied world gave the pleasure of belonging to individuals who rarely belonged anywhere. Because he was the founder, curiosity would run high on the reasons for the break-in. Five members messaged him within a half-hour, and he brainstormed with them for two more hours, expecting even more discussion with others in the next few days.

At 11:30, pleasantly high with drugs and ideas, he dressed in an elegant midnight-blue Indian *lungi*, chosen in honor of Schopenhauer's cultural fetish. He packed a small overnight bag and put on a light topcoat to reduce his visibility. Then he called his chauffeur and set out for Union Square.

CHAPTER 11

Smart Mouth

A few minutes after Wiley and Dave left Borstal's, Gloria excused herself from her friends. The bar was still stirring with the impromptu concert, but she knew that she would eventually have to answer to Manuel for the conversation with Dave in the booth. With Wiley's song reverberating in her body, she quickly said her good-byes and asked the bartender to get her a cab.

At the Empress, she took the elevator to the restaurant on the 30th floor. She confirmed a reservation made under the name Blue for three; the hostess assured her with a too-knowing smile that they had not yet arrived. When Gloria asked to be seated at the reserved table, the hostess politely demurred and suggested that she wait at the bar. Gloria turned away. Was the hostess identifying her as a single Latina in a late-night restaurant looking for lonely businessmen and tourists to ply her trade? Her friends said she was paranoid, but they knew little about the habits of men in fancy hotels in San Francisco. Probably the hostess didn't want to seat her without the entire party present, but she couldn't be sure. She walked to the elevator. She would wait for Dave and Wiley in the lobby.

When it came, she sped downward in what felt like free fall. She spotted a small seating area where she wouldn't be bothered and bought a copy of the morning's *New York Times* from a newsstand outside of the closed sundries store at the back of the lobby. The highbrow newspaper would help her to fend off any offensive inquiries from passersby. Then she ordered a large coffee from a hostess serving the lounge and sat waiting for Dave and Wiley.

The coffee was delicious and she ordered another. The Empress Hotel, despite its safety and elegant service at any time of the day or night, was not her favorite place. It held too many sordid memories, but seven years ago, it had brought her an exceptional piece of good luck when she first met a man named John White, alias Joe Diamond. She sat back and stared at the high ornate ceiling covered with florid murals. That encounter had been rank, but also the luckiest of her life. The memory of that night flooded back.

* * *

Gloria sat curled up on a plush sofa in the living room of an elegant junior suite on the 20th floor of the venerable old Empress Hotel. The suites were very expensive and often hired by the week or weekend by corporations and nonprofits for favored clients who liked comfort and private high-end parties at night while they did deals during the day. The party this night was for two, Gloria and a special client, John White, referred to her from an escort service named Ideal Nights. As always, the client was told that what they did sexually was up to her.

The curtains had been left open to reveal a large expanse of startling clear moonless sky replete with brilliant stars. She stood and walked closer to the window to see the lights of the city below, and beyond the dense hillside city to the dark expanse of bay made visible only by the lights of the Golden Gate Bridge on the Pacific Ocean. Looking past the north end of the bridge, she could see the dark bulk of the Marin Headlands, the half-circle of lights defining Sausalito, and an occasional mast light from boats anchored out in the bay.

The great orange bridge never ceased to amaze her. After a year in this city, she had yet to cross it on foot or even in a car; she only gazed at it from the San Francisco side when walking with friends around Lands End and Crissy Field. They teased her about a fear of heights, and she didn't dissuade them from their idea. She was simply waiting for the right moment, a time when she was ready to "cross over" to a new life that didn't include the tribulations of her current disaster. Waiting for her new client, she knew the right moment was still far in the future, but looking out at the spectacular beauty in front of her, she promised herself that it would come.

There was a chime at the door. Reluctantly, she turned away and walked across the room. She looked through the view hole on the door and saw an intense-looking man waiting expectantly.

She took a good look at herself in the mirror near the door. She saw a beautiful young woman unmarred except for some worry lines on her forehead and at the corners of her eyes. Rouge and deep red lipstick brought out the dusky complexion that was her birthright. She had large fake rubies on her earlobes and several ropes of fake pearls playing around her full breasts, which were half-covered by a red blouse with an open neck. Her skirt was maroon silk, and she wore white sandals on her bare feet. She was always amazed at how well she looked the part she was now playing.

She held out her hand to John White as he walked in and looked her up and down with evident pleasure. He took her by the hand and walked her to the sofa.

"Hello, Gloria," he said jauntily, completely in control. "Your real name? I like to get these things straight at the beginning."

"It's mine and I'm real."

"Smart mouth and very pretty. Nicely dressed too."

He put his hand on her thigh over her skirt and watched her reaction. "Good. You're young but not shy." His unblinking, knowing eyes provoked her. "You're used to doing this."

Gloria nodded despite herself. She was not averse to sleeping with the men who bought her time, but her role did not require it. She poured him a glass of French Champagne from the open iced bottle she had prepared for his coming. She replaced it in the silver bucket on the glass table in front of them. She watched him try it.

"Want some?" he asked. "It's good."

She smiled, poured herself a glass, and then sipped it slowly. "Glad you like it, John."

"Good and cold. Still bubbly. You must've opened it just before I came."

"And you were on time."

John looked her over again. "I know you're very young, Gloria. How long have you worked for Ideal?"

"Long enough."

"You have an interesting way of talking. Very sure of yourself. Ideal told me you were 21. I'd say just barely. I imagine you've spent a couple of difficult years to gain such confidence. How did you get hired by such a well-known escort service? I'm always interested in the background of the women I get intimate with."

"Remember. That intimacy will depend on me, John."

"Of course it will. Ideal was very clear about that. Would you like to go to a late-night spot after we finish this superb Champagne? It's a way of having clean fun and your getting to know me better."

She disliked his cockiness, and she did not find him physically attractive—she hated his mustache—but there was an energy in his words that made her curious in every way. More than curious, she thought, as she monitored her body's reaction to him.

"I don't mind talking; it's your time, John."

"It is indeed. But it's your time as well," he said confidently, "a precious commodity you should treat with the utmost care and consideration. You're a delicious woman," he continued, in a tone blending arrogance and generosity, "but you'll taste even better if I know some of the ingredients."

Gloria was amazed at how easily he was controlling the direction of the evening while allowing her to make all the decisions. Fortunately it was a direction that she, and her body, now seemed to favor. And Gloria very much wanted to talk to this man who used words so well. Furthermore, she saw no reason not to tell him some of the truth.

"I left my adoptive home in San Diego at 14 and kicked around the streets. I took odd jobs, trying to finish high school. It wasn't easy, and I began working part time as a dancer in a club to pay the rent. People there would ask me out for more than lap dances, which was against the rules, but occasionally I'd go with them and it was fine. Made me feel like I was a girl, if you know what I mean. Of course the money was great, and I needed that. I never got in trouble.

"Then I met a married guy who wanted me as a regular girlfriend. Like a mistress, he said. The people at the club got wind of it and threatened to fire me. They were my security, and so naturally I was scared. I mentioned it to him the next time he came to the club. He thought for a while and said I'd be getting a call from an escort service, Ideal Nights. That way I could quit the club and be available to him. He didn't mind my taking other work. And he said Ideal was high-class and protected its employees."

John finished his glass of Champagne and motioned for her to pour another. Good choice. I bet you don't work as hard as you did before. I never understood what women got out of lap dancing."

"That's easy. Control. Men in my control." She smiled at her comment. She'd never said that out loud before, but it was true.

"You like that, Gloria. That surprises me. Most beautiful woman like being controlled by men."

"I guess so," she said, feeling very young and outclassed. "I don't think of my work that way. Mostly I like the money. Ideal takes a 40 percent cut, so I depend more on tips."

"I'll bet you do. And thanks for telling me so much about yourself, Gloria. I know you don't have to if you don't want to."

"But I want to." She put her hand on his knee. He held it there for a moment and then moved it up between his legs. Why not? she thought. Without quite making a decision, she already knew how this night would go.

John didn't move against her hand. "Gloria, your talk is exciting. You're exciting. You know I'm a businessman and always looking for a good prospect. Who knows? Maybe I'll buy the company and put you to work for me. Maybe I'll buy you." He laughed too loudly. "Just kidding."

She laughed with him and gently stroked his prick, which grew larger under his pants. "Ideal gives me the protection I need, John. They screen the clients. They give me a pager in case I get into trouble. That's a lot. I plan to stay with them. But tonight, with you, could be fun."

She raised her leg and put it over his thigh, straddling him. "You want more Champagne or more of me?"

"You, Gloria." She moved on his thighs suggestively, and her skirt rode high on her hips.

"Very nice move. You give me no choice. To the bedroom with you."

She rose and hugged him. He moved away and led her through the door. "Any questions for me, Gloria? You've been very good answering mine."

"None." She wanted to ask if he was from out of town looking for adventure or escaping from his wife. She guessed he was local. Could be a great client, she thought. Could be another regular for her.

"You have a gorgeous body," he said, when she had undressed. "And you are very young." He caressed and then licked her pink nipples. "And never been pregnant. You're really quite perfect."

She helped him to undress. When he immediately began roughly caressing her vagina, she slipped away and pushed him on his side. She had made a mistake in not going to a club when he had suggested it. She began oral sex, hoping to get him off quickly. He seemed to relish whatever she did with her mouth and tongue, but he never came close to coming, never even had that light sticky fluid that came right before men got off. After a long while, her tongue got tired and she let him enter her. He pumped her for a long time, and she pretended to respond and even tried to fake a climax to get him off. It didn't work. He took more and more control, switching from one variety of sexual acrobatics to another, soon including deep anal penetration. Then he suggested a variety of fantasies, which she carried out to the best of her ability. But despite all her moves and a great deal of time, he stayed hard and eager but never came.

Eventually, to her great relief, he returned to simple missionary intercourse, but it went on and on, and after a while, the repetition began to hurt her insides.

She stopped moving and deliberately made eye contact. "Look, is there something you want from me that I'm not doing? You're very big and this is uncomfortable. I'm not enjoying this at all."

He was annoyed by her question. "Your enjoyment is not my concern. This is your job, isn't it? And as a matter of fact, there is something you could do better. What turns me on most is watching you come. I mean really come, not faking it like you've done a couple of times. A genuine big orgasm. Screaming and kicking or singing, whatever you do. Just so it's real."

Gloria wasn't surprised. Most men liked that but rarely asked for it. But it was something she didn't like to do, particularly not in front of a guy with an aging body and a mean mouth. But this guy was definitely someone who wanted his way, so why not? She closed her eyes and imagined some of the young men on the San Diego beaches, and with lots of pressure from her fingers, she succeeded in generating a few real spasms and whimpers, which she exaggerated as best she could.

He was watching her when she opened her eyes.

"That's much better, Gloria. But didn't I say I need you to look at me when that happens?" He smiled derisively. "Well, it's true. Don't I look good to you?" He stretched his body and held his still-erect penis in his fist. "I bet you were thinking of some hot girl. Or maybe your brother or father."

"You're a shit."

He smirked. "Good! Real sounds and real emotions are what I want, Gloria. So try to come again, but this time with more feeling. And with your eyes open."

"My vagina's bleeding." She showed him her fingers, which were smeared with blood. "And this isn't my period." She was near to tears. "You have to pay me a lot more to continue. It's been three hours."

"Get me off a couple of times," he drawled. "I've told you what works for me. And I'll give you a great big tip that Ideal won't need to know about."

The hour was pure hell. All he wanted to do was watch her masturbate, and his increasing condescension as she tried and failed made any real excitement impossible. He seemed to know when she faked, and eventually she gave herself up to every perverse movement he ordered. He watched intently while drinking Champagne and playing with himself. He never came.

She lay exhausted and humiliated on the bed. "You need to go, John. You can watch me sleep instead of fucking myself. I don't know what your problem is, but I can't help you."

"I don't have a problem, Gloria. I just love giving girls like you a hard time. See, before I arrived, I took a very high dose of Zoloft. It's an antidepressant, which in that amount stops men from having orgasms for about four hours. It's your time to watch, sweetie." He jerked at his penis for 30 seconds and ejaculated into his hand, which he dried on the sheet.

He stood next to the bed and looked down at her. "This was great, Gloria," he said with a sadistic chuckle. "And don't worry, I won't call you again. No fun. You'll know my tricks, won't you?" He left the bed, gathered up some of his things, and walked into the bathroom, not closing the door. She heard him pee and then turn on the shower.

He had taken his wallet and watch with him but left his pants and jacket. Furious, Gloria went through his clothing and was rewarded with a business card tucked in the inside pocket of his jacket, displaying the name Joe Diamond in raised letters. It said he was CEO of a company called the Molecular Institute in San Francisco. She put the card under the crumpled sheets.

He came back to the room and dressed. "This has been nice, and you've been a good sport. I'm not a bad guy, Gloria. At least not as bad as some. Take my advice: You're smart. Think about what you're good at and use it. And I don't mean sex, because that's not it."

When he was dressed, he put some money in an envelope from the hotel desk and left the room without looking back.

"Thanks," she said to his back. When the door closed, she opened the envelope. In it were two $20 bills. She screamed in fury and then desperately searched through the sheets for the crumpled card. It looked genuine, but it was probably another one of his mean tricks.

CHAPTER 12

Tengo Miedo

Gloria gradually emerged from her remembrance and checked her watch. Dave and Wiley were 10 minutes late. She'd give them another 15 minutes and then leave. She studied the empty lobby again before settling back into her chair and what she remembered of the next time she saw Joe Diamond.

She sat on the only comfortable sofa in an ultra-high-tech room on the 45th floor of the Transamerica Pyramid waiting for her interview. She walked to the window for a better look at the spectacular panorama, but the building was swaying in the moderate wind. She went back to her sofa; she felt safer seated.

The impact of that evening with "John White" had never ended. It wasn't just about his cruelty and pleasure at her humiliation; it was his so outwitting her that really stung. It was being so seen, so played, so used. She wanted to take revenge, maybe blackmail him. All the girls at the clubs wanted to do that but rarely tried. It was too dangerous. When she had been hired by Ideal Nights, she was strongly cautioned never to deal with clients on her own. She knew that if she threatened him in any way, she'd be fired, blackmailed, or arrested, whichever came first.

So she kept his card on her nightstand and waited for him to return. True to his word, he stayed away. Then she waited for time to bring relief. Often she would stare at his real name, Joe Diamond, before going to sleep, thinking of what she would do to him if she got the chance. But always afterward she'd have a dream of painful images from her past: a little girl desperate for help in a gutted village, fragments of abuse in the orphanage in El Salvador, her adoptive father's humiliating comments about the blood of her first menstrual period, and the fear and loneliness of living on her own.

Then one night she dreamed that she was walking on the village road of her childhood. Her feet were wet; there was a river of blood running in the grooves of mud. She knew for certain that it was her parents' blood, and she began collecting it in a holy vessel, which she put on her church altar. Next to it appeared a wreath of new spring flowers collected in an earthen pot. She took one of the flowers and placed it in the lapel of a fashionable new business suit she was wearing.

She liked the dream and kept thinking about what it might mean. That she must no longer be a victim. That she must grow up and stop taking the easy way. That she must start using her body, her beauty, and her mind to get what she wanted. That someday she would be able to cross the great Golden Gate Bridge and begin her new life. What had John said as he left? "Figure out what you're good at and use it."

A plan of how to accomplish that gradually emerged. She reduced her plan to a short list of actions and followed it step by step:

First step: Check out the card she had stolen and find out if the Molecular Institute and Joe Diamond, alias John White, really existed. Gloria used her computer to do a search and found its website. And Joe Diamond was indeed its listed CEO. The company's offices were in Mission Bay. Next day, Gloria walked from her apartment in the Mission to check the place out. It occupied one of the low-rise buildings located near the new UCSF campus. There was security at the door, an older Hispanic man she was sure she could con. She walked home feeling better than she had in months.

Second step: Get an appointment to see Joe Diamond. After several calls, she spoke to his personal secretary, Anna Montez. From her accent, Gloria knew she was Salvadoran, too. And although neither said anything about it, she knew that their common Salvadoran heritage gave her an edge for receiving an appointment with the big man.

Final step: Make the most of that appointment.

* * *

"He's giving you ten minutes," Anna said in accented English, barely looking at Gloria from behind a large computer screen. "That's a standard interview for new customers. I've told him you are the daughter of the head of a big construction company in Central America, just like you said."

"Good. Thanks, Anna." She was around 40, pretty, and expensively dressed, and she wore a midsized diamond with a wedding band.

"Of course I don't believe you," Anna said easily. "Not for a minute. I know you're just like me. We both come from some poor village up in the mountains of our country. I hate to say it, dear, but whatever you are planning won't work. Joe will see right through you. He'll get that it's a scam pretty quickly. He's very experienced at handing all kinds of ... hustlers. The deal is for you not to include me in your pitch."

Gloria was silent and then shook her head slightly. "You're misjudging me, and I'm holding some cards. But thank you for helping me."

Anna pivoted in her chair to face Gloria and finally switched to Spanish. "You've got some kind of guts. A job is what you're after, right?"

Gloria nodded.

"Well, who knows? I got you this chance. Don't embarrass me—or yourself. He uses one of the offices on the first floor to meet unknowns. Doesn't want anyone in his lab upstairs. Security. So you're only half in the door."

And then Anna was walking her into a small office toward Joe Diamond, whom she knew as John White. He sat behind a tidy teak desk in its center, facing the picture window. When Gloria looked at him, she felt a rush of confidence. She had seen his aging body and knew his petty sexual trick. All she had to do was stick to her plan. When he finally turned, his eyes glinted with attraction that was followed swiftly by recognition. He pointed to the seat opposite his desk, dismissed Anna, and shut off his phone. He was very still and silent, watching her closely. But his eyes flickered with interest, not fear. Gloria withdrew two business cards from her purse, one wrinkled, the other brand new, and put both on his desk.

"You know who I am," she said as innocently as possible.

He glanced at his card. "Of course. The naive young woman at the Empress. An interesting night."

"I want help, a way to get out of my current life."

Surprised, he sat back in his chair and eyed her suspiciously. Then he picked up Gloria's business card and looked at the name on it. "Gloria

Garcia. So you weren't lying about its being your real name. You're obviously not the daughter of some construction magnate from Central America."

"Dr. Diamond—"

"You can call me Joe. We've been … close. OK. Get to the point. And don't even think of blackmail. It won't work."

"I know. That night, I couldn't please you. Now I'd like to try."

"I told you I didn't want a return ticket."

"I haven't heard from you for six months, so I believe you. But I'm also sure you put in a good word for me. I got a number of good clients after that night."

"You picked that up, did you? Good for you. I felt you deserved someone you could lead around by the nose. I was asking a lot. You deserved a reward," Joe said. "How on earth did you find me? Ideal has good security for top clients like me. Oh, the card …"

"I found it in your jacket pocket. Did you leave it there for me?"

"Good question." He cocked his head, considering. "Maybe."

"I looked up your company on the Internet. I like what you do, what I can understand of it. Basic research and new drugs for serious illnesses. Who wouldn't like that?"

"Please, Gloria." He snickered under his breath. "This is the interview you asked for. You've got ten minutes to explain why I should give you a job. Begin by telling me what I need that I don't have." He sat back smugly.

Gloria had not expected this. "Security," she blurted out. "Your secretary is fine, but the guy at the door was easy. So I want you to train me in security. I'd be good at it. I know how to handle tough guys and rich guys and most people in between. I need some school skills and some technical training."

"Security, huh? Good for you. Maybe I've thought too little about it. Always assumed I'd know when trouble was brewing." He leaned back in his chair and swiveled it toward the window. "You probably conned Anna to get you in here. That's another good trick. You want to tell me how?"

Gloria was silent.

Joe smiled. "Right answer." He turned his back to her and then spoke to the brilliant view below: "Well, why not? You're much better off under my wing than running around alone, Gloria. I owe you a tip for a night's action, which I thoroughly enjoyed. And somehow what happened has changed you, right?" He turned to face her. "So here's what I'll do. You quit your job with Ideal and clean up anything you do or use illegally. I don't want to know. Take six months and come back with a clean physical exam and one or two Internet courses in business under your belt. Then we'll see."

"I've done all that, and only men with letters after their name can afford six months without pay."

He eyed her carefully. "Do you have a record?"

"There was never anything major."

"I'll check on that too."

She knew he was blowing her off. "Be my guest, but Joe, six more months is too long," she said evenly. "I'm clean now, and I've been taking courses for a year."

"How long do you need?" he asked quietly.

"I'm ready today. I wouldn't have come here unless I was ready to go. You know that!" She returned to being meek. "What do you think, Joe? Don't you trust me?" She smiled girlishly.

"You'll need a lot of training, Gloria. You'll need a college degree, probably in police science. You'll need to be good with a computer. You'll need some languages besides English and Spanish. MI will soon do business all over the world."

"I can't promise Chinese or Arabic."

He laughed. "Not bad. Maybe I didn't take full advantage of your skills."

"Not part of that deal, Joe."

"It could take four years to complete what I want. You could work here some of that time. It's a large investment for me and hard work for you."

"I don't want to keep on making money at places like men's clubs and Ideal."

He thought for a moment, and then, making up his mind, turned his chair to face her squarely. "Fair enough. I'll go the whole way. I'll pay the tuition and have Anna show you around." He looked at her sharply.

"Another question. Why do you think I'm being so generous?"

"Because you're a player," Gloria said immediately. "And you like my style. Back there in the Empress suite, you saw someone worth playing with. I didn't win, but neither did I fold." All at once she felt totally alive.

He pursed his lips. "It's my game that you're in now, Gloria. Don't ever forget that, or you'll lose everything. Now our ten minutes are up. Leave your address and phone number with Anna, and we'll call as soon as we check out what you've said. That's it."

Gloria left the room without shaking hands. She could have fallen into his arms in gratitude, but showing how much it mattered wasn't part of her scenario. She made it to Anna's desk and the sound of his door closing, and then burst into tears.

Much later that night, she thought that the interview had been her first moment of adulthood.

* * *

Gloria glanced at her watch again. Ten more minutes had passed. Perhaps they weren't coming. She should leave, but the memory of Wiley stopped her. She needed to see him again. She'd give it another 15 minutes before she got a cab to her apartment.

Twenty minutes later, Gloria began folding her *Times* and considering where the bathroom was and how she would get the information she needed about Wiley and Dave to MI. By missing this appointment, they had become prime suspects for the break-in.

Just then, a heavyset man entered the lobby at the head of a group of people. As they came closer, she thought he looked Russian: squat, tough, built like a bull. Then she realized that she had seen him before. He was one of the few friends of Joe Diamond's whom she had seen. His name was Zvi; she had heard Joe call him that when signing him in at MI. She had asked Joe who he was, but Joe said that he would personally vouch for the man. He was off-limits to her. But no one was off-limits to her. So she had tried to get a make on him and failed.

Walking behind Zvi were two olive-skinned little girls, seven to nine years old, their heads down, half-hidden behind Zvi's bulk. At the end of the line was a small, squat woman, Asian or South American, dressed in a severe business suit and chunky black shoes and wearing wire-framed glasses. She was followed by a tall, thin olive-skinned Latino man dressed in a dark business suit.

The group headed toward the elevator. Gloria tried to imagine a happy family returning from a late dinner or show. Probably the kids would want to watch a little TV and be tucked in by their parents and kissed on their foreheads. But Zvi didn't fit the picture, and neither did the couple, hardly loving parents in her eyes. Gloria remembered what it was like to go somewhere with bullying attendants who controlled instead of caring. Just then, one of the children spoke in a high voice, which carried across the room. She heard Spanish, "*Tengo miedo*," then an angry hiss from the woman: "*Silencio*." The elevator doors opened and the children were pushed in. She glimpsed their faces looking back, helpless, clearly frightened to be there. A happy family? No. Their expressions were frozen in forced compliance, their eyes vacant, their mouths closed against words, their hands clenched in despair.

Gloria stood up and quickly moved toward the elevator's open door. The tall man saw her movement and gave her a warning glance. She felt a wave of fear pass through her, along with another memory of the orphanage in El Salvador. The elevator doors closed. She watched the floor indicator slowly move across its half-circle. It stopped at the 29th floor.

She returned to the sitting area and tried to relax. She had no idea what to do. The image of Wiley floated into her mind again. He didn't need to use the muscle he had; it was just one element of him that added to his presence as a strong man. He had managed a group of hostile men with such ease, singing his way out of Borstal's without throwing a punch! Why was she so obsessed with him? Sexual attraction for sure, but there was something even deeper that reminded her of her father.

Wiley was a natural leader. He would know how to assess and handle what she had just seen.

She sat staring at the lobby entrance, wishing he and Dave would appear. Instead, a familiar man came through the revolving door. She brought the newspaper up to her face as she watched Joe Diamond move swiftly to the elevator. Like the group before him, he looked around carefully before pressing the button. What was he doing here? Probably dinner at the same restaurant where her reservations waited. She watched as he entered the elevator and the doors closed behind. The floor indicator showed the floors as the elevator ascended. It was going up to the top and the restaurant … no! It stopped at the 29th floor as it had with the other group.

"Gloria." She recognized Dave's voice as he entered the hotel. Wiley was with him. "Sorry to keep you waiting. Getting here took longer than we thought it would."

She stood shaking. "I don't like to be kept waiting."

"Sorry," Dave said again. Her shaking increased.

"I told you I don't like to be kept waiting," she said, looking at the thick rug beneath her.

"C'mon, it's more than that," Wiley spoke for the first time and held out his hand. "Gloria, we haven't really been introduced. My name is Wiley, Wiley Stone."

Gloria took his hand. It was huge. She felt encompassed by all of him.

"Your hand is shaking," he said, still holding on.

Gloria looked up into his face, deciding. She could get away if she continued to feign annoyance. She could just walk out the door.

"Right now I just want to go home, OK?"

She looked at the door, but Wiley's hand restrained her. "It's very late. If you're leaving, at least let us get you a cab. It's our fault you've waited."

She looked up into his face and realized that she didn't want to be alone. She wanted help. "A family just came through the lobby and took the hotel elevator, except that it wasn't a family," she blurted out. "Two frightened little girls with parents who weren't their parents. I think one of them was a friend of my boss at MI. A Russian called Zvi. There was something very wrong with the scene. It may sound stupid, and I'm probably imagining the worst possible scenario … but the children seemed like prisoners."

"This is a pretty fancy hotel for what I think you're implying," Dave said. "But I imagine it's got plenty of high-toned crime as well."

"At first I thought they were a family. Tourists out with their kids for a late night in San Francisco. But then I saw the faces of the children. They were frightened. They desperately didn't want to get in the elevator with the people they were with."

"But how could you be sure?" Dave asked. "The kids wanted to stay up after an exciting night. We've all been part of that situation as kids or parents."

"Not all of us, Dave," Gloria said sarcastically.

"Go on, Gloria," Wiley intervened gently.

"One of the little girls said something in Spanish, '*Tengo miedo*,' in a small voice, and the 'mother' tried to shut her up just before the elevator doors closed. It means 'I'm scared.' I was sitting here deciding what to do. I kept thinking of you, Wiley—that you would know." She looked up at him again and realized that she was still holding his hand in a tight grip. She dropped it slowly. "That's when Joe Diamond walked into the lobby and went to the same floor as they did, the 29th."

"Joe Diamond, as in Debra Jean's Joe Diamond, as in your boss at MI?" Dave asked in surprise.

"Yes." Gloria stopped. "I'd love to believe that all this is a coincidence." She thought for a moment and frowned. "Actually, it was you, Dave, who suggested the Empress."

Wiley looked into her eyes. "No. That's the wrong direction, Gloria. Dave and I are not in the child-abuse business. What were you going to do?"

"I sat here trying to figure that out and getting nowhere. I couldn't just barge into a strange room, and the hotel security has no reason to check. Still ..."

"We need to be certain."

"But what can we do? It could all be my paranoia."

"Perhaps. But Dave invited you here to find out what you knew about Debra Jean. That's why we're interested in MI. She told us a story about Joe and Paul Stokes that makes your 'paranoia' more plausible. But even if it's all fantasy or has a good explanation, none of us are going to feel good until we check on those children."

"We could call the police—" Gloria said hesitantly.

Dave interrupted, "They'd never believe the story, and without some evidence of a crime threat, they won't respond. And you'll almost certainly lose your job if you're wrong."

"Or right, for that matter," she added. "This is more important than my job."

Wiley smiled down at her. "But we may be wasting time. Look, we don't use the police in something so circumstantial. But you were here. It's your call."

"If not the police, then what?"

Dave studied her face. "I have an idea, beginning with my keychain," he said. "But it won't make the police or the hotel happy."

"Dave's ideas are the kind that no one else has but that always work," Wiley said as he and Gloria followed Dave to the elevator. "So don't worry, Gloria. We're in good if eccentric hands. As an All-American end, he never dropped the ball."

CHAPTER 13

Snuff Film

Joe Diamond stood with his back to the closed door and looked around the beautiful newly redecorated suite on the 29th floor, the highest residential floor of the Empress Hotel. He was in his element. He had been in many spectacular hotel rooms, but only the Four Seasons in Beijing and the Trump Tower in Manhattan could rival this. The strains of Mozart's last quartet played softly throughout the room. The furnishings could have graced the empress's chamber in the Forbidden City, and the view through the large windows of the twinkling hills of the city, the Bay and Golden Gate bridges, the dark water, and the soft glow of Sausalito and the Marin Headlands beyond was truly extraordinary.

All this was overshadowed by the quality of the people gathered here, all members of Sons of Mozart. The room held Zvi and ten other of his favorite players, and this particular game was something darkly delicious. He had no doubt that the greatest composer, the greatest prodigy of them all, would have enjoyed it as much as the group here tonight.

The two beautiful little girls were tied to what looked like elementary school chairs, the kind he had regularly defaced in his few years at public schools in New York City. Their wrists were secured to the chairs' wide arms by a thin rope, which then had been looped around their flat chests and fastened at the chairs' backs. They were gagged with translucent tape, although Joe was sure they were too frightened to scream. They made quite a picture: frightened, innocent, naked, and very beautiful.

The people nearest the children were a surgeon and his wife, a famous dominatrix. The pair were well known to Joe and the others, famous on the West Coast for what they called their life-and-death child pornography ceremonies. The tools were displayed before the children in frightening clarity: scalpels, probes, two sharp knives, two small axes, and two syringes. There were also bandages, tourniquets, many large towels, disinfectant, and cleaning spray. And there was photographic equipment.

Joe was not sure how the evening would play out. His presence as the SM founder was probably an added excitement to the group and might increase the stakes and fun, but he also knew that many of his members could match him in accomplishments as well as perverse inventiveness. Prodigies knew control, and this group of prodigies had long ago decided to be victimizers rather than scapegoats, which meant great pleasure for themselves and a lot of pain for others. Everyone here knew how to do pleasure—and pain—in style.

He had missed the beginning of the show but guessed that the girls had been told to empty their bladders and bowels before they were tied to the chairs. Watching the children's acute embarrassment was usually an exquisite part of the preliminary fun. The group had probably used the children's humiliation as a backdrop to discussing how far to go tonight. This was not a group that cared about democracy or about limiting their options. From out of this discussion one of the Sons of Mozart would be chosen, and he or she would then claim absolute authority to make the final verdict on the fate of the girls and their hands.

A gong sounded, signaling the beginning of whatever had been decided by the chosen one, a tall, elderly woman who was CEO of a large retail conglomerate. She walked slowly to the surgeon to communicate her desire. Joe watched as he gravely nodded his head in affirmation and then flashed a smile as he walked ceremoniously to the operating field and its collection of implements. He gloved his hands and chose one of the sharp knives and held it aloft. The children's eyes showed their fear. A thin stream of urine spattered the wood floor under one of the girls. The group quickly surrounded the children. The dominatrix slowly put on gloves and began swabbing the children's wrists with disinfectant from the table.

Suddenly, a loud, shrill tone pierced the room. Joe recognized the sound of a fire alarm. Part of the game? No. It came from outside the room, in the hall or an adjacent room. As the sound continued and everyone's attention was reluctantly drawn away from the tender flesh before them, Zvi walked to the door and carefully opened it. The sound immediately grew louder. Smoke curled through the door and with it the faint smell of burning fabric. He hurriedly closed it. The implications for the group were ominous.

Everyone looked to Joe. He responded by taking command. "The hotel staff and the police will be here in a few minutes to check on the fire," he said calmly. "Now, everyone out except the children. All except a few of you must use the stairs. Stagger your re-entrances on the lower floors, wait a few seconds, then keep going, if possible on another staircase. Leave by the basement exits."

He thought for a moment. "I assume that whoever made the reservation used a pseudonym."

A quiet "Yes" came from somewhere in the room.

"The children stay?" their procurer asked hesitantly.

"Their fate was already sealed when they entered this room," Joe asserted. "I assume they don't know who we are or speak English well enough to give descriptions."

"No problem there."

"Then let's get out of here."

With a glance at the children, the surgeon and his colleagues gathered their instruments quickly and left first, followed immediately by the rest.

*　*　*

Twenty feet away, at a corner of the same floor, Wiley, Dave, and Gloria watched from a service alcove as the smoke spread through the corridor and hotel guests milled in the hall in bathrobes.

"Recognize anyone?" Dave hissed above the din of the jangling bell as a phalanx of men and women in flamboyant dinner dress left one of the rooms and walked toward the bathrobe-clad guests who were waiting for an elevator despite warnings to the contrary. A few waited with them; the others headed for the stairs.

"My God, yes," Gloria whispered. "I think so, anyway. It's hard to be sure with all the commotion. The couple I saw in the lobby with the children." She stared intently through the smoke and pointed. "That looks like Joe and Zvi. I can't be absolutely sure. They're facing away from us, walking toward the stairway with the others." Two chimes announced the arrival of elevators, and they moved toward the opening doors. "It's them," Gloria said, and launched herself into the hall.

Wiley's hand shot out and grabbed her shoulder, easily pulling her back into their hideout. "Hold on. Our first job is to rescue the children if they're still here. They're not in the hall. Maybe they were left in the room."

They watched as most of the crowd piled into the elevator; the ones who couldn't find a place headed for the stairway.

Dave spoke sharply. "Right now, someone from the hotel is climbing 28 floors of stairs to find out what's going on. They won't be using the elevators in case there is a fire. Let's get those children. I'll bet they're in the room where the couple came from."

Gloria ran toward the room, Wiley and Dave behind her. Sprinklers were going off all around them. She tried the door, but it was locked.

Wiley slammed the door with his shoulder, but it was far too solid. "Dave, you can get us in, can't you?" he said.

"No problem." He already had a knife opened and pushed a thin blade into the lock. The door opened after a brief manipulation. The room showed signs of a party: ashtrays, furniture moved about, an open window. The two children were in the middle of the room, gagged and bound, shivering with fear.

Dave and Wiley rushed toward them, but Gloria got there first. She spoke softly in Spanish as she removed the gags. "Get blankets from the bedroom, and find water!" she yelled. Wiley ran for the supplies as Dave cut their bonds with his knife and briefly checked their bodies.

"They're physically OK."

"Thank God," Gloria said. "I'm going to try to get an address." She kneeled to talk to the girls, and one of them said something in a low voice.

"She says that those people were trying to hurt them."

"Could she repeat anything to the hotel people or the police? They'll be here in a moment."

Gloria asked a question of the children, and they nodded their heads. "These kids are petrified, but yes, I'm sure they can," she said.

"Brave girls," Wiley said as he covered them with blankets. He handed Gloria glasses of water, and the children grabbed them from her hands and gulped them down.

"Have the sprinklers taken care of the fire?" Gloria asked.

"There never was any danger," Dave replied. "Just the smoke alarm I set off with some burning cloth, lining from my jacket."

"But where are the hotel people, Dave?" Wiley asked. "Doesn't this alarm go directly to the police station?"

"When I activated the smoke alarm, I also cut the connections to the lines to other floors and to the outside. So the alarm is sounding only on this floor, and the hotel won't know until the guests have alerted staff. That was bound to happen, but I wanted to make sure."

He moved to the phone, dialed, spoke into the receiver, waited a moment, and then hung up. "They know at the desk. The police are already on their way up. Everyone will be here very soon. We should leave while we can. It will present big problems for all of us if they don't like what we're doing here."

Gloria spoke again to the children, who nodded. She hugged them both and hesitantly followed Dave and Wiley to the door. She looked at the girls and trembled slightly. "I'll stay with them."

Wiley said, "Tell them that other adults will be here in a moment. Tell them to tell the story to anyone who will listen. We'll leave the door ajar and hide back in the service alcove. Then, when we are sure that they're taken care of, we'll leave by the service stairs."

"But why not just stay with them?" Gloria implored.

"I can't tell you what to do," Wiley said. "But we need to stay out of the way of the police if we're going to figure this out."

He and Dave walked to the door and back to the alcove. Gloria reluctantly followed.

"Do you live alone, Gloria?" Wiley asked, huddled with the other two in the alcove.

"Yes. I have an apartment in the Mission."

"It's going to be tough being alone after what we've seen. There's plenty of room on my Sausalito barge. Debra Jean will be over in the late morning to discuss our progress, so Dave's sleeping over as well." Wiley watched the elevator intently. "Dammit, where are they?"

Gloria was shivering. "These kids, and Joe being with them. I can hardly believe it." She smiled wanly.

"This was probably a snuff scene," Dave said soberly. "We may have just saved those two children's lives."

"Look." Wiley pointed as the elevator opened and a cohort of security men and police came charging into the hall, looking confused, and then headed for the open door.

"Let's get going," Wiley whispered intently. All three moved quickly to the stairwell at the end of the hall and crouched out of sight as the security men reached the door. "Dave, you go first and get a cab. I'll stay with Gloria till we're sure the kids are taken care of. Pick us up at Post and Taylor."

"Five minutes," Dave said and left.

"OK," Wiley said to Gloria, and took her hand. "We'll just pretend we're a couple, but let's not get stopped. Lean on me a little, as if you are in shock. We'll take a stairway and be gone."

Gloria did as she was told.

CHAPTER 14

Bonding

The sun was high overhead as Wiley sipped his first latte of the morning from his heron-watching post on the upper deck of his barge. He stretched and felt the stiffness in his legs from the short night on the sofa. He had given Gloria his bed, and Dave curled up in the corner of the living room with his sleeping bag. It was very hard for him not to think of the lovely troubled woman alone in his bed. She had lapsed into silence on the ride to Sausalito, and then passively accepted his bedroom and closed the door. The barge had always been an island of sanity for him, he thought. Perhaps it would help Gloria.

The horrible scene of the night before had its aftershocks in him as well; the abuse and torture of children was an image he would never forget. It brought his own losses to the forefront of his mind: his father's murder, the devastation of his mother after his father's death and the fracturing of her always-fragile hold on sanity. Now she lived in the chronic ward of a psychiatric institution, a shadow of her former self. He had left his home ten years earlier, a functional orphan. Sausalito, this barge, his friendship with Dave, and their mission in Revenge, Inc., were what kept him going.

He put aside his melancholy and turned both hands toward the sun and stretched. Before falling asleep, Dave and he worried together about the implications of how they had handled the events at the Empress, especially how they had dealt with the children. Should they all have stayed waiting for the police, as Gloria had wanted? His gut had told him that leaving unrecognized was the right choice, and Dave had agreed, especially once Gloria recognized Joe Diamond and Zvi in the hall. It was not an easy call, and he fell asleep praying that the children got the help they needed after their ordeal.

The great blue landed on a nearby rock, searching for a late breakfast. Wiley watched it take its silent hunter's pose. After a few minutes of willed catatonia, it gathered itself, spread its graceful blue-gray wings, and flew off to a better site. With a sigh, Wiley looked at his own full table, the product of a quick trip to Mollie's earlier that morning. It had been a long while since he'd hosted a champagne brunch, California style: fresh orange juice; lox, onion, tomatoes, bagels, cream cheese; fresh muffins; and Napa bubbly—to his taste as good as the French variety in all but name. He was excited, as if he were readying for a party rather than preparing to strategize about how to deal with Debra Jean's needs and the horror of what they had witnessed, including the revelations about Joe Diamond.

Gloria appeared at the door to the deck dressed in the clothes she had been wearing last night, and he instantly recognized where that excitement lay. She was barefoot, carrying her high heels. Wiley couldn't help noticing the sexy way Gloria filled out her clothes and how good she looked in the daylight on his boat.

"Sleep well, Gloria?" he asked, as Dave appeared from the kitchen and handed her a homemade latte with extra foam.

"Fair. Bed was great. Thanks for that, Wiley, but I had nightmares. I got up at sunrise and came out on deck. It's so beautiful. You're lucky to be here."

"Early morning is the best time: quiet, swaying boats, the light and colors …"

"It reminds me of home," she said, taking a seat next to him facing the water. "El Salvador. I grew up in a little town in the hills above the water. My family would sit together and watch the sunrise before going to work or school. We used to call the sun 'our great golden fish.'"

"Sausalito sunrises are the best around here," Wiley said.

"It beats not sleeping. The sky in the early morning holds charcoal blue and the color of fire together," Dave added.

"I've never felt like I deserved Marin. It's so beautiful … and privileged. The Mission, with all the different Spanish-speaking communities, is great, but it's still city life."

"Meaning too many people, or is there something else missing?" Dave questioned, joining them at the table.

"My childhood spoiled me with small-town life and sunrises up close. Sausalito has both. This barge, being with both of you. It makes me feel connected in a way I haven't for too long. Crossing over to a new life without giving up the best parts of the old."

They sat quietly for a while, listening to the waves lapping against the boat's hull. "Nothing like this in Dolores Park," she added, relishing her coffee.

"It is a strange coincidence that those children at the Empress came from El Salvador," Wiley said, reluctantly breaking the mood. "It probably helped you to make contact."

"But listening to their pathetic words in the lobby, '*Tengo miedo*,' I almost lost it. God! I really hope they're OK."

"Not to worry," Dave said reassuringly. "I checked with one of the police dispatchers I know as soon as I woke. There was a note on the blotter. They're back in the foster home where they were living. It's a good place, a private home owned by a retired couple who take in small groups of children for the city welfare services. It's extra income and they're treated well. It seems the girls went with a larger group of Salvadorans, kids and adults, to a cultural event earlier in the evening and never returned home. The couple was frantic and so were the chaperones. They called it into the police, but nothing was done except an immediate neighborhood search. Apparently the police routinely wait 12 hours to check on missing persons, even children. And—get this— there was no mention of an investigation of the events at the Empress."

"That can't be," Gloria said angrily.

"It happens. Don't worry. I'll follow up on it."

"Me too. Get me their address and I'll talk to the kids. See what kind of help they need after such a trauma." She smiled. "You're good at this, Dave. Dealing with the smoke alarm, getting into the room so fast, having contacts with police." She smiled more broadly. "As you know, security is my expertise, so if you ever need a new job ..."

"Dave does everything well," Wiley said, winking at Gloria. "It's humbling working with a partner with so much talent."

"And friends know that he keeps me around because I make him look better than he is," Dave said drolly. "Even when he was the great All-American quarterback, I covered for his overthrown passes, converting them into touchdowns with great catches."

Wiley rolled his eyes. "Don't overdo it, Dave."

"Someone has to bring you down. I mean, you're six-foot-seven, a perfect physical specimen, smart, cultured, not to mention possessing the intangibles of leadership and an instinct for winning. The coaches always knew you'd make the right decisions. All they knew about me was that I delivered the touchdowns."

"You're strange for white guys," Gloria observed. "Competitive and loving. Not at all like the gringos I've been around before."

"Not like at MI?" Dave asked. "My God, the group we saw last night could give the devil a run for his money."

"I still can't believe I saw Joe and Zvi coming from that room. I was pretty tired and spacey. I almost believe I made it all up."

"Memory can play tricks, Gloria," Dave said dryly. "But you saw them."

"It's just hard to believe," she flared.

"Tell us more about MI," Wiley said quietly.

"MI is basically Joe and Paul. They and their company are fantastically successful. Colleagues treat them with awe and respect. They are great scientists, but they also get the job done."

Wiley placed his hand over hers and leaned toward her. "Debra Jean will be here in a minute. An honest assessment of Joe and Paul will really help. And do I need to add that it might prevent other kids and women from getting hurt?"

"Look, I hate what I saw, and I gather Debra Jean is in trouble, but give me a little time." Gloria pulled her hand away. "I need to keep this job, and I owe Joe for giving it to me."

"Your call, but after what we saw, covering for Joe doesn't seem like your style," Wiley said.

She drew her chair closer to him. "You're right. I'm just nervous. Look, I don't know all that much. Joe is the leader, the idea man, and also the one with the giant ego." She blushed, dropping her gaze. "I always assumed the worst with guys like Joe. I have good reasons." She paused, using the last sips of her coffee to regain her composure. "Now

95

Paul is different," she went on. "He is a little like you, Dave: a jack of all trades, gets things done no matter how difficult. Very smart. And he's also a pretty decent guy. He's always treated me well."

"But Joe and Paul are a pair, right?" Dave said. "One could be covering for the other."

"Yes, and they are a very loyal pair. Paul once told me that their relationship went back to their time at a high school in New York City for gifted children. He never said what it was, only that it joined them completely and still does. I don't understand the culture of young men in this country, so I won't even guess what they were talking about. But neither has ever been in trouble with the law. I've checked."

"What else?" Wiley asked. "You've seen them in action."

Gloria began rocking slowly back and forth in her chair. "I've never thought much about what makes them so special together. Paul takes Joe's superiority for granted." She stopped rocking. "I have tapes of their conversations together. It's part of routine security I've set up there. When they're alone, they're not always so harmonious. But what good partnership is?"

"It would be great to listen to those tapes," Dave murmured.

"Unfortunately, those tapes belong to my company," Gloria said without hesitation. "Anyway, they're not as useful as you'd imagine. Joe and Paul edit what they say because they know I'm listening."

"People give away a lot about themselves when they try not to," Dave said, looking over his shoulder as Debra Jean crossed the thin wooden bridge to the barge.

She mounted the stairs and greeted Wiley and Dave. Wiley gave her a hug and then turned to Gloria. "You remember Debra Jean from MI?"

"Of course." Gloria extended her hand to Debra Jean, who clasped it warmly. "You look great. Much better than during those last months at MI."

"Appearances are deceiving. It's been two years since I left, and I'm still on my knees. That's why I am working with Revenge, Inc."

Wiley nodded. "Dave and I will find some hot coffee for you. Let you both get reacquainted." They both left for the kitchen.

"I never understood what made you leave," Gloria said with genuine concern, "and I was sorry to see you go. By the way, since you left, all our other PhD hires have been men."

"No surprise that," Debra Jean said sarcastically, sitting down at the table next to Gloria.

Gloria nodded.

"But why are you here, Gloria?" Debra Jean asked. "How do you know these guys?" She pointed to the kitchen, where they had gone for her breakfast.

"I was investigating a data break-in. We thought the attempts were about company secrets. As a former employee who was dismissed, you were actually a suspect. Then Dave showed up, wanting to talk to me about MI, and I met Wiley." She blushed.

"You like him," Debra Jean stated. "Most woman do."

"He's something else."

Wiley came up the stairs with a flask of coffee for the table and sat next to Gloria. Dave followed with two glasses of orange juice and sat next to Debra Jean. "This is an amazing spread," Debra Jean said, appraising the full table.

"Standard fare for us," Dave said, deadpan.

Gloria grinned. "Good try, Dave." Then she turned to Debra Jean and said more seriously, "I know this discussion is about you, and I don't want to intrude, but after what I saw last night, I think I can help you."

"We're going to need all the help we can get," Wiley said.

"Well, I can't imagine why you shouldn't stay," Debra Jean said. "I've always liked you, Gloria."

Dave said, "Debra Jean, we think we've seen another piece of Joe Diamond's pattern of behavior, the kind of thing we wondered about when we first heard your story. Frankly, it's very extreme. It changes the meaning of what happened to you."

"You're scaring me, Dave," Debra Jean said.

Wiley said, "We think that Joe Diamond is involved in abusing young children at the Empress hotel in Union Square. Maybe even making a snuff film."

"Snuff films are where people are killed or maimed while others watch," Debra Jean said in disbelief. "You can't be saying that Joe Diamond is involved in that."

"It's likely."

"My God," Debra Jean said in horror. "And you're also saying that what happened to me is part of that pattern. But compared to snuff films, what happened to me is so minor."

Dave nodded. "Abuse is a repetitive pattern with a long continuum of behavior. I think your own reaction at Jardinière was an apprehension of real evil, the kind that Gloria and Wiley and I saw last night."

"I think I should know what happened to you, Debra Jean," Gloria said quietly. "It would help me to understand …"

"More than that. It's something you need to know," Debra Jean said, and quickly described the scene at the table.

"Why didn't you turn them in?" Gloria asked.

"My personal reaction to abuse is also repetitive," Debra Jean said. "It's something I know too much about. I nearly failed psychiatry in medical school because I couldn't listen to patients who had experienced psychological trauma without becoming anxious. Luckily I was good at psychopharm and diagnosis. I mean, no one flunks out of medical school because they can't pass psychiatry!"

"Research must've been a blessing for you," Gloria said.

Debra Jean stared at her. "You understand, then. Yes, it was my salvation, until Joe and Paul decided to get rid of me. I know that what happened in Jardinière triggered something else, something much deeper, though whether it's about me or them I just can't tell. But how many people freak out for two years just because some guy puts his hand where he shouldn't?"

"It wasn't just some guy, Debra Jean." Gloria frowned anxiously. "It was one or both of your bosses."

"He's your boss, too, Gloria," Wiley said.

"That's true, but it was more about what could have happened to the children."

"And that your boss is a monster who's also a genius, not to mention holding a lot of cards in your life." He looked at Gloria and Debra Jean. "You both share that particular fate."

Debra Jean leaned far back into her chair and twirled her empty cup around and around in her hands. "It's unbelievable. Where do we go from here?"

Gloria looked over at her. "Somewhere very dangerous, I'm afraid."

98

Wiley looked over at Dave, who nodded. "One thing is sure: if you are still interested in pursuing this, Debra Jean, we're with you."

"I'm in," she said, and for the first time in two years felt a cloak of darkness lift from her shoulders.

CHAPTER 15

Montrachet

D ebra Jean finished dressing for the San Francisco Opera. She checked her tickets, face, and outfit as she left her condo. If clothes mattered, she'd be OK.

She felt like a sexy woman for the first time in as long as she could remember. That had begun at the Sunday-morning Sausalito meeting with Wiley's decision to take her case, and her own to take on Joe and Paul, wherever it led.

It was good to have Gloria along, and not just because she was a woman. Debra Jean imagined that Gloria would have taken the situation at Jardinière and turned it into a ball-crushing event for Joe and Paul. Well, like it or not, she was a spoiled, overachieving daddy's girl, and she had blown her career because she couldn't fight back. She climbed into her Lexus SC and headed for the opera. The money he left her had made her effortlessly rich but no less professionally empty.

Tonight, though, she was a woman dressed to attract and seduce, and someone had better notice, if only the parking valets at the restaurant.

The target of her preparations was Paul Stokes. A little research had confirmed that Friday was a night out alone; he had a single subscription and a first-row center orchestra seat. She wondered if he himself sang. In her experience, it was singers who most enjoyed that nearness to the stage. They liked to watch the sound apparatus, the way the singers' tongues flicked their upper teeth for crisp Ds and Ls and curled low and deep to elicit the maximum resonance on the big vowels and high notes. For that intimacy, close seats sacrificed something of the drama and spectacle afforded by a larger view.

She negotiated through the usual late-afternoon traffic jam to the Bay Bridge and the chaos of the multilane toll plaza. Once she worked her way onto the bridge itself, the traffic moved smoothly. The sun was still high enough to infuse the Golden Gate Bridge with incandescent light contrasting with the green hills and blue water that it spanned. And just north of the bridge, she could see tiny Sausalito, her new repository of hope, nestled at the bottom of the Marin Headlands.

As she drove, she wondered how Wiley and Gloria's relationship was working out. The spark between them was obvious. She remembered the rumors of how Gloria had gotten her job as head of security at MI. Something to do with sleeping with Joe Diamond and exacting a price. Probably a bit of anti-Latino racism, she thought; Gloria had more than held her own against consultants, scientists, and Joe and Paul.

Debra Jean felt she had begun to change since coming to Revenge, Inc. Look what she was into now. OK, it was straight out of her mother's playbook: seducing a man whom she shouldn't. Paul Stokes, celebrity scientist, Nobel Prize contender, was married and a possible collaborator in a variety of horrors, and she was still after him. Well, she didn't believe any of the really bad things. She was very sure that belonged to Joe, and this date would give her a chance to prove it!

After exiting the bridge, she drove up to Market Street and made the straight run toward the Civic Center, where San Francisco's Opera, Symphony, Ballet, and Conservatory were all located. A mile to the southeast were the UC Mission Bay campus and biotech firms, including MI. She felt a stab of anxiety. This was the geography that had been her life until Joe's finger penetrated her and propelled her to reenter the hysterical world of childhood.

The welcome sight of the Opera House and Davies Symphony Hall rescued her from the depressing reverie. She turned right on Larkin and left on Grove, and pulled up in front of Jardinière. The scene of the crime, she thought. The valet took her car, and yes, he gave her an appraising glance as he held out his hand for her keys. She smiled with more confidence than she felt. Men often looked her over. So what? Bottom line, guys always left her for another woman. Case in point: Her ex-husband had left her for a charming surgery resident. He had gotten bored with her endless need for reassurance. Mommy dearest, what have you done to me!

Don't go there, she thought. None of that was going to help with Paul tonight. She knew that he had been attracted to her when she was at MI. And she'd seen his interested look when he saw her at the opera two weeks before. Tonight she wasn't going to shy away as she had then. She was going to be a provocateur, a cultured woman who was not afraid to ask the hard questions and show that she was available.

The fashionable restaurant was half-full at six, and the rest of the opera and symphony crowd would be arriving soon for the eight o'clock curtains. Food, music, and sex, or at least sexy conversation: that's what she wanted to add to her life, hopefully with Paul as companion.

She had asked for a table near where they had sat together that fateful night—straight counterphobic strategy, the kind she had learned about in cognitive behavioral therapy in medical school. She could feel a twinge of anxiety as she climbed the circular staircase to the region of trauma. That was OK too, she thought. Perhaps it would give her a frenetic edge that she would need to attract him.

And there he was, as expected, sitting alone at one of the smaller tables for two at the edge of the railing overlooking the bar, a floor below. Debra Jean smiled as she went past him. He looked down, as if he were thinking of something important. But then after she was comfortably seated, she heard footsteps behind her. Bingo!

"Debra Jean! It *is* you. I'm sorry to be rude, but I didn't recognize you at first."

Liar, she thought. "Well, that's not surprising," she said out loud. "It's been a while."

"Wasn't that you at the Shostakovich opera? I caught a glimpse but wasn't sure."

She didn't answer directly but just smiled up at him as he babbled nervously, wondering how long he would stand there before inviting her to his table.

"An amazing opera, *Lady Macbeth of Mtsensk*," he continued, seeming oblivious to his awkward situation.

"Yes. The tale of woman as scapegoat," Debra Jean said. "Pertinent, I would say."

He looked warily at her. Wrong move? Only if she continued to be the good girl with him. She repositioned her body to show off her figure and waited.

"Why don't you join me for dinner?" he said. "We can catch up."

She waited a beat. "Sure, Paul."

The waiter, experienced in the ways of single diners, had intuited what might happen, and there was a new setting at Paul's table. The sommelier was waiting at a safe distance.

"What a nice invitation," she said as she settled into a chair opposite him.

"We're both alone, so … can I order wine for you?" He turned to the man, whom he addressed by first name, and together they decided on the wine. Neither man had looked at the wine list. Paul murmured the names of the wines almost to himself when the sommelier left. "Is that OK, Debra Jean?"

"I'll see when I taste it."

"We haven't talked in almost two years," Paul ventured.

"Since you fired me."

"That's not exactly the way it was," he said solemnly.

"Really. I'd be glad to hear your version of it, but that's what happened to me." She couldn't stop herself. "Didn't it all start here at this restaurant?"

"Something happened, that's for sure. But I never understood what."

"And you never asked."

"What I remember is you standing and everything flying off the table. Then you began screaming and ran down the stairs. Not like you at all. I'd never seen you hysterical before."

"Hysterical isn't my thing, but there was a good reason."

"Was there?"

"C'mon Paul," she said sarcastically. "You expect me to believe you had nothing to do with what happened?"

"That's right," he said. "Look, let's not rehash this right now. We're both going to the opera tonight. *The Marriage of Figaro*."

"One of my favorites."

"It's one of Mozart's masterpieces. Let's not spoil it for each other."

"In most circumstances, you'd be right," she said, hesitating. "But Paul, this isn't one of them. I can only stay at the table with you if you promise to answer one question. It's not about science or research."

"If I can. Try me."

"That night at the table."

"Yes."

"What do you remember?"

"Not a lot. We were asking you to change the direction of your work. You got angry. What happened next was a complete surprise to me. It looked like sheer panic."

"Paul, do you remember where I was sitting?"

"Yes, at that booth right over there." He pointed toward a plush red seat across the aisle. "With Joe and me."

"More specifically?"

He thought for a moment. "I can't remember the exact seating. Is it important?"

"I was sitting between you and Joe, wedged pretty tightly between the two of you. So tightly that I couldn't react when someone put his hand between my legs. Not on my legs, between them. High up. And the hand kept moving, Paul. It kept moving higher until a finger was inside of me. The hand belonged to either you or Joe. Did you flip a coin to see who would have all that fun at my expense?"

Paul gasped. "That's crazy, Debra Jean. You're saying Joe did that to you?"

"One of you. One of the ugly things about that particular event was that I didn't know which of you was responsible. Or why. Only that it was happening."

After a long silence, Paul spoke tersely. "It's something he could do but ..."

"But?"

"It's hard to explain."

"You mean you don't want to explain."

"Yes, that's right, Debra Jean. I'm sorry. I can't say more."

"Then I can't sit here with you. You owe me something."

"Look, I've answered your question," he said slowly, in obvious pain. "It wasn't me, I promise you that."

"I want to believe you," she said sincerely. "And sitting with you is nice."

He reached out and gently placed his hand on top of hers. "Ditto both statements, but believe me, Debra Jean, this is totally new."

104

"But you said it's something Joe could do."

"Yes."

"OK." She sighed. "In deference to Mozart and us, I'll try to leave it there. For now." She gave his hand a quick squeeze, then let it go. She studied the menu, working hard to hold back from crying openly. It didn't work.

"God, I hope I can trust you," she said, looking up at him, letting him see her tears.

Paul looked away, obviously embarrassed by her emotion. "I'm sorry you had to go through that."

She nodded, appreciating his inference. "So am I. Now let's eat, and I'll tell you why I picked this opera for our first dinner together."

"You're stalking me." He sounded serious.

"Kind of." She looked at him and broke into a giggle. He frowned, then suddenly joined her laughter, and for a moment they were deliciously out of control.

"OK," he said when they had both calmed down. "I always knew you were interesting, but not quite like this."

A warm pink glow spread across her upper chest and cleavage, as it always did when she blushed. She was embarrassed, hoping that her light makeup gave sufficient cover for her obvious excitement. "So do you want to know how the opera fits our subject?"

"I'm all ears."

She smiled. "Give it a try, Paul."

"OK, I love a puzzle. Hmmm, *The Marriage of Figaro*." He thought for a moment, and then his eyes brightened. "Is it possible you're thinking of the *droit de seigneur*?"

She smiled appreciatively. "Not bad." She paused. "Yes, I'm thinking about the *droit de seigneur*, the traditional right of a noble to take the bridegroom's place on the wedding night of his female subject. Figaro was the nobleman's servant who was about to marry Susanna, when she pointed out that she was going to be legally raped by his own boss."

"Susanna had her eyes wide open. But you're making the analogy with what happened to you here. You promised we wouldn't go there … for now."

"Well, let's consider it an operatic metaphor. You both invited me to dinner to tell me that I couldn't continue my research. MI was the fiefdom and I a lowly postdoc, a servant forced to do her masters' bidding, which in medieval times included serving the lord's physical needs. Apparently that custom hasn't stopped."

"Now wait a second," Paul said.

She continued as if she hadn't heard him. "And so, like Susanna, I was sexually propositioned. At least Count Almaviva wooed Susanna with courtly chivalry. I was just diddled in public!"

"You're very clever," Paul said. "So now you, like Susanna, want revenge. You obviously are very good at interpretation of librettos. What you've got to believe is that I'm not the Count."

"Unfortunately, this is more complicated than whose finger it was. You were involved just being there. And with what happened at MI afterward."

He turned away from her. "You're not keeping your promise. I don't know what you want of me, Debra Jean."

"I'm not sure I do, either. I know that Susanna didn't panic the way I did. She and Figaro didn't sulk for two years or wait to get even. They acted."

"Mostly to save his honor."

"And hers. And because he cared about her and was brave and smart, he manipulated the Count at considerable risk to himself."

"I'm to be your Figaro to your Suzanne," Paul said helplessly.

"That would be interesting," she said, looking him straight in the eye, and then broke into a lascivious grin.

The wine came, a Montrachet, and hot rolls were placed on the table. "I'm sorry to disturb you, but if you want to make the opera, I'll need to take your order now," the waiter said with a wry smile.

"Yes, of course," Paul said. They made their selections, and the waiter left.

Paul turned to Debra Jean "Do you still want to … "

"Be here with you? Yes, Paul."

"There's a lot in my relationship with Joe that you don't understand," Paul said sadly. "Figaro was a servant. He could have lost his head if he displeased the Count."

"I'm not Figaro. I'm not a hero, but I am horrified at what happened.

106

I'm not going to forget what you've told me. Trust me on that."

"OK. Your apology is helpful."

"There's always been a lot going with us, Debra Jean," Paul said.

"And it always felt positive to me until that evening. And afterward. You didn't exactly help me to keep my job, Paul." She sighed. "What's really embarrassing is why it's taken me two years to have this conversation."

With that, Debra Jean felt better. She had said what she wanted to say. It was all going faster than she had imagined. He was vulnerable, and there were secrets he wouldn't share. She wondered how far to push their mutual attraction. She smiled inwardly thinking of what she imagined Gloria would do.

The waiter returned with their entrees and again reminded them of the time.

Debra Jean picked at her food. "Have you ever had an affair, Paul?"

"Is that a random question or … or what?" Now it was he who was blushing.

"I've heard rumors," she said carefully. "There are rumors about you, Paul—even about you and Joe. And of course, any friend of Joe's can't be that straight."

"Joe's the genius; I'm just an ordinary guy."

"At least you play it that way."

"No. It's true. I learned early in my work that I'm not capable of taking the kinds of risks that great science requires."

"No risky science, no risky affairs. You leave it all to Joe?" she asked quizzically.

"I'm not gay, if that's what you're hinting about."

"I've never thought you were gay. But I do wonder what you do for fun. Your marriage looks distant, from what I've seen."

"But I am married."

"No children."

"Sharon didn't want to raise them alone, and my life in science didn't promise much room to help." He looked into her eyes.

She held his gaze. "Married without a child. Some women would say you're still in play."

"Why are you coming on to me, Debra Jean?"

"Why not? I'm a free woman. But if you're afraid, perhaps we can leave it at being friends. Go to the opera on Friday night. I doubt if Sharon would mind that. I'd like much, much more."

Paul's face grew red as the blush spread through his cheeks and into his ears. He finished off half a glass of wine in a gulp. "You don't want to get too close to me, Debra Jean," he said, lowering his eyes.

"And why is that, Paul?"

The waiter approached with the check. "Your curtain is in 15 minutes, sir."

Paul sighed with relief. "Do you know the Intermezzo Lounge?"

"I've seen it from the Opera gift shop. Never been inside."

"I'm a big patron: first-row seat and an automatic membership to the Intermezzo. Guests are allowed. Why don't you meet me there at the second intermission. By then, Figaro and Susanna will have worked their particular magic on the Count."

"A rendezvous at the opera," Debra Jean said dramatically. "To us!" She raised her glass and drained it.

Paul paid the bill and then escorted her down the winding staircase and out into the night air. The parking valet at the door who had seen her come in alone winked at her. Well, why not? she thought as she took the hand that Paul offered. All told, it had been an excellent dinner.

CHAPTER 16

Sentience

Joe Diamond anxiously paced his office at MI, reassessing the damage to his usually orderly world wrought by the events at the Empress Hotel ten days earlier. The unlikely fire there had aborted a well-earned night of pleasure. The children had been rescued, but Joe was sure that the Sons of Mozart members who put on the event would control any incriminating information. The night had been a bust, but he, Zvi, and his collaborators in Sons of Mozart had escaped into the night with no negative consequences likely. A different kind of drama than he had bargained for, but surprise and risk were very much to his taste.

But not with Paul. Paul was his security blanket. He needed the scut work of graduate students, the shackled brilliance of postdocs, but it was only his gifted, hands-on colleague who really counted. Everyone else was replaceable.

Paul Stokes was his only friend, and that was what mattered most, although he was a critical resource at every level of their scientific partnership as well. He was comfortable in maintaining political relationships in the MI lab as well as vital ties with private and public science and the managing committees and granting agencies that were so necessary in the scientific world.

In the social world of science, Joe knew he was a miserable failure, not for lack of skills but because he fundamentally didn't care about anyone, Paul excluded. This knowledge had come early; as a senior at Harvard College, he had lost control of his experiment to an august chemistry professor. For weeks, Joe sulked, obsessing about revenge.

It had been his work; the professor had simply taken it from him, as was his due, and yet no one cared. Students hated getting ripped off by elders, and his peers should have supported him, but he was unable to inspire them with the importance of the issue—or himself.

Joe was in despair and tried to find an answer in books. He scoured Widener Library and the Harvard Business School library, devoting weeks to studying strategies of great leaders of the past. Then when he was about to give up his search for answers, Robert Oppenheimer was appointed visiting scholar at Harvard, in residence at Adams House, where he lived and took meals with the students, including Joe. Oppie had been a fine scientist, but it was his leadership skills that were legendary. At the atomic bomb project at Los Alamos, he had collected the greatest physicists of his generation, many with genius far beyond his own, and subtly bent them to his will.

Joe became a regular at biweekly lunches with Oppie in Adams House. He hoped to gain knowledge about control strategies and instead learned about what the great man called *sentience*, a deeply felt relationship with other humans, complete with the emotional cost of those bonds. Oppenheimer was loved by all because he loved them all. When Joe tried to imagine feelings like that and failed, he understood that he could never emulate the charismatic leadership that he so admired in the great man.

Sons of Mozart was his only success without Paul, whom he knew could never stomach its purposes. It was always Paul who smoothed away the effects of Joe's abrasiveness, holding his labs, institutes, organizations, and bankers together. It was Paul who took the heat and provided the sentience that Joe was missing.

Joe knew that this collaboration was at risk. The silken thread of control that Joe had spun around the adolescent boy he befriended in high school was beginning to fray.

But Debra Jean Lieberman? "Why her?" he cried to the diploma-heavy walls and picked up his pacing speed. What was he missing about her? She was such an unlikely siren, Joe thought. He had assumed that the muse of men like him and Paul would be someone extraordinary.

But deep down he knew that Paul wasn't at all like him. When Joe went to the opera, it was only to hear the most gorgeous divas sing great arias. When he drank wine, Joe wanted the intense fruit and nose of the most sublime Burgundies. Sex was interesting only when it emphasized the perverse. Paul stayed away from all these edges; he could watch the San Jose Opera as well as the Met and be satisfied with a cheap Chianti or Riesling. His taste in women was notoriously pedestrian. Yet Joe knew there was an unsatisfied hunger in the man, and he knew better than to second-guess the vagaries of infatuation. Debra Jean had a major-league mind—and good-enough body—and she must still hold a grudge against Paul that could perversely give both these mild people a bite of passion.

Joe relived the memory of Debra Jean's soft genital skin beneath his finger. As he had hoped, tweaking her nether parts had uncovered the large reservoir of self-denigration that lurked just below the surface. Unfortunately, he was sure that she would tell Paul what had happened in the restaurant, and Paul would recognize Joe's MO. His meeting with Paul would take care of that as easily as he had taken care of Debra Jean!

Unless, as he now suspected, Debra Jean was not alone. There was one part of the Empress incident that didn't hold together. One of the Mozart group had discovered that the alarm that went off on the 29th floor had not been forwarded to the hotel manager or the police station. Someone with an electrician's bent had tampered with the alarm system. Its malfunction had not been a chance occurrence; it had served someone's purposes.

So there was no fire, just a plot and a threat that could well have to do with the snuff-film party.

He walked through the door at the side of his office to the large workspace crammed with half-worked-out ideas and experiments. Something was obviously missing in his analysis of the succession of events. Gloria had assumed that the data probes were industrial espionage, but there were other possibilities. Suppose the attempted break-in, the false alarm, and Debra Jean's sly seduction of Paul, if that's where it went, were connected by an X factor, still unknown? What if there was a pattern of interconnection in all these events that he had not yet discerned? Joe froze in mid-stride, concentrating hard.

When he mentally returned, he saw that Paul had entered their shared space unseen and now was sitting watching him. Joe walked to within a few inches of Paul and took the offensive.

"You've been busy, Paul," he said, with genuine anger.

"Thanks to you, I'm always busy with something."

"I meant at the opera."

Paul observed his friend thoughtfully. "So you know about my meeting with Debra Jean?"

"Anything you do is bound to enter the gossip circus."

"Debra Jean was eating alone in Jardinière, and I asked her to join me. Seemed like the human thing to do." Paul looked away, conscious of his half-truth, and decided to take on Joe directly. "We got to talking and she told me about your little sex game with her at Jardinière." He paused to calm himself before continuing. "What she said is true, isn't it? It smacks of the things you do to people. I'm just surprised that you would risk ... everything for something so childish."

"Her personality and response were carefully calibrated to my action."

"How can you be so sure of yourself?"

"Because I'm always right about this sort of thing."

"Even if that were true, it was cruel, Joe. It almost destroyed her."

"Destroyed her? She's not a child, Paul." He laughed.

"But getting her to leave MI was the goal."

"Yes. And since when were you such a fan of hers? We both agreed about changing the direction of her science."

"I didn't agree to your humiliating her."

"It was a turn-on for me to see her blush and get so angry. You're upset because I got there first."

"You're pathetic, Joe. It can't go on."

"It can. And it will. You mean *you* can't go on."

"Perhaps you're right. That is what I mean."

"Paul, you've known about this side of me for years. Are you going to hurt our relationship because of a woman like Debra Jean? By the way, in most eyes, the adultery you're planning with her is a far greater sin than anything I did under the table to our precious virgin."

"If I have an affair, it won't be just about sex."

Joe walked slowly away from Paul and peered down through the large picture window at the Mission Bay complex. Bullying the man wasn't helping. It was time to change tactics.

"Look, this doesn't have to become a fight between us. And you know I don't care if you have an affair with Debra Jean. But Gloria said she was a prime suspect in the data break-in attempt. So shouldn't we both wonder about our former postdoc's motivation with you now? This is her second time of opera-going on your subscription night. Maybe it's not just your body she's after."

"You're being paranoid."

"Perhaps, but let's make sure. Suppose I ask Gloria to investigate Debra Jean: check her phone calls, have her followed, see who she's contacted in the past month, that's sort of thing."

"If you must. She's no threat to us."

"How do we know? Someone is after us, and Debra Jean is at the top of the list. Remember, we've licensed two new drugs in the last six months. MI is worth many millions more now, and that will quadruple if our IPO goes well."

Joe left the window and stood behind Paul, putting a hand on his shoulder. "You're losing sight of the big picture. It's not just one drug that we're talking about. Our new delivery system is a multiplier for all drugs. We've discovered how to introduce photosensitive molecules into the body that are able to piggyback on any biologically active molecules. That means we can follow a drug's progress in the bloodstream and lymphatic system, and activate it when needed. The possibilities are limitless. It's going to revolutionize the treatment of many diseases."

Paul squirmed in his seat. "I know the science and its practical value."

"Security at MI becomes even more important." Joe paused, trying to understand Paul's mood. "For God's sake, let yourself enjoy our achievements. Forget about a lightweight like Debra Jean. Energy, excitement, potency, beauty—it's all available for people like us." He let his voice grow darker. "Do you remember that day when we brought Judith over to your house when we were in high school? You picked her up and then brought her to us. She was so young and luscious. Her breasts were just budding under her soft cotton T-shirt. Remember how she had painted flowers across her chest to hide her nipples?"

"You don't need to do this, Joe."

"We had so much fun together, Paul. Remember how we put on that first Simon and Garfunkel album, and Judith stripped to her underpants and asked us to take them off for her—slowly?"

"Let you take them off."

"And how we flipped a coin to see who would go first, and you won? And how you were so frightened that I had to hold your hands behind your back while Judith reciprocated? And how surprised she was when your perfect penis was limp and soft and so little compared with mine, even when she put it into her mouth? Judith and I laughed at that, and you began to cry. We tried to be nice to you, but then we got going and forgot about you. You were watching us when your prick turned hard. I understood immediately and began fucking her for you as well as me, just to keep you turned on."

"Come on, Joe," Paul said weakly.

"Judith came and so did I, although there was barely enough semen to justify my condom. But Judith wanted more. Actually, it was more of you she wanted. You were why she was there, not me. So after she and I finished, she came on to you. She tried everything she could think of, but you stayed soft. A very inventive girl, actually, but it didn't take long for her to intuit what I already understood: that I, not she, was your excitement. You're not gay, Paul—something far more interesting, as it turns out. So I mounted her and you instantly got hard; then we made the switch. We worked it out together, didn't we? You were a Venus's-flytrap for the girls, but you needed me to get off."

Joe saw that Paul's face was covered with sweat. "And now you want to desert our relationship for Debra Jean? Try to be serious."

Paul slouched down in his chair, searching for the courage to face Joe. "We both know how we fit together, Joe," he began. "You won't understand how painful it has always been for me."

"Pain and pleasure aren't opposites, Paul." He leaned forward, both hands on the table.

"I don't like the way you inflict pain, now or then," Paul said angrily. "Look, Joe, I'm still part of your scene. Now I want my own. I should have stopped all this long ago."

"But you didn't," Joe prodded. "And you can't." He straightened and let his voice deepen. "Enough of this. I want to know what you are really saying to me, Paul."

"Hearing about what you did to Debra Jean pushed me over an edge. It's over."

Joe saw the determination in his friend's face. "You want to disband our relationship."

Paul shook off the comment. "I'd like to make our break a smooth one, for you and me."

Joe looked at the ceiling for a moment and then pushed a button on the desk. "Gloria, can you come in here for a moment?"

"What are you up to, Joe?" Paul said warily.

"What you've already agreed to: spying on Debra Jean."

"Putting Gloria on Debra Jean won't change anything."

"Maybe not, but the woman's got you wrapped around her little finger. Before you go off with her, I want you to see who she is. And for both our sakes, I want to know who's putting her up to this."

"It won't make any difference."

"We'll see," Joe said briskly. Gloria's heels clicked in the corridor as she approached.

"I don't want to be in on this conversation. I'm leaving."

"Suit yourself. But do me a favor. Don't do anything impetuously until we've both learned more about what's going on. Because something is!"

There was a knock at the door, and Joe moved to answer it. "Paul," he said over his shoulder, "it's been an amazing partnership. If you need to go your own way, go. Perhaps it's time. I know you're disgusted by my habits. I don't always like myself. It's just … who I am."

"You'll always be important to me, Joe."

"Just wait to see what Gloria finds out about your new flame."

"No matter what she finds, it won't change my mind." And he walked out of the room.

CHAPTER 17

Silken Threads

Wiley woke up feeling irritated. He needed to move his body. He thought of Gloria as he had every day, waking up from the very bed she had occupied—alone.

He decided on a long run with the Ferry Building as his goal. It was ten miles and as beautiful an urban landscape as he could imagine. The route was mostly along the water: Sausalito's waterfront, the Golden Gate Bridge, the Marina Green, and the long stretch of piers would take him two and a half hours.

His plan had been to catch the ferry back to Sausalito at 1, but when he arrived at noon, he decided to stroll down Market Street instead. He liked the way his jogging clothes set him apart from the dark-suited businessmen walking purposefully between financial and corporate offices. He decided to stop for a coffee and newspaper, and spotted Starbucks on all four corners of the first main intersection. He ducked into one for coffee, a scone, and the *New York Times*. A half-hour later, he continued his walk on Market and then took Second Street down to Mission Street. Gloria again came to mind. He could say he was nearby and invite her to lunch. The idea brought a giddy sexual rush. He felt like a kid.

He stopped and pulled out the cell phone tucked into a side pocket of his shorts, and dialed the MI number. He gave his name to the receptionist and asked for Ms. Garcia. She answered on the second ring.

"I'm in the neighborhood."

"On business?"

"Sort of. Lunch?"

"Sure. Borstal's in a half-hour." She laughed. "You know where it is."

* * *

Borstal's had a few outdoor tables and served a drinkers' lunch—hard-boiled eggs, simple sandwiches, and a good homemade soup of beef and barley. Gloria arrived a few minutes after Wiley, dressed in a tight black skirt and sweater covered by a stylish leather jacket. He was painfully aware of his running shorts and sweat-soaked T-shirt.

"Just ran in from Sausalito," he said hesitantly.

She smiled flirtatiously. "I hope I'm worth the effort, Wiley."

"Actually, I didn't know I would end up here."

"Don't apologize. I've been thinking about you too. I'm glad you made it so soon. I only hope Manuel doesn't show up."

"He had a right to be annoyed."

"I'm not anyone's property, certainly not his."

"But you are family."

She nodded appreciatively and turned serious. "I know. There are a lot of displaced people in the Mission, people who have been here a long time and still feel they don't belong. I'm a good example. *La familia* works for us."

"Sure."

"I still long for El Salvador." Gloria leaned back in her chair to catch the sun. "So what brings you here—besides me?"

"I could make up something," he said honestly. He watched the bronze in her hair sparkle in the sunlight.

"Thanks for that. God, your size still amazes me."

"It's not the easiest attribute to carry around. I can't fit into most beds. Airline travel is difficult. I sit in the back of movie theaters. People are always asking me if I'm a basketball player. Should I go on?"

"But it also has its advantages. When you and Dave go places, the waves of humanity part. It wasn't just your tenor voice that got you out of Borstal's that night."

"Size definitely has its advantages."

"I'll bet the women like it."

"Sure they do." He looked her over. "You're a beautiful woman, Gloria, so you know the problems. How can we help asking ourselves if they like us just for our bodies?"

She smiled. "Thanks for the compliment." She stretched provocatively in her chair. "I try not to hide what I have to offer. But I know what fantasy the women are having." She pointedly provocatively at his flimsy running shorts. "Not that it really makes a difference, in my experience."

"There is no simple correspondence," Wiley said sheepishly, aware of his own growing excitement. "You know the worst thing about being so tall?" he said. "I never feel completely held. There are always big parts of my body getting left out."

"On the other hand, your girlfriends really get to snuggle." She gave him another one of those flirtatious looks. "You're a sexy guy even when you're embarrassed." Then she said directly, "Look, Wiley, you must know that I like you. And right now I'm loving teasing you, but I also can see that it's making you nervous. I'm happy to leave your body alone and get on with why you came."

"This is a pretty crazy conversation."

"The way we met hasn't had a normal moment," she said wryly. The street was filling with men and women on lunch breaks. "So what about some food before it gets busy and we get sillier? I thought I'd go for the soup and a beer. Let me order. If anybody remembers you, they might poison the soup."

"OK. And this is business, so the tab is on me."

She seemed amused and signaled to the waiter, who was watching them suspiciously from behind the door. She frowned and then spoke to him in rapid Spanish. He left without a smile.

"They remember you, all right."

"Another disadvantage of size."

"But I think the soup will be clean." She caught his eye. "Did you really run all the way here just to take me to lunch? It must be 20 miles."

"More like 10. I often run into San Francisco and take a ferry back. But then it occurred to me …"

"That I was here."

"And that you said you needed time to decide on your relationship with Revenge, Inc. What you decide is important to our case. Debra Jean called me after meeting Paul at the opera. She's pretty sure that Joe is the one who molested her at Jardinière."

"I'm glad she's working with you guys. She needs to get a good handle on what happened to her and what she's going to do about it," Gloria said. "And you have a great gift, Wiley. You make even scared people like Debra Jean feel secure."

The waiter brought the soup and a large pitcher of beer. He put the pitcher in the middle of the table with two iced glasses next to it.

Wiley poured a beer for both of them and stretched out his legs as he drank. Gloria couldn't help staring at the vast expanse of powerful muscles that unfolded from beneath the table.

"You said you might help us, Gloria."

"A qualified yes to that. What happened with Debra Jean is unfortunate but not worth losing my job about. But seeing those children in the hotel suite, those horrible knives on the table ready for 'use,' definitely is. The two are related in my mind. So of course I want to help. I can't work for a man who's involved in what I saw at the Empress."

"Your role at MI will be a big advantage."

"It's also got complications. That's the 'qualified' part."

"I understand."

"I could just leave MI, but I'd never get another job at this level. He'd see to that."

Wiley waited.

Gloria looked up into his eyes. "Look, Revenge, Inc., is a great idea. You're very good at what you do. And Dave, well, he's one of a kind. But Joe—he's something else. He's beyond genius. He scared me even before I knew about his extreme pleasures, and I don't scare easily. And then there's Paul. They're a brilliant pair."

"You still include Paul in this? How involved do you think he is?"

"Everyone says he's been around Joe for all of his adult life. That makes him guilty in my mind."

"Could Joe operate MI without him?"

"From what I've seen, Joe uses Paul and Paul submits. He's a sweet guy and very talented, and of course he gets a lot from being with Joe. But believe me, Joe could go it alone."

"Except he doesn't."

Gloria put her hand on his arm and squeezed it in frustration. "Wiley, you're not listening to me; you don't understand who you'll be dealing with. I'm worried about you."

"You handle him."

"Well, yes. That's what I'm good at." She pressed her lips together in a pout. "I do. And I admire you. You are a smart, hunky gringo who's found a way to help others. But don't get cocky. You've got blue eyes and white skin and height and good looks. No matter how good you were on the football field, you're not a match for a super-genius like Joe. An evil one to boot."

"So you're afraid that Revenge, Inc., will go down, and you'll lose your job and maybe more."

"Also you'll get hurt. That matters to me, too."

"Don't forget about Dave. And you."

She glared at him. "I know I bring a lot to the table. I have access to everything in that company, and there is my own tape collection of Joe and Paul's private conversations. With Dave's help, I can figure out a lot more from the computer files."

"What do you want, Gloria?"

It was her turn to be quiet.

He took up the slack. "It's my job."

"Is it really just a job to you, Wiley?" She touched his forearm again.

"No. Does that matter?"

She smiled again, this time with a hint of mischief.

Wiley flushed. "I'm going to freeze in these damp clothes."

"My apartment's nearby. I can lend you some of my father's clothes. They'll be way small, but they'll keep you warm. I can drop you at the Ferry Building when you need to go."

"That's very nice of you. But don't you need to get back to work?"

"Sure I do, but my Latino hospitality comes first. Besides, you're a suspect, so getting to know you better *is* work." She rubbed her palm over the muscles in his arm. "If we're going to have any chance against Joe, we'll need to put everything on the table."

"Remember that this is also about Debra Jean."

She nodded and got up from the table. "Let's go." She placed a hand on her hip. "And remember, sometimes a shower is just a shower." Then she began walking slowly down the sidewalk in the direction away from her office.

Wiley reached into his wallet and put a $20 bill next to the check. He quickly caught up with Gloria. She reached out her hand to him. Wiley took it. "I am good at keeping things simple," he said. "Like showers."

"Let's keep this afternoon focused on getting you warm and dry, and learning to trust one another," she said as they walked. "I don't mind simple."

* * *

Dave was not surprised to see Wiley sitting at an outdoor table at Borstal's talking with Gloria. But he was astonished to see his friend being completely unaware of the watcher staked out 50 feet away from him. As a quarterback, Wiley had been famous for his peripheral vision, a talent that had saved him from many a sack. Obviously Gloria had considerably narrowed his gaze. Dave decided against contacting Wiley by cell phone. Better to sit tight, protect his friend, and watch him make a fool of himself with the new girl in town.

Earlier he had seen Gloria leave MI's building and head in the direction of Borstal's. A few minutes later, Joe Diamond emerged from the same door. Almost immediately, a long black car pulled up, and a squat muscled man in a chauffeur's uniform got out, leaving the motor running. He stood on the curb next to Joe. The two men talked for a few minutes, and then Joe went back inside the building. The chauffeur leaned in to shut off the motor but left the car where it was. Then he walked quickly away in the direction in which Gloria had gone. Dave followed him. The chauffeur took up a position diagonally across from the Borstal's doorway, and then moments later he seemed to change his mind and entered the bar. Dave found a busy building entrance where he could see inside and remain hidden.

When Wiley and Gloria walked off together heading away from Borstal's and MI, the chauffeur followed on foot, and so did Dave. Wiley and Gloria walked a half-mile to a working-class neighborhood in the Mission and entered a two-story converted Victorian. Dave and the shadow took up positions a block from one another. Probably Gloria's home, Dave thought. After ten minutes, the chauffeur pulled out his cell phone and made a quick call. Five minutes later, an Eldorado SUV drew up next to him. The chauffeur walked back the way he had come. Some sort of tag team. Dave called Wiley.

Wiley answered on the second ring. "Dave."

"You busy?"

"Just getting started up here."

"You're being watched by two of Joe's lackeys. Only one is here now."

"Thanks." There was a brief pause, and Dave could hear Gloria's voice saying something unintelligible.

Wiley came back on. "OK. You stay where you are. I'll be down in ten and walk back to Borstal's. Gloria will follow five minutes later and return to MI. You follow her and make sure she gets back without trouble."

"They probably will follow you. The guys are both built like tanks. Even you—"

"Don't worry about me," Wiley interrupted. "Let's meet back at Borstal's when you're through."

"I like cloak and dagger, but is Borstal's a good idea?"

"We're friends of a friend, even if we are the enemy."

Dave heard Gloria's voice. "She says the bar has a back room. Let's meet there." Wiley hung up.

Dave waited until Wiley walk out the door. He was dressed in clothes many sizes too small for him and looked wrung out. Makes sense, Dave thought. He had run 12 miles and probably just gotten laid.

He watched Wiley walk swiftly in the opposite direction from MI. The driver got out of the SUV and followed Wiley until he reached the end of the block and turned the corner. On cue, Gloria exited the building. The man hesitated, and then took out his cell phone as Wiley disappeared from view. The man listened on the phone, waited while Gloria crossed the street, and then took off at a fast run after Wiley. Bad move, Dave thought. You've lost them both.

Dave shadowed Gloria back to MI. He stopped a block before the entrance as she disappeared through the door, and then waited. The chauffeur appeared and waited at the entrance of MI. When Gloria didn't leave the building, he got into the car and drove off. Dave waited a few more minutes and, seeing no one, sauntered back to Borstal's.

The room was more than half-filled with Irish men, a late-afternoon drinking crowd, from the sounds of it. A smaller number of Latinos were in a separate group at the bar. The Irish bartender looked him over as he entered and then pointed toward a door. Both groups of drinkers watched him carefully. A few of the Latinos mumbled his name in greeting, and others nodded in recognition. He opened the back door to a large empty room, probably used for private meetings and parties, where Wiley sat nursing a Guinness. He looked like a giant homeless guy. Irish hospitality, Dave thought. He appreciatively greeted his friend with a big hug and took a big gulp from the other large mug on the table.

* * *

Gloria watched as an in-house message appeared on the screen on her desk. "We have a problem." It was signed "JD."

She walked the two flights up to Joe Diamond's office and knocked.

"Come in." Joe was at his desk poring over papers filled with equations.

"You want to see me, Dr. Diamond?" she said easily. "What's up?"

Joe pointed to the sofa to the right of his desk. She sat down. He got up from his desk and sat at the opposite end of the sofa. "You are, Gloria. Where were you just now?"

"Doing my job," Gloria answered immediately.

"Meaning?"

"At Borstal's with a guy, the friend of that man I met at Borstal's Friday night who said he needed to talk to me about MI's security. I assumed it related to the attempted break-in at MI."

Joe said, "Go on."

"He said he was a computer consultant. Said he had tried to get into our system but failed. He said he found a weak spot that he wanted to tell me about. It's a way to get new business."

"Smart and stupid," Joe mused. "You believe him?"

"It's something people do. I decided to check it out further and took him up on his lunch invitation. While I was at Borstal's, your chauffeur, Peter, was watching me. The man I was with spotted him too. After lunch, I took him to my apartment."

"Explain, Gloria."

"It's a way to get information."

"Did you get what you wanted from the guy?"

She smiled. "It depends how you mean that. He's very tall and sexy." She looked at Joe, trying to make the comparison crystal-clear.

"Don't mess with me, Gloria. I don't care what you think of me. What matters is that I'm your boss."

"The guy was amazing. At least six-foot-seven and built—nothing like him where I come from."

"Stop putting me on."

"Well, I don't like being followed, especially by my boss and his lackeys. It slows me down. Security is my job; let me do it." She paused to let that sink in. "We got to my apartment, but then I saw one of your cars drive up and another ghoul get out."

"I see."

"Unfortunately, the guy noticed, too. I mean, either your guys are amateurs or they want to be seen. Either way, it was unproductive. It cooled things down between us. Made him suspicious; he left before I got what I wanted." She left her meaning ambiguous.

"OK, I'm sorry about that. But it felt necessary. There's too much going on that I don't understand."

"Well, if you let me do my job, I could've helped. It's why you pay me."

Joe took a minute to straighten the papers on his desk. "What did you decide about the guy?"

"Nothing yet." She smiled. "Don't worry. He'll be back. We both didn't get what we wanted."

"I get the picture," Joe said, nodding. "OK. I'll call off Peter and Zvi." He leaned over and patted her on the knee, and Gloria put her hand over his for just a moment. Then she left the room, carefully closing the door after her.

Joe sat quietly, watching her go. She was tough and confident, and her explanation seemed plausible, if unorthodox. He loved her hard comebacks when he pushed her. She was very good to look at and knew it. While it was true that security personnel could easily be turned for a bit of money, Gloria had a lot more to lose with MI than she could possibly gain from passing on information about MI.

But he was not satisfied with her explanation. Her luncheon date, Debra Jean's dinner with Paul at Jardinière, and the fire alarm at the

Empress could not be isolated events. But he was still without a connector, the X factor. What could the intruders be after? All the new drugs were well into the commercial pipeline, and it was unlikely that anybody but the most experienced scientists could see the possibilities in his new work. Something else was going on.

As always, the challenges interested him more than the outcome. He was fascinated and slightly anxious about the puzzle of unexplained events and his inability to penetrate their meaning. Well, anxiety about loss of control was an issue for all prodigies, at least the ones who joined SM. Members of that group had outfoxed their parents and teachers and even their therapists by developing powerfully assertive identities. Mozart, the gold standard of the genius prodigy, had famously turned the tables on his father-mentor. Or had he? Joe tried to imagine the early years of that struggle. Perhaps Mozart would have felt the same kind of anxiety as Joe felt now, the kind when you couldn't grasp the largest picture. Which meant you couldn't protect your flank.

Paul posed the real threat to him. He always had. Joe was bound to him by silken threads, invisible and unfelt until he pulled against them, and then they cut into him like steel. The thought brought a sharp jolt of fear. Was he forever to be hostage to his emotional need for Paul? If he lost Paul, he would be in real danger.

His mother once told him that all his brilliance would someday be rendered useless by the emotions of love. Even as a little boy, he knew she was talking about her own unrequited love for him, the dark, impenetrable magical child that she had brought into the world. But she was wrong. After all, he had freed himself from her. Separating Debra Jean from Paul should be just another iteration of a strategy well known to him.

Although it was still early in the afternoon, Joe put away his papers. He called Peter and gave him the night off. He had a lot of thinking to do, and there was plenty of time for a long walk to his apartment in North Beach. There were the lecture and business dealings in Beijing this weekend. And he would put out his worries to his brain trust, the SM group. They always came up with a few right answers.

CHAPTER 18

Threesomes

Debra Jean closed the door and surveyed a standard room on the third floor of the Travelodge near the San Francisco Airport. Nothing special, she thought, just a king-size bed, some pleasant pictures on the wall, privacy, and a good shower. But what else did they need except themselves?

She sat down on the edge of the bed and began chewing her cuticles. Not cool, she thought. She had seen the kind of woman Paul admired in Jardinière and at the Opera House the previous week. They were pretty and chic and shone with excitement, in contrast to her own dependence and depression.

She freed her hand from her teeth and pushed it down between her legs. She'd been in a chronic state of sexual excitement ever since Paul had passionately kissed her goodnight at her car after the opera and proposed this meeting.

Two nights ago, a dream had released her sexual longing in a climax that awakened her from sleep. Another climax followed, and for the next 45 minutes she gave in to her fantasies of Paul and an almost continuous orgasmic plateau. In her sex class in med school, such experiences were described as sexual pathology, a female variant of male priapism. She remembered treating the male variety in the ICU as an intern. What had begun as sexual excitement ended in the emergency ward as overwhelming pain and panic. It took a strong intramuscular sedative to calm the patient and his penis. But her own experience had given her continuous intense pleasurable climaxes. So much for pathologizing the good things in life. It was only when her hand and thigh began to cramp that she had reluctantly used scotch and a Valium to bring herself down.

This afternoon would bring the pleasure of two bodies to her and an exponential increase in joy.

She decided to undress and meet him here naked. She took a long, warm shower, dried off, and smoothed on the lotions. Naked, she lay down on the bed, draped a sheer pearl-hued silk robe on the lower half of her body, crossed her hands over her heart, and waited.

Things were looking up—first and foremost, sex and a relationship with Paul Stokes. She also needed information about Joe and MI. The two goals, sex and revenge, almost coincided—almost because Paul's character and motivation, despite his apologies and explanations, were still unclear. He had, after all, been involved in her downfall at MI.

She looked at the clock. He was ten minutes late. She closed her eyes and imagined Paul: his easy way of holding her arm as they strolled to their seats in the opera. Her excitement grew as she imagined what would happen when he joined his body with hers.

There was a knock at the door.

"Just a minute!" she cried. She rushed to the bathroom to inspect her face. The sexual flush and faint perspiration looked alluring.

Holding her robe up to her body, she rushed to open the door. As he entered, he looked her over appreciatively. "A naked woman. A beautiful naked woman. What a sight! Exquisite. I haven't been able to stop thinking about you since the opera, and for good reason."

Paul put two bottles of champagne and his overnight bag on the floor. She took a step toward him.

"Sorry to be late. The flight from L.A," he continued, holding her off. He nodded toward the champagne bottles. "These will need ice, Debra Jean," he said. It was only then that he opened his arms to her.

Twenty minutes later, Debra Jean lay in bed next to Paul, who was staring up at the ceiling. The champagne in the ice bucket was still unopened.

"So now you know me better," he said.

"You could say I know you for the first time." She leaned over him and kissed him on the lips, then gently slid her hand down his chest and played with his bellybutton. "There's always Viagra, Paul."

"I've tried Viagra, and it rarely works."

"Guilty about Sharon?"

"Hardly. Sharon and I haven't had sex in years."

She thought that one over. "But you look so devoted to one another."

"We are, in a way," he replied. "You know how she follows me around at parties? Everybody thinks she's trying to keep her man away from other women. Well, that's true, but not because she's worried about losing me. Actually, she's trying to save me from an encounter like this one. She doesn't want me to feel impotent and get more depressed than I am now."

Debra Jean took his hand. "That's both sick and sweet. Forgive my curiosity, but what does she do? For sex, I mean?"

"I'm sure she has lovers. I certainly hope so. But we don't talk about it."

She placed her hand on his languid penis. It was beautiful, so perfectly shaped in repose. But it had shown no hardness despite her ministrations.

"Is there anything more I can do?"

"You've done everything I can think of, and more. You're great, Debra Jean. I hoped that with you …"

She pointed to herself, saying, "This lack of excitement must have something to do with me." She heard the desperation in her voice.

"No way. Look at you, your breasts, your thighs. You're perfect." He turned away. "I just don't respond."

"How can that be, Paul? I've seen you excited. Not sexually, but I've seen you come alive in the laboratory. I remember when you took the whole lab staff out sailing. Your smile, your forcefulness, your body, your humor—in every way a gorgeous, potent man."

"You remember that?"

"I remember how sexy you looked." She blushed.

"I felt that way, and it was all about you."

"But then what are you talking about? And what's happening now?" She heard the anger in her voice as she spoke.

"It was genuine." His body shivered slightly. "But replay that scene in your mind. Who was at the helm?"

Debra Jean thought for a moment. "Joe Diamond. I remember being surprised that he was such a good sailor. Not compared to you, of course." She frowned at him. "What are you saying?" She took her hand away from his penis. "Is he your lover? Are you gay?"

"No. We've never been involved sexually—not directly, at least. It's something else, more subterranean. It's something he has that I need. It sounds crazy, but it's all too real."

She sat up on the bed and tucked her legs into a lotus position. "I'm sorry, I don't understand."

"I've learned to accept that nothing happens to me—down there—without him."

"So you're saying that if Joe were here, you'd be excited, capable of having sex with me."

"Yes." His penis began to grow, and he quickly put his hands out to cover it. "There's your answer."

She looked down at him, then away. "I still don't understand, Paul." She cuddled against his chest.

"Joe and I went to the same high school. Bronx Science. I was dating girls—chastely, actually—and one day he was with me at my house with one of my girlfriends. We all got slightly drunk and I discovered"—he looked down—"this truth." They both watched his penis grow to a size he could no longer cover. "A lie detector for my need. It all works very well when he's involved."

Debra Jean frowned. "And you don't get an erection without Joe?"

"I know it sounds incredible, but there it is. It's complicated because I feel connected to women, not men. When I was younger, he sometimes tried things with me, but I hated it." Paul shivered slightly. "It's not his body that turns me on, it's his energy. It's only when that electrical charge gets into me that I can come alive: with women, with ideas, with everything."

"So why are you here today? It was your invitation," Debra Jean said, trying to bring compassion back to her voice.

"You're so special. After our kiss, I decided to give it a try."

"Obviously I'm not special enough," she said angrily.

"Believe me, it's not your fault, Debra Jean. It has nothing to do with you."

"Two years treating suburbanites in Walnut Creek has taught me more about bizarre sexuality than I ever wanted to know. But this thing with Joe is right up there. And you're saying his effect is not just about sex …"

"Right—it's about everything. Work, colleagues, reputation—all are tied to him. It's about life."

She disentangled herself from his body and rolled onto her back. "And these 'threesomes' with Joe, do they still go on?"

"No. Joe's gone to … other things. I was never very interested in drugs, and they became critical to his scenarios. S&M, too. It felt filthy, the kind of thing where you want to wash for a long time afterward. But that didn't mean it didn't turn me on. I just found it too disgusting to act on it, and, later, to be there at all."

Debra Jean leaned over and kissed him again. She placed her hand on his groin and let her fingers cup his penis. The skin was so soft. All she wanted to do right now was stroke it.

"Do you miss it?"

"What I miss is good sex with a woman I care about. That's why I'm here this afternoon." He put his hand over hers. "But it's not going to work." He paused and then said, "I also came here today to tell you again how sorry I am about what Joe did to you at Jardinière."

She pulled the covers over their nakedness. "I'm just glad you weren't involved with what happened."

"But I was there. In a way, it was the same old scenario …"

She could see his penis grow under the sheet. She frowned, trying not to look. "I had a crush on both of you—Joe for his mind, you for … well, everything. I'd have gone for you if you'd asked. Or him. How strange is that?"

Paul looked at her. "I don't want to share you with Joe."

"Now I think Joe is disgusting."

Paul was silent.

"What he did shamed me horribly. He knew exactly how to hurt me, like I was some kind of puppet."

"He always knows …"

She propped her head on an elbow and looked Paul straight in the eyes. "Frankly, I'm used to disappointments in love. And I can't keep guys for very long, so I hit and run. I can't stand getting left."

She leaned into him again. "It must be about hero worship, the sexual turn-on you feel around him. When Joe hired me, I felt a buzz. Stronger than a drug. I wanted to take him inside me any way I could—his ideas, his energy, his flesh. I feel that way about great composers. I want to take their music inside me—an elegant phrase, a complex rhythm, a crazy orchestration. If Mozart walked into the room, I would prostrate myself on the floor and beg."

"Necrophilia?" he joked.

She laughed. "Joe lives in a world of compressed energy. He's like Bach: creativity that doesn't stop. You say you don't want his prick inside of you, and I believe that. But what you want from him isn't far from that."

"You've got it," Paul said. "And what started off as a kind of hero worship is now an addiction. He's the passion in my life."

"But you've got a lot of your own passion."

"All in the service of—"

"Joe. Yes, I get that you feel that way. And now you're here, and Joe isn't with you, and you can't get it up unless you imagine he's here. And as much as I want you, I'd rather have nothing sexual from you than have him here, even in fantasy."

"I thought you said you wanted us both that night at Jardinière."

"As I also said, things have changed." She got out of bed and put on her robe. A waste of a beautiful outfit, she thought, as she opened the champagne, poured two glasses, and put the bottle and his glass on the table next to his side of the bed. She sat down by him.

"Paul, would you like to have sex with me?"

"Shhh. Of course. You know that."

"Would you leave Joe if you knew that could happen?"

He had to tell her. "I told him I was leaving him several times this week. I told him it was because of what he did to you and the way I felt about you. He wasn't worried. I've tried to leave before. He told me that you wanted something from us, from MI. He said I should find out what you were up to, and then, if I still wanted to leave, he wouldn't try to stop me. Maybe that's another reason why I'm here."

"He's right."

"He's always right, damn him." Paul swung his legs down, sat on the

131

other side of the bed away from her, and grabbed at a sock. "Look, I'd better leave."

"Listen to me!" she said sharply and took a long gulp of champagne. Then she leaned across his body, letting her breasts touch his back, and poured more into his glass. "There is something I haven't told you."

Paul picked up his other sock, stood, and began to gather the rest of his clothes. "Which is?"

"Slow down for a moment. Pretend that you got laid. This is important. I need to tell you some things that aren't pretty."

"I see. About Joe, I'd guess."

"About all three of us. Look, I still don't know why I fell apart that night at the restaurant. I don't know why I was so passive afterward." She pulled him back onto the bed. They sat next to each other, finishing the champagne. "I should have been able to treat what he did like a really bad moment, file a complaint at UC, demand an apology, and more." She burrowed closer to him. "Instead, I lost my job and my pride and stayed depressed for two years. Then suddenly I got angry. I don't know why; it just happened. I wanted revenge."

"Revenge? Come on. What's that about?"

She looked at Paul. "I'm a little drunk, but I'm serious. Just like I'm still serious about you—an overeducated, sexually fucked-up Nobel Prize wannabe." She burped. "You're handsome even with one sock on, that hangdog look on your face, and a limp prick." She hiccupped. "God, did I say that?"

She got up and sashayed in front of the mirror opposite the bed. "It's a shame that my lover can't get it up even when I'm at my prettiest."

"You are beautiful, Debra Jean. And sexy."

"You don't know how hard it is to feel sexy after two years in exile from all that." She went back to the bed. "You didn't mention smart. I can design a good experiment. I have a good strategic sense. How could you get rid of me?"

"It shouldn't have happened."

"In Walnut Creek, when I got angry, you know what I did? I thought about revenge. I thought about how I could get you guys on the rack. I prepared like I would for a complicated experiment. I read detective novels. I dreamed up arcane strategies for torture. But with all I knew, I still couldn't come up with a good plan. Not if I didn't want to go to jail or get mixed up with hoodlums."

"Hoodlums. That's a strange word. Do you know any?"

"No. That's exactly the point. I don't, except through movies and books." She giggled. "I became obsessed with revenge. A few months ago, I took a vacation to Seychelles and met someone who seemed to know something about revenge. The someone turned out to be the future president of the country. His name was Xavier Le Grand. Great name, eh?"

"What were you doing with the future president of Seychelles?"

"Jealous, Paul?" She put her head in his naked lap and smiled up into his face. "I was on vacation on La Digue, one of its islands, at a gorgeous hotel and decided to go to a political rally in town and seek out some local color. We talked after his speech. I was the only white person there, and maybe he was tired of the partying that was the heart of the rally. He asked me to dinner. I agreed and got pretty tipsy, just like now. I told him what was bothering me, the revenge thing. He picked up on my story and gave me the name of someone he thought could help. Someone in Sausalito, of all places. His name was Wiley Stone. So I contacted him when I got back here, and I hired him and a man named Dave Blue. They're partners at Revenge, Inc. They played football together a decade ago. They were first-round draft picks. But there was some sort of scandal."

Paul finished his champagne and put the glass on the table. "Of course I remember them. And you're saying they're running some scam out in Sausalito."

"Scam isn't a nice word, Paul."

"Wait a minute. A little more than a week ago, someone tried to break into MI's files. Could that have been connected to them?"

"Actually, they couldn't get into your files. But they didn't seem to care. Wiley just wanted to stir you guys up. He thought that how you reacted might tell him something. By chance they discovered something awful." She sat up straighter and took one of Paul's hands in hers. "About Joe."

"What about Joe?"

"Wiley, Dave, and your head of security, Gloria Garcia, saw Joe

133

leaving a hotel room with some other people." She hesitated. "Inside, two naked little girls were bound and gagged. They found surgical tools and a set-up for filming. Probably had to move fast."

"My God!" Paul exclaimed. "Are you sure Joe was there?"

"Gloria saw him with one of his friends. Dave had created a diversion, which saved the children," Debra Jean said.

"Who else knows about this?" Paul snapped.

"That's the wrong question, Paul."

"How sure are you, Debra Jean?"

"Better question. I wasn't there, so it's just hearsay. Does that make you feel comfortable about your partner?"

"No." He moved away from her.

Debra Jean stood up and without looking at him went to the bathroom to dress. When she came back, Paul had not moved from the side of the bed. She went to the door.

"Sunday morning there will be a meeting on their barge in Sausalito, where you can learn more. Frankly, I don't want to give you the address now, meaning I don't trust you completely. But think about it. You have my cell phone number. I'll even pick you up. Just call." She opened the door.

"Debra Jean …"

She closed the door on his pleading voice.

* * *

Dave sat in his car across the street from the entrance to the lobby of the Travelodge. Zvi was also there, sitting in an Eldorado SUV parked a block away on the other side of the street. Both of them saw Debra Jean walk out the door and head for the parking lot. She got into her Lexus, opened the sunroof, and drove swiftly out of the lot. Zvi just sat there and waited. Dave stayed, too.

Fifteen minutes later, Paul emerged from the same door. He got into his Targa and left. This time, Zvi started up his SUV and followed Paul away from the hotel at a safe distance. Dave drove to Joe Diamond's apartment building on Green Street in North Beach. There was a doorman and obvious video cameras, which meant even more security inside. He didn't need to risk being caught. Not yet, anyway.

Dave headed back to Sausalito. He stopped at the Liquor Barn to buy a good Oregon Pinot for Wiley and whoever might be with him.

CHAPTER 19

Shadow Men

Joe Diamond leaned back in a deep armchair and sipped a well-aged and particularly delicious Drouhin '84 Corton Charlemagne thinking about the upcoming trip to China. Zvi was in a smaller room off Joe's bedroom, setting up floor mats and a massage table for the evening workout. Joe called for him to come in. What happened at the Empress required a tougher approach, and Zvi would be the right person for the job.

"I need you to help me while I'm gone," Joe said easily. "Primarily to control the aftermath of the Empress. Also to clarify who we're up against in the break-in and whether there is a connection."

"Perhaps it relates to the events at the Travelodge," Zvi suggested. "Debra Jean had Paul alone there for some time. She's a clever woman. Paul might like her type," he said with obvious disdain. "She has the motivation to hurt you."

"Go on."

"Paul worries me, Joe. He knows too much about you and could inadvertently pass it on to whoever is interested in MI. The tall man is our best candidate for that. We underestimate him."

"But what is he after?"

"What about the new drugs you're synthesizing in China?"

"In the long run, they are worth a fortune. Only someone like Paul, and possibly Debra Jean, would understand why."

"I don't think data theft for money is Debra Jean's style," Zvi murmured.

"It's definitely not about money," Joe said. "She had a very wealthy father. … Anything is possible, which means we know nothing. It's imperative that I know what she's up to. I don't want Paul involved in her schemes."

"Don't worry, Joe. I'll have a few days to check on them before he joins you in Beijing. Once he leaves, we'll focus on the woman."

"Good." Joe brought out a second bottle of the Corton. He settled down in a chair opposite Zvi, pouring two glasses. "Relax. Taste this, my friend. The fruit and finish are amazing."

Zvi looked at the bottle. "A great year. A privilege to drink."

Joe nodded. "What happened at the Empress was a fiasco and a tragedy."

"And the tampering with the smoke alarm suggests a non-chance occurrence," Zvi added.

"I agree. If it connects to Debra Jean, she must be working with someone experienced."

"I doubt that it's just the tall man," Zvi said.

"Why do you say that?"

"I had a feeling of being followed at the Travelodge. Someone else was there. Not him."

"Who else would be interested? It makes little sense. You saw my query on our SM site about these issues?"

"Yes." He went around to the back of Joe's chair and began kneading his shoulders. "Anything interesting come of that?"

"Not yet. There are many offers of help."

"They'll come through," Zvi reassured Joe as he dug his knuckles into Joe's back. "They're the very best."

"I know that. But so far, there is very little to go on."

"Could it be someone in SM itself?"

"There's never been a problem of loyalty."

"It's always possible. Snuff films are not everybody's fare, even in our group."

Zvi's hands were strong and skillful, and Joe sighed contentedly. "Thank God you're not a moralist like some of our American members."

Zvi signaled Joe to lie down on the sofa and disrobe. His strong hands prodded vital points on Joe's naked back.

"You've taught me so much about my body, Zvi, and you've made great discoveries in the field of somatics. You named the field. You are almost as famous as I am."

"Yours is the more important contribution, Joe. Still, we help each other. You never considered the body as real until we met. Now it is much more important to you, eh? I still remember that extraordinary SM camp in the Sierra where we first met. It was your first experience with sadomasochism."

"And I will never forget the hooks in your back, Zvi, and the way you used them to drag a heavy tree limb up a steep mountain road. Such discipline."

"Tonight I will give you more pain than you have ever felt. It will be my pleasure. And yours."

They both smiled as they walked toward Joe's bedroom.

"You must watch Paul carefully," Zvi insisted. "We all have a weakness, and he is yours, my friend. But don't worry. I will find out what he's up to."

"Try not to hurt him."

"But that is the point of tonight. You must trust me with what is precious to you. The one on the bottom must learn to trust. That is the risk and reward. You will imagine my following Paul as I work on you? Perhaps hurting him a little."

"Tonight I will trust you, Zvi, as never before. But tomorrow you must do my bidding."

"Of course," Zvi said. "But do you believe me?"

CHAPTER 20

Running Uphill

Wiley and Dave jogged up through the town of Sausalito toward the headlands munching on fresh muffins from a local bakery. They crossed under the freeway that divided the town from the park to connect with the steep wooden steps of the Morning Sun trail and on to a seven-mile loop circumnavigating the southern hills of the Marin Headlands. The first three miles was a steep uphill to a communication tower.

"So. What happened?" Dave began, puffing slightly as he stretched out to match Wiley's longer stride.

"You're asking about what happened in Gloria's apartment?"

"It's my job to know how my partner is treating an important source of information—and potential pleasure."

Wiley pulled ahead again. "You're curious about sex," he said over his shoulder. "We were together. At lunch, we talked some about MI, Debra Jean, how she could help us after what she saw at the Empress. She's going to be a major asset. She saw I was cold from the run and invited me to her apartment, and I took a shower. She gave me some of her dad's clothing. Right then you called. We left when we learned that one or both of us were being followed."

"That's it? Too many spaces in that narrative, Wiley."

Wiley further increased his speed.

"Running away won't help you," Dave said as he pushed to keep up. "Want my thoughts?"

"Can I escape them?"

"You can't run that fast. Gloria is our best link to Joe and Paul. She likes you. We need to separate Paul and Joe. Paul likes Debra Jean. So we invite Paul to our meeting with Debra Jean tomorrow, and Gloria should be there, too." A large jackrabbit hopped ahead on the trail.

"One part of that is easy—Gloria. I haven't felt so interested in a woman for a long time. I'll ask her to our breakfast."

"Great. Debra Jean will invite Paul. She mentioned that she had that in mind."

"We've got to move with this. It's beyond the contract with our client."

"I know, man." Dave smiled. "Race you to the top. Last to the tower buys beers for a week." Wiley nodded and they took off.

Dave edged Wiley toward a patch of poison oak covering the trail. Wiley had to do a delicate right pirouette to avoid brushing the poisonous weed and lost a few steps to his friend. Dave stayed ahead until they reached the high wooden fence protecting a 25-foot white metal tower shaped like a phallus, surrounded by seven electronic modules that looked like robots. Forty years earlier, they had been the electronic controls for a Nike missile installation to attack the Russians; now, post Cold War, the units made up a sending and receiving radio dish that helped local ships to navigate through the Golden Gate.

Both men vaulted over the six-foot fence and raced toward the tower. Their hands touched its metal surface simultaneously.

Wiley drank some water and then handed the bottle to his friend. The recent rains had turned the land into a sea of emerald green dotted with wildflowers. The brown deer and coyote trails were barely visible in the profusion.

"All this fantastic wilderness so near a big city—it still amazes me," Dave declared.

They stood silently for a few moments, taking in the scenery, and then Wiley said, "I meant it when I said that I really like Gloria."

"What's not to like? She's got that Latino vivacity. She is tall with an amazing figure and legs long enough to accommodate even you. She handles herself with grace and intelligence."

"The lunch, the afternoon in her apartment. Something new happened inside of me, Dave."

"You mean beyond the situation. You're in her apartment and strip off your running shorts and sweaty T-shirt in the living room and walk naked to the shower, wondering how much she's watching. Nice and seductive."

"You bet, even if it's your fantasy. Perhaps you made that call a little earlier than needed. 'Fess up."

"Perhaps I did. It did seem a good idea to tell you there was a watcher as soon as possible."

"Gloria is a gift to men; she may not go for me. I'm not that unusual."

"Come on, Wiley. You must be like a white god to her."

"And you're being racist."

"Maybe, but I'm also being realistic. Remember I spent time with her friends at Borstal's, and you stand out from her male buddies—by at least a foot." Dave held out his hand for the water bottle.

"Actually, if she gets involved with us, it will be because of the way we rescued those kids." Dave took a swig and returned the water, which Wiley emptied in a gulp. "Snuff films aren't what we signed up to investigate," he said.

"It's all intertwined."

Wiley nodded. "Joe is our subject and object. It all revolves around him."

They walked around the tower, enjoying the 360-degree panorama of the Tiburon Peninsula, Mount Tamalpais, and the Pacific Ocean, with Point Reyes and the Farallons in the distance.

Dave stretched his arms toward the sun and then touched his palms to the ground. "When we accepted Debra Jean's case," he began, "we guessed that what happened to her at Jardinière was just the tip of a huge iceberg. Now we know that's true. What's really amazing is our presence at the Empress that night. That had to be pure luck. Or pure fate."

"With MI's head of security, no less," Wiley agreed.

"And that kind of synchronicity creates confusion," Dave went on. "What happened there had no obvious links to Debra Jean." He dropped to his knees and pushed up on his hands so that his head was on the ground and his feet were balanced against the tower wall. "Except Joe's perverse tastes," he continued, walking on his hands, circumnavigating the tower. "Lousy view from down here." When he was finished, he arched his back and did a graceful back flip, landing neatly on his feet.

"Which means that our case is suddenly about homicidal child abuse rather than inappropriate sexual advances and hurt feelings."

They walked toward the other side of the circular clearing. "And we are breaking the law by not reporting what we saw."

"Remember, the authorities have all the relevant information that we have."

"Except Joe's presence on the 29th floor," Wiley pointed out.

"We don't have actual proof that he was in that room," Dave said. "He could have been somewhere else on the 29th floor. The police will check who was registered in the hotel that night."

"You're hedging," Wiley said.

"I know."

"We're right on the line, Dave. We've been there before, as in not telling the police about the threat to my father."

Both men were silent. They walked to the fence on the other side of the concrete clearing, vaulted over the barrier, and made their way up to the fire road.

"Sorry, Wiley, but this is nothing like what happened to your father," Dave said quietly.

"I know," Wiley said. "But there is a lot at stake. Joe and his friends could continue their evil doings. Gloria could lose her job by helping us, or she could report us. Even talking with Paul could implicate us in a major crime. Taking on Joe … we could be in over our heads with this one, Dave."

"We always feel like this at the beginning of a case. Don't worry, Wiley. I'm with you. That gives you a leg up on anyone."

Wiley clapped Dave hard on the back and began jogging down the fire road, which snaked to the valley below.

"You and I invented Revenge, Inc., to provide legal alternative justice and revenge, which in itself challenges conventional ethics," Dave said. "This is the kind of case that it was designed for. I think we should at least wait till our meeting tomorrow and see how things play out before we change course."

"Gloria said the same thing," Wiley muttered.

Dave arched his eyebrows but said nothing.

"Which brings us back to the big picture again. We have one abusive episode with Debra Jean and another far more malignant one at the Empress. How do they fit together?"

Dave pointed to the valley below them. "Look down there. It's wilderness now, right? But if you look closely, you can see some small fruit trees and the remnants of a broken-down fence. Seventy years ago, that fence was a large corral and the trees part of an orchard. The stream that ran along this valley once served a large herd of cattle and an entire ranch community. And that patch of color at the bottom? It was a garden of roses and hyacinths, the rancher's wife's contribution."

"The relevance?"

"Thirty years ago, developers were going to build a town of 70,000 here. That would have destroyed one of the most beautiful spots on earth, not to mention creating an endless traffic jam at the Golden Gate Bridge. There were some demonstrations, but there was no plan, just sentiments. Then a few wealthy private individuals who were worried about their homes in Sausalito took matters into their own hands. They used their financial clout to hold up the bank loans long enough for the federal government to make a park for hikers from the suburbs and schoolkids from the city to enjoy. And beautiful Sausalito still is beautiful. A good outcome."

"At least from our point of view."

"But you see the analogy, Wiley. We've run into something that obviously goes far beyond what Debra Jean brought us. You and I know that we are not going to run away from what we saw at the Empress, but that doesn't stop us from doing our best for Debra Jean. And we have to make sure she understands that."

"So our strategy is to stay with Debra Jean and wait for the larger atrocities to emerge more clearly," Wiley said.

"Right."

"It's about outwitting Joe at both levels, isn't it? I wonder if that can be done."

"Not our easiest assignment. One unpleasant fact is that there were others in that hotel room, which means that Joe has an organization behind him. He could be the center of a snuff-film industry and God knows what else."

They reached the bottom of the hill. There was a rhythmic roar from the southwest, breaking waves a half-mile west at Cronkite Beach.

Wiley looked north at the long, steep uphill climb. "Like it or not, we're back in the big leagues."

"We've been there before, Wiley. We belong there."

They started up the hill together, the final leg in their seven-mile run. Twenty minutes later, they were at the stairway path down to their car.

"Tomorrow morning, I think you should follow me to Gloria's," Wiley said, taking the stairs down three at a time. "See if anyone is watching us. Then, assuming Debra Jean is going to pick up Paul and bring him to the barge, make sure that no one is staking him out at his house when Debra Jean picks him up."

"Great," Dave muttered, close at his heels. "I'll be driving back and forth across the Golden Gate Bridge all morning."

"Definitely. And Dave, watch out. This case is heating up. If there is a watcher, he's going to be well chosen. Hit him before he hits you."

"The last time we were in a brawl, you chose to sing a Spanish song to your green-eyed love. Now you want violence?"

"Different circumstances. Down the stairs is the official end of this morning's race."

"I didn't know we were racing."

"Sure you did. If you win, you can have my gun."

"You don't have a gun, Wiley." Dave looked puzzled.

Wiley smiled at his friend as he sped down the stairs. "That's why we need to keep in shape."

CHAPTER 21

Sex and Violence

The next morning, Dave followed Wiley to Gloria's apartment and tailed them back to the bridge. As he had expected, he saw nothing suspicious. It was Paul who had been followed by Joe's men after meeting Debra Jean. Putting off his trip to Beijing would heighten suspicion further.

Dave's route took him up the steep hills of Pacific Heights. He parked on Gough next to the park and opposite the C. G. Jung Institute, where he occasionally attended seminars. Paul's mansion was on the bay side of Jackson a short walk from the institute. There was a smattering of wealthy homeowners already on the street: joggers in their 20s; a few elderly couples taking a morning constitutional; mothers, fathers, and nannies pushing baby strollers along the lovely tree-lined streets with bay views that made the neighborhood one of the prime locations in the Bay Area. His lanky six-foot-five frame attracted an occasional glance from young mothers and single females—it was depressingly easy to tell the difference. He decorously ignored both.

He walked to Buchanan and took his time scanning the neighborhood for either of the two men he had seen in front of MI, Gloria's apartment, and the Travelodge. A block and a half west of Paul's house on Jackson he saw Zvi sitting in a parked black Eldorado SUV. Dave crossed the street behind a jogger and headed up Buchanan toward the depressing gray concrete buildings of California Pacific Medical Center. Now he had to find Zvi's backup. Picking up his pace slightly, he crossed through the hospital campus and headed toward Fillmore, the busy upscale shopping street that serves the social needs of the denizens of Pacific Heights.

On his second pass of Fillmore, he saw a man fingering a cell phone, dressed incongruously in a black suit, sitting at a table outside of a coffee shop at Fillmore and Jackson. Dave recognized him from the stakeouts at both Gloria's apartment and the Travelodge. Satisfied, he circled back through the medical campus to Buchanan. He punched in Debra Jean's cell phone number. She answered as she was entering the Broadway tunnel, five minutes from Paul's house. He told her about Zvi's stakeout and asked her to park near Buchanan and wait for him to check in before approaching Paul's house.

Dave decided to disable the SUV, as both a warning and a way to protect the upcoming meeting on the barge. He took two small thick-bladed knives from his pocket and walked down Buchanan to Jackson and headed east. The SUV hadn't moved, and Dave could see the faint shadow of someone in the driver's seat. Almost certainly Zvi.

Hidden by a passing car, Dave crossed the street and, bending low, walked behind the SUV. Dropping to his knees under the SUV's high fender, he jammed a knife into each back tire. He rolled to the right away from Zvi's mirror, pocketed the knives, and crouched, listening for movement. The air softly hissed from the tires, and Dave tensed to make his getaway. Too late, he heard the car door open.

From his perch, he saw the heavyset man emerge from the car, already stabbing at his cell phone. When he saw Dave, he rushed around the back of the car and then, without hesitating, launched himself at Dave, who bent low to meet him, his right shoulder cracking hard against both shins. Zvi fell backward, and Dave thrust his head up between the man's legs. The man grunted with pain but deftly grabbed Dave's neck, and with strong, thick fingers he began pushing a thumb in, aiming for the carotid artery. Ducking his head to loosen the grip, Dave again aimed his head at the man's groin. This time, Zvi was ready. Using his thigh to block the blow, Zvi leveraged his thick, squat body against Dave's, forcing him to the ground, crushing his neck between powerful fingers in a death grip. Dave arched his body backward and pivoted slightly, changing the balance enough to jam his right elbow into the top of the man's right eye. He could feel a slight give in the delicate, eggshell-thin orbit bone, then a soft crack. With a cry of agony, Zvi fell toward him. Dave pivoted again and launched a spinning kick at

146

the man's ankles. He heard Zvi's head crack against the side of the car as his heavy body fell to the ground and was still.

Dave checked his foe, who was unconscious but breathing, blood leaking from his eye socket. He looked up and down the street for possible witnesses. The street was clear, and he quickly checked the man's pockets. Empty. He took the cell phone still clutched in the man's fist. Without looking back, he rapidly crossed the street and jogged back up Jackson to Buchanan, to where Debra Jean was waiting.

Dave told her to wait for a call before going on to Paul's house. Without explaining further, he walked to Jackson and Fillmore. Zvi's backup on the other side of the street seemed to be immersed in the sports section of the *Chronicle*, his cell phone still on the table in front of him. Dave turned left on Fillmore and walked uphill for 100 feet. Then, in an impulse of mercy, he pressed the redial button on the cell phone. He could hear a ring down the street and watched as the black-suited man brought the phone to his ear.

Dave immediately clicked off. The man shook his head, looked at the cell phone, and then got up from the table and walked in the direction of the Eldorado. Dave bought a paper in a local magazine shop and then jogged through the medical campus to his own car on Gough. He drove down to Jackson and looked west. The Eldorado was still there. He could see the man running toward it.

Dave drove the few blocks down to the Marina, parked, and waited. Ten minutes later, he drove back to Jackson. The Eldorado was gone. There was no ambulance, not even a crowd to mark the site of violence. He called Debra Jean and told her to pick up Paul; then he headed down to Lombard and joined the traffic going to Marin. He'd been amazingly lucky, in both the fight and its aftermath. He rubbed his sore elbow thinking of the powerful hands clutching at his neck and his own extreme response, using a capoeira move appropriate for the deadly street fighting in Rio. An image of the naked children tied by their arms to the chairs and the surgical tools on the table flickered in his brain. There might have been less lethal ways for him to react to the bull-like charge, but at the moment he didn't really care.

Waiting at the last signal before Doyle Drive and the bridge, he pressed the menu button on the stolen cell phone and glanced at the contact list. There were numbers and addresses stored there, a bonanza for the case.

* * *

"Where's the bathroom, Wiley?" Gloria asked, smiling breathlessly down at him from her perch on his naked lap. "I'll need to freshen up before the others come."

"Probably more than that," he said, enjoying her breasts hanging near his lips. He thrust his pelvis tentatively upward, testing what was left of his desire. Well sated, he noted with some sadness. "Down the stairs at the end of the hall. Or use the one in my office. It's got a Japanese-style douche."

"How convenient. You treat your women well."

"Is that a problem?"

"I'm not complaining." She eased her body from his loins, grabbed her clothes in one hand, and, her bottom swaying suggestively, sauntered toward the bathroom. He watched her go, feeling the ember of longing beginning to rekindle.

It had happened again, he thought, a carbon copy of their first explosive tryst in her apartment almost a week earlier. He had taken a shower and dressed with some of her father's clothes. He had asked her for some hot coffee to warm him up, and she had brushed against him on her way to the kitchen. His sexual response had been so intense that he heard his breath catch in his throat, and when she turned to see what was the matter, he grabbed her in his arms. She placed her hand low on his belly. They strained toward each other with an intensity he hadn't experienced since his college days. The call from Dave had come minutes after the climax of their frenzy.

Today they had time and used it, moving beyond bursts of lust to a more languid experience in each other's arms.

He looked at his watch. It was 11:30, time to prepare for the noon meeting with the others. He picked up his pants and went to his closet to get some clothes. She was just leaving, and he leaned down to kiss her on the lips as they passed. The bathroom smelled of Gloria and sex. He ran a washcloth with cold water over himself, changed into fresh jeans and a warm sweater, and hurried upstairs.

She was standing outside on the deck looking at the water. If he put his arm around her waist, it would start all over again. Instead, he turned away, headed toward the kitchen, and began gathering food for their brunch. Gloria went down to help him, but she too was careful to keep her distance. For the next ten minutes they worked together to transform the outside table into an eating and working space.

Wiley's cell phone rang, and Dave's picture appeared on the small screen. He walked to the railing. "Wiley. Listen up. Paul and Debra Jean should be arriving momentarily. I'll be a few minutes behind them."

"How did it go?"

"They weren't followed, but the cost was high. I'm fine. I'll tell you more when I get there." The phone clicked off.

Ten minutes later, the five of them were talking animatedly on the deck. With Gloria acting as hostess, the pitcher of mimosas was emptying quickly.

"You look terrible, Dave," Wiley said out of earshot from the rest of the group. "And there is blood on your shirt."

"A souvenir of the fight. I'll change downstairs. By the way, Wiley, you look pretty relaxed, given that your best friend is bloodied and bruised."

"Sex will do that." Wiley blushed.

Dave waited, amused.

"I couldn't tell you yesterday about what happened in her apartment. It was too private, uncertain."

"It's OK. I'm glad it's continuing. It's good for you."

"Now tell me what happened."

Dave quickly summarized his morning encounter with Zvi.

"We'll need to go over this in detail with the group," Wiley said. "It might give Paul a heads-up about his friends."

"They're going to think I'm a hit man!"

"Or their savior."

"After the fight, I took Zvi's cell phone, and I glanced at it coming over. There were calls to the Empress Hotel before and after the events

149

of that night. Several were immediately followed by calls to another number, which I tried. I got an answering machine. Joe."

"It's the link we needed. Joe, Zvi, those children—all connected," Wiley affirmed. "Anything else I should know?"

"One other thing. After the fight, I parked at the Marina to get away from the scene and cool down. When I returned, maybe ten minutes later, Zvi's Eldorado was gone and the street was empty. The backup at the coffee shop must have somehow gotten Zvi into the car and found help."

"No ambulance, no police, and no witnesses on the street. If no one was looking out the windows, you may have gotten away clean."

"I hope so. But here's what's interesting. I hurt the guy, and he needed treatment. When you hit someone where I did, he's likely to have some cerebrospinal fluid leaking through the torn sinus membranes. At a minimum, he'll need IV antibiotics as a prophylaxis against brain infection. He could need surgery. I called California Pacific Medical Center right down the street and spoke to one of the ICU nurses. No emergencies at all in the hour when it happened. No admissions, either. I tried the several other ICUs nearby. Nothing."

"Which means …"

"A private clinic ready to go. Clearly a very elaborate backup."

Wiley nodded. "It's like the way the Empress was handled. Every contingency is covered. Whoever 'they' are, they're efficient and careful." Wiley thought for a moment. "There were ten or so people at the Empress. We only know two of them. It could be quite an operation, especially if they were filming."

"You the one who wondered if we were in over our heads?" Dave mumbled. "Or was it me?"

"It's where Debra Jean's case has taken us."

Dave nodded. "We're going to need all the intelligence we can get, starting with the group right here. So let's ply them with food, coffee, and champagne, and see what we can find out. And work on Paul."

"But first you need to change your shirt, Dave."

"I'd also like to check out more of what's in Zvi's cell phone."

"That can wait. I'll need you at the meeting," Wiley said. He punched Dave lightly on the chest. "You made some tough choices, my friend."

150

"I was in danger, and those kids were in my mind."

Wiley paused, holding his friend's eyes in a tight gaze. "We may be overmatched, Dave, but don't forget about our secret weapon."

"What's that?"

"You mentioned him on our last Headlands run. His name's Dave."

CHAPTER 22

Vendettas

D ebra Jean stood by the railing and watched Wiley and Gloria emerge from the kitchen carrying a large tray of freshly toasted bagels, which they added to the table in the center of the upper deck, already loaded with food. It was clear to her from their behavior that the two were lovers, and she felt no jealousy.

She remembered sitting around Saturday afternoons in college watching him on TV. She was not much of a football fan, but it was easy to chime in with lewd jokes from other horny coeds about his amazing body. Now she wondered what it was like for him to be six-foot-seven and a national hero by the time he was 20. She did an Internet search of his name, which brought up hundreds of articles from newspapers and sports magazines. With Dave Blue as his star end, the team had been invincible and also exemplary: there were none of the usual scandals that plagued athletes unprepared for notoriety. Then a day after his team won its conference championship, Wiley's father committed suicide— that was the newspaper version, anyway—and all the superhero stuff crashed when Wiley and Dave both refused to play in the Rose Bowl. Eventually, the story was dropped except for the occasional nostalgic commentator wondering where the mighty duo had gone and bemoaning their loss and their betrayal. Well, Debra Jean thought, they were here on a Sausalito barge inventing Revenge, Inc., and at her service, thank you, although in a far different way than her adolescent jokes pointed.

Without the uniform and the game, it was easier to see the true source of Wiley's charisma. He always focused on the task, probably just the way he had done as a quarterback. Her problem was his concern, and that commitment to her had already helped. She could see changes in her own behavior, in the way she handled Paul, and there were other signs of her increasing self-confidence. Last night she had a dream of molecules circling and careening in space until they gradually formed more and more meaningful and beautiful patterns. All this was accompanied by one of her favorite Bach cantatas. When she woke up, she reread her unpublished manuscript that had been headed for *Nature*, the one that Joe and Paul had refused to support. She checked the online medical library and found no follow-ups on her ideas, just as Joe had threatened. Sad as that was, it also gave her another chance. After two years of sulking, she wanted back in.

She left the railing and sat at the table to talk with Gloria and Paul. He was his usual self, dressed in expensive jeans, a white T-shirt, and a blue sailing jacket. When she picked him up at his house, there had been a friendly European-style kiss but little affection or talk on the short drive across the bridge. He all but ignored her once he came on board. He greeted Gloria as an employee. He focused entirely on Wiley, grasping at his every word, acting more like a fawning groupie than a famous scientist doing her a favor just by being there. Again she felt no jealousy—to the contrary. She hoped that Wiley would inject Paul with some of what Joe provided, and then she could reap the benefits in bed and beyond. She reminded herself that whatever Paul's importance, this meeting had to be about her. It was hard for her to remember that, but she knew Wiley would, and that made it easier.

* * *

"Greetings and salutations to you all," Wiley said when they had all settled on the upper deck. "My partner, Dave, will be here in a minute; he's washing blood off his shirt from an earlier encounter." The group was instantly alert. "But more of that when he returns.

"This meeting is about helping Debra Jean. Revenge, Inc., which owns this barge, where I live and work, holds what we call strategy meetings for our clients. We try to include relevant people," Wiley said, gesturing to Gloria and Paul. "Our first job will be to clarify our relationships and different motives for being here."

"Let me interrupt on that idea, Wiley," Gloria interjected. "I think everybody here knows that Paul Stokes and Joe Diamond are my bosses at MI. I am head of MI's security, which means that I may have a conflict of interest during this meeting. I want to make it clear, especially to you, Paul, that I will honor the responsibilities of that role as much as possible. The reason for my being here is personal, specifically what I saw at the Empress Hotel. I'm not sure if you know …"

"Debra Jean told me. It's very hard to take in," Paul said. "Obviously I need to hear more. That's a big reason why I'm here."

Dave's voice echoed from the stairwell. "Dave Blue here, and sorry to be late, all. But I bring a gift." He walked over to where Gloria and Debra Jean were seated and with a loud clunk placed a cell phone on the table. Then he bounded to the deck, pulling on a T-shirt, his hair still wet from a shower. He poured himself some coffee with one hand and simultaneously grabbed a bagel, somehow slathering it with cream cheese, lox, tomatoes, onions, and capers with the other.

He went back to the table and pointed to the cell. "Evidence from a difficult encounter earlier this morning." He looked at Wiley, who nodded for him to continue. "The memory bank of this little box will interest all of you. And perhaps clarify your motivations for coming, Paul, which I heard a bit of on the way up." He paused and looked around at the group. "You want that I continue?" he said with a smile.

Wiley shrugged to the group. "My partner is always valuable but rarely coy. I think he's nervous. Go on, Dave. We all need to catch up on what we've missed, including the blood on your shirt when you arrived and of course the cell phone."

Dave stood over them and began with a flourish, "First, a party trick to get things going. I've written down some phone numbers that I took from this cell phone. Gloria and Paul, would you do me a favor and take a look at them? Tell us what you see." He handed a slip of paper to each of them.

Paul looked at the list for a moment. "The ones I know offhand belong to Joe and Peter, Joe's personal chauffeur." He looked at the list again. "But I'd have to check those numbers against my own phone list to be sure. I also think the phone belongs to Zvi, one of Joe's colleagues."

Dave nodded. "Understood. And you, Gloria."

154

"I also recognize Joe's and Peter's numbers and Zvi's cell. And there are other familiar ones. I need to check them against my own lists. But there is one other number that I know well. I've dialed it many times in the past week. It's the exchange of the Empress Hotel."

Wiley watched Paul's face change color, and he turned to Debra Jean. "This would be a good time to know what you told Paul."

Debra Jean said quietly, "I told him what we saw at the Empress."

"Does anyone know Zvi well?" Dave asked the table as he took a seat.

"Yes," Paul said uneasily. "I've met him often, although I know little about him. He's part of Joe's private life."

"What about you, Gloria?" Dave questioned. "How well did you know Zvi before you saw him at the Empress?"

"As Paul implies, he's something of a mystery man," Gloria said. "I'd love a shot at what's inside that cell phone. When I asked Joe about Zvi, he ignored me. He's a physical therapist in San Francisco with a big reputation."

Wiley glanced at Dave. "You need to tell us what happened this morning."

Dave held up the shirt he had in his lap. It had a dark reddish stain across the front. "Zvi's blood. So, very much my business, Paul," Dave said, turning to face him. "I was sitting in my car watching Zvi watch your house when—"

"Why were you watching my house?" Paul interrupted angrily.

"You'll find out, if you let me continue," Dave said.

Paul pushed back his chair and rose from the table. "I shouldn't be here."

Wiley leaned toward him and extended a long arm, touching Paul's shoulder. "Paul, I'd appreciate it if you could stay for just a while."

Paul looked around the table, focusing on Debra Jean, who nodded to him. "OK. But only because of wanting to help Debra Jean."

"I appreciate that, Paul," Debra Jean said.

Wiley kept his hand on Paul. "Zvi was watching your house, Paul. Doesn't that bother you?"

"I'm surprised. He is a very strange man, a prodigy like Joe—but that's not unusual among Joe's friends. He's around Joe a lot; I've assumed it has to do with his profession. Sometimes he answers the phone when I call Joe's apartment."

"Thanks, Paul," Wiley said, guiding him back to his chair.

Paul said, "What could this possibly have to do with your both spying on my house?"

"Listen and learn," Dave said, taking a big bite out of a fully loaded bagel. He began talking with his mouth half-full, keeping his focus on Paul. "Zvi was sitting in an Eldorado SUV watching your house when I arrived. So, not wanting to be seen, I kept moving and checked around the perimeter. Sure enough, Joe's chauffeur, the man we know as Peter from his cell phone, was sitting at a coffee shop at Fillmore and Jackson a few blocks away. He was obviously running backup for Zvi, just as he probably had at the Travelodge where you and Debra Jean had a rendezvous."

"Wait a second!" Paul cried out. "How do you know that?"

"Zvi followed you after you left the motel," Dave continued, ignoring the outburst.

Paul turned bright red. "Assuming you're telling the truth, how do we know he wasn't tailing Debra Jean?"

"It was you he followed from the motel, not Debra Jean," Dave said drily.

Gloria intervened. "Paul, as you know, Debra Jean was a suspect in the data break-in. So maybe the two men were doing a job for Joe without me or you knowing."

Paul shook his head in disbelief. "You're saying Joe is using Zvi and his chauffeur to follow me? I can't believe he's that suspicious."

"When both of you left the motel, no one trailed Debra Jean. She just went on her way," Dave repeated. "You were the target."

"Maybe he saw you there, Dave, and was trying to protect me from you!" Paul said, his face full of rage.

Debra Jean turned to Paul. "We're all trying to figure out what's going on. You could be helping."

"OK. You all think I'm trying to protect Joe. Maybe I am. He had reasons to be wary. He asked me about my rendezvous with Debra Jean, so he obviously was watching me and maybe using Zvi to do that. I thought I worked it out with him. I guess I haven't." He stopped talking and looked thoughtful.

Debra Jean snarled, "So much for privacy. No wonder you're so embarrassed."

156

Paul dropped his gaze to the deck. "But why did he continue to have me followed this morning?" he added, almost to himself.

She opened her mouth and closed it.

"Enough," Dave drawled. "What's clear is that Joe has been watching everybody he can think of. I also saw Peter watching Gloria when she met Wiley at Borstal's for lunch."

Wiley said, "I was followed when I left Gloria's apartment. All this can't be routine, can it, Gloria?"

She shook her head. "I'm completely out of this loop."

"Let me add something even more disturbing," Dave said. "The men watching your apartment, Gloria. One of them was also at the Empress with Joe that night. I wasn't absolutely sure, so I didn't mention it. But this morning there was no question that it was the same one who was there. Zvi." He clenched his jaw, remembering his own savage attack on the man. "Zvi's cell phone tells us that he called the Empress several times before the events of that night." Dave shivered. "He was probably setting up the soiree and the snuff filming for the group, which included Joe.

"All this is a backdrop to what happened: the surveillance and the memory of Zvi at the Empress. Anyway, when I saw Zvi and his backup watching Paul's house, I called Debra Jean and told her to delay picking you up." Dave paused. "Then I returned, and Zvi was still in his car. I wanted him to know we were there."

Gloria grasped the edge of the table. "And you did that while he was in the car?"

"Hear me out," Dave said, and described the fight. "That's how I got hold of his cell phone. Zvi went down hard and cracked his skull on the car. I checked him. He was unconscious but breathing. His eye was in bad shape. I went through his pockets, which were empty, and took his cell phone."

"Are you saying that all this happened next to my house while I was waiting for Debra Jean?" Paul said, amazed. "Are you sure no one saw you? It's got to be all over the neighborhood."

"I ran to where I could see the coffee shop and hit redial. I could see Peter pick it up and leave at top speed, heading in Zvi's direction. I think no one saw me, Paul."

Wiley said, "What did you do then?"

"I sat quietly at the Marina and looked at the bay and the boats. I returned in ten minutes to check. Like I told you, Wiley, there was no sign of Zvi, Peter, or the car. Then I checked several ICUs and emergency care facilities in town. He hadn't been admitted anywhere."

"With that kind of injury, he couldn't have left on his own steam," Debra Jean said. "Maybe he wasn't as hurt as you're saying, Dave."

"Dave's elbows are like chisels, so it's safe to say that Zvi's in big trouble," Wiley said emphatically. "That's how he got past the linebackers, who wore the equivalent of body armor."

"It did inflate your passing stats."

"Boys," Debra Jean and Gloria said almost simultaneously.

"Girls don't understand," Dave said, nodding to Paul. "It's our male language when we're anxious. Thank God I didn't know he was once a European wrestling champ. I was obviously very lucky to get in the blow that I did." He turned to Paul. "I'm sure he couldn't have moved on his own, and he needed a hospital. It's amazing that there was no one on the street when I returned; maybe passersby thought he was just drunk and homeless. Peter must have taken him to a private clinic. Meaning a great organization designed for secrecy."

"Just like at the Empress," Gloria observed.

"You're quite a convincing storyteller, Dave, but maybe it didn't happen exactly the way you said it did," Paul said sarcastically. "Let me deconstruct your little morning myth for you." He adjusted his chair to face Wiley. "For starters, Peter and Zvi may have been out of line doing all that watching, but they didn't commit a crime. Dave did begin it with knifing the car tires. Zvi sensed what you were doing. He was defending himself. He was already a villain to you because of the Empress, perhaps another exaggeration."

Paul continued, shaking his head angrily, "As I understand it, no one can be sure they saw Zvi or Joe leave the room at the Empress. All of you are just guessing, based on your own biases. The phone calls to the Empress may have been about something else or even about the fire alarm itself, say to check on a guest or a friend staying there. Frankly, your conjectures wouldn't hold up in a freshman chemistry lab."

"What a defensive prick you are," Debra Jean said.

"I'm not saying that Joe's a saint or hasn't been involved in very bad deals in the past. But you're the criminal in this episode, Dave. Someone may be severely injured because of you. My God, you may have killed the man."

"You're brilliant and logical," Debra Jean spat out each word, "but you use your mental skills to deny whatever scares you. Next you'll be blaming Wiley for what happened at the Empress. You're just covering up for Joe wherever you can." Her voice darkened. "You need him for lots of things, remember?"

"No fair, Debra Jean," Paul growled.

"Your beloved partner was into a lot of things besides photoactive molecules: some innocent children's bodies, for starters."

"This is unbelievable," Paul said. He rose and stalked toward the stairs to the lower deck. "I didn't come here to be victimized. Joe has flaws but is also a great scientist, and his work has saved a lot of people."

Debra Jean glared at Paul, then rose out of her chair and charged after him.

Dave grabbed her wrist as she went by. "Wrong move."

"You're right about that," Paul said, turning his back to her like an arrogant matador. "I'm getting out of here. I came here to help, but all of you are trying to hang Joe, and you want me to be the executioner." He walked rapidly down the deck stairs and then hesitated as he stepped onto the small bridge connecting the barge to the dock. He shouted up at them, "You're making Joe into a monster! You are saying that the man who is about to win a Nobel Prize is a sexual criminal! I've known him since we were kids in high school. Sure he could be mixed up in a whole lot of things, but don't you think I would have known about child murder? Why don't you tell the police, if you're so worried?"

"You're smarter than this, Paul," Debra Jean said sadly. "I told you what he did to me at Jardinière. Small potatoes compared to the Empress, but not to me. It was my body he was violating."

Wiley rose to his feet and went to the front railing, looking down at the dock where Paul still lingered. When he spoke, his voice was quiet yet resonant. "You're right, Paul. We are guessing. We need more evidence; we all need to understand what this is about before we pass judgment on Joe. And that requires some investigative work … and your help."

159

He vaulted to the gangplank and landed softly next to Paul. "You can't imagine the impact of what we all saw in the hotel room. Gloria saw Zvi with the children in the elevator. Adding that to what happened to Debra Jean at Jardinière, there is a pattern here that none of us can walk away from. Dave and I spent a great deal of time deciding whether to take this case. There are questions that need answers. You have the most to gain by getting to the bottom of this."

Wiley looked down and caught Paul's gaze. "Answer me honestly: would you bet against what's being said about Joe?"

Paul answered with a long silence.

"You know you'd lose. The more we look, the more we find, and the more we see is covered up. I don't know whether Dave overreacted, but it's amazing that, desperately in need of medical attention, Zvi completely disappeared."

"And how do we know Dave checked everywhere?" Paul said uncertainly.

Wiley looked down into Paul's eyes again. "This is the moment— yours and mine. You need to level. You know Joe better than anyone. What do you think is really going on?"

Paul replied cautiously, "I'm a scientist. I believe in its rules. Inference isn't good enough; there needs to be independent data that implicates Joe in order for me to stand behind that conjecture." He turned away from Wiley and put his head in his hands. "You're all saying he was at the Empress and in the room with the children. And of course I believe Debra Jean about what happened at Jardinière."

Wiley gently urged him back across the bridge to the deck of the barge. "Loyalty to a friend is commendable." Wiley cradled Paul's elbow in his hand, and the two walked slowly up the stairs.

Paul reluctantly freed himself from Wiley's grasp and walked over to Debra Jean. "Whatever we find, you've got to believe that I was never a part of any of this. I didn't know that horrible stuff with children was happening."

Debra Jean sparked, "You're so worried about yourself, Paul. What about me, and most of all those children? You know a lot about your friend that you're not telling us."

"He's my friend." Paul groaned.

160

Debra Jean nodded sadly. "Joe owns you, and you won't fight back."

Paul slumped back into his chair. "I'm here, aren't I?"

"Yes, you are, and that took guts," Wiley said, nodding. "When Revenge, Inc., takes a case like Debra Jean's, we don't usually go out and hurt people, as happened this morning. We try to open up all the avenues we can, to push a little and see where it goes. Sometimes people push back, victim or perpetrator, and that's usually when the situation clarifies and when the action potentials appear. That's our strategy. Revenge may end in a physical act, but most of all it's a psychological process of discovery."

"That sounds suspiciously like Dave," Gloria quipped.

"Or Socrates," Paul said, smiling for the first time.

"Two of my favorite philosophers," Wiley admitted.

"Learning about your partner through Dave's eyes can't be easy for you, Paul," Gloria said. "And don't forget, you and Joe are my bosses. My livelihood is at stake here." She took Wiley's hand and squeezed it hard. "We all know that Joe is a charismatic guy, but I can't forget that he was at the Empress and in that room."

"I'll bet you never question his authority," Debra Jean said to Paul.

Gloria added, "I've never seen you go up against him."

Wiley circled the table with his long arms, as if encompassing the group. "Paul is Dave's and my guest on this boat. He came at some risk. It took courage, and he's learning a lot that's got to be upsetting. So let's all give him a break."

"You're both right," Paul said, and turned to Debra Jean. "I really wanted to keep you on at MI, but I couldn't make it happen."

"My God, to think I was worried about protecting you!" Debra Jean said, and was overcome by a wave of hysterical laughter. Paul put a hand on her forearm, but she flung it away. Her laughter turned to sobs.

Gloria got up from the table, walked over to Debra Jean, and stood close. She kneaded Debra Jean's shoulders until the sobs subsided. Calmer now, Debra Jean spoke again. "Paul, for the last couple of years I've been a doc in Walnut Creek treating sniffling kids and alcoholic executives. I've stayed sane by imagining that someday you would want to work with me again and support my research. And really like me."

"That could still come true, Debra Jean," Paul sighed. "So where do we go from here?"

Wiley leaned forward. "When Joe hears about Zvi, he's going to be very angry."

"And suspicious," Gloria agreed. "And he'll never believe that the fire alarm at the Empress was a random event. He'll look for the big picture, and that's bound to include some of us." She sat up straight, suddenly all business. "The good news is that all this surveillance means that as of yesterday, he's still in the dark and trawling for data."

"We still don't know why he's been following you, Paul," Wiley said.

"I think I do," Paul confessed. "A few days ago, I told him I was leaving MI." He paused, watching the group's surprised reactions.

"What happened after you told him about leaving?" Wiley asked.

"He was upset. He asked for some time to check out Debra Jean and you, Wiley, so that I could have all the data to make my decision. As usual, I gave in. I can't believe it led to his following me."

"Gloria," Wiley said, "you've watched Joe and Paul interacting for a few years now. Is he just keeping tabs on his partner or something more?"

"I believe he would be decimated if Paul left. A man like Joe, a prodigy with all his defenses up, has to have life support. Coming from somewhere. You're it, Paul."

"Don't kid yourself about my importance," Paul shot back. "I'm his lab tech and an old friend."

"It's not about work; it's about relationships," Dave said pointedly. "Wiley, I hope you're getting this, because it opens up certain possibilities in our revenge scenario."

"It does indeed, Dave," Wiley said.

"Now I'm lost," Gloria said. "What are you guys talking about?"

"Until now, we've just been reacting to events and collecting data," Wiley said. "But if Dave is right, we have a shot at moving toward a plan of action."

"Joe and I are just friends and scientific colleagues. I think you're implying that there's something sexual and romantic between us," Paul said angrily. "No one here cares about facts. There's nothing like that going on."

"I believe you, Paul," Wiley said. "We're just brainstorming. So let's change the subject. ... Debra Jean, how do you feel about Joe now? You know so much more than when you came to Revenge, Inc."

"I still hate the man for what he did to me. And now to others," she said irritably. "I want him to suffer."

"What will it take to get even? A first approximation."

"How can I know that, Wiley? Getting even. Revenge. It's hard to think about making it real."

"But you have to," Dave interjected. "Your fantasies and nightmares are real, the posttraumatic ones that haunt your sleep."

"It's strange. They're almost gone since I met you guys."

"Makes sense," Dave said. "You've changed so much since you started this process, Debra Jean. Whatever was suppressed is rising to the surface. All that new energy at your disposal."

Paul lurched out of his chair again. "Are you talking about concrete revenge just for what Joe did at Jardinière? What about what you did to Zvi, Dave? Who do you guys think you are, anyway?"

Wiley pressed on. "Gloria? Where are you with this?"

"I have no problem with revenge, Wiley. The guy's evil."

Wiley looked at Dave, who nodded affirmatively.

"So now there's just you, Paul," Dave said. "You've taken a few hits here and survived. We don't need for you to take sides yet, but we need to be able to trust you."

Wiley spoke up. "No, Dave. It's the other way around. He needs to trust us."

"But how can I?" Paul said carefully. "I can barely understand what you're talking about."

"It's not about understanding Joe. It's more about acceptance." Wiley spoke softly now. "It sounds to me like a big chunk of your life is hostage to your relationship with Joe. There are a lot of victims in this story, and in my mind, at least, you and the children are at the top of the list."

Paul sighed deeply. "I arrive in Beijing on Tuesday. My first decision when I leave here is going to be whether and what I tell him about this meeting. After that, I just don't know."

A tinny rendition of "Green Eyes" broke the silence. Wiley and Dave began to laugh as Gloria grabbed for her purse and cell phone. "I'm sorry, guys—private joke." She smiled up at Wiley as she hunted for the phone; then she looked at the tiny screen. "My God, it's Joe." She punched a key and walked to the edge of the deck, out of earshot.

"Well, it's time for a break, anyway," Wiley said. "How about we come back in an hour and a half. Everyone willing?"

There were nods from all around. Dave began clearing the table, and Debra Jean helped him. Both headed for the kitchen.

"I'll stick around," Paul said, watching Gloria. "Maybe just to learn what Joe has to say."

Wiley turned to Paul with a glint in his eye. "Good idea. Look, I need a moment with Dave, but I have a better idea. If you'd like, we can take a spin on the bay in my Aries, a two-man Klepper kayak the Germans invented. It's the wooden kayak lying on the dock just past the barge. Take a look." Wiley pointed down the dock toward the water.

"I will. I've always wanted to see one of them, Wiley. If I remember, it can be taken apart and carried in backpacks."

"When I was a kid, my dad and I would take trips together down the rivers in western Pennsylvania that I'll never forget."

Paul went to the railing and looked down to where the kayak was tied to the dock. He made awkward paddling motions with his arms. "It's tempting, but it's been a while since I've used a double paddle."

Wiley moved to stand next to him. "So what about it?"

"Sure, as long as you take the stern."

"Getting out on the water in this gorgeous light might bring a new angle to old perspectives. Beauty always clarifies issues for me. Dave says that beauty and truth build on one another."

"So did Plato. Dave's in good company."

"Shall we meet in, say, ten minutes? I'll bring some beer if you like."

"Beer in a kayak? The bay isn't that calm."

"You're a very careful man, Paul," Wiley said with amusement. "We'll be safe enough. With the underwater built-in pontoons, there's little chance of capsizing."

Paul took off down the stairs just as Dave was coming out. "I'm going kayaking with Wiley."

"A little piece of Wiley in the afternoon, eh?" Dave rejoined.

Paul smiled. "Shakespeare, *Henry IV, Part 2*." He skipped down the stairs and disappeared.

Dave stepped onto the deck and sat at the table. "The Klepper, huh. Good idea, Wiley. He was like a little boy just now. My diagnosis, by the way, is acute father hunger. If he's going to come over to our side, he's going to need you close by."

"I know. While I'm gone, watch out for Debra Jean. She's so much in her head."

"Yes," Dave said. "Gloria's there already. Said she'll report on the conversation with Joe when we're all there. I loved the way she comforted Debra Jean and just held on. 'Something in the way she moves … ,'" Dave crooned under his breath. "The meeting was great, Wiley. You led us all the way."

"There's a team developing; only some members don't know they're on it yet."

"They're getting the idea, but a lot is going to depend on how you do with Paul in the kayak."

Wiley headed down the stairs for the bathroom. "It's like a chummy huddle before a big play."

CHAPTER 23

Two in a Boat

Wiley held the Klepper steady against the dock as Paul lowered himself into the bow seat and mimed paddle strokes in the air. He squatted alongside the boat and handed Paul a life jacket. "We've only got an hour, so we'll head south along the shoreline toward the center of town and return through deeper water." He thrust a long arm across to the opposite side of the hull, placed his right foot on the wood frame, and gracefully swung his body onto the seat. His long legs just fit behind Paul's seat. "I'll take us out alone. Give you a feel for how it handles."

Wiley shoved off from the dock, propelling the craft past the large yacht tied at the end of the pier. Using deft strokes of the double paddle, he guided the boat into the open water.

"OK, Paul, now you try. I'll keep us balanced. The blades are skewed 15 degrees from each other; that's to decrease air resistance in heavy weather. They require a slight wrist roll as you move from side to side. It's awkward at first, but you'll get used to it."

Paul played with the paddles in the air and gradually established an even rhythm; then he dipped each into the water and pulled. The boat moved smoothly through the water. Wiley barely had to touch his paddle to the water to keep them on course.

"You learn very fast, Paul."

"I've sailed a little on the bay, and I learned how to handle a canoe at summer camp as a kid. But I've always been very comfortable with the physical world: fixing things, making them work."

"Me too. My background was in engineering before I took on Revenge, Inc. Debra Jean said you are the pragmatic part of the team with Joe. I guess I didn't fully take in what that meant."

"She's more like Joe: concepts, theory, and experimental design. My work is both experimental and technical, old-fashioned bench research. I'm most comfortable with bubbling beakers, a few petri dishes, and an old column chromatography setup. Of course, I work with high-tech equipment as well. In today's world, people do most of their research in front of a screen."

As Paul talked about the new science, Wiley gradually picked up the pace, leaning into his own strokes. He was already enjoying the subtle rhythm of the double blades dipping silently through the rippling water. Paul reacted by strengthening his strokes, gauging how to tip the paddles so that they caught the water in position for the next strong pull.

They were making good headway. To the right was the northern waterfront of Sausalito—houseboats, restaurants, and the elegant Yacht Harbor, where a few famous Silicon Valley billionaires housed their sleek vessels. In the water around them were a variety of anchor-out boats: inexpensive yachts, funky tugs, a few houseboats. Farther out, open water rippled a darker blue, reflecting the strong current from the Golden Gate. The mountain-shaped Angel Island loomed a couple of miles off.

"I haven't been out on the bay for many years," Paul mused. "I used to go sailing with Sharon, but that stopped several years ago."

"How long have you been married?"

"Almost 20 years. We met when I was in medical school and married when I graduated. Sharon was a surgical nurse who had a nice way about her. She also made a good salary when I really needed that. We were well matched as a couple, but Joe has always been my best friend. What about you, Wiley—ever been married?"

"No. I'm still learning about women. My last relationship ended badly six months ago. Gloria and I are just beginning one, as you probably observed."

Wiley wanted Paul to talk, but he could feel his own desires well up as he paddled with the older man. As an only child, he had had a close relationship with his father and was used to being alone except when playing team sports. Now his friendships were mainly with Dave and Xavier Le Grand, who lived 9,000 miles away in Seychelles. Dave said this was because he missed his father but didn't want to replace him. That and the guilt.

They were passing Sausalito's downtown now. Wiley glanced at his watch as he leaned harder to the left with a circling stroke, gradually turning the kayak at a right angle to the shore. He could see Paul using his own paddles to make the turn. "You're really good at this, Paul. I think we can make it across the Raccoon Strait and see Angel Island up close. There'll be a current and some rough water, but the view will be fabulous. There is usually a sea lion or two hanging out at the rocks next to the island. What do you say? Of course, we might end up swimming."

"You're the skipper, but I'd say let's go for it."

Something about the way he answered made Wiley feel like his teacher. And yet the man was 15 years his senior and a candidate for the Nobel Prize.

"I thought you didn't like risks."

"Joe and Sharon say that all the time to me, and it's usually true. This is embarrassing to say, but I think it's you, Wiley. I have this feeling that nothing bad is going to happen as long as you're with me. It feels that way with Joe too. His scientific judgments are spot-on; he is almost always right."

"You think?"

"Stupid, eh?"

"I'd say his ethics are a different matter."

They were in the Gate current now, and Wiley had to pull hard right to not get swept toward the bridge. "I know a lot about making the wrong decisions."

"That's hard for me to believe. I remember you in action. I watched you lead Purdue to three national championships. On the field, you were a perfect quarterback. I doubt if the coaches called in many plays."

"Not by the time I was a junior. That's not the kind of decision making that I'm talking about. You probably read about my father. There were rumors that he died because of me. They weren't just rumors. I made a very bad decision, which he paid for with his life."

"So you still blame yourself?"

Wiley had turned the kayak directly into the current, and Angel Island was looming ahead. They were both paddling hard. "That's a strange question. Debra Jean says you are a scientific genius and a great physician. So how can you believe that I would ever stop blaming myself?"

"Maybe you're being too tough on yourself."

"Maybe you're being too easy on yourself."

"You mean like not factoring in Joe's extracurricular activities?"

"I know it's not simple or easy. For example, you could have supported Debra Jean when she was under fire. But you didn't."

As the current increased, Paul bent lower in the kayak, straining with each stroke. "I've never been able to take on Joe. I just don't know how. But since we're about ethics, Wiley, what about Revenge, Inc.? A lot of people would say that even contemplating revenge multiplies the victim's problems, let alone doing something about it. What about turning the other cheek or including forgiveness in Revenge, Inc.'s action principles?"

"Try selling forgiveness to most of the families of 9/11 victims or those whose children were kidnapped. Contemplating revenge allows forgiveness to be a real decision."

"Why not be a therapist?"

"I'm all for reflection, but most therapists stop way short of what's needed. In dealing with abuse, the human animal requires redemptive or vengeful action as much as or more than insight, even if that needs to comes first."

"Well, you've obviously thought about what you're doing."

"With all respect, I wonder if you have done the same. You seem so defensive about Joe's behavior. Like just now."

"That's sure what everyone around the table was implying."

Both men were paddling furiously as the bow of the kayak dipped low, crossing through the current.

"I guess if I were to believe what you're describing at the Empress ..."

"You know it's the truth. You're afraid to believe it."

"Anyway, I'm not responsible for all of Joe's deeds."

"Cain and Abel. Guess who killed whom?"

"That's overdoing it, Wiley. Anyway, I sure picked a winner as far as my career goes. I've always thought that was the most creative thing I did in science."

"Finding Joe?"

"Yes. Strictly speaking, he found me. Sure, he cuts some corners, but most really creative people do, and with him the good works outweigh the bad."

"You buy that?" They'd turned toward home, now moving swiftly with the incoming tide.

"Look, he has earned me the respect of scientists around the world."

"All true—"

Paul interrupted, "Did Debra Jean tell you what happened at the motel?"

"Not explicitly. I gather it didn't go well."

"That's too mild. I was impotent with her. Funny, I thought she'd told you." Paul pulled hard on the paddles. "I really don't know why I'm talking to you this way, Wiley. I know you're trying to influence me to take your side."

"It could be your side." Wiley feathered his paddle in the air and let Paul guide the craft toward the barge. They paddled in silence for a long time, reveling in the wind, sun, and sparkling water.

It was Wiley who broke the spell as they headed toward the barge. "Paul, we've carved out a great hour for ourselves with the help of this glorious bay and its currents."

"Best hour I can remember for months."

"I like it when a common purpose brings friends and colleagues together."

"The team football captain speaks!"

"Absolutely. We've joined in a two-man team around this kayak, Paul. It felt like we could paddle this thing up to Oregon."

"We could."

"Maybe we will someday. Maybe that's the way it feels to you when you and Joe do science together."

"Maybe at the beginning, but now I'm too much part of his journey. Can you imagine not being able to get it up without him around?"

"That's a big price to pay for a friend. But women undo me all the time." The tension broke, and they laughed until the boat rocked.

"Keep your eyes on the goal. We'll be in Richmond if you don't watch out."

"This has been great, Wiley. I could use more time with you." Paul was in full control as they headed toward the forest of masts that marked Wiley's harbor.

"I've rarely had such a famous traveling companion," Wiley quipped.

"Me neither," Paul said with a smile.

CHAPTER 24

Joe and Niccolò

Dave spotted Debra Jean walking up from the waterfront toward Bridgeway. He hurried to catch up. "Mind if I join you?" he said as he moved alongside her.

"I'd like it. Paul and Wiley are off on the water, and Gloria is in a marathon talk with her boss, meaning Joe."

He smiled down at her. "You think you're being ignored?"

"It had crossed my mind. This was supposed to be my show, but events have changed that."

"I'm here and it's still your show, Debra Jean. Fate has added a few twists and turns." There was lots of bike traffic on Bridgeway. They stopped at a crosswalk and watched a cloud of colorfully dressed bike riders sail past without a glance.

"I guess they think they own the place. The cops won't bother them because the merchants like them."

"I love Sausalito," Debra Jean said. "Since working with Revenge, Inc., I've come here to Sushi Ran, just up the street, and Le Garage, north on the docks."

"Great place for croissants in the morning."

"And I've strolled through the tourist areas." She put her hands on her hips and eyed him jauntily. "You must know it so well. Take me somewhere special?"

Dave put a hand on each of her hips and turned her toward him. "Yes, lovely lady. I will take you away from all of this—the traffic, the masses of people, the hurly-burly of Sausalito life. Let me show you the byways, the dark alleys, the drug dealers, the aging artists and eccentric shopkeepers." He continued the rhetoric, his voice pitched to serious Bogart. "Stay here with me, Debra Jean. We could make a life, a good life together."

"Just the two of us." She mimed his theatrical stance and giggled. "Oh, I'd like that, Dave. But how could I leave Walnut Creek and its alluring suburbs and romantic urban blight?"

The light changed, and they crossed Bridgeway and walked south in silence. "Tell me something, Debra Jean—do you think Paul is telling the truth about not being involved in what happened at Jardinière?"

"Depends on how you define involvement. I don't think he consciously knew what Joe was doing, if that's what you mean." She looked away. "Paul's a strange guy. His work is precise and elegant. And it's no small feat to partner successfully with great scientific geniuses."

"A very large one. I'm working on my own hero worship."

"Wiley?"

"None other." Dave pointed to a hill and the sign that read "Napa Street." "We'll go up here."

"That grade defines steep. It's the reason they put cable cars in the city."

Dave switched to his Clark Gable voice. "I can carry you up hill and dale."

"I'm in good shape. Physically, at least."

"Actually, you're in great shape physically. If you weren't a client …"

"You're putting me on."

"You sure?"

"Xavier did imply that your relationship with at least one client wasn't exactly pristine." She stopped to catch her breath. "Believe me, I can tell that I'm not the kind of woman you're attracted to."

"If that's true, it's my problem, not yours."

They clambered to the top of Napa, and Dave set a fast pace up the more gradual incline of Filbert.

"Would you have taken my case if you hadn't known about the Empress, Dave?"

"I think so. But we knew from the start that there would be something big and dirty attached to what you told us. Unfortunately we were right."

"You can't imagine Joe's intensity, and I know only a small part of him."

"So where does Paul fit with our evil genius?" Dave asked.

"I think you were right just now on the barge. Paul is the guy who makes Joe feel human. I never thought of Paul that way because he is a scientific force in his own right. But he's lived off of Joe's brilliance for his entire career. That's the quid pro quo."

Dave slowed to let Debra Jean catch her breath again. "Another 50 yards and we'll be more or less level." They walked on for a few moments. "We need Paul's help to get to Joe."

"And that's why Wiley's with him now."

"Male bonding. It runs the world."

"Pretty manipulative."

"Except that Wiley really likes him. That's why it will work."

"It won't work, Dave. Paul has no real men friends besides Joe."

"Never underestimate Wiley, Debra Jean. Or yourself. We're counting on you for help with Paul."

"Sex was a bust," she said sadly. "I was little more than a shoulder to cry on."

"Are you still interested in him?"

"I'm not going to tell you."

"Aww, c'mon."

They had reached a flat stretch about halfway to the top. All around were houses with great views of the bay, precariously perched on the steep hillside. Angel Island rose like a volcano from the water.

Debra Jean pointed to one of the smallest houses. "How much?" she ventured.

"Two million, give or take a million," Dave said.

"Wow. They look pretty ordinary."

"Except for the views. That and ten minutes from San Francisco. Doesn't get much better for most people. If we kept walking up for a few more minutes, we'd be at the edge of the headlands and the best hiking in the Bay Area. But we'll save that for another time. OK?"

"I won't forget the invitation."

They ambled back down the hill.

"Debra Jean, I need to know more about what's happening with you and Paul."

"Really, Dave. You get off on voyeurism? It's none of your business."

"Wrong on both counts. Isn't it obvious that I'm more exhibitionist

173

than voyeur? Unfortunately, Paul's psychology is a key to how we proceed."

"I'm afraid to ask how that works. Let's see how with the women he's attracted to, like me."

"One way into a man's psyche. OK. Shoot."

"Lots of guys are attracted to farmer's-daughter cheerleader types like what they see in me. I buy into their attraction every time I can. When I catch them getting bored, which they always do, I get rid of them in self-defense."

"That's therapy talk. Victim talk. You're accomplished, gifted, and rich, and you're looking more like a fighter every day. Look at the way you climbed that hill. Body straining, heavy breathing. Very fetching."

"I'd love it if I had suitors who'd talk to me like you do." She looked over at him coquettishly. "Still not your type?"

"That could change," Dave said coyly.

She stopped in her tracks. "But it won't, right?"

"It won't. This is all about Joe, remember? That's why we need to know about Paul. If Wiley's kayaking adventure is the male-bonding part, you're our Mata Hari."

"You really said that. You're so bad."

"Paul is Joe's weak spot. It is likely that Joe is afraid of your influence on his friend."

"Well, I wish I had more influence. I think I'm a little bit in love with Paul. But I can't imagine that he cares for me at all."

"I know he's married."

She stopped and looked up at him. "You're kidding about this Mata Hari stuff, aren't you?" Dave kept walking, and she followed hesitantly. Her face was burning.

"No," he said over his shoulder. He stopped and waited. "You need to put aside being a good girl on this one."

"This walk, Wiley's outing—you're both so manipulative."

"We're doing a job—for you."

"You're saying I have to change to become a more predatory creature."

"'Assertive' is a more appropriate term."

"The way you talk about it is so mechanical."

"That's because I'm not half in love with Paul," Dave said gently.

"Once revenge is let loose, it has a way of getting out of hand. So we try to do our homework, understand motivations, all to get a little control over the uncontrollable."

"What about you this morning with Zvi? You were way out of control."

"Depends on how you feel with a fist around your neck and a thumb on your carotid. But you're right. 'Out of control' has already begun. Joe won't back down. He won't want to lose Paul. If Paul is on our side, we've got a wedge into him—that wedge is you. It's a beginning."

"Prince Machiavelli of Sausalito?"

"Niccolò Blue at your service."

* * *

Gloria said good-bye to Joe and put down her cell phone. Everyone was gone from the upper deck. She prowled through each room of the barge just to make sure. From habit, she checked out Wiley's office on the lower deck and tried to open a few drawers. All locked. She didn't try to jimmy them, though her new assignment from Joe more than justified it.

She said "Hello?" loudly, but no one answered. They'd all left without checking on her. She climbed the stairs again to the upper deck, poured some coffee, and took another bagel. Her adoptive parents in San Diego called them Jew food. Thinking about that now made her nauseous. How could she have ever loved them so much? How could they have treated her so badly in the end? That was too easy a question, she thought. Her story was so stereotypical: the needy traumatized orphan becomes a sexy adolescent, and the family who rescues her betrays her. It hadn't been rape or even major abuse. But it had been enough.

She thought back to the morning when her relationship with her "second family" tanked. Her mother had been out for a church meeting, and she was in the kitchen making breakfast when she felt her father's hand on her bottom, then on the front of her T-shirt just where her breasts had begun to show. He pushed himself up against her, and she yelled, calling him a bad name. He moved away quickly, using his hands to cover evidence of his excitement. She yelled louder. He became afraid and tried to calm her. Out of nowhere, the old language from the orphanage returned with a vengeance. She shouted Spanish obscenities in his face, words he didn't understand, and then raced for her room and locked the door.

When her mother returned from church, Gloria told her what had happened. She responded so sympathetically at first: she had listened, held her, and then confided her own secret, the reason for the adoption. It wasn't just Christian kindness, she said, rescuing Gloria from the grim orphanage. They couldn't get pregnant, and the tests revealed that it was her husband who was sterile. She got the results in the mail and told him that it was her. She refused to go back to the doctor and steered the conversation about children toward adoption.

"You see, we have to protect men," she counseled Gloria. "Men are weak and childlike. You provoked your father. You flaunted your body in front of him. He couldn't help himself. Now the best thing you can do is forgive him."

But she couldn't. She didn't even try. Six months later, she left them both and struck out on her own, which led nowhere until she met Joe. And despite all his sexual weirdness and general unpleasantness, he lived up to the bargain they had first struck. Joe kept his word to her.

He was a good bet for her future and not a man to double-cross. He knew she was competent, and he had just asked her to go to Beijing and handle his security. His offer had been overwhelming. If she accepted, he would double her salary and give her a fat bonus at the end of the trip. Pretty sweet, Gloria thought. And there was every possibility of keeping what she had gained.

What did Wiley and Dave have to offer, compared with all that? They were good people: sharp and strong, too, and they were dead right about Joe. They had charmed a bunch of brotherly Latinos without a drop of blood or a broken bone in a bar famous for its brawls. Dave had put down Zvi, which was nothing short of amazing. Sex with Wiley was great, and she really liked him. But most important, Dave and Wiley had stopped those two children from being horribly maimed or killed. And now they were trying to bring Joe down.

"Which he deserves," she thought.

But some of the lessons she had learned about life did not include believing in good people.

She took her coffee cup to the deck rail and threw the dregs into the water. Her body still tingled from the early morning's go with Wiley. What she really wanted to do was think about him and what they had done together. She knew a lot about sex, but she had never let the pleasure turn her head; with Wiley, her own needs mattered most. She had needed to get him to her apartment, and she had needed to get her hands on him in the boat. She needed him again right now.

It was not just his extraordinary body. It was also something about the way he made her feel in her head and heart.

> *Aquellos ojos verdes*
> *de mirada serena,*
> *dejaron en mi alma*
> *eterna sed de amar.*
>
> Those green eyes
> with their serene gaze,
> they left in my soul
> eternal thirst to love.

She felt the song he had sung to her vibrate in every part of her body. She could not believe how much she wanted him.

CHAPTER 25

Achilles' Heel

Wiley eyed the group as they took their seats at the table again. They had changed, becoming much more than the collection of individuals who had begun the day together. They were, as Dave and he had hoped, becoming a team, and now it was his job to point them toward an intent that would subsume their disparate motivations.

"It looks to me as if we're ready to see what kind of common purpose we can live with," Wiley said to the group as they watched the fog come across the bridge and headlands. "But let's begin by catching up." He turned to Gloria. "Dave said you had a long talk with Joe."

She opened a bottle of Dos Equis fresh from the fridge. "Too long for my comfort! But his offer was interesting. He wants me to go to Beijing ASAP. His offer was to expand my job to include his security, and he's doubling my salary."

"Personal security was probably Zvi's job before this morning's encounter," Dave said. "He's out of action. I must have really hurt him."

"Did you accept his offer?" Wiley asked.

"Yes."

"You're not sure what that means, right?" Dave asked quietly, staring intently at her.

Gloria stared back.

"You're way off-base Dave," Debra Jean said angrily. "Gloria is with us."

"It's not that easy, Debra Jean," Gloria said with a note of sadness in her voice. "Dave's right."

"I understand you've got a lot to lose," Debra Jean said, feeling exposed. "But those kids?"

Gloria laughed. "Let's say I really want to go to Beijing, and I like the big raise he's offering. And I can be a good actress, but it's going to be very hard to fool him."

"Don't underestimate your skills, Gloria," Dave said.

"Is that a compliment?"

"Of course."

Paul came alive and leaned into the conversation. "You work for me as well as Joe."

"And you're a nice guy," Gloria said. "Can I be honest, Paul? In practice, Joe is the only boss who counts."

"I see." Paul returned to his reverie.

"I'm relying on you, Wiley," Gloria continued, a blush spreading under her dark skin. "If I work with Joe, I'm going to need lots of help."

"Joe will pick up conflicting loyalties," Wiley said. "If you're going to survive in the role, he has to believe you're with him. And that means—"

"A double-agent solution," Dave finished the sentence, rubbing his hands together, pleased. "It's difficult to pull off, but it serves what we're doing."

Gloria nodded her agreement.

"Joe's offer could also be a ploy to get more information and control you," Dave said.

"He's obviously suspicious," Gloria said. "He wants to make sure that I'll remain loyal to him. He wants to know everything I know."

Wiley added, "He needs information, and he also needs a new security person to replace Zvi. So it works for him and it works for us. Treacherous for you."

"It's part of what Joe does to people," Paul said thoughtfully. "Puts them in a double bind."

"Gregory Bateson thought that created schizophrenics," Dave said absently. "He was mostly wrong, but what an idea."

"Tell us what else he told you, Gloria," Wiley said.

Paul intervened. "Remember that I'm still here and still your boss. And Joe is my colleague and friend."

Debra Jean almost flew out of her deck chair. "Dammit! She's ready to put herself on the line for us! While you—you're Joe's slave." She shrugged in despair.

179

"Please, Debra Jean," Paul bleated.

Dave said, "That's what happens when we make demigods out of humans. The price of worship is feeling like children."

Paul shifted uncomfortably in his chair. "Enough. I'm not here to be your punching bag. Go ahead, Gloria. I obviously need to know more."

"Joe's penchant for watching you is nothing new. Just now, he told me to keep a special eye on you, Paul."

"Which is why he was following us," Debra Jean said. "You still don't get it. This is all about you."

"That can't be right. I've never felt that important to Joe, and certainly not as a security risk."

"Victims rarely understand their importance to their abuser," Dave said.

"Phew. You're always a step ahead. Explain," Paul said uneasily.

"It's an emotional equation. The scapegoater needs a goat or he's out of business. Joe needs his victims, and he knows just how to create them. He's got a huge amount to give and does so unsparingly. But there's a piece of jagged glass in every Halloween apple he offers."

"Your explanation works for me," Debra Jean said. "I've sure been there."

Wiley turned to Paul. "Does any of this apply to you?"

He considered for a moment. "You're saying I'm important to Joe because he needs a victim as well as a support system. It's a funny way to describe my role. Anyway, it comes with great perks." He laughed quietly.

Dave said, "The cross of gold. It's still crucifixion. I'd hate to go to Beijing without your knowing that."

"You're going to Beijing?" Paul asked, bewildered.

"As far as I'm concerned, we're now in the process of negotiating our mutual commitments. Our task is to help Debra Jean, protect Gloria, and learn more about Joe. Where else can we do all that!"

"Well, I wish it were in Paris or India," Dave said, grinning. "Beijing sucks. It's polluted, self-satisfied, and boring. If I'm going, Debra Jean will have to spring for a really good hotel. One of our clients said it has a passable Four Seasons."

"That's where Joe and I are staying," Paul said. "Gloria too, it seems. It's quite passable, Dave," he added drily.

Dave turned to Paul. "You're a man of culture. I'll bet you like good art. There must be some wonderful paintings hanging in that mansion of yours. Do you know David Hockney's collage of his old mother in a blue raincoat sitting on the gravestone? There's a pair of brown wingtips in the lower left corner, signaling another perspective. We gradually understand that it must be the artist's own shoes and that the grave is his father's. Hockney is saying, 'This is not just a family portrait. I'm in this picture, too.'" Dave paused for emphasis. "That's what I want from you—to be in the picture."

"You're too young to be giving me advice, Dave," Paul retorted.

"Sorry, Paul. He's right," Wiley said kindly. "It's showtime."

"I know, Wiley." Paul addressed the group with a touch of formality. "But the truth is, I just can't fully commit. Not yet. All I can say is that I won't give you away, and I will do my best to help this group learn more about Joe."

"That's a good start," Wiley said.

Dave said, "Our team in college would always say that we played our hearts out for the man. It wasn't the coach we were talking about. It was Wiley, in case you missed the reference. He's hard to turn down: he grows on you, and he's always on the winning side."

"Enough of the hype, Dave," Wiley said. "Look, Paul, what I said earlier about finding a common purpose—that's the most important thing."

"OK, here's something. I'm leaving for Beijing tomorrow," Paul said. "I'll be giving a keynote address at the Biogenetic Conference there on Wednesday morning while Joe negotiates deals with pharmaceutical manufacturers interested in our drugs. On Wednesday afternoon, we fly to Chongqing, and we board a cruise ship. We're booked on the *Viking Century Sky*, a five-star Three Gorges tour ship, courtesy of a small group of key principals who will be our scientific and business advisers in China." He considered. "It won't be hard to find."

"Have they taken the entire ship?"

"I doubt it. It's not that high-level. They probably just took the best rooms."

"Joe wants me on board," Gloria said. "He said I could book myself a room, so there must be more available."

"Thanks, Paul," Dave said. "The rest of us should be on that ship."

Wiley looked out at the water. The sun had erased the fog, and the bay reflected the hues of the coming sunset. "It will put a lot of pressure on Joe. You'll learn a lot, and so will we. What do you think, Paul?"

"It scares me."

"It could be romantic," Debra Jean said, smiling sweetly at him. Hope springs eternal, she thought.

"Well, I like the idea, Wiley," Gloria said. "I'd feel safer with you guys around. Joe's going to be much more dependent than he is here. There'll be these mysterious tall Americans close up, not to mention Debra Jean hanging out with Paul. Lots of pressure, lots of unknowns—what everyone wants, right?"

"OK, we've got a plan of sorts, with room to play," Wiley said. "Paul and Gloria are going to meet with Joe in Beijing, and Dave and I will stay out of the way until we board the ship in Chongqing." He smiled. "I've always wanted to see the Three Gorges Dam. I've been hearing about its inevitable construction since I was a kid. My dad did some consulting there when he was young. He used to show me pictures. You remember, Dave. You've seen them in the display case behind his desk."

"I remember."

"This is going to cost a lot of money," Dave added.

"That's what daddies are for," Debra Jean said. "Anyway, the Three Gorges has been on my list for a long time, too. And there's bound to be a lot of interesting men on board." She winked at Paul.

"Aiee," Gloria breathed, shaking her hand at the wrist. "Paul, you'd better make your move."

"Me too," Dave exulted. "This trip is going to have it all: exotic places, an incredible group of people, heroes, heroines, and villains. Hopefully no deaths on our little adventure," he added quickly.

"What about airplane seats?" Debra Jean asked jauntily, growing into her role as financier. She took a long slow inventory of the way Wiley's and Dave's legs stuck out from the table. "Do you and Dave need first class?"

"We don't fit well into coach, so if it's possible, yes."

"Done."

"Goody," Dave said.

"Gloria?"

"Not your concern. Joe's already put me there. He chose the first flight going to Beijing."

Paul laughed despite himself. "I've got to warn you, Joe is not going to come apart just because he feels pressure."

"Depends on where it's applied," Wiley said.

Dave turned serious. "You're the pressure, Paul. Joe's Achilles' heel."

CHAPTER 26

Yearnings

Wiley stretched his long legs as far as the seat would allow, then curled an ankle over the farthest corner of the footrest. The plane from San Francisco was five hours over the Pacific Ocean, less than halfway to Beijing, and hours of discomfort loomed ahead before they arrived and connected directly to Chongqing.

He turned to Dave and said, "We're both too tall even for first class."

"You especially."

Wiley continued to search for comfort. Two rows ahead, he could see Debra Jean and Paul talking quietly, their heads almost touching.

"Before my siesta, anything on your mind, Dave?"

"Beijing, Gloria and Joe's relationship, Joe's reaction to finding Debra Jean on the cruise. For starters. Not to mention how Debra Jean and Paul will do in bed."

"Goodnight, Dave. As always, I count on your dreams to help."

"Reality works too. I can't wait to see Joe's expression when we all show up in Chongqing."

* * *

"What do you think of the intrepid pair, Debra Jean?" Paul asked, pointing over his shoulder as he closed his eyes and settled into the reclining seat.

"I think they're both pretty wonderful," Debra Jean said sleepily from the same vantage point. "They make me feel secure and a bit inadequate."

Paul clicked off the overhead light. "Me too. You know, I watched every game they were in, along with most of America. All those college football championships. They were a fabulous duo." He yawned and adjusted his night mask. "Dave was acrobatic and eccentric, just like he's being with us. But Wiley was always at the center. He was the perfect leader: inspirational, smart, and a great natural athlete. He'd have a plan and the team would follow him, and he and Dave would deliver the goods. He was the model for every son in the American suburban family, and most of their fathers."

"Somehow I can't see you sitting in front of the TV in a wife-beater with the guys, putting away cans of beer."

"The details are off, but I did watch every one of Wiley's games. I wanted to be just like him."

"You're something of a hero yourself, Paul," Debra Jean said. "For starters, you're an extraordinary scientist."

"I'm competent, that's all." He shrugged dejectedly. "You and I both know I'd never be anything without Joe."

Debra Jean began to object, but he stopped her. "No, that's the truth. Wiley was my hero because he was always his own man. Even the coaches knew that. He made it on his own. He knew what he had to do to make winning happen."

"And what about Dave? Another hero?"

"A black sheep with every skill in the book. A little less for me to identify with, but boy did I want what he had."

"You mean Wiley?"

"Yes. Or Dave; I'm in love with people who have enormous talent."

"Like Joe."

"Exactly."

"Why? Why do you give yourself away?"

"That's the story of my life."

"Dammit, Paul, what stops you from starting a new story?" She reached across under the blanket and placed a hand on his thigh. "I've always wanted to get well laid in foreign lands. Beijing would be great. You're my best candidate."

"You're making me nervous, Debra Jean."

"Jesus, take it easy. For the time being, you're safe."

185

"Joe is always around, even when he's not."

"That comment makes me sleepy."

Paul went on as if he hadn't heard. "Everybody's counting on me to do something. You, Wiley, Joe, the Nobel Prize committee, even Gloria. Joe's a rotten pervert, and the Empress probably happened the way Wiley described. But I'm meeting Joe in Beijing, and I won't even ask him about it. What does that say about me?"

"Pathetic. You can't be that much of a coward."

"You're not listening to me. You want to believe I'm someone else. For an hour, kayaking with Wiley, I felt like I was inside of me, not him. It didn't last long, and it's just hero worship with a different hero. The same old pattern."

"Joe makes you paranoid about everything," Debra Jean said dejectedly. "You're sharing a room at the Four Seasons. He's going to know."

"I've booked adjoining rooms for us. Now I think we should go to sleep." Paul pulled his mask down, pushed two yellow plastic earplugs into his ears, and turned away from Debra Jean, leaving her alone with her reading light.

"Paul," she said to the back of his head, "let's at least put on a good show. There's a lot more at stake for both of us than our relationship."

"I can't hear what you're saying," he mumbled. "These earplugs are pretty good. We'll talk later."

But she knew he had heard. Talk wouldn't be good enough. Not for Joe and not for her.

CHAPTER 27

Double Agent

loria pressed a button in the electronic pad next to her plush first-class seat. The gears hummed as the seat back moved into the required upright position. She raised the window shade and saw the diffuse smoky glow of China's capital. She checked her watch. Exactly 14 hours had gone by, and the Air China jet was descending swiftly to land exactly on time.

The flight had been like a vacation in a fancy resort. She'd slept seven hours, aided by a flute of champagne, a glass of a French Burgundy with a delicious dinner, and a flat bed. She would have liked to see at least one of the 120 available movies, including several in Spanish. Instead, she had used her waking time studying files that Joe had faxed before she left.

Her immersion in luxury, work, and sleep had been a convenient escape from thoughts of difficult times ahead. As Dave said, her loyalty to Joe was likely in question. Because Zvi was out of commission, he needed her for routine security. But he had hired her to keep her close, the best possible damage control.

The plane rolled to a stop, and as a first-class passenger, she moved rapidly through the disembarking, baggage claim, and customs procedures. The last time she had crossed an international boundary had been as a scared little immigrant girl. She had carried one worn suitcase on a flight from San Salvador to San Diego with a picture of a strange white couple who had sent a note in pidgin Spanish saying they would take care of her forever.

As she emerged into the arrival hall, a tall tuxedoed Chinese man held up a sign with "GLORIA GARCIA" emblazoned in gold capital letters on a shiny wooden placard. She approached as he surreptitiously matched her face with a picture taken from his inner jacket pocket. He stepped toward her and respectfully spoke her name. After he had confirmed her identity, he took her bags from the trolley and helped her into the backseat of a long black limousine waiting in a VIP position at the curb.

She must have dozed during the ride from the airport, because suddenly she was at the Four Seasons Hotel following her bags up the express elevator to a 40th-floor suite larger than her apartment in the Mission District. The porter called her attention to an envelope with her name on it on the desk in the living room. She took out a $10 bill she'd carefully prepared for this moment, but he motioned for her to put it away. "It's already taken care of," he said in perfect English as he softly closed the door.

She surveyed her new home with delight. The appointments were elegant, and the urban view from the large picture windows across the room was dazzling: giant buildings, glittering lights, and a profusion of neon signs in Chinese and English. It dwarfed San Francisco's downtown skyline ten times over. Every building looked brand new.

She stared at the scene for a long time and then reluctantly picked up the envelope, just as the phone rang.

"It's Joe Diamond, Gloria. Welcome to Beijing. Hope you're comfortable."

"Thanks," she said. "It was a great flight, and the room's perfect."

"Good. Are you too tired to talk tonight?"

"I slept on the plane."

"Room 4001, just down the hall. Shall I ring for some food?"

"No food, thank you, but I could use a beer. Mexican if they have it."

He laughed. "Perfect."

"Give me 15 minutes."

"I'll be waiting, Gloria," he said as she put down the phone.

It was too easy to slip into her careless business relationship with him. She would need the memory of two shackled children and Wiley's body to remain vigilant.

Twenty minutes later, showered and dressed in jeans and a sweater, she rang the bell of room 4001 at the end of the corridor. The door was open for her, and she instantly regretted her apparel as she stepped into the most luxurious setting she had ever seen. It was a corner room; there were floor-to-ceiling windows on two sides, and the walls were hung with beautiful paintings and tapestries—worth a fortune, she imagined. Three separate islands of sofas and soft chairs were placed for the view and designed for intimate comfort. Through a smoked-glass door she could see an opulent high-tech kitchen and formal dining room. There were no bedrooms in sight, but she guessed there were at least two, maybe more.

Joe pointed to a chair next to a long, low marble slab, where a tall frosted glass and the bottle in a silver bucket awaited her, along with a short stack of papers.

"Brandy or beer, Gloria?" he asked as she scanned the room. "I have the best China can offer of either."

"Beer would be great."

"A Corona for you, Gloria." As she walked to the chair, the diffuse lighting of the room changed in relationship to her location, while a soft spotlight followed her route through the otherwise subdued surroundings. She sat, and Joe joined her in an opposite chair, warming a half-full brandy snifter in his hands. The situation reminded her of the night she had met him. Not a pleasant memory.

Joe was not a handsome man. His hair was cut close to his skull, and his too-ordinary face and carefully clipped mustache were unappealing. The opulent setting and his clothing—maroon silk lounging jacket, matching pants, and moccasin-style slippers—could not hide his short stature and awkward body movements.

But all that mediocrity was overwhelmed by the amazing crackling energy radiating from his hands and eyes, a powerful force simultaneously frightening and seductive.

"You look worried," Joe said, picking up her mood. "Something wrong? Whatever you need, let me know, Gloria."

"No. Everything is fabulous."

"It's all designed to impress, to let us know that China is rising and the Chinese are to be treated with respect. Our hosts, the entrepreneurs who are partnering with MI, are obviously intent on pleasing. They have many plans for MI's China branch."

"Are we dealing with local business or the government?" Gloria said, forcing herself to identify with her job.

"Americans have asked that question for a generation now, with no clear answers. It's the wrong question. Think Party and you'll get it right. It's an octopus with many tentacles. You'll be meeting five top scientists and several highly placed government officials with industry connections. Earlier tonight, I met our administrative contact, a woman named Song. She is definitely government and Party. Quite attractive in the Han way and a very high-level security person. She has given me carefully edited CVs of the five Chinese 'scientists' joining us on the cruise. They're in a packet in that stack in front of you. There is also an itinerary of the trip."

"Do you trust Song?" Gloria interrupted, needing to find her voice. She was feeling overwhelmed.

"That's the kind of question I trust. Song is Party. Period."

She leaned forward, crossed her legs, and folded her hands on her knees. "You said my job is to take care of security."

Gloria felt a wave of fatigue come over her as she sipped the beer. She reverted to the necessary administrative details. "I'll begin by establishing a working relationship with Song and her colleagues. And do they speak English?"

"Assume that they do," Joe replied with a tight smile.

"Right."

"Song will help us as long as there is no conflict with her party's needs. There is great harmony between our interests and China's."

"Yet you brought me here as security. There is something to fear."

"Of course, Gloria."

"Some of the problems you foresee are beyond the obvious?" she persisted.

He frowned, raising the brandy to his lips. "I think you know that already."

"It would be helpful if I understood more clearly …"

"Clarity is the problem," Joe said, sipping the amber liquid after rubbing the edge of the glass back and forth on his lower lip. "I'm still tracking incidents, random occurrences that can't be arbitrary. I doubt if all of it relates to the China deal."

"Why is that?"

"The amateurish attempt to break into MI's data system; that's not at all like the Chinese. It's also hard to imagine their hiring the kind of low-level person you described." He paused, watching her. "But what happened to Zvi is a different order of operation. It could be their handiwork, all right."

Gloria waited expectantly. It was Joe's first trap.

"In case you hadn't heard, Zvi was attacked. He was seriously hurt and is recuperating. The attacker was definitely not an amateur. You are his replacement."

"You're implying that I can't match his experience."

"Unfortunately, that's true."

"His injury makes you more vulnerable? But for what motive?"

Joe sipped his brandy. "Those are my questions, too. There are many possibilities. For example, Song informed me an hour ago that Paul is bringing Debra Jean Lieberman to China. She'll be staying at this hotel. He personally made the reservations for her to join our cruise. It was embarrassing to learn that from Song before Paul told me."

"And you see Debra Jean's relationship with Paul as a problem to you?"

"Her presence here makes no obvious sense, and it's hard to believe that it's just a sexual fling. She's very plain."

"Not to some people," Gloria said tentatively.

"Good. I want your opinions, Gloria. I may not be a good judge of such matters."

"I need to understand why Debra Jean was kicked out of MI. She was a favorite of everyone, including you and Paul. Then, suddenly, she was out of favor and her behavior disintegrated. I have found little in her history that explains why. I need more, particularly if she's now in bed with Paul."

"Fair enough. She began with us because we saw a talented scientist with great promise. Postdocs often go through negative spirals, particularly those that have rapid success as she did. She couldn't hold the pace we needed, so she blamed her bosses. Not atypical of young scientists with an early history of success."

"Also a profile of a woman bearing a grudge."

191

"Exactly. Debra Jean was a good young scientist but unfit for our company. Scientists who don't fit in often bear grudges. However, they rarely act on their feelings. They need references and our good will to get another job. So we rarely hear from them again. That's the way it usually works. Debra Jean could be an exception." He frowned. "If she's behind the break-in, it's not about money. But what?"

"Anything else about her, Joe, that might give her a motive?" Gloria asked, her concentration failing with jet lag.

"She is a privileged woman and feels entitled. She lost a great deal when she left MI, perhaps enough to make revenge an obsession." Unexpectedly, Joe smiled. "But the attack on Zvi doesn't match Debra Jean's timid profile."

"What about Paul? He knows she is a suspect, and yet …"

Joe looked away but didn't manage to hide his strong feelings. "It is hard for me to believe that Paul is part of this."

Gloria waited a beat and then moved on. "What about Song? Could she be connected to Paul?"

"Unlikely." Joe finished his brandy. "One more thing. The man you brought to your apartment. We know he is part of this, and from what you described, he has the physical attributes to put Zvi in the hospital. Do we know anything more about him?"

"Very little from formal sources. A football hero, a fallen idol, then a dropout. But he must be smart and strong; after all, he outmaneuvered your personal surveillance," Gloria murmured appreciatively. "Unfortunately, I didn't complete my own appraisal of the man."

"That was my mistake and your loss. He obviously still captivates you," Joe said with a hint of sarcasm.

Gloria sipped her beer. "Anything else I should know, Joe?"

He hesitated. "The Nobel. It could be a factor. Perhaps someone does not want me to get it."

"I don't see …"

"I don't, either. The Chinese would benefit from our prestige. The same is true of everyone at MI. But it's a giant independent variable that we need to keep in mind. It is a competitive prize of great value."

Joe checked the bottle of brandy on the table and found it empty. "You look tired, Gloria, and there's a lot to do." He handed her a folder.

"Song's briefing to me. Wednesday afternoon we fly to Chongqing to board our cruise. In your papers, you will find a manifest of the other passengers on the cruise. The *Viking Century Sky* can hold 306 passengers, but most of the passengers on our cruise are from Taiwan. I don't think we need concern ourselves with them. We'll be focused on the Europeans and of course the Americans: room assignments, relationships, background, all of that."

Gloria took a sip of her beer and said, "I'll need Song's cooperation."

"I'll make sure you get it. Relax and finish your beer," Joe ordered and handed her a small pill. "That and this sleeping pill will do wonders."

With a start, Gloria recognized the Quaalude he handed her and quickly palmed it, downing her beer to cover her action. Joe didn't show if he noticed, but he put on some music and kept up a steady chatter, presumably waiting for the drug to take hold. Finally she got up to leave, saying, "I'm exhausted."

He rose too, walked over to her, and put a hand on her shoulder. "I'm open to your staying the night," he said matter-of-factly. "Sex is said to be good for jet lag. We could make up for our first night together."

She kept her exterior calm. "I like my privacy, and I'm here to work."

"I assure you that any intimacy between us wouldn't affect our work relationship. On the contrary. It was there from the very beginning."

"Dr. Diamond, I must decline."

"Fair enough."

"I appreciate the offer. The assignment you've given me is daunting. Perhaps pleasure will come afterward, Dr. Diamond." Despite herself, despite what she knew of his tastes, she felt an unexpected wave of attraction. His energy was overwhelming and erotic. Thank God she'd dodged the Quaalude.

"It will take all the energy I have to do the job," she said finally.

"No problem. By the way, I like your word, 'pleasure.' Be assured that pleasure or not, I am very satisfied with this meeting."

"I appreciate that."

"Goodnight, then."

Gloria rose to leave. "Goodnight, Dr. Diamond. Thank you again."

"I think I've made a good choice," Joe said, almost to himself, and walked Gloria to the door. He saw her out, then returned to his seat and refilled his brandy snifter. He still had no idea whether she was working for or against him—or both—but either way, she'd be useful to him. She was smart, she would provide information, and she could be controlled.

He thought again of his invitation to her and shuddered. He had made a mistake. He had wanted someone in his bed, but it wasn't about sex, a need he could fill with a phone call to the desk. It was to fill the ache of loneliness that had permanently settled in his chest since Paul had distanced himself. Asking her to stay had reduced his power with her and increased his own discomfort.

Joe twirled his glass, inhaling the scent of paradise. He sipped the smooth liqueur slowly, swirling it in his mouth before swallowing. Suddenly he saw what he had missed. Gloria had not seized on the advantage that he inadvertently offered by suggesting sex. In the language of chess, she had refused his sacrifice. And that meant she was in the grip of a strategy that went beyond simply influencing him. "I wonder what that could be," he said aloud to the empty room.

CHAPTER 28

Coal Dust

From their cab window, Dave and Wiley gazed incredulously at hundreds of gigantic high-rise apartment buildings disappearing into a bleary horizon along a river clogged with junks, fishing boats, steamships, oil tankers, and pleasure boats.

"The mind boggles," Dave said. "I knew that Chongqing was huge, but I imagined something spread out, like L.A. or Cairo. This defines human density. It makes Manhattan look like a Lego model."

"It's a new species of city," Wiley said. "I wish my father were here to see it. He loved large-scale projects, and this one would have taken his breath away." He turned to the cab driver. "How many people live in Chongqing?"

"Thirty million, maybe more," the driver answered in thickly accented English muted by the thick mask he wore over his nose and mouth. Looking out the window, Wiley saw that most of the shopping pedestrians crowding the wide streets in the early evening wore similar protection. Yellow-gray haze shrouded the lower half of the buildings and blanketed the streets. And he knew that the visible gases were only part of the problem in this vaporous evening.

Wiley opened the window to sample the air. By his second breath, his throat burned and his chest tightened. It was worse than their short layover in Beijing. He quickly closed the window.

"Makes me glad I quit engineering," Dave gasped. "Imagine coping with this monstrosity."

"Well, we don't choose our villains or where they hang out," Wiley said. "Maybe Chongqing is Joe's kind of place."

"Could be." Dave coughed noisily into his handkerchief. "Did you know that the Japanese bombed this city into rubble in '42? Made slaves of the prisoners they didn't kill."

"Talk about a phoenix rising from the ashes," Wiley said. "The shoppers look happy enough if you assume that people are supposed to wear masks. Another thousand years on this planet and we'll be growing filters in our noses. By the way, I'm assuming that the hotel has a gym. There's no way to exercise in the 'fresh' air."

"It's five-star Marriott, standard around the world," Dave said. "So it will have a pool, a weight room, massage, and probably yoga and t'ai chi classes."

Dave leaned back into the hot plush seats and began reading from the Lonely Planet guide he had brought. "Listen to this. The gorges are worth the trip, as is the Three Gorges Dam. But watch out for pneumonitis and white clothing. The river is lined with coal mines belching black smoke and other noxious fumes. I think the writer had a chip on her shoulder."

"Back home, the air can be pretty filthy, too. Remember Pasadena, where we played against UCLA? Your last pass of the first half. The ball disappeared into the smoke and haze."

Dave burst out laughing. "And the smog was so thick that the defenders never saw me. I didn't even have to run a pattern."

"You exaggerate. But don't forget that the U.S. of A. is still the number-one polluter on earth. We need to stop feeling like superior Americans."

"You're the patriot, Wiley. I'm just a wandering Jew on loan to whatever country I'm allowed to stay in. The best case is, I help it prosper, then move on. The worst case is pretty bad."

"Sure, but don't your people own most of the polluting factories, besides controlling the media and the banks?"

"It's good to clarify our prejudices." He looked fondly at his friend. "You're my people, Wiley."

"And you're my favorite minority, Dave. A minority of one."

The taxi slowed, pulled off into a tree-lined driveway, and pulled to a stop at the entrance to an elegant hotel, a Marriott fronting the river.

"Thank you, Debra Jean," Dave said as the doorman opened the taxi and a flock of bellboys converged on them, vying for their luggage. "It must be 95 degrees with 100 percent humidity, not to mention what's in the air." He turned to Wiley, who was calmly surveying the scene. "We need to make sure we have a room high enough to be above the densest part of this pollution."

Dave and Wiley strode across the luxurious lobby toward the registration desk. "The rooms next to the elevators must begin at $750."

They waited impatiently in the check-in line crowded with Japanese men in dark suits and a few Europeans in more casual wear.

Wiley took a brochure from his pocket and scanned it. "The *Century Sky* is an ultramodern ship, and our cabins are deluxe, hopefully meaning air-conditioned." He wiped his face, which turned his handkerchief gray. "Anyway, the river should cool things down *au naturel*."

"I doubt it. It's a gorge. Probably traps the heat. But the guidebook says the scenery is great, especially on the few days when the air's not shrouded in sulfur dioxide."

"I get the pessimist's picture, Dave. Remember, this isn't a vacation. We're getting paid and doing our job."

When their turn came, the woman at the console offered them a 10th-floor standard room with two double beds. Dave leaned close and asked her for oversize beds and a higher floor, and after a brief conversation, they were upgraded to a 40th-floor river-view two-bedroom suite with king-size beds.

They headed for the elevator, where two men waited with their bags. "What did you offer her, Dave?" Wiley asked as the express elevator doors closed.

"Nothing but a little touch of Dave in the night." He shrugged his shoulders. "Actually, I did it all with just a smile and a wink."

The suite was huge, and they quickly settled into their sumptuous bedrooms. Dave found some excellent single malt in the freestanding bar, and they sat around an engraved glass table facing an enormous window. The view through the filter of smog below them was of the river life—commercial boats and docking facilities and laborers servicing both. Above them, the sky was clear and bright blue.

Dave looked around. "It's all standard Marriott fare, right down to the face creams," Dave said, looking at the hangings on the wall. "Except for the Chinese artworks, we could be in Chicago."

Wiley's cell phone chimed. "It's Gloria," he said to Dave. He listened for a while before speaking quietly into the phone, "I'll put it on speakerphone."

"Hope I didn't wake you guys." Her voice sounded tired and hesitant. "I can't sleep, and I really needed a familiar voice. Jet lag, I guess. You there, Dave?"

"Hi Gloria," Dave said. "Glad you survived the trip."

"Oh, I loved the flight, and now I've got this great room—"

Dave interrupted, "But before you say anything more, is there any chance he's monitoring this call? Wiley's phone is clean, but—"

"I've checked my room with a device that I brought from San Francisco. One generation beyond what Silicon Valley exports to China security. Good enough for you?"

"I'm a believer, Gloria. You're now speaking to a humble man. How's Joe? Any problems when he briefed you?"

"Should we be worried about you, Gloria?" Wiley asked. "Does he trust you?"

"As much as he trusts anyone. At the end of our work session, he wanted me to stay the night."

"Damn. Why would he do that?" Wiley asked.

"Come on, Wiley. Why do men ask women to stay the night?"

"I'm asking about motivation."

"I turned him down, and he was matter-of-fact about it. Like it was a potential business deal and no hard feelings. It was presented with interest but without emotion. I could have been a pack of gum."

"More games?" Dave asked.

"Maybe. But more than that, Dave. A little like the autistic kids I volunteer to be with once a week. Something's missing emotionally."

"Therefore Paul," Dave said.

"During the proposition, I kept having images of those kids tied down and those knives next to them on the table."

"A really great woman," Dave mouthed to Wiley.

"Which brings me to another question. He'll want me to investigate all the Americans on board. To stay in his good graces, I'll need to tell him as much as possible about you guys. Our little group needs to understand that, Wiley."

"As long as you call the group 'ours.' Best that he doesn't find out about Revenge, Inc."

"Don't worry, Wiley."

"This is all about increasing the pressure on him. We want him to feel increasingly isolated, and Paul's the key to that."

"Pressure! Dammit, Wiley, we need a lot more than that," Gloria said angrily. "You're dealing with a criminal pervert, and your plan of attack is to increase the pressure by isolating him from his friend."

"Wars have begun with less, Gloria. We start there; we poke and prod; we test his defenses. Don't worry. There's going to be plenty happening before the cruise is over."

"Believe Wiley on this one," Dave told her. "He has a way with winning strategies. And Gloria, watch yourself."

"Thanks."

Wiley turned off the speakerphone and walked to the window. He said a few more words into the phone and then disconnected.

Dave joined him, and they gazed out at the city. "It sure isn't Sausalito."

"More like a gigantic Indianapolis."

"We're lucky. Gloria's a professional, and she's clearly on our side," Dave said. He dropped to a crouch and circled 360 degrees on the heel of his left foot, using his right foot as a lever, then completed a counter-clockwise circle on his right foot. "You've got yourself a winner, Wiley."

"I haven't gotten her yet."

"Then you don't know women," Dave said with a shrug. "By the way, if I'm gone when you wake up in the morning, I'll be buying some protection and surveillance devices. There's always a black market in a city like this."

Wiley finished his drink. "Great. I'm going to check out my bed. You staying up?"

"I'm going to celebrate." He broke into a wide smile. "Hey, Wiley! We're in China. It's a first. Revenge, Inc., has gone international."

"You're such a kid, Dave."

"We're coming up in the world." He punched Wiley lightly in the gut and sang the first few bars of "The Internationale."

"You need some sleep."

"Maybe, but enjoying my excitement comes first. I'm going to check out that woman at the desk who liked my smile, find the real China."

"She's probably a spy. See you in the morning, Dave."

CHAPTER 29

Impotence

Debra Jean woke slowly, stretched luxuriously, and then thought of Paul and was simultaneously aroused and depressed. Here she was, in what should have been a dream: China, Beijing, the top floor of the Peninsula Hotel in a super-luxurious king-size bed overlooking the Forbidden City, and an attractive and available man who cared for her in the adjoining room. Their bedrooms were separated by two thin doors, and she had left her door unlocked and open, but there had been no dark lover in the night creeping between her sheets … and legs. She touched a pad on the control panel on her bedside table, and a soft whir began in the voluminous folds of cloth that slowly parted to reveal an enormous window. Outside, the sky was a pearly gray sprayed yellow.

Sex, revenge, and a reluctant lover; it all came together in Paul. Sex with Paul and destroying Joe, two birds with one stone. And all she had to do was what came naturally. She looked at the clock at her bedside: 9:30 Wednesday morning. She got up from the bed, grabbed a robe, and stood at the door to his room. Silence. Should she knock? Was it worth what might happen? Well, she thought, she had to try again, and not just because she was horny and wanted him. It was part of the plan, and she could wait. The foreplay should come from him.

She tossed off her robe and walked across the room to check out the view below. A mirror on the wall stopped her progress. She studied her compact, shapely body in profile. She turned full-face to admire herself. She would never be a skinny model showing off lingerie and sheer blouses in fashion magazines. But there were no unsightly childbirth lines above her groin. Her skin was luminous, and her breasts and thighs were full and firm, sensuous enough to attract most men. She parted her legs and playfully wiggled her hips. She had all the moves. She was a sexually experienced woman in her prime who attracted men—that is, until they left her. She always felt that they were right in leaving her. In her mind, there was always someone better than her. Like her mother, she thought with a sigh.

She stood at the window and looked out at Beijing. Through the haze she could see the familiar outlines of Tiananmen Square, the world-famous symbol of failed revolution. Sightseeing there would be de rigueur, and it could be a good excuse for calling him. She walked back to the door. Still no sound there. She tapped her chest: no self-esteem here.

Her mother's living legacy, she thought angrily. Her mother ruled, just like Joe ruled Paul. And she had dampened any hint of femininity in Debra Jean from the time she could remember. Her father could have helped with that, but he was afraid. Mother had threatened and sabotaged that in every way she could. Later on, when DJ was blossoming in high school, her mother would show up in a towel after a shower, or short shorts from a tennis match, whenever boys visited her. They never stayed too long after these encounters with her mom; they all said it made them feel uncomfortable. DJ was sure it was because the comparison between mother and daughter was so unflattering. Now Debra Jean understood that her mother was envious of her youth and privilege, and getting rid of her father and then her boyfriends in a manner that was cruel and effective was meant to leave her defenseless, a victim.

Dave was right about the change in her. She was part of a team that she had initiated, and her assigned role in it was to help loosen Joe's control over Paul. She could feel the anticipated pleasure of seeing Joe squirm. Wiley had asked her about an endpoint. She could feel how much she wanted to degrade him; she wanted to feel power over him. Did she want to take a whip and chains to his body or just see him disappear in disgrace? Most of all, she wanted the power to choose what would hurt him most when the time was ripe. And she wanted him to know that she was at the bottom of it.

Well, next door was what could hurt him most. She pushed down on the handle. Surprisingly, it opened to her pressure. Had he thought of entering her room, unlocked the door, and then chickened out? At the other end of the spacious room she saw his form in bed, shaped by quilts and sheets. He stirred as if sensing her presence.

"Paul," she whispered, approaching the bed. He didn't move. She got in beside him. There was no movement: asleep or faking, she couldn't tell. He was deliciously vulnerable. What would he want? This was every man's dream, wasn't it?—a naked lover entering through the warm haze of sleep to caress and arouse. It was certainly one she had hoped for last night.

The warmth of his body and the situation increased her excitement, and it was all she could do not to press her body hard up against his butt like some rutting animal. She stopped herself. This was a different kind of man than the men she found in bars or on the Internet dating services. "Paul," she said softly. She placed a hand gently on his naked hip. He stirred and rolled over on his back.

"Debra Jean?"

"Are you expecting someone else?" she said lightly and lay still next to him. How could he resist her in this situation? She moved her hand to the front of his thigh. In response, he stroked her gently along her hip; then he rolled toward her and touched her belly with a single finger.

"Sexy," she murmured. She could feel his penis against her thigh, and it didn't stir. "Any plans for today, Paul?" Pragmatic me, she thought, but anything to keep him near.

His finger continued to stroke her in maddening half-circles. "I haven't spoken to Joe yet," he said in a voice still filled with sleep. "I don't know how he'll react to your coming with us. I'm sure he knows by now. He won't be happy."

"What are you going to do?"

"About what? Everything is up in the air."

Not really, she smiled to herself at the pun. "About Wiley, about what you've learned. About me." It was an effort to keep her voice even.

He looked directly into her eyes. "You're such a luscious woman. But Joe's going to call pretty soon. There's a lot for us to do about our biotech startup and factory."

She felt his beginning arousal and moved to put space between them.

His erection pushed between her legs. "Don't bring Joe here," Debra Jean said quickly.

The phone rang.

"Don't answer yet," Debra Jean said.

"I want to." The phone was on her side of the bed. He leaned over her, balanced on an elbow, and pressed a button for the speakerphone.

"Paul." A deep voice echoed through the room.

"Joe. I'm here."

"Welcome to Beijing. I wish you had called when you arrived."

"It was too late, Joe."

"I'm in room 4001. You should come here as soon as you can. There's a lot to go over."

Paul was pushing into her. She resisted, though she was overcome with desire.

"I know," he said. "I'll shower and dress and be over in a half-hour."

"And Paul, about Debra Jean. I hear she's coming with us to Chongqing and will be your guest on the ship."

"Yes," Paul said. He pushed at her resistance.

Joe waited before continuing. "Well, you must have your reasons." The phone clicked off.

Paul entered her with a powerful thrust. She sighed with pleasure. He turned his face away as he began to move inside her.

"Paul. Wait."

"Shhh. This is what we both want, isn't it?" She could feel his muscular bottom moving like a piston on her hips while his arms and chest held her in a vise.

"Yes. But ..."

"I'll stop if ..."

But there was no way she could stop now. Whatever had been unlocked was far too powerful. Was he Joe? Was she Joe? She didn't want to be in either of those fantasies, but her body didn't seem to care. "Look, Paul," she said frantically as she felt her own excitement reach toward him, "I don't want it this way."

"But I do!"

She closed her eyes, feeling the pleasure and the disappointment. She shuddered with his last spasms, a small pleasure, a cry or moan, she couldn't tell.

He let go of her and rolled onto his back, still breathing in gasps. "I'm going to try to get away from him, Debra Jean. Any way I can."

"Do me a favor. Don't shower, Paul," Debra Jean said impulsively. "It may sound crazy, but I want you to remember my body smells, and Joe needs to know. In fact, let me come with you. We can talk to him together. Threaten him with what we know."

"I can't do that. Not yet." The muscles in his back tightened. She knew he was pulling away.

"You mean you won't," she said to herself. Then to him, "I'll be here when you get back. Whatever the fantasy you were acting out, Paul, that was also you in your body, and I want more of that."

He stood up, nodding, and turned toward her. Their eyes met. "I do, too. But I can't do this again until I'm free of him." He turned away from her and began to dress.

When he finally left, she sobbed into the sheets, adding her tears to the wetness of their lovemaking. As the tears dried on her face, she grew cold. She mustn't kid herself about a future with him. But she would play this out in the hopes of binding him to her. It was her only leverage, and she would use it to get Joe. That was really why she was here, wasn't it?

CHAPTER 30

Surveillance

Dave and Wiley sampled the sumptuous buffet breakfast in the hotel dining area and then strode out into the bustling street markets of Chongqing: Dave to search for surveillance equipment—miniature cameras, microphones, and some simple debugging equipment—and Wiley to reconnoiter their cruise ship on the river port. They agreed to meet at the ship as soon as Dave found what he needed.

The *Viking Century Sky* was easy to locate. It was the shiniest structure on the busy riverfront, a brand-new luxury liner clearly designed for privileged Chinese and high-end tourism. Preparations for the afternoon sailing were in full swing, and streams of shirtless workers hefted materiel up gangplanks directed to the ship's hold. Looking up at the ship, Wiley was reminded of the high-rise Caribbean cruise ships, the kind that docked in places like Montego Bay and Bermuda and spewed thousands of tourists onto the streets for a few hours of shopping and sightseeing. As a younger man, he had observed these scenes with disdain, vowing that he would never be a pampered passenger on such a vessel. But now, sweating in the hundred-degree polluted air, he found himself dreaming about air-conditioned glassed-in balcony cabins, clean air-filtered exercise rooms, and luxurious dinners.

A rope extended across the walkways leading to the passenger areas. They were early and no passengers were in evidence. Wiley walked up the wood platform hoping to be spotted by one of the ship's security personnel. Sure enough, a small, attractive woman in a well-pressed ship's uniform ran down to intercept him. She stopped a few feet above him on the ramp.

"Can I help you?" she asked in perfect English. Wiley introduced himself as a passenger needing to check out the ship's accommodations.

"My name is Ms. Song Lee. I am in charge of administration on the ship. Boarding time is 4 p.m. Use the name Song."

"I had hoped to have a look around before that." Wiley stood his ground. "My height may affect the sleeping arrangements."

"That is very sensible," Song said curtly. "Many of our passengers are Taiwanese." She tried a smile. "No need of extra length for them."

Wiley smiled back. "At least one other passenger does." He nodded at a tall figure making his way along the wharf toward the ship.

Dodging porters, Dave walked up the gangplank. Wiley introduced him, and Song offered to show them around.

They had been placed on the middle deck, down two floors from the upper observation areas. It was large enough, with two standard-size single beds. Dave stretched out on one of them. His calves hung over the edge.

"Wiley will need even more bed to accommodate."

"I am embarrassed," Song said, staring a moment too long at Dave's body. "I will find something better."

"I am told that China is particularly sensitive to favoritism," Wiley offered. "We do not want to offend your values."

"That is true, but a guest's comfort is also important." Song guided them up the metal stairs to look for a better suite.

"We are grateful for your help," Dave said.

They climbed one flight to the upper deck. Song showed them a suite that had a common living room and two bedrooms, each with a king-size bed.

"This will work well," Wiley said.

"Then I will arrange it."

Song seemed hesitant to leave. She walked them up another staircase, which ended in a luxurious hall with red plush carpeting. Antique vases and statuary lined the walls. "This is the observation deck, which is for government officials and their guests; it is strictly off-limits to everyone else once the cruise begins. We have 14 deluxe suites for our VIP passengers. The private exercise room, pool, lounges, work room, and banquet room are modeled after our emperors' palaces."

"There was surveillance in the part of the ship we were just in, but I don't see any cameras here," Dave said. "Does this area of the ship extend beyond your authority?"

Song eyed him suspiciously. "These guests have their own security personnel."

"Of course." Dave nodded understandingly and then smiled. "I don't suppose you have a room up here for us."

"Assignments on this deck are made by high government officials," Song said, her voice neutral. "Two American scientists hosted by Chinese colleagues are on the list, but neither of your names is included. Sadly, you will have to remain below."

Song guided Dave and Wiley to a lounge area with a large window framing part of the Chongqing skyline. "San Francisco is a small village in comparison," she said proudly. "Sausalito would fit on half a city block."

"You have studied our bios carefully," Wiley said pointedly.

"Not just yours. This trip is highest security."

"The American scientists?" Dave suggested.

Song looked surprised. "Of course. They are known around the world for their groundbreaking work."

"Scientists are rarely treated as VIPs in the United States," Dave explained.

"Americans are not an intellectual people. That is not true of Chinese," Song said with pride.

"Ignoring your cultural revolution, I agree," Dave said.

"I must get back to my staff," she said, closing the subject. She led them out of the lounge and onto the open deck. They were immediately beset by the din of the city and the oppressive heat.

Song straightened her shoulders. "I'm glad to meet both of you and happy to have found more comfortable rooms for you. I have learned that both of you were well-known athletes in your country. Perhaps you work for your government in some capacity, as many of our athletes do." She stopped and searched their faces. Finding no response, she continued. "In any case, Chinese officials love to hobnob with celebrities, and if you like, I will obtain invitations for you to some of the VIP parties."

Wiley smiled. "Athletes make good ambassadors." Then he added more seriously, "There is one thing more you can do for me. It's a private matter. It has to do with Gloria Garcia, the American guest who is berthed in the observation deck."

"I've seen photographs of all the passengers. Ms. Garcia is strikingly beautiful."

"She also is working for one of the American scientists," Wiley continued.

Song stiffened. "We know."

Dave intervened. "Song, Ms. Garcia and Wiley are interested in one another for many reasons. He would like her well treated."

Song spoke carefully. "I will keep a special eye out for her, but a word of warning to you both: On this cruise, we have 90 Taiwanese, 30 French people, and a few Americans. Our focus is on the two famous American scientists. They are very important to our future. I have come from Beijing to add depth to our excellent security services."

"And that is why you are spending so much time with us this afternoon?" Dave asked.

"Very observant, Mr. Blue. Both you and Mr. Stone, as well as Debra-Jean Lieberman, were flagged for attention. I have been asked to learn all about both of you, make contact, and stay close. I hope our security needs do not interfere with the pleasure of your trip." She bowed slightly. "Now I must leave."

"It is a great pleasure to have met you," Wiley said.

Song guided them down to the main deck. "At 7 p.m. there is a welcoming dinner, when you will meet your fellow passengers. Ciao."

After Song was out of earshot, Dave led Wiley down the gangplank to the dock. "So what do you think, Wiley?"

"Lots of information and a much better room."

"And being conned," Dave said, donning a face mask. "Probably all three," he added, entering a crowded street with Wiley close behind.

"How was the electronics shopping?"

"Productive. I did see a great open-air fish market. I didn't recognize too many of the edibles, but they could be delicious."

Wiley made a disagreeable sound. "To you! I assume the ship's cooks are fonder of international cuisine. Four days is a long time to survive on nameless creatures from the deep."

They reached the food market, and Dave pointed to corn roasting over an open fire. "Hungry? I've pretty much mastered the currency." He gave the woman tending the food a small bill and held up two fingers. She gave him the ears of corn in waxed paper and handed him back change.

Wiley took a big bite. "Pretty good." He munched for a while. "So how do we get to Song, Dave?"

Dave picked up two cans of Pepsi from another stall and paid. "If she's really a Party member, it could be a first."

"The attraction of power," Wiley teased.

"Let's get back to the hotel. I could use a workout at their gym and 50 laps in their pool to clear my head … and lungs. We board the ship at 4 p.m."

"What happened to our penchant for exploring the real China?"

Dave looked around at the teeming streets. "Another day. A different country."

CHAPTER 31

Isolation and Encounter

Joe Diamond was unprepared for the increasing depth of loneliness he had felt since boarding the vessel two days earlier.

He sat on his stateroom balcony, windows open to the cool early-dawn air, watching the *Viking Century Sky* depart from the small harbor where it had anchored for the night. The scene on the wide river—aging junks in slow motion, commercial trawlers and small motorboats churning the water, the omnipresent coal barges—gave little visual respite from the heat and smoke of the day when the sun was blazing. But there was no surcease from the acute discomfort that regularly woke him at 4 a.m. with anxiety about Paul and his link with the puzzle of the Americans' presence on board.

These painful emotions surprised him: it was an inevitable part of the experience of an only-child prodigy and one that he had welcomed. But despite their unique gifts, prodigies desperately needed human comfort. True, some were geniuses at relationship, devoting their lives to healing and advising. But most prodigies suffered intensely from their superiorities. A significant minority chose suicide—cowards whom he disdained, men and women unwilling to face the challenge of being different from the rest of humanity. Others deliberately hid their talents within the ordinary population. But the real heroes of his subspecies were those who, like himself, actualized themselves to the fullest, no matter the personal cost.

He, Joe Diamond, had willingly sacrificed camaraderie for the pursuit of greatness. He hadn't conquered loneliness—his relationship with Paul was proof of that. Until this cruise, he hadn't realized how dependent he was on the crutch of this special friendship. Herodotus said that everything changes—everything—but he had never included his relationship with Paul in this famous credo. It was Paul's familiar presence that kept him safely in the world, and it was Paul's recent disaffection that had created his current crisis. The others in his life—the loose federation of the members of Sons of Mozart, his scientific colleagues, Zvi and Peter, a few favorite whores—all provided a utilitarian service. Paul was alone in the give and take of love. Joe never contemplated losing him.

It was imperative to regain his friend's loyalty, and that meant it was time to prepare the ground for action.

The air outside was growing hot from the fast-rising sun, and the fumes rose like avenging witches from the awakening river. Joe retreated to the air conditioning of his suite. Then he rang for coffee and settled back into a plush easy chair. There was a soft chime at the cabin door, and a formally dressed server brought coffee and sweet rolls. Joe sipped the coffee and began to pace. When had he last seen Paul, other than at official meetings? Not since their confrontation before leaving for China. Since then, Paul had barely spoken to him. He was obviously spending time with Debra Jean. Joe had also seen him chatting with Gloria and with Dave Blue and Wiley Stone, the other Americans—even with a few of the Taiwanese.

He should be in the VP dining room enjoying the lavish buffet and gathering data about the strangers in his midst, but he couldn't bear the chance of meeting Paul and Debra Jean together. Taking the last of the coffee with him, he lay on the bed and propped a pillow under his head. Was this another one of Paul's feeble attempts at separation, a phase in the cyclical slave–master relationship that Joe had painstakingly fashioned? Of course, the slave—the bottom, as it was called in SM circles—always had the ultimate power. But Paul had never understood, let alone used that leverage.

Joe wondered how Debra Jean had managed to hold on to him. He had always assumed that she was a weakling; hadn't she rolled over like a child when he embarrassed her in the restaurant? Obviously he was missing something very important. He nodded off, only to wake with a hypnagogic image of an ugly woman staring down at him and laughing derisively. Frightened, Joe quickly left his suite to check out the observation deck. The barely hidden cameras and microphones mounted on the ceilings of passageways and public rooms accosted him at every turn. He had assumed that his own room was bugged. He felt too vulnerable; the Chinese had long experience reading the faces of Westerners. His image would be analyzed for signs of weakness, and now all his feelings were too strong for him to hide effectively.

He ordered a beer and a sandwich at the observation deck bar and decided to face his fears directly by eating it in the restaurant area on the main deck. He took the stairway down three floors. Paul and the other Americans were absent. The food he ordered was served at an isolated table. There were the usual obsequious nods from the staff; he was sure the help sensed his disquiet.

He finished his meal quickly and continued his walk. Thus far, his best thinking place on the ship had been at the stern of this deck, and he ambled there with the remains of his beer. Passing by the foredeck, he saw passengers gathered to look at the famous scenery, beautiful deep gorges on the western shore, reflecting water framing jagged green hills that had been the object of every artist's vision of China for 20 centuries. It was beautiful and evocative, but he was too preoccupied to enjoy it. Looking away, he reached the edge of the back sun deck, where the low railing allowed a direct view of the churning water flushed from the large engines throwing plumes of mist high into the air. He liked the fierce bubbling whoosh of noise surging around him. No audio surveillance was possible here, he thought.

It was broiling in the midmorning heat and light, the sun a copper disc veiled by dark gaseous fumes pouring from the large coal-processing plant on the hill they were passing. Joe wiped the sweat from his forehead with the back of his hand. It came away black. The factory being built near Hong Kong to manufacture the drugs synthesized at MI would add its own noxious fumes to the environment, but that was modern China—cheap and dirty, capitalism at its primitive best. He didn't mind dirt, and he would enjoy the profits from the new pharmaceutical factory that would add its smoky by-products to the others.

He stared into the exhaust and let time go by. When he finally looked up, he was alone. Facing toward the water, he took a small wad of shredded dark green coca leaves from his pocket and added a bit of white lime from a pill case, wrapping the mixture in ordinary tobacco leaves. He pressed this between his gum and cheek, and let the saliva activate the mixture. Coca leaves made a good tea; unaltered, the only psychoactive drug was the mild stimulant of theophylline, analogous to caffeine in coffee. But adding a strong alkaline substance such as lime activated the cocaine molecule in the leaves. Within seconds, he felt a slight numbness in his mouth and the beginnings of cerebral activation.

He smiled delightedly as the high of cocaine amplified associations, the intensity of data points making connections more evident. Maybe now he could pull together the events over the last two weeks and make them meaningful.

The antidepressant effect of the cocaine also changed his dark mood. The shroud that had enveloped him lifted, and the names, facts, and inferences joined in a swirling dance. Gloria, Song, the Chinese scientists, even Paul and Debra Jean had roles and relationships in the roiling mix. But what about the other Americans listed as passengers? Wiley Stone and Dave Blue stood out from the background noise. Of course he knew of them from his sports betting days. He knew a great deal about Stone. Could they be the wild cards, the missing variable in his unsolvable equation?

Use the drug, he urged himself. Think. According to Gloria, Wiley Stone was the tall man who had approached her outside of MI. Dave Blue had had no registered business she could find, but he had attempted to make contact with her and hadn't tried to hide his attempts to hack into the MI computers. She assumed that their presence on the ship had something to do with the earlier thwarted data break-in.

The important new data point was this connection to their past. And that they were still a team ten years after leaving Purdue.

But what did they do together? Gloria had said that they were trained as engineers, but she had found no record of actual work in that field—in any field, for that matter. They were public figures in college because of their fame as football players. That would help if he needed to confront them because—and here was cocaine prodding his memory—neither man could possibly know about his own relationship to their last football game. His secret weapon, he thought, rubbing his hands in glee.

OK, now, don't leave it there. What else could he infer? If they had been trained as engineers, there might be a connection to their interest in biotech data, even to hacking MI's computer system. What about the lack of a history of work activity? He knew that the death of Stone's father stopped Wiley's football career. Stone's father had been found dead at his desk with his own pistol near him on the floor, but there had been speculation that odds-making pros were involved. Well, they had, Joe thought, rubbing his hands together again. Where was Dave in all this? A loyal friend? A secret bond?

After the death, they had both dropped out of sight. Gloria had found a sizable bank account in Stone's name at Wells Fargo. Deposits were made by hand in the Sausalito branch in personal accounts. Stone paid taxes on a houseboat berthed in Sausalito, to which he had title, and he had a P.O. box there as well; Blue showed no regular address.

Did they have secret government jobs? Midwestern athletes were prime recruiting objects. Stone and Blue could have been approached early in their careers. Joe could feel his mind racing out of control, connecting every lead, relevant or not.

But that idea was hardly farfetched. A man like Stone would need revenge for his father's death. Government connections might bring the illusion of possibility. It could explain why a college friend like Blue could be drawn into the drama. Someone was behind their trip. Someone was paying them to follow him all the way to Beijing and find out … what?

He pressed the last jets of fluid from the wad between his gums. Concentrating on the water swirling below, he widened the possibilities. Perhaps Sons of Mozart was under government investigation. That could connect the fire at the Empress with the break-in at MI and even with Zvi's ambush. Possible except that SM had far-reaching contacts throughout the government. Someone would have been alerted to an ongoing investigation.

Was he correct in leaving out Debra Jean? Was there more to her presence on this trip than her budding liaison with Paul, and could it be related to Stone and Blue's mission? Was she working for the government even while she was a postdoc at MI, and had her hysteria at Jardinière been part of a long-term plot to entrap him? Was everything connected by the common thread of a plot against his company?

Joe recognized the paranoid thinking and disconnected inclusiveness characteristic of excessive cocaine use. As the New Age gurus ceaselessly intoned to hungry acolytes, the fluttering of one butterfly's wings affected everything.

Sure, and knowing every possibility was knowing nothing!

Joe stretched his body against the railing and aggressively rubbed his jaw. He deliberately slowed his breath. Wiley Stone and Dave Blue. His mind centered on Stone and his still-unrevealed relationship with the man. If activated correctly, Wiley would fall meekly into his hands.

He felt a presence behind him and turned to find Wiley Stone's enormous figure standing calmly nearby. Frightened, he backed against the railing. More paranoia coursed through him. That was the drug speaking. Stone was simply seeking him out, making his move. The game was on, and the mystery man would soon reveal himself. But Joe would have to keep this first conversation between them very short. The cocaine was still in his system at a level that made him far too unreliable to get the most out of this encounter.

"Wiley Stone? Joe Diamond here." His words flew into the sky and were lost in the intensity of the high noon.

"*The* Joe Diamond? At last we meet." Wiley was mocking him.

He struck back. "Hardly by chance. You seem to have followed me halfway across the world." His own voice sounded loud and high and distant. He glanced at the tall man backlit by the bright sun. Looking up at Wiley, he was all but blind. His pupils must be pinpoints. He tried to converge them into focus and instead saw revolving pairs of colored scintillations of light and fragments and shapes.

"That's true, Joe. I'm here to talk with you about very serious matters." Wiley's voice echoed with resonance. His backlit shape looked like some gigantic Mephisphelean body mask.

"Serious matters. Very deep stuff for an ex-football player. Like what?" Joe's voice belied the calm he sought to achieve.

"Like who. Certain people come to mind. Debra Jean, for one."

Joe relaxed.

"Paul too."

"Paul? I don't want to talk about Paul with the likes of you."

"But I do. I want to talk about Debra Jean and Paul—about Paul especially."

Joe felt his jaw and stomach spasm. His breath came with difficulty. His cocaine trip was definitely spinning out of control at just the wrong moment. And Wiley was sure to take advantage.

He summoned up his unspent energy. "I'm feeling sick, Wiley. It's probably the sun. We'll talk later."

"Afraid of me, Joe?"

"Unlike you, I don't have the body of a trained gorilla. I'm just not in shape for this climate. If you want to talk, I'll be here tonight. Make it seven."

Before Wiley could respond, Joe moved away, almost losing his balance. Wiley put out a huge hand to help him. Instinctively Joe reached for it, but he caught himself on his own and hurried away. Wiley was left standing there with his arm outstretched.

In Joe's mind a bell chimed. "Wiley Stone, first round, the winner."

CHAPTER 32

Boy Talk

A short time later, Wiley and Dave were exercising on the brand-new elliptical bicycles in the well-equipped gym.

"Keep your voice low, Wiley," Dave said under his breath. "I'm hoping the noise of the exercise machines and air conditioning will cover most of our words."

Wiley nodded. "I found Joe by the back deck. He sure didn't live up to his reputation. He seemed sick or scared. Almost fell as he was leaving. And dammit, where were you, Dave? You knew where I was going. You were supposed to shadow me and help as needed."

"I'm sorry, Wiley. As I was leaving my room, Song knocked on the door and insisted on talking with me. I had no choice but to hear her out." Dave looked away and upped his pedaling rate.

"What happened?"

"Her eyes offered what her body resisted. In other words, she's the kind of woman who could fall hard for a guy like me."

Wiley remained quiet concentrating on his cycling.

"OK. I should have sent her away and found you. I was walking out the door when she knocked. She said she was delivering an invitation to a party, but now I wonder if her timing was deliberate."

"Interesting. What about the party?"

"Apparently, passing through the locks of the Three Gorges Dam has become a ritual, like crossing the equator. The Chinese with rooms on the observation deck are having a private shindig, with us as the guests of honor. Aging football stars still have cachet over here."

"What did you say?"

"Nothing out loud. I mentally batted my eyelashes and willed her to want me."

"After that!"

"I told her that I was a terrorist."

"I don't believe you."

"The truth. Teasing is the quickest way to disarm an uptight woman. She looked worried at first but eventually got the joke and laughed. It made her face look fetching. I then told her that we were interested in Dr. Diamond. I said there were reasons to believe he was involved in illegal activities. She looked surprised. I kept smiling and looking at her soulfully, that kind of thing."

"And?"

"Maybe she was breathing a little faster …"

"Go on."

"She said that investigating Dr. Diamond was not in her job description. Protecting him from foreigners who might work for a U.S. government agency was. She gave me an ominous stare, which was a lot more fetching than her mask of perfection. I told her that she looked sexy when she was trying to frighten me, and she blushed and left."

"And your working hypothesis?" Wiley asked.

"This is a big job for her. China has a major investment in Joe and Paul. I think she really believes we are working for the U.S. government."

"Why didn't she just ask?"

"Maybe she wanted to keep me on the hook. Underneath all that stylized posing beats a hot body yearning for my touch." Dave suddenly turned serious. "What happened between Joe and you?"

"His speech was choppy and fast, like he was on something."

"You're saying Joe was high?"

"He was clenching his jaw while talking," Wiley replied. "Pinpoint pupils. Muscles jumping."

"Cocaine or amphetamines," Dave said. "But the consequences of being caught are awesome."

"He's not supposed to be risk averse. I mentioned Debra Jean, and he relaxed. Then I tried Paul, and he panicked. Couldn't hide his reaction except by saying that he was sick. Suggested we meet again this evening and left abruptly."

"So we guessed right about who threatens him."

Wiley nodded in agreement.

Dave lowered his voice to a whisper. "Do you think he knows about your liaison with Gloria?"

"No idea."

Dave wiped the sweat off his face and chest with a towel on the console. "Maybe you just caught him unawares, or it could be a trap. Either way, he's giving us a way in, which we need."

"Right. We need to talk with Debra Jean, Gloria, and especially Paul to see what they can add," Wiley said. "What about surveillance?"

"I've been working on that," Dave said. "With a little tinkering, I can get us a few hours of quiet." He grinned at Wiley. "I'll bet you've already figured out something that puts you off-camera with Gloria."

Wiley stepped into the pedaling while increasing the pitch of the machine. Globules of sweat pooled on his upper lip and shoulders. "I haven't worried too much about it."

"If they're watching, it must make Joe furious."

"Pressing Joe is our strategy."

"You absolutely sure Gloria is on our side?"

"Yes. You worried?"

"I'm cool if you are," Dave said easily. "But we should stay alert. Your next meeting with Joe is important. When he leaves the *Viking* day after tomorrow, he walks away from us. Once that happens ..." Dave wiped his face again with a wet towel.

Wiley nodded. "In the meeting we focus on Paul."

"Right. And keep Debra Jean in the picture."

"She's paying the bills."

"And plays the key role in separating Paul from Joe," Dave said. "I happen to know they're together in her cabin right now."

"In which case Paul may be feeling another kind of pressure," Wiley said drily.

Dave nodded. "He has a lot of accomplishments and credentials, but with women he's more a puppy than a man. Debra Jean is sexy but insecure. It's still not a great combination."

Wiley stretched and got off his bike. A river of sweat poured down his abdomen and thighs. Dave followed suit.

"There's no one I know who's better at doing alpha male stuff than you, but be careful, Wiley. I'll time our meeting so that you can rehash what happens with Joe."

"Don't worry, Dave. I'll be on guard," Wiley said as they picked up their towels to leave.

"Shower and sauna?" Dave asked.

"Great idea. I have something else to run by you."

The showers were lukewarm and the sauna was very hot. Dave used the rheostat to turn the lights down to an orange glow. The small room became a dark cave. "No camera in here. So what's on your mind?"

"Since I arrived in China, I've been dreaming about my father almost every night. They are all variations on his dying. Gloria says that I've woken her up crying his name."

"Sorry, man, that can't be fun. A place like this, the river, the dream of a great dam finally realized, all of that has enormous psychic power. You are revisiting where he spent a good part of his early 30s, just the age you are now. No wonder he's so present."

"Well, I'm feeling him. Not just in the dreams. He was in China as a warrant officer for the U.S. Army. We had a small presence here, mainly technical. I remember his telling you and me about it and the picture of him on this river. I see it in my mind all the time. It's in black-and-white, but the gorges are unmistakable. There were fewer towns and almost no coal plants, but it's the same place."

"That's reason enough to dream of him. But what about his dying?"

"I don't know. It was even present when I was talking with Joe."

"Dreams of death can mean many things," Dave said.

"Mostly I'd like to stop them." He fell silent and buried his sweaty face in a towel.

"I think the dreams are a warning," Dave said. "Something we're not seeing. Someone at risk."

"But who?"

"The end game is upon us, Wiley. It's always full of surprises. We'll just have to stay alert and be paranoid as hell."

CHAPTER 33

Butterflies

I t's just no good, Debra Jean," Paul said, pointing to the flaccid flesh at his groin. "You've been great, but without Joe, it's not going to work."

They were lying together on the king-size bed in Paul's luxurious stateroom. Through the curved glass window of the private balcony he could see a late-afternoon fog on the surface of the river, smoky wisps drifting along the water and merging with the yellow haze. The room was icy cold from air conditioning; opening the window had irritated their throats, and turning off the ventilation had sent the temperature soaring.

Debra Jean caressed his chest, combing through the brown hair with her fingers. "We have tried everything. Everything I know, anyway. 'Kama Sutra Defeated.'" She looked at Paul's dour face. "The humor doesn't fit, does it? This must be so humiliating for you."

"I'm beyond humiliation, Debra Jean."

Debra Jean rolled onto her back next to him and stretched down to her toes. Her muscles tingled, but she felt little sexual frustration. It wasn't erotic anymore. She rose on her elbow and kissed his mouth, then laid her head on the cold sweat of his belly, nuzzling his pubic hair with her nose. "There is a bright side to this, you know," she said as she used her hand to roll the lengthy penis from side to side with no visible response. "I've never been so intimate with any man before. Guys get hard, and then they push and prod and come. Or don't. Even the best lovers rarely take the time with a woman's needs." She put her fist around his penis, then eyed the hole at its tip and pretended to look inside. "I've never had time to explore a guy's penis like this even in a medical exam. They don't stand still for it." She grinned and playfully squeezed the shaft.

"Hey, that hurts."

"Have we tried pain?"

"Yes. Body and psyche."

"I'll be more gentle." She put her hands on his balls and played with the fine black hairs that curled from the prickly skin. "Every once in a while, when I do a rectal exam with some young guy, I tease him a little—like this." She touched the line of flesh from the base of the scrotum to just inside his buttocks."

"You could get sued," Paul said, laughing.

"Nah. They don't even keep a nurse in the room for women docs. Besides, almost every man likes it. They'd never say anything. They blush and try to hide their erection. It's kind of cute. I just go on and finish up the exam."

"You're full of mischief, aren't you? The men you take to bed must love you."

She stopped playing with him. "They do at first, but within hours or weeks, they stop being interested. Several guys have told me that I put too much into it, like I'm desperate to keep their attention. I guess I'm doing that with you too."

Paul stared up at the ceiling. "You could see it like that, but to me it's more like you're taking pity on one of your patients." He shivered. "The past two days have made me more guilty about what Joe and I did to you."

She said, "These last weeks, I wondered if I could take you away from your marriage. I even felt a little guilty. But there's no real marriage to break up. You're wedded to Joe."

Paul's penis stirred. Debra Jean sighed heavily. "Dammit. You're going to teach me to hate sex as much as I hate Joe. Do you wish he were here, Paul? Fucking me? I'll bet he's good, like he is at everything else."

His erection grew even larger. "Horrible, isn't it? I'm one of Joe's most successful experiments. He's put an electrode in the pleasure center of my brain and has his finger on the stimulator, whether he's around or not."

She pulled away from him, lay back, and doubled a pillow under her head. "It reminds me of *The Collector*, that great John Fowles novel."

"I barely remember it from college ..."

223

"You should look at it again, Paul, because it's your story. The protagonist collects beautiful butterflies; his passion is to capture and control beauty. Eventually he substitutes a beautiful woman—puts her in a cage and won't let her out."

"And you think I'm like that woman?"

"He's collected you for the pleasure of controlling you. In the process, he's robbed you of your life force. I know because I have my own personal version of being controlled. Mom. My mother hated my developing body, so she seduced my boyfriends. I'm still recovering from that one."

"Christ, Debra Jean."

"She was a pro. If she were in a village in Africa, she'd have cut off my clitoris. Joe's almost as good at it as she was. In a couple of nasty minutes, he put his middle finger in the center of my life. But now I see he's had 28 years to hone his techniques on you." She sat up straight and pulled the covers over her chest. "You, me, those children: he's got a whole world of abuse going, and you're the only one who can stop him, Paul. That's what Wiley's strategy is all about."

He sat up with her. "What does Wiley have to do with it?"

"You're the leverage, Paul." Debra Jean took Paul's face in her hands, silently asking him to understand. "When I first contacted Revenge, Inc., it was very personal, Paul, very personal revenge. It was about what Joe did to me and what I wanted to do to him. But after what we found out, it's no longer simply a woman confronting a man who abused her. I want to destroy him, Paul. You've got to find the strength to leave Joe. And Wiley believes that will be his undoing."

"No one can do that. It's hopeless."

"Revenge of the scapegoat," she said. "Not hopeless. Very much to the point."

Paul waited for more, but she was silent. He sat up and began pulling on his socks.

"Leave it alone, Debra Jean. I don't want to see you get hurt."

She swung her legs out of bed and grabbed her clothes on the way to the bathroom.

"Please, Debra Jean. Plotting your revenge may be changing you, but it won't affect Joe. I've watched him walking through the ship. He's in a trance. It's more than intellect. It's almost sensual. I've seen him this way before. That's his problem-solving behavior, and when he figures it all out, he'll attack like a demon."

Debra Jean was silent.

"He's desperate," Paul struggled to continue. "I can feel his loneliness. Wiley's right. We're joined at the hip. He is afraid of losing me. I'm all he has."

Debra Jean turned at the bathroom door, throwing her clothes on the floor. She faced him, legs slightly apart, hands on hips.

Paul turned away.

"No. Take a good look. I want you to know what you're missing because of him." She swiveled her hips provocatively. She held her breasts in the palms of her hands. "C'mon, Paul. Aren't I worth taking that risk?" She waited, but he remained silent. "No. Well, then, guess what? I'm no longer yours to play with." She sashayed toward him, swaying seductively. "Take a good look at what you've lost. All this jazz!"

* * *

Two floors below in the security room, Song huddled over piles of audiotape transcripts from the ship's surveillance microphones. Below each stack was a précis of results from the sampling software that she had keyed to Joe Diamond.

"It's just as he implies," Song said to Yang, the technician staring at a screen and pulling out data. "Stone and Blue are repeatedly slandering him." She read a tagged segment out loud. "They claim he was at the Empress Hotel in San Francisco making a snuff film. Obviously the claim is preposterous. Most of the others are as well." But why would they slander him so blatantly? she thought.

She smiled. "So I have plenty of evidence of verbal threats. Wiley Stone and Dave Blue are strong and smart." She sighed and concentrated on the situation. "We will bring in more security by helicopter. Please send a message to Shanghai to that effect. I will sign it when it's ready. What is the ship's travel itinerary for tomorrow."

"We dock at the bridge at Fengdu in the early morning," Yang replied. "Most of the passengers will visit the smaller gorges to the west. You scheduled yourself to lead a tour to the new city on the eastern bank of the river, the one that is handling the dislocated river people. After both tours return, we begin the last leg of the trip to the Three Gorges Dam."

"Good. Schedule the security to arrive when the guests are off ship." She turned away and left the room.

CHAPTER 34

Assault

The evening air was hot and still, and the rising moon shimmered silver on the banks of the Yangtze. It was gorgeous and it was ugly, Wiley thought, as he walked toward the sun deck to keep his appointment with Joe Diamond. Tonight there were no factories belching black smoke; instead the ship was gliding through an agricultural area dimly lit by fires and kerosene lanterns in the villages that were high enough to have escaped the previous floodings of the river. He looked up at the sky. He could see stars for the first time since he'd been on board.

These scenes, the gorges, the peasant life next to the river, and the imminent view of the world's largest dam were the climax of the trip, but Wiley longed for the crisp, clean air of Sausalito and the sight of a great blue heron seeking out fishing grounds near his barge. It had been a difficult voyage, and not just because of the mission of Revenge, Inc. The heat and pollution were bad enough without their being forced to listen to propagandist lectures about the new dam, blasted on ubiquitous tinny loudspeakers every afternoon. There was no doubt that the project had captured the country's imagination and the environmentalists' ire. It was like the days of Noah, he thought. "And the great river rose and flooded the land."

He had grown up watching his father's architectural projects—small, intimate affairs serving the needs of their rural Pennsylvania community. But he also grasped his father's yearning for a great project, and this one defined that need. As a young architect, he had volunteered to be attached to the beleaguered Chinese government stationed in Chongqing, a small American presence in the holdout capital during the occupation of Sichuan. Wiley wondered what his father had said to the Chinese engineers. Perhaps the geographical site of the Three Gorges Dam grew out of those conversations.

Wiley still remembered how his father, always a quiet man, would become uncharacteristically voluble when describing the magnificent river and the potential of a great dam for China and its people. He would carefully take down the picture postcard, the one he had mailed to his young wife from China with a black-and-white picture of the most famous of the gorges. With great patience, he would answer his son's questions about his voyage down the great river. Sometimes he would go to a locked case and take out the pistol and bullets he had carried on the river trip, the gun he had brought home as a war trophy, the same gun that his murderers would turn on him after the fateful football game was won by too many points.

For a brief moment, he heard the song his father laughingly sang to him when the story was over and the guns replaced in their case. "I want to get you on a slow boat to China, all to myself alone."

Far too good for the son who had betrayed him and brought about his death, Wiley thought as he made his way along the railings to meet Joe. For the first time, Wiley understood that love for a suffering friend had bound Dave to him just as tightly as fear and compassion for Joe had co-opted Paul.

The moon dipped under a cloud, and a light wind ruffled the water as he reached the back of the boat. He felt undermanned and vulnerable and wished Dave was with him.

* * *

From a room nearby, Joe Diamond stood watching the ship's surveillance screens: The first showed Wiley climbing the stairs to the sun deck and, finding it empty, looking distractedly out at the river. Three of the other screens were playing well-edited videos: Wiley and Dave in the gym, barely audible over the whirr of bikes, Gloria and Wiley hugging each other in bed, Paul and Debra Jean's depressing conversation in Paul's room. He had been watching for several hours, gleaning what he could for ways to deal with his coming encounter with Wiley. The missing piece was still Wiley and Dave's relationship with Debra Jean,

228

and he was sure he could squeeze that from Wiley tonight.

Joe had taken a sound reading from the camcorder at the stern where Wiley stood. The engine and the swirling water were more than enough to drown all but shouted words. He did not want their conversation available to anyone, particularly Song. She was already in his pocket, and he wanted her to remain there.

Joe finished reviewing the last tapes and pressed the stop button. He left the surveillance room and took the outside stairs to the back of the sun deck two at a time. Wiley stood at the railing, and Joe had a moment of doubt—his size was daunting—but that didn't last long. This time he was ready. He had taken the measure of the man and knew he would prevail.

He moved directly to the railing. Neither offered to shake hands.

"Such a beautiful evening, Wiley," Joe began.

"As a tourist, I would agree."

"But we both know you're not just a tourist, Wiley. Actually, it's one of the things I need to know: why you are here. Or should I say, why you, Dave, and Debra Jean are here."

"Without granting your speculation, why do you think, Joe? You must have some hypothesis."

"A few, none confirmed. Someone spent a great deal of money bringing all three of you here. When I return to San Francisco, that information will be available to me, but I was hoping you could enlighten me yourself." Joe paused, following his strategy of limiting their height difference by focusing on Wiley's hands. A darting glance to his eyes at the critical moment would be enough.

Wiley remained silent, looking down at the river and the receding shoreline.

"Cat got your tongue? Playing it coy? No rush, Wiley. Whatever your reason for being here, this scene, the gorges in their full glory, will remain in our memories." Joe spread his hands, palms up. "And I don't mind being with you at such a poignant time. Actually, I was looking forward to it. I've had so little company the past few days. Debra Jean has fully occupied my colleague Paul. But of course you know that." He looked up suddenly, but there were no clues in Wiley's face.

"Such control." He continued, "This cruise would be more exciting with some good conversation. I thought Gloria would help, but she has provided little in the way of information. It is clear that she prefers your company to mine." He leered at Wiley before continuing. "And of course my Chinese colleagues are all business and no pleasure. At least they won't share any of their pleasures with me."

"Or you with them," Wiley commented evenly.

"What do you mean?" Joe asked. Suddenly he was alert to the new theme and, seeing its possibilities, put out a feeler. "Oh yes, I understand. You have fantasies about my sexual habits. Perhaps you imagine that my Chinese hosts would try to find ways to fill them. I've heard about the repetitive slander in the tapes of your shipboard conversations. Why would you be peddling such lies, Wiley? Is it part of a strategy against me that you, Dave Blue, and whoever you are working for have developed?"

Wiley's voice turned sarcastic. "Men who have talents are often the victim of their vices. Yours are probably more extreme than most, maybe the kind of extreme behavior that should send you to a locked psychiatric ward."

"What are you up to, Wiley?" Joe said, mocking him slightly. "Why the character assassination? Industrial espionage? Working for the CIA? Lies and threats fit their style. That might explain the lack of a work history for the past ten years—starting immediately after your father committed suicide."

Wiley could feel his own anxiety surge. "I don't need to catalogue my work history to you, Joe," he said grimly. "Or have you characterize how my father died."

"It's hardly a secret," Joe said. "But you can't blame me for being testy, with you and your friends maligning me and my company at every opportunity. Why?"

"I think you know."

"Hasn't it crossed your mind that you may have been given false information that has colored your opinions?"

"I've thought about that possibility," Wiley said. "I'm a long way from home, at considerable expense, which means I've already made my decision. So have the others with me."

"I appreciate that information. Shall I present an alternate view of things to you? Will you listen with an open mind?"

230

"You're asking me if I am a fair man."

"Exactly. Perhaps it will help you to know that the great Wiley Stone was a hero of mine. I watched many of your games. I was delighted with the way you could invent truly audacious plays from the line of scrimmage. It's what made you great. You had good coaching, and your talents made winning look easy. In my opinion, it was your intelligence, your ability to change your mind in a flash of insight, that made your team so successful. You were a great artist. I've always thought the best athletes are that."

"So now I am intelligent and an artist. If you were a friend and there was a pitcher of beer, I might enjoy this conversation, but right now I am not with a friend, and I have other plans for our time together."

"You can leave anytime, Wiley. However, I believe I have not mentioned my main hypothesis for your presence on this cruise, which I know will interest you very much." He paused briefly to establish a rhythm. "I should warn you, it depends on exploring a subject that won't be pleasant." Joe continued to look at the water. "See, your presence here, well, I think it has a lot to do with your father." He didn't need to check Wiley's response—he knew that this was a surprise. He paused again, this time long enough to underline his point, and then continued in a slow and measured tone.

"Your attempt to characterize me as a child abuser, a snuff film maker, and God knows what else seems an extreme strategy to me, given the lack of evidence. You have something in mind that eludes me. Something unresolved. That led me to consider the death of your father, the large unresolved issue in your life. I've spent a lot of time on the Internet going over old newspapers and magazines and various other ways of reviewing his history. I have my own very personal memories ..."

Joe looked at Wiley's hands. They were white-knuckled on the rail. He laughed. "I see you want me to go on. When your father died, the sports media and eventually the general media began asking quite reasonable questions about his death. They had a right to know; you were a genuine American hero and very newsworthy, and he was a well-respected architect with a national reputation of his own. He had served his country and community loyally—in fact, one of his assignments was right near here in Chongqing." He waited a beat. "Did you know that,

Wiley?" He could see that Wiley's hands were bracing for more control.

"Of course you did. Anyway, the articles focused on your father's good character, as well as his apparent lack of suicidal motivation and the fact that there wasn't an adequate police investigation. One reporter mentioned financial problems in your father's architectural firm; another found evidence of marital difficulties over an affair. Your mother never disputed the claim of suicide or family troubles. As you well know, she became uncommunicative after the death and has been in and out of psychiatric hospitals ever since."

"My mother and father won't be part of our conversation," Wiley said with studied calm. "It upsets me to hear you mention them. I can only assume that's your motivation."

"To upset you? Not really. I'm the one under pressure here; I figured out that much about your strategy from the tapes I've watched." Joe moved closer to his prey. "As it happens, I have valuable information for you. Those journalists who questioned the depth of the investigation? They were on the right track. The police efforts to find out what happened were aborted prematurely. Whoever killed your father had enormous power and connections and used them. As it happens, I know a little something about that. Listening now? Of course you are.

"After you quit football, you were no longer a hero to your fans," Joe continued. "Americans love their sports heroes but don't like to feel used, meaning when their heroes don't play along with their God projections. You let them down, and they began to hate you the way sycophants hate when they are deceived. So you became something of a pariah among the rural rednecks, especially when you didn't play in the postseason games or honor your commitments to the pro teams. That was unsportsmanlike and, what's worse, un-American."

"The point, Joe," Wiley interjected, trying to regain some momentum.

"The point. Well, for starters, it couldn't have been fun being hated after you were the pride and joy of football fans for four years."

"People should have understood," Wiley blurted out. "My father's death—" He stopped abruptly, suddenly aware of the trap.

"Death. An apt phrase. I think you knew it wasn't a suicide, Wiley. And most important, you knew who was behind the murder of your father." Joe paused, waiting for a response that didn't come. "Yes, you knew." He went on. "You knew, and that knowledge made you ashamed. The media were correct when they declared that it couldn't have been a suicide. They were right in pointing out that it wasn't your father's style; he was an extraordinary man and I suspect a wonderful father. Right? He was so thrilled with what you did in sports. He was proud of your commitments. He was happy with you, Wiley. And happy with your mother. You and your friends and teammates mattered so much to him. That was his way, the American ideal that he had honored all his life. You fit the culture that your father honored with all his might. You were making his dreams come true so close to home, and you felt his pleasure. It made you like a god, head in the clouds, feet planted firmly on the ground, your body spanning earth and sky. You represented the best that the heartland could produce—a Purdue engineer no less. A man's man, you were the best and the brightest. You were very much his son, and more than his son." Joe stopped. Wiley's breathing was irregular; his hands shook slightly. Joe glanced up. There were tears in Wiley's eyes.

"You knew that the Mafia killed your father," Joe stated emphatically. "There were others who knew. In fact, I knew. You see, I bet on football in Las Vegas. I bet on that fateful game. I knew what was going down.

"That last championship game was a problem for the professionals. Your team were such favorites that the big money needed a few points shaved in order to make a killing. Only you could deliver those points. They decided to get to you through your father. They came to you and threatened him and then sat back and waited.

"I don't know if you told him. If so, I can imagine his anguish. But I doubt if he told you to betray your commitments to your team and fans. I can even imagine you kept it all to yourself except for Dave. Perhaps you didn't believe they'd go through with it. Why ask? You knew what your father would say. He was a war hero, after all. That gun was out of its case, the bullets waiting for a home." Joe raised his head and for the first time in that conversation looked directly up into Wiley's eyes. "But here's the kicker, Wiley. Whatever did or didn't happen between you, I don't think your precious perfect touchdown throw to Dave Blue was worth the risk to your father's life."

"You bastard," Wiley said, lunging forward and grabbing Joe's shoulders. Joe lurched backward with the impact, and his knees gave way. He fell hard against the railing as Wiley's bulk pressed him toward the churning water.

"Get away from me!" Joe screamed. Wiley backed up, and Joe, losing his balance, teetered on the edge of the low railing, then tipped over it, slowing his fall only by hooking one elbow over the railing.

"Hold on!" Wiley yelled and, steadying himself on the deck, grabbed at Joe's shirt and belt until he got a grip on both. Then he lifted Joe in the air and heaved him away from the ship's edge. Joe landed on the deck with a crash and lay still, breathing hard.

He was scared but not hurt, and his mind immediately focused on what had just happened. The opportunity provided was immense. The thought calmed him as he rose unsteadily to his feet. "You fool. Killing me won't get rid of your guilt about your father. That's yours forever."

Wiley cowered against the railing, afraid to move or talk.

Joe advanced toward him. "Why are you here, Wiley? I demand to know. Is it about Las Vegas? The gamblers? Your revenge?"

"What are you talking about?"

"Why else would you pursue me unless it was about your father? And you're right. I was involved in your father's death, but not in the way you imagine."

"How are you connected with my father?" Wiley asked incredulously.

Joe's panic was gone. He relished the man's pain. "I'm connected through sports betting. That's how I know about the circumstances around his death."

Wiley slumped farther down against the railing. He forced himself to evaluate the situation. Joe had to be frightened by the violence of the encounter. He had been a hairsbreadth from going overboard and into the vessel's motor. Was he lying? Wiley doubted it. Joe was using the information to manipulate him, but that didn't make the information any less true.

Wiley slowly nodded his head. He was being drawn inexorably into a game of wits that Dave had warned him against. He should turn his back on the man and walk away, but he couldn't do it. He needed to hear what Joe had to say. He really had no choice.

Joe smiled at the turn of events. He spoke calmly with righteous authority about an important truth. What matter that he would also benefit?

"Despite the lies you've been told about me and are telling others, I've done nothing wrong. Your witch hunt will have to stop. This is China. I'm very important here. If this continues, you and your friend won't be safe."

"What about my father, Joe?"

"Quid pro quo."

"For what? Why should I believe anything you say?" Wiley stormed back. "I was there at the Empress, Joe. I saw those children. I know what you're capable of."

"The Empress!" Joe said in amazement. "A threat to children. You think I was involved. Look, it's true that I was at the hotel. I was on the 29th floor of the Empress, but not with those poor children. When I heard the fire alarm and had to leave sweet Lilly, my favorite call girl, among others—"

"You're lying. I saw you in the hall outside their room. Dave Blue and Gloria saw you, too, and recognized your friend Zvi."

"No, Wiley," Joe said patiently as if he were talking to a child. "You prejudged me. You decided I was abusing the children and told Gloria and maybe even Paul that I was involved. Zvi and some others were with me, including sweet Lilly. It was a sex party, for God's sake. Strictly adult." He stopped and looked up at Wiley. "But are you implying that you are the one who hurt Zvi?"

"Dave, actually."

"Then I can assume that maiming Zvi was part of your revenge, for your father? If so, you have done him a great and wrongful harm. Your misinterpretation has left him paralyzed and half-blind, recuperating in a medical clinic in San Francisco."

"Dave and I saw you come out of that room, Joe."

"There was thick smoke. People were milling through the halls. We were in a suite a few doors down, and I got out of there as quickly as I could. Not because I was involved with those children. I wasn't. But because I didn't want any publicity about my night's activities. Even in San Francisco, my tastes in matters of sex are exotic, and prostitution is nominally illegal, so I protect myself. I'm not into child murder."

Wiley looked down at the man lecturing to him and suddenly felt confused.

Joe pressed his advantage. "You need to help me here, Wiley. You really think I'm a sex pervert? Up to this moment, I thought you'd been told that I helped kill your father and that's why you're here. Given your current aggression and its potential consequences, it wouldn't hurt to tell me what's going on."

Wiley was silent, again wishing he'd brought Dave. "I never thought you killed my father, Joe. I don't understand that part of what you're saying …"

"Wiley. Listen to me. It's simpler than you think. There's a bit of truth in all you've been told. When you hear the whole story, you are going to feel like a fool for coming all this way for nothing and becoming involved in trying to defame me. And if you'll listen, I am going to feel a lot better as well. Being throttled by you is an experience I don't want to repeat."

"I didn't throttle you, Joe." But he knew he had.

"I'm sure you know there are cameras on board, and the whole episode was recorded. He waited a beat, then continued. "OK. Let me tell you about gambling, the Mafia, Las Vegas, and the facts behind the game that changed your life. But first I need to give you some background."

"Joe!" Wiley said. "It's not what you think."

Joe interrupted angrily. "You're in no position to say that anymore." His voice took on a more conversational tone. "Indulge me for a moment. It will be worth it. … Imagine what I've felt like on this trip. Imagine how frightening it is to be investigated by people I don't know, by a person I have hired to protect me, and by my own closest colleague. I'm an unusual man, Wiley. An eccentric but I don't deserve your tactics. The Nobel Prize, my friendship with Paul, my basic research, my financial future, my medical discoveries—you're challenging them all. Then imagine how it felt to be attacked by a man who is a foot taller."

"I'm sorry about what just happened," Wiley said slowly, struggling once more to gain some control of the situation. "But you're still way off base. I can assure you that my presence here has nothing to do with my father's death."

236

"Good try but not very convincing. I'll tell you all about Dad as long as you promise to keep that temper of yours under control."

He walked away from the ship's railing and faced Wiley from a distance. "You see, it's not a pretty story."

CHAPTER 35

Confusion

J oe peered down into the turmoil of the dark water, churned to a boiling foam by the ship's large engines. He was keenly aware of a similar turmoil in the huge man looming next him, and he knew that he had to be watchful. He had planned this story carefully, a narrative and an endgame that would convince, control, and subdue. The worst was over, and Wiley's recorded attack on him had ended up playing perfectly into his hands.

He paused, searching for the correct voice. "To understand how I came to learn about your father's death, you must understand more about my background. I was a graduate of Harvard Med and earned a PhD in molecular biology from UCSF. Even before that last degree, I had already published some of the most important work in my field, but I was still a postdoc and despite my successes had no authority. I still had no lab space of my own. "

"Joe!"

"I understand. I should get on with it. Right?"

"Right," Wiley answered sullenly.

"But I've asked you to be patient, Wiley. This is hard for me too. OK?"

"OK, Joe."

"Molecular biology was a hot field. I didn't have enough money to fund my own research, and I knew it would be years before I got the grants that provided the space, equipment, and staff that I needed. My salary was $50,000, barely enough to live on. I had money of my own but needed some of that to fund my own company.

"I chose what I was doing because it held the greatest intellectual challenges for me. In the 19th century, I might've chosen music or philosophy, but now science alone can truly challenge great minds. Of course I knew that eventually the status and money would come. But it was humiliating to be under the thumb of dull but well-connected professors who had little creativity but lots of administrative power."

Joe took a slow, deep breath before he continued. "I don't know what you know about prodigies, Wiley. Perhaps you were one, if we include somatic intelligence in the definition. The way you used your body on the football field, not to mention the way you saved my life, is a kind of genius, at once thrilling and beautiful. When I watched you play, so smooth and sure, I often thought of the way I used my mind. Does that make sense to you?"

He looked up into Wiley's eyes, hoping that Wiley could be drawn into his narrative. He was amazed at how much he wanted the big man to like him. Wiley showed no interest in him, only in what he might say. He could feel how vulnerable he was to the special charisma of the man, the intangible essence that made some into great leaders—the qualities he didn't have, he thought darkly. Joe turned to look at the water and with a sigh continued.

"Perhaps someday you might tell me how it feels to be such a great athlete. But to do that, you'll need to trust rather than condemn me. I would like that."

"Why is that, Joe?"

Joe laughed out loud. "Even in the age of Steve Jobs, superior intelligence is ridiculed, especially before the money rolls in. Science fairs, math contests, a few gigs at designing computer games—big deals for some but no girls waiting in your hotel room. And sure, getting into Harvard was a good beginning—they pretty much recruited me—and it gave me some extra prestige at my high school graduation, where garnering every academic award possible hardly mattered more than winning the tennis trophy.

"Harvard was actually a pretty dull place. It may be the best school in the country, but it wasn't geared for the likes of me! I did enough work to get As and concentrated on other things, games mostly: chess, poker, go, and computer games."

Wiley stirred again. "This is boring, Joe. Things were tough for the nerdy prodigy, OK. You were smart in high school, the brightest kid at Harvard. But you were too young to date and probably afraid to shower with your classmates because you had no pubic hair on your balls and a pencil for a dick. God knows what that did to your psyche.

"We've got to move on before I get really angry." He took a deep breath. "I won't rescue you the next time."

"Listen up, Wiley," Joe said imperiously. "This is all important to you and your dad's memory, so cool it." He waited a few beats, then continued. "What I learned in college and medical school was that my gifts included a proclivity for competition. I loved games of skill."

"At least the ones you could win."

"I know this all sounds like bragging, but I guarantee it's all leading to your father, Wiley. I knew a lot about games where skill and smarts were useful. Las Vegas gambling, for example. You might think Las Vegas is for suckers. Right? Not for people like me. So that's your first link. I'm sure you know that football is big-time among the odds makers. Gambling is not an enterprise that relies on chance. We're not talking slot machines here, where there's no way to take advantage of the laws of chance. But when there are objective mathematical laws running the game, people with my brains have a great advantage. Games like blackjack, for example, are almost all about memory. Perfect for mnemonists."

"Help me on that one, Joe," Wiley said.

"Mnemonists? They're people who remember everything they see or hear. Mastering the math of blackjack and counting cards with a good memory is fun, but it didn't take long for casino owners to catch on. Even now I can't enter a blackjack game without having two goons at my elbows. But poker is a different matter. Once you master the odds of getting a flush or two pair, it's all about the laws governing competition: betting, bluffing, and dealing successfully with the anxiety of risk and reward. Poker, the stock market, team sports, and war—those are real-life games in which winning depends on the psychology of competition."

"Joe ..."

"Before you attack me again, you should know it's paydirt time for you. You see, I was deeply involved in mob-dominated sports betting when you were a college football star."

Wiley made a noise in his throat.

"I see I have your attention again." Joe looked up at Wiley. "You do need to relearn the kind of patience that served you so well as a quarterback." Their eyes met, but Joe dropped his first. It wasn't time for another challenge.

"I'm going to tell you about your father and the Mafia. In college there was a weekly poker game with the best players on the campus. Word got around about my talents. I was invited as a freshman, a big honor, although I was already a celebrity because of my age. We were all clever enough to master the odds, so winning was entirely about psychology and bravado. I was a consistent winner, but there were others who had more emotional power to bring to the game, and they were the bigger winners. So I moved on.

"I wonder how much you know about sports betting. Probably very little, and, sadly, I suspect that your lack of knowledge cost your father his life. So I'm going to educate you, even if it's too late.

"Player statistics and position match-ups are important, and there are banks of sports fanatics and computer types who provide data to the big betters. Leveraging outside information is one game changer. Creating new conditions is the other.

"The bookmakers make the odds based on betting. There are clever ways to consistently beat them. The easiest way is to know something that others don't. That's where good information comes in. Nonpublicized injuries, personnel changes, and alterations in the emotional stability of the coaches and key players are some of what's available, and they can make a big difference in the outcome of every game. Unlike ordinary gamblers, even the savviest ones, organized crime has a big advantage. Bribing, threatening, and even injuring key athletes and coaches are some of the best ways to significantly change a game's outcome. Crime becomes an independent variable that regularly affects the outcome of games.

"I was a regular player, and I did well, particularly in betting on football. I knew the stats and had good intuition, but I had no access to game-changing info. So I began offering my mathematical and memory skills to gamblers with crime connections in return for occasional tips: things like which players were being pressured to drop a few passes or fumble on a hard tackle. Soon my winnings increased precipitously, as did my personal jeopardy. Working for organized crime has inevitable risks. I wish I could tell you that I was ashamed of links with the Mafia and other criminal syndicates. Those feelings came later, particularly after your father died.

"As you can imagine, the national college football championships are big gambling events, but they are also difficult to influence, particularly on the player side. The potential future rewards for college athletes are vast; promises of huge signing bonuses and high salaries in the pros make them immune to all but the crudest threats. And in those last few months, team spirit and the joy of winning a national championship really count. You'd be surprised how much loyalty to team and coach still matters. Rule of thumb for the really big games is patience. Wait for the right person and the big opportunity, and seize the moment with gigantic bets.

"That's where you came in, Wiley. You were a perfect mark. If your performance were to be compromised, even a little, it would make a big difference in the game's outcome. Best of all, no one would ever imagine your taking a fall. Wiley Stone, the All-American Hero, on the take? Forget it!

"But before the last game of the season, your name came up. I knew that you had never been in play before—too risky because of your personality and stature—but I figured the stakes were high and something could happen. I was sure the Mafia was thinking that way, too, so I kept my ear to the ground and called in favors."

"Get to the point," Wiley said disgustedly.

"You ready? Then on to the kill! Thursday, two days before the big game on Saturday, Wiley Stone's name was on everybody's lips. Not in the usual way—like the guy has a cold, or his girlfriend isn't putting out, or he's having a fight with his coach. They were working on turning you. I could feel it.

"So I emptied my wallet and spent a night with one of the girls who belonged to the mob. At 4 a.m., she told me that your father had been threatened. By Saturday morning, I thought I knew what you were facing. The Mafia was interested in you, and the odds on your team's winning with a decent point spread dropped precipitously. Everybody was betting you'd throw the game to save your father from danger. I made a big move, but not in the way everybody was going. I bet you'd beat your point spread. I bet against your dumping the game. Why? Simple. I bet on your romance with loyalty and your father's pride in his son's character. I bet on what your father might tell you to do and on your love for him. And so I won big. Very big.

"That's the story, Wiley. Just that. I had nothing to do with the Mafia contacting your father."

Wiley stood suddenly and peered down at Joe. "If you did …"

Joe took a step back, smiled furtively, and then moved closer again. "But here is where I can help, Wiley. The men who set up the deal are still out there. I can help you find them. Maybe that's the good news for you, maybe not. What I'm telling you now is to back off on the lies and threats, on character assassination. It's way off the mark. I wasn't involved in his setup or his death."

"You're the one who is off the mark."

"Really?"

"Yep. I'm not lying to you, Joe. My coming here has nothing to do with my father in the way you imagine. It has everything to do with you, but again not in the way you believe."

"But it must! Why else could you be here? I never bought that you were some ex-jock government agency hire. That was just to smoke you out. Look at your reaction to what I said about his death. And you want me to believe that revenge is not your motive."

"My emotions are real. Your logic isn't."

Joe began talking faster. He struggled to keep control. "You think I got away scot free. Almost true, Wiley. That night a bunch of tough guys came to my room and asked me what I knew. I told them the truth. They weren't happy with my explanation, but they weren't ready for another scandal, so they just roughed me up bad and banned me from Las Vegas sports betting for a year. I landed in the hospital for a week. To them, that was leaving me alone."

He paused for effect. "I was the one who got it right. Not them, not you and your father. I walked away with some bad bruises and a couple of million dollars free and clear and never looked back. I made a fortune on a clever bet and your father died. And now, ten years later, someone, maybe someone from the mob itself, has set you up with a false story and you're after me. I have no desire to be your target. That's why I'm telling you the truth about who it was that spoke to your father. I have the names. All you have to do is ask.

"I put the money into high-tech stocks, which went through the roof. That fueled my exit from academia, and the rest is history." Joe raised his eyes to the big man. Wiley looked away and glanced at his watch. "Thanks for the confession, Joe. I hope it worked for you."

"What I've just told you is the truth. I took a risk. I could've gotten killed. What you did that afternoon, well, I won't judge you. You were young. You didn't have the information or experience to make the right choice. I'm offering you payback and an end to the need for revenge that you've let run your life. I'll give you the men who did this to you. All I want in return is for you and the rest of your buddies to stop hassling me." Joe swallowed. "And to leave Paul alone."

"And the Empress, Joe?"

"I already told you why I was on that floor and what I was and wasn't doing. That kind of scene you're talking about is mob stuff. Even if I were interested in little girls, which I'm not, I certainly wouldn't put myself in their gun sights for a night out. People who deal in vice have long memories."

"I don't believe you, Joe."

"Occam's razor. Nothing else makes sense."

"Go through the possibilities again. Maybe you'll catch on."

"You're lying," Joe said, trying to keep his voice steady. "And you owe me."

"No I don't." Wiley turned away and studied the churning engine exhaust fouling the water. He looked up at the dark sky and the beginnings of a full yellow moon rising over the river. He desperately wanted to know more about his father's murderers. In that way, he had lied to Joe. He was here because of his father, but not in the way Joe thought. He was here because Revenge, Inc., was the only story that mattered after his father died.

Joe had dreamed up an elaborate scheme because he couldn't believe that what he had done to a lowly postdoc might still be an issue. He couldn't understand that someone would be outraged by his behavior and want to help her or that it could point to other crimes like the Empress.

Could Joe be telling the truth about that? He said he had just been in another room on the same floor with a favorite prostitute and other partners, including Zvi. That was his alibi. But how much coincidence was acceptable? Dave had told Wiley that he was a great quarterback because he saw the whole picture like no one else. He didn't need to have experienced coaches call in the plays. His instincts were better than those of any team of analysts. Everything he had heard, beginning with Debra Jean's story and ending in this conversation, told him that Joe was at the Empress, and those children, not "sweet" Lilly the hooker, were his sex party.

Wiley turned back to Joe. "I'm going to give you a hint about why I'm here."

Joe smiled up at him appreciatively. "No need, Wiley. I can see by your reactions that you're telling me the truth—that your presence is not related to your father, nor are you an investigating government agent. So there's only one motive left. I had rejected Debra Jean's complaints, so it's got to be her." He threw his hands into the air in a gesture of helplessness. "It must be about Debra Jean. Losing her job. As absurd as that is, there's nothing else I can think of."

"It's more than the job, Joe. Firing her was your right. Yours and Paul's."

Joe looked at Wiley in amazement. "Then what? Questioning her publications? Changing her research tasks? Not rescuing her from Walnut Creek? As you say, people get fired."

"Something else, Joe. You knew how vulnerable she was, how she idolized you and your work, how hard she'd fall. You should have treated her better."

Joe leered at him. "Why? Because she's smart and had some good ideas? No, you're still holding out on me, Wiley. What else is there?" He waited, unsure of what he was missing.

"You remember Jardinière, Joe. The celebratory dinner marked by abuse and humiliation."

Joe opened his mouth in astonishment. "You're worried about what happened in Jardinière? What did she tell you? That I put my finger in her twat and she jumped out of her skin, spilling an excellent Latour in the process? Absolutely true. No excuses. But the context, Wiley, the context. She came on to me. I was just responding to her moves, and she didn't like my style. I felt her. She was wet and ready. Lots was going on inside that uptight body of hers."

"You were her boss. It's called abuse, Joe," Wiley said with more certainty than he felt.

Joe held one finger in the air and sniffed it appreciatively. "Believe me, she was more than ready. Anyway, you don't know the scene, Wiley. Postdocs are fair game, but so are their bosses. Dammit, Wiley, you were a hero once. You know the way girls come on to their jock heroes. Think of me as a science jock, the biggest one in the Bay Area. My mind is every bit as exciting to eager young professional women as your body was to your coed fan club. Not to mention my millions and what I can do for their careers. Just being near me is enough to turn their heads. Can you tell me you never took advantage of, shall I say, your charisma? Power and sex are part of life, my friend."

He looked at Wiley with condescension. "Have I got it now, Wiley? A woman's honor at stake. Robin Hood and the Knights of the Round Table all rolled into one romantic package. If that's why you've come to harass me in China, then you're a fool."

"Your value system may be different than mine—and Debra Jean's," Wiley said evenly.

"Please. Save me your moralizing. It's all about your father, but not in the way I thought. You're obsessed by what you did. It's made you a revenge junkie. Might even use your services someday. But all for a finger up Debra Jean's cunt? She's not even a virgin, and you're hardly an innocent.

"You said your father's death wasn't behind this, but I'm not buying that any longer. You've never gotten over it because you're overwhelmed by guilt. Now you're out of control. Your friend Dave attacked my security man and friend in San Francisco. He's someone I care about personally, and he's still in the hospital. If you're involved with that, watch out, because Dave tried to break into my company. Zvi was following up on that. Nothing nefarious in that.

"A last warning, Wiley. Leave Paul alone. Do that and I'll just walk away from all this, including Dave's attack on Zvi and your assault on me. If you want, I'll throw in the names of the Las Vegas gamblers. I'll never bother you again. But push Paul, and you're playing with fire."

Wiley took a long look at the dark river in the moonlit landscape and then turned back to Joe. It was not an easy face to read. "I'm going now, Joe." It was all he could say. He had no idea how to separate fact from fiction. Joe was tough, crude, and convincing. Somehow Joe had nailed the problem: he was a revenge junkie. No one else had put it so clearly. He walked away, leaving Joe at the railing. Joe was right about him. He didn't know why he was there.

CHAPTER 36

Strategy Session

Wiley stumbled back toward the main deck until he found himself in the narrow corridor leading to his room. He felt around in his pants pocket for the key and came up empty. He tried the other pockets with no better results, and then patted down his shirt pockets. No key. He heard a jingle at his side. Looking down, he saw the metal key dangling from his left index finger.

His conversation with Joe made him yearn for a hot, cleansing shower. A shower to wash clean the gray residue from a day's pollution on the Yangtze and the residue from Joe's insinuation and his own confusion. A shower that wouldn't begin to touch the slime in his brain. The trouble was, he wasn't sure whose slime it was—Joe Diamond's or his own.

He placed the key in the lock, then hesitated before turning it. Dave had been dead right. There was no way he should have taken on Joe alone. The unnerving look into his own past that Joe had brought, all that Joe had said about the circumstances around his father's death, and even his rhetoric about Debra Jean had left Wiley shaken and vulnerable. Some of Joe's perspective had the ring of truth. Certainly the story about Wiley's father felt true. He had described the essence of the father-son relationship as if he had been there.

Changing his mind about the shower, Wiley withdrew the key and walked the few steps to Dave's entrance to their suite. Better to talk about his conversation with Joe while it was still fresh. He stopped again. Did he hear voices? Suppose Dave had a woman in his room. He'd give Dave a call first.

He crossed back to his own door. First that shower, then a call to Dave and a possible debriefing. He unlocked the door and heard voices. He entered the living room and saw that it was full: Dave, Debra Jean, and Gloria, even Paul, who sat somewhat apart. Dave waved him in and then turned back to the group. Then Wiley remembered the meeting that Dave had asked to be held after his encounter with Joe. Not his usual style to forget a scheduled rehash—more of Joe's residual effect on his psyche.

"Wiley!" Dave barked from his chair. "We've been waiting and worrying. So how did you survive the evil genius?"

"Barely," Wiley answered, standing on the threshold of the room. "And badly."

Dave, seeing Wiley's unease, walked to where he waited and embraced his friend. "I'm here for you, man," he said softly.

"I could use a drink."

"That bad?"

Wiley nodded his head like an embarrassed child. Dave continued to eye him. "You look like a man who's taken a beating. Not like you at all, Wiley. Let's both get a beer and talk. You don't need to face this group now."

Wiley shook his head. "A beer and talk, yes, but I need to tell everybody what happened."

"You're sure?" Dave asked gingerly. "I could debrief you, and then we could share it."

"What happened has to be shared, and the sooner the better. It affects everybody. I'll get washed and be back in a couple of minutes." He flashed a brief smile. "And make sure that beer is ice-cold and plentiful."

* * *

When Wiley returned, he took the seat on the sofa next to Gloria. He put his arm around her. She pulled him toward her, whispering affectionately in his ear. Then she did her best to cradle him in her arms.

"Stop staring, you guys," Wiley said from his comfortable perch as he leaned farther back into Gloria's arms. "My first rule of good leadership is to take care of the leader. That's me. And after talking with Joe for almost two hours, debriefing begins with healing. Why don't you fill me in and let me soak up Gloria's balms."

Dave nodded. "Sure. Tell me when you want to take over."

"OK. I'll just listen for a while." Wiley lay back and closed his eyes.

Dave began. "Exhibit A," he said, pointing to Wiley. "Here we see the dire consequences of a conversation with Joe Diamond." He looked around the room, frowning. "We all need to check in. It's our first real discussion since we arrived." His eyes rested on Gloria. "You especially. Can you do that without disturbing our love-starved hero?"

"Sure." Gloria's posture changed slightly, but she stayed close to her man. "First day on board, Joe and I talked at some length. He asked for background information on the three of you, so I filled him in without giving him anything he couldn't find in his own computer databases. Later on, Song and I met to collaborate on security issues on the ship. I didn't tell her anything she didn't know, and she was equally guarded with me.

"We agreed on a daily briefing," she continued, "but that never happened. I'm definitely out of the loop. I'd guess it was Joe's decision. I can understand if he knows about this." She kissed Wiley on the ear.

"He does," Dave said. "They've got surveillance all over the ship. We have to assume we're on camera most of the time, folks. I used what I got in Chongqing to clear this room and the corridor, but they'll pick up the negative signals, so it won't last long."

"I don't like the idea of Song watching," Gloria said.

"Uptight defines her," Dave said regretfully. "But there's hope."

"Her vibe is racist," Gloria went on. "She thinks Latinos are inferior in the workplace because they have so much fun."

"You mean it isn't true that all Latinos are warm and sexy, love their families, and go to church?" Wiley teased from his reclining position.

"Racist white boy." She pushed him away, then reconsidered and cuddled him again. "Bottom line is, Joe and I haven't been alone since the second day of this trip. He simply has stopped using me in my job. But the trip hasn't been all bad." She smiled at Wiley. "There's love in this group, and that counts for a lot."

"It does," Dave said. "Your loyalty to us is a big part of Joe's isolation, and that's the name of our game plan so far." He glanced over at Wiley before continuing. "My turn to spill all. My biggest achievement is getting our meeting tonight together without full court surveillance." He paused. "Let's see. What else have I done? Wiley suggested I try to co-opt Song. My words, not his, by the way. But my charms have been useless ... so far."

Debra Jean spoke up for the first time. "Why so much interest in Song? How could she help us?"

"We're working on isolating Joe, right? He doesn't trust Gloria, so Song is his main link to information and security."

Wiley opened his eyes and looked around. "Paul. Glad you're here. Anything you want to add?"

Paul returned his gaze. "I've barely talked to Joe during the whole trip, except for formal business meetings the first two days. I've spent most of my time with Debra Jean—"

"And I with Paul," Debra Jean interjected. "But that's not because of Joe."

"Say more," Wiley said.

"Well, things have changed. My motives for signing up with Revenge, Inc., are still there. I'm still angry at Joe, but I don't obsess about him as much. Nothing like when I first came to see you. But that doesn't mean my mind's not on revenge. Joe's a part of a larger picture. I've been having all these memories."

"What memories?" Dave asked.

"Very personal ones. I'd rather wait to talk about them."

"Your call," Dave said. "Ready, Wiley?"

Wiley nodded. "Where to begin ..."

Paul came out of his slump, looking animated. "I have some questions. I'd like to know what you thought of Joe. I was hoping that you and Joe would talk and get along. Then we could put this vendetta to rest, especially after what Debra Jean just said."

"You're misinterpreting me, Paul." She glowered at him.

Wiley leaned toward the group. "You've described him accurately, Paul. He's a powerhouse: shrewd, aggressive, and tuned in." Wiley reluctantly extricated himself from Gloria and sat up. "He got to me pretty quickly. He knew a lot about my past, and he used that information unmercifully. He led me into the most degrading parts of my personal life, questioned my value as a human being, and denigrated all my work for the past ten years. I wouldn't call that getting along ..."

"Wait a second," Dave interjected. "What's this about your work? Does he know about Revenge, Inc.?"

251

"Joe's a click away from figuring it out. He completely denied any connection to what happened at the Empress. He told me that he was down the hall at a party with a prostitute, which was why he left so quickly. … He kept focusing on why I had followed him to China. At first he was way off, but by the end of the conversation, he seemed to have homed in on something closer to the truth."

"Did Joe have any idea why I'm here?" Debra Jean asked, a quaver in her voice.

"Before our conversation, he was in the dark about why any of us are here. Me especially. I was his target. You barely came up. I was the one to bring up Jardinière and its aftermath."

"I don't like the way that sounds," she said.

Wiley let that hang in the air.

Dave broke the silence. "He didn't deny any of it?"

"He said she made a pass at him. He assumed that his response was what she wanted."

Debra Jean turned beet red.

"You OK?" Wiley asked.

"Of course not. But go on."

Wiley continued, "He said you were a clever enough postdoc, but letting you go was routine with young scientists who didn't fit into the program. He said that you came on to him, like many other attractive postdocs who wanted something from him. To him it was all part of the sexual politics of science. As I said, he implied that all you had to do was tell him to stop or find a more conducive venue."

"Nice," Gloria said under her breath.

"Bottom line, he couldn't accept that it was your concerns that had brought us here. He's partially correct, you know."

Debra Jean sat up straight, suddenly ablaze. "Meaning you and he don't take what he did to me seriously. He got you to join in his male trip, didn't he?"

Again Wiley was silent.

"Maybe he's right," Debra Jean said, her stomach knotted with anxiety. "What happened wasn't such a big deal." She had tears in her eyes.

Wiley looked at her carefully. "When you first visited Revenge, Inc., in Sausalito, we agreed to work with you. What happened to you still feels important. Don't be confused by comparisons about what else we found about Joe. With the behavior you described, there had to be much, much more. We told you that from the beginning."

"I guess I should take that as an expression of faith," Debra Jean said.

"He's very cagey," Dave said, breaking the mood. "He's saying, 'Sure, I'm a bad guy, but I'm not that bad: I like prostitutes but not children; I'm only slightly out of line with Debra Jean, and it's done all the time.' He works on making you feel stupid for accusing him. I'll bet you ended up feeling guilty about suspecting him of anything."

Wiley turned back to Debra Jean. "He certainly made me doubt why I am here."

The room was quiet. No one moved except Debra Jean, who turned away from the group.

Wiley looked at Paul. "Do you have anything to add?"

"Like telling us why you look so angry," Dave said.

"I'm more sad than angry," Paul said. "Listening to Wiley describe his conversation, it all sounds painfully familiar."

Dave moved swiftly to a kneeling position on his chair. "Wiley, I need to say something here."

"We all guessed that!" Gloria rejoined.

Dave winked at her. "It's like you brought Joe's spirit down here with you. It's affecting our whole group. Sure, Debra Jean isn't the child victims at the Empress, but she's important. And by the way, so are those children. Soon we'll be writing them off, too, along with Debra Jean."

"Is he strong enough to affect all of us through a short contact with Wiley?" Gloria asked.

Dave moved again, to sit cross-legged. "Only if we let him."

Debra Jean eyed Wiley and Dave in turn. "From the beginning, you both told me that revenge is never a straight line. What Joe did to me took two years of my life. To him, it was just one of his little games, but it destroyed my world. What he did to me feels different now, though. You said that revenge is a psychological process that can be transformative. Well, it's happening. This may sound foolish, but I can almost feel myself ... evolving."

There was a long silence. Dave finally broke it and turned to Debra Jean. "That's a fantastic comment. Now how do you want us to proceed? Do I need to mention that it's your dollar?"

She stood up and began to pace. "Learning more bad things about Joe hasn't made it easier for me. I'm one of his victims, a very minor one compared with others, probably tons of others. It takes a lot to believe that I still count. But that's what Revenge, Inc., does, isn't it? You offer your revenge clients the possibility of action, but only along with some big-time reflection."

"Right. So I take it your revenge fantasies are part of what's transformed?" Dave asked.

"Like the one where I cut off his nuts?" She supplied graphic hand motions. The room dissolved in a chorus of laughter. Dave said, "Yeah. That one."

"When I began this process, all I wanted was to get even with him. Activating that idea has led in very strange directions: the Empress, Paul, China, and a lot of soul-searching."

"Soul searching?" Dave questioned.

"Well, I always had fantasies about Paul. Maybe I showed some of that, and it got picked up as flirting and made Joe jealous and me more attractive. It wouldn't be the first time that happened between friends."

Gloria laughed. "Come on, girl. You and Paul were part of the company gossip way before all this happened."

Debra Jean blushed. "I knew that."

"Me too." Paul echoed.

"I was angry with Joe at Jardinière, but later on maybe I was even angrier at you, Paul. I never thought it was you who touched me, but I sure felt you betrayed me. I was losing my research, my job, and you did nothing to stop it. It was easier to blame Joe for fingering me in a restaurant, but it was your doing nothing that really hurt."

"And if things had worked out for us on this trip," Paul asked, "would you still want to hurt Joe?"

"Yes, and as Wiley keeps telling us, taking you away from Joe is here-and-now revenge. Two birds with one stone, so to speak."

"Exactly," Dave said. "So, should we enjoy the rest of this trip and go home? Which is why this whole issue of what happened at the Empress keeps coming up. Wiley, do you believe what Joe said about not being in that room with the children?"

Wiley looked uncertain. "He said I had it all wrong, that the smoke in the hall made it impossible to see who was there. He could be right. I never actually saw him leave the room where the children were. Can anyone say they did? Dave? Gloria?"

"I can't be absolutely sure," Gloria said, "but I know he was behind it."

"What about you, Dave?" Wiley said.

"No. I didn't see him leave that room, but like Gloria, I have no doubts about his role."

Paul stirred from his lethargy and began talking from a whisper deep inside. "That's the trouble here. It's always been more about those children than what Joe did to Debra Jean. And now it turns out that there is no proof that Joe was involved in what happened at the Empress."

Wiley turned to Paul. "You know Joe so well. You've told us he was involved in bad things. The children, what we described —is that something he could do? Your judgment is important here."

"I just don't know. How can I know that? I wasn't there."

"We need your opinion, Paul," Dave said angrily. "You know more than you're saying about your colleague."

"Why push him, Dave?" Debra Jean said. "He's doing his best."

"Speaking of action, you put a man in the hospital, Dave," Paul said.

"Where he belonged," Dave muttered.

"But there's no absolute proof about the children," Paul retorted.

Dave stood and circled the room. "Answer my question, Paul," he snapped.

Paul was quiet, his eyes opaque. Dave looked at him in disgust.

"Take it easy, Dave," Wiley said. "Paul's been with us all the way in this. Besides, we're not a hanging jury that decides who's guilty and who's innocent. Debra Jean is our client, not Paul." He leaned back in Gloria's arms and continued. "Look, guys, we're all in this together. Revenge uncovers our most powerful emotions. Dave always says it pushes at the line between fantasy and action, and we're at that line right now."

Gloria said, "I'm sympathetic to what happened to you, Debra Jean."

"Thanks, Gloria."

"But it's not why I'm here. That scene in the hotel room haunts me and conjures up all the loss, all the evil I've lived with since the death of my parents: the destruction of my village and home, the outrages at the orphanage, not to mention the hypocrisy of my 'Christian' adoptive parents. I want revenge on all of them. So yes, I'm biased.

"And I know that Joe was in that room." Gloria's body tensed with anger, and her voiced was bitter as she remembered their first degrading encounter. "Believe me, I know. I saw Zvi with the children, entering the hotel and herding them into the elevator. I don't know what to do, but I can't leave it alone and play nice as Paul suggests."

Paul stood and faced down Gloria. "What can you possibly know about my friend? It's all bullshit." He turned to the group. "You're all part of a very dangerous charade! You're using sex, bad childhoods, job losses, whatever you can think of, to destroy someone who has done more good in the world than all of you combined."

Dave stood and moved to block Paul. Then he caught a warning glance from Wiley, turned away from Paul, and went back to his seat. Wiley freed himself from Gloria's arms. "Paul, you're saying that Joe is a stand-in for all our revenge needs. It's possible."

Paul's voice was cold. "Wiley, that's classic scapegoating. I'm not going to be part of labeling my friend a criminal based on flimsy data and supposition."

"Even if he is, Paul?" Dave said.

Paul half-stood up and then slumped back, his hands folded across his chest with an air of defiance.

Debra Jean turned toward Paul and stroked his cheek. "We all know who Joe is. What we've seen is more than enough for me, and I'm including what he did to you, Paul. It must be hard to take a good look at your best friend after all these years." She shifted in her seat. "It's had its good side, too. It got us into bed together and brought you into my heart."

She smiled and turned to face Gloria. "I'm not planning to spend all my days as a doc in Walnut Creek, and I'm not going to let my science be sidetracked again by some man I treat like a daddy. I've got a problem to solve in molecular genetics and the money to start my own lab. If you're up for it, you can manage my empire."

"What you really need is someone to manage your love life." Gloria chuckled and stroked Wiley's thigh with a long painted nail.

"That too. So, as you can see, Wiley, I've got what I wanted from

Revenge, Inc. I'm not sure what comes next in my life, but I know now it can't just focus on making Joe a better man or figuring out how to destroy him."

"So we're back to the top, Debra Jean," Wiley said. "Your contract with Revenge, Inc., is almost at an end."

"I know. I need to talk with Joe first. After that, I have some plans that I think I can carry out all on my own."

Dave said, "I'm glad, Debra Jean. But Joe may have other ideas. He's not finished with us, and what he has in mind may not be pleasant."

"Talking with Joe might help," Debra Jean said hesitantly.

"And have some unintended consequences. Revenge cuts both ways. He's pretty angry."

"Exactly right." Paul stiffened.

"Maybe I can cool him off," Debra Jean persisted.

Gloria stirred. "Joe may not be finished with us. Well, I'm not finished with him. Debra Jean can have her conversation, and you guys can terminate the contract, but Joe isn't going away for me."

"She's right, Wiley," Dave said. "There's a decision here that is not about our contract with Debra Jean."

"Right now I need to get a shower and some rest," Wiley said.

There were footsteps at the door, the sound of a piece of paper being slipped under it, and footsteps again, disappearing down the hall.

Dave sprang to his feet, walked quickly to the door, and picked up the note. He looked it over and sighed with relief. Then he walked back to the group and said, "Shall I read it? It's from the ship's tour manager."

"Of course," Gloria said.

"'To our guests,'" Dave began. "'Tomorrow morning at 10 a.m. we will be offering two outings: a boat trip to a small gorge off the river, and a walk to the new city that our government has built to resettle villagers on the riverbank. Please sign up with the purser if you are interested in either outing. Tomorrow evening we will reach the dam. It takes several hours to go through the great locks. Plan to be on board. It is a sight you will not want to miss. During the passage, there will be a party hosted by our cruise company, to begin at 7 p.m. We hope it has been a pleasant journey so far. The best is yet to come.'"

"It's signed 'Song Lee, Administration,'" Dave said. "So there's an end game brewing for all of us."

They split up quickly with little talk. Paul and Debra Jean left the room first. Gloria clung to Wiley, sensing his exhaustion.

Dave stood and began to stretch. "Wiley, we need to talk."

"Sorry," Wiley said, putting an arm around Gloria, "but it's going to have to wait till the morning."

Dave looked at the romantic pair. "Play before work. OK. Watch out for any hidden cameras."

"Get out of here, Dave," Wiley said affably from the couch.

"I'm going to take that tour of the new city. I need a word or two with Song."

"Is this about our case?" Wiley asked. "Or are you testing whether she's interested in you?"

"All of the above and more. This project has been a cause célèbre for environmentalists around the world. Would you believe I'm interested in the effects of the dam on the river people?"

Wiley said, "Social consciousness is part of your heritage."

"What's his heritage?" Gloria asked as Dave left the room, carefully closing the door behind him.

"I'll tell you later," Wiley said, taking Gloria's hand and leading her to the bedroom.

CHAPTER 37

Best Friends

Joe stared at the large plasma screen mounted on the wall of the security room. "Well, at least now we know a little more about the Americans," he said to Song, who was listening intently through earphones. "Your idea of slipping a tiny mike under the door with that tourist update was inspired. It's too bad we could only monitor the end of the meeting."

"We have the audio until then," said Song, "and of course we have a visual of your earlier conversation with Stone. It's one of the few places on the ship with good video surveillance. But of course you know that. You knew that when you chose the meeting place."

"I try to be careful with everyone, including you, Song."

"Our camera captured him threatening you. You were very close to going overboard, and with the propellers so close … At first viewing, it shows Stone as a violent man trying to kill you. Were you frightened, Dr. Diamond?"

"I was in danger, but I was never frightened."

"We have more than enough to arrest Stone and hold some of the other Americans as accomplices."

"Not yet, Song," Joe said quickly. "But we do need to be ready for more violence."

"I already radioed Shanghai police for a security team. They'll be here in the morning. In any case, there will be an interrogation."

Joe smiled. "Your call. By the way, who dismantled the surveillance during that meeting?"

"Dave Blue. He did a very good job," she said admiringly.

"Why didn't you stop him?" Joe asked.

"He would have found out. We wanted the meeting to take place, and we wanted something on him."

Joe nodded and looked up at the monitor. "I take it someone will keep a close watch on Stone tonight."

Song acknowledged his request with a grimace. "I doubt that we'll learn much. They'll be in his bedroom all night."

"Turn up the volume. They'll have a lot to say to one another." Joe stood up, an amused smile playing on his lips as he thought about his conversation with Wiley. "You've done a good job, Song. But we still don't know what Stone and the others might be planning. Keep on it. And there's also Blue. He said he's signing up for the visit to the new city that you're leading."

"People who choose my tour usually do so for political reasons or to emphasize their social conscience when they return home."

"Yes. That could be Blue's motive," Joe said. "San Francisco is a very liberal city, eager to find fault with others."

"He should worry about his own country," Song said angrily.

"It's also about you. He said as much at the end of the meeting, remember?"

She shrugged. "My office asked me to see how the new city is faring. And the trip works out well with our call to Shanghai. It might make things easier if we don't have to deal with Blue and Stone together."

"I'm sure your men can handle themselves with unarmed Americans! But you didn't answer my question—is Blue interested in you? Are you interested in him? You might find him attractive."

"You think so?" Song rose to her feet and walked up to Joe. "I agree with your taste. Dave Blue is very attractive, but so are you, Dr. Diamond." She lifted her eyes to his. "Unlike Gloria Garcia, I don't mix business and pleasure, nor do I use my body as a means for gathering information."

"You're careful, Song," Joe said, smiling.

"Perhaps too careful. That's what you're implying." She looked meaningfully at him. "But it's safer. You can be sure that Dave Blue will not get what he may want from me."

"Apparently neither will I," Joe said under his breath. "Goodnight, Song."

Joe left the surveillance office and walked slowly up the stairs to the observation deck and his room. Song was more unsure of herself than she showed, he thought. He wondered what Song planned for Wiley's inquest after the trip was over and whether he should watch. There would probably be nothing subtle about the encounter.

His room was an icebox. He turned off the air conditioning, opened the sliding glass door to the balcony, and stepped out into the balmy evening. The sky was clear. The almost-full moon lit the river. Many lights dotted the cliffs above the flooded riverbank. New life was already springing up in a land with far too many people.

He walked back inside and closed the sliding doors behind him. The room was already hot. He turned the air conditioning back on and used the bathroom. Then he lay down on his bed and closed his eyes, mentally reviewing the tape he had seen of the meeting. Unfortunately, Paul's face and body were often hidden. The camera had shown Debra Jean making several little speeches with obvious emotion. Paul had listened, looking more forlorn than interested. Joe felt pity for his friend's sexual humiliation. Why had he repeatedly submitted to failed encounters that threatened a generation of friendship?

From Paul's face, even without words, it was clear that he had not betrayed Joe to the group. But Joe also saw that Paul's loyalty to their relationship was slipping. His presence at that meeting was evidence enough. Paul was on the edge of leaving him, Joe thought, and despite Paul's impotence, Debra Jean was the catalyst. The two of them had not been close at the meeting—no passion there, like that between Wiley and Gloria—but they were definitely comfortable together. The end of the meeting made it pretty clear that punishing Joe and usurping Paul's loyalty to him were their goals. They all had to be dealt with, or the painful vacuum in his chest would never go away.

He settled on 10 milligrams of Valium to move him past anxiety into sleep.

CHAPTER 38

Sick at Heart

It was still early in the morning when Song, in a staff uniform of white shirt, brown shorts, and brown baseball cap, guided three sturdy Taiwanese couples up the gravel road that led to the new city poised on high cliffs overlooking the river. A fierce purplish sun shone defiantly through the chemical haze rising from a factory downstream. Across the river, the *Viking Century Sky* was docked at the riverside quay under an old steel bridge, now disgorging Taiwanese and European tourists to waiting motorboats for the trip down a small tributary leading to the famous Wu Gorge.

Dave, taking long sips of coffee from a paper cup, loped across the bridge next to where the *Viking* was docked, in pursuit of Song's tour group.

Once he reached the other side, Dave slowed his pace to match the group's and then kept his distance. The new city was still under construction. Large stone boulders, rolls of wire mesh, piles of steel girders, the detritus from cement mixers, and garbage of all kinds blocked parts of the road. White dust and the omnipresent black coal particles hung in the air, creating a visible shimmer. But despite the contaminated air, it felt good to be outdoors, away from the boat. Dave busied himself with watching the slight provocative sway of Song's hips far out in front. Her simple unisex uniform made her look far more feminine than the tailored suit she wore in her more official capacities on the ship.

After a half-hour march upward, Song detached herself from her Taiwanese charges and fell back to join Dave.

"Up late, Mr. Blue?" she said, eyeing the empty paper cup in his hand.

"I'd be sleeping in if it weren't for this tour ... and please call me Dave." He crushed the cup and put it into a pocket of his shorts.

"I will try, but my job requires formality."

"What exactly is your job?"

"Tour guide, of course. That's why we are both here. And I hope you will find this tour and the rest of the trip very interesting," she said cheerily.

"I've been following the progress of the Three Gorges Dam project ever since I was in engineering student in college. The construction of the largest dam in the world is a very big deal, and I'm grateful to be here for the opening. The decision to relocate a million and a half of your own people, not to mention the possibility of an ecological disaster, is also of great interest to me. My God, nothing in large building enterprises has happened like it since Nasser dammed the Nile River at Aswan."

"Most of our American and European tourists criticize us rather than trying to understand our country's needs." She paused. "Americans and Chinese have much in common. We both love 'big.' To me, your country is a land of big skies, skyscrapers, long cars, and huge shopping malls. It is our turn now; the dam is our flagship toward the future."

"Have you been to my country?" Dave asked.

"No. But I've studied a great deal about it. It's our model. The speed of development in the 19th and early 20th centuries was breathtaking, and no one complained about pollution except the immigrants who labored for you. Perhaps you do not know that many Chinese immigrants lost their lives building your transcontinental railroad."

"You've had a difficult history with colonial powers, including ours."

"We need to be strong so that we will never be dominated again. China also needs sources of power that don't pollute." She wiped her hand across her forehead and pointed to the black grime on her fingers. "The Three Gorges Dam will help our people, although it is a hardship for some. The greatest good for the greatest number is official government policy. Most tourists prefer beautiful scenery to social exploration, and I can't blame them."

"The Wu Gorge on a cool riverboat seems far more appealing," Dave said as he plodded up the path, sweating profusely.

"Then why have you come here this morning?"

"I've told you, Song. I am interested in the dam and its effects on the local population. But I am also interested in you."

"So you are a social activist?" she asked, pointedly ignoring his personal reference.

He nodded. "But my interest is also about the extinction of beauty. I'm glad to be here before the river reaches its full height and the gorges change forever," Dave said. He felt unexpected pain at the thought, and it showed in his face.

"It is sad when you say it that way," she said slowly. "But the dam itself is an amazing structure besides its great economic importance."

"You're determined to be a proper tour guide."

She blushed. "But that is my job, Mr. Blue. You have no idea how hard I worked to get here."

"And of course I do not believe it's your only job, Song."

She was silent and began to walk away from him toward the group.

"OK, then," he called to her. She slowed. "Do your job. Tell me about this city above us. What does the very best tour guide in China, and one of the prettiest, say about that?"

She smiled. "She would say that it's a great success. All our tour guides are told to emphasize that."

"Do you always spout the official policy and follow orders?" Dave asked.

She looked sternly at him. "I'll be happy to tell you more than the official line if you stop being so sarcastic. But to the second point, I don't know what you mean by following orders."

"With all respect, Song, I think you do."

She tossed her head as if shaking off the idea. "Building the dam was first proposed in 1919 by Sun Yat-sen as a method of flood control. The coming of communism, and Mao, and then the Cultural Revolution intervened. Sun Yat-sen's vision reemerged when we began our accelerated development in the early 1990s."

"Accelerated development? I'd call it an explosion! Chongqing blew my mind."

"A peasant's city, Mr. Blue. Wait till you see Shanghai." She spoke with enthusiasm. "But the dam has had problems, and not just in engineering. The project has been plagued with cost overruns, unsafe working conditions, and corruption and bribes of every description. Public works projects seem to bring out the worst of us in our country."

Dave said, "A couple of years ago, a tunnel collapsed in Boston because of shoddy materials. The contractors are probably sunning themselves in the Cayman Islands."

"I read about that." She smiled. "Unfortunately, we often copy rather than learn from your experience. We had other problems—political problems. Our relationship with the Soviet Union, for example. We've done much better without their engineers, and with some help from the Americans and Europeans."

She pointed far downstream at the brick-red arc spanning the river. "Perhaps you are familiar with that structure. It is based on the famous Golden Gate Bridge in your hometown. Does it look like it, Mr. Blue?" She sounded like a little girl.

"Very much," Dave answered sincerely.

"We call it the New Rainbow Bridge, and it is a symbol of hope for this project."

As they looked at the bridge, Dave moved his arm so that their hands touched. She didn't pull away. She was so much more free and open compared with how she had been during the brief visit to his room. He wondered what had changed. "We should continue to walk," she said. "It's another half-mile."

"And you must return to your other guests. But before you go, tell me more about how this new city came about."

"We first thought that the village people could be moved uphill from the flooding area."

"So what happened?"

"Too little land. Our engineers vastly underestimated the height of the flooding river."

"Typical. Our engineers' motto is build first, then worry about the consequences."

"Ours too. It was decided that building a new city was a better solution."

"And how is it working?" Dave asked, looking at a remarkably stylish apartment building coming into view above them.

"We don't know. That is part of why I am here. We misjudged the psychology of these people. They are river people and rural farmers. They have no experience with cities."

"But surely there were some cities on the riverbanks."

"A few, and the people who lived there were not peasants but wealthy landowners. In the new city, they were the ones who got the best new apartments. The poor were sent elsewhere or crowded together in the small apartments."

"You are certainly being very forthcoming this morning," Dave marveled.

"Well, why not? It is my job to answer your questions."

Dave smiled. He touched her hand again.

Song tilted her face upward to look directly at him. "I'm sorry. People will see us and will talk. Let's catch up with the rest of the group." She set off, and Dave walked slightly behind her.

"At least finish the story."

"I'll have to stop when we reach the others. The Taiwanese require positive stories, so we tell them of our successes."

"We call that propaganda."

It was her turn to smile. "We call it 'simultaneous truths.'"

"And therefore many falsehoods."

"It's an art form in China. Perhaps it's harder for Americans to understand. You are a more straightforward people."

"Blunt, you mean. We're pretty good at just plain lying," Dave said. "But the truth works for me. Always has, fool that I am."

Song said, "One of the many truths about these new cities is simple: they are full of troublemakers. Many are not river people. Perhaps they use one local relative to gain a foothold; then they bribe officials. Once they get an apartment, they bring their 'extended family,' who are rarely family, just strangers who pay large bribes. Besides, farmers have a cultural prejudice against working in the mines. There is little effort to retrain them in something palatable. The government turns a blind eye to who comes and goes. Labor for mining coal is our top priority."

"I see."

She seemed to feel compelled to talk. "We copied your idea of creating freestanding space to encourage spontaneous community activity.

Unfortunately, some of our younger citizens turned those spaces into Internet cafés, which support drug use and insurrection."

They stopped to rest and gaze at the river far below. The boats on the Yangtze looked like toys floating in a small stream. Dave estimated they had climbed more than 1,500 feet in the blazing heat.

She looked ahead at the rest of the group. "As you can see, the Taiwanese are also resting too, so there's no rush."

"So the rural people here fare poorly."

"They rarely stay. They are very unhappy in this kind of environment," Song said quietly, not hiding her sadness.

"I'm sorry, Song."

"It was the natural fallout from our policy of many truths. We did what Chinese governments have always done, what was done to my family two generations ago."

"So your family was relocated to keep them quiet?" Dave asked, increasingly confused about her motives for this talk but sensing that the story was important to her.

"My grandparents were linguists. During the Cultural Revolution, they were labeled as counterrevolutionaries. They were taken from their university jobs in Beijing and sent to the countryside to teach and work the land. They barely survived. My parents grew up as farmers and I saw their unhappiness. I wanted to change things. Many in my generation do. We put up with a great deal to have the kind of life our parents lost."

Tears in her eyes, she walked rapidly away from Dave, heading for the rest of the group. He watched her open her pack and distribute snacks. Then she returned and handed him an apple, some crackers, and a bottle of water.

He thanked her. "I appreciate your confidences."

"Just because I confide in you, Mr. Blue, do not think you are so special. I often tell Americans this story. I have learned they are moved by it."

"Clever of you."

She stood looking at the river. "You seem like a decent man, but it is hard to have a good conversation with you with such secrets between us. For example, I would appreciate knowing if you are employed by your government."

"I do not work for my government, Song," Dave said. "My presence here is all about Joe Diamond and what he's done to others."

"Why do you keep saying that to me?"

"Because it is true. He may be valuable to your country, but he's an evil man, and he will bring his vices with him to this country, Song. He torments children in ways you don't want to hear about."

"Is that why you are all here?"

"That and other things he's done."

"Wiley Stone too?"

"Perhaps. Why do you mention Wiley now?"

Song hesitated. "I do not trust him the way I trust you. I feel you and I … are similar, capable of great depth." She turned away from him, embarrassed. "I think Mr. Stone knows nothing about difficulties such as we have experienced."

"'We'?"

"Yes. I feel you know about being a victim."

"You're wrong about Wiley, Song," Dave said as he followed her uphill. "He is more like you than you think."

She turned back to him. "Please stay for the tour. I will speak English for your benefit. Most Taiwanese will understand."

Dave felt caught up in her feelings. "I'd prefer to wander and see the new city for myself. Is that OK? Is it safe for me?"

"Yes, of course. Foreigners are not the targets of people here."

She walked slowly away, this time without looking back. Dave stared down at the river and the New Rainbow Bridge. He felt a twinge of homesickness for more familiar waterscapes of the Marin Headlands and San Francisco.

The river was filled with boats, probably the result of increasing traffic near the dam. Dave took out a pocket monocular and scanned the plethora of boats. This was not his childhood picture postcard of Chinese junks and scrap metal vessels. Here were medium-size container ships and huge barges loaded with coal. He scanned the horizon. There were a few specks in the sky coming upriver, probably commercial flights from Beijing and Shanghai headed for the dam's headquarters at Yichang. Seeing the planes made Dave feel uneasy and disheartened. What had they accomplished here? The conversation with Song had been sweet but led nowhere. Wiley's strategy had been too imprecise, Dave thought. Joe easily withstood the pressure they were able to bring.

He caught up with the group, but Song was speaking in Chinese and barely nodded. Dave left them standing together and took one of the side streets away from the river. The air was cleaner up here, away from the river industry. Most of the traffic consisted of motorcycles pulling carts. There were large islands of public space: patios and gardens lined with stone benches, small working fountains, and even some modest sculpture. A few people loitered on the streets, which were practically empty now; probably everyone was at work. He imagined clandestine meetings monitored by government spies. He imagined aggressive arrests and dispersal by tear gas and clubs. He slowed to a walk. Above, on top of the hills, were fancier high-rise apartments and a few private villas commanding the best views of the river.

Rejoining the road, he saw people congregating in what looked like a small shopping center. It had the low-class ugliness of an American strip mall. Bicycles were parked in front of the small shops. No one bothered him; few even looked. Why not, he wondered? How many six-foot-five white tourists had they seen?

Thirsty from the climb, Dave entered a store that looked like a 7-Eleven and bought a bottle of water. The clerk was polite but taciturn. The people in the streets continued to avert their eyes. Lured by the sound of children playing, he turned inland again and followed the chatter. Across a wide street, he saw a two-story building and next to it a large playground. Children in clean uniforms of white shirts and blue pants were playing on new equipment identical to that in suburban parks in the United States—made in the same Chinese factory, Dave thought. The children looked alert, healthy, and well behaved. He peered in through the wire fence and waited. After a little while, two eight-year-olds sidled over and peered furtively back. A stern adult quickly followed them and motioned for them to come away. So much for meeting the natives.

Dave followed the fence around the playground, beguiled by the similarity of the children's features, so different from the population of a similar school in San Francisco. There were no white faces, no black faces, no Indians or Southeast Asians or Japanese or Pacific Islanders. But there was something else. Despite the homogeneity, there were no outright similarities. Then it struck him. There were no brothers or sisters and no sibling behavior. It was a schoolyard full of one-per-family children. In this schoolyard was the new heart and soul of China, the behavioral legacy of the one-child policy, and a new and unknown variable for the generations to come.

Dave walked back the way he had come, looking for Song and the Taiwanese. As he approached the river, he heard the drone of an aircraft. It came from a transport-sized helicopter flying low over the river, toward the New Rainbow Bridge. With a sense of foreboding, he took out his monocular and followed the machine's progress in the air. It circled the docking area and then swooped over the *Viking Century Sky*, anchored on the far bank, and landed on a patch of yellow grass nearby. Dave did not wait to see who would emerge once the craft stabilized. He knew. He scanned the pedestrian walkway along the river for Song's baseball hat but couldn't find her. He raced through the streets, finally locating the group at another small shopping center a few blocks away.

"Song, I need to talk to you."

She ignored him.

"Please."

"What?" she said with a smile.

"That helicopter."

"What helicopter?"

"You must have heard it—a large military helicopter is landing 100 feet from the *Viking Century Sky*." Studying her reaction, he handed her his monocular. "Here, take a look."

She turned away from him and back to the group.

"Why is it there?"

"I don't know."

"It's about us, isn't it? About Wiley and me."

"Why would you think that?"

He raised his voice loud enough that the Taiwanese could hear. "Song, why is that helicopter landing next to our cruise ship?"

As he had intended, the Taiwanese turned toward her. He hoped they thought it was about them.

"You're behaving rudely, Mr. Blue." Dave took two steps toward her and grasped her shoulder. "I want to know."

"Let go of me, Mr. Blue!" Song cried, trying to duck away from him. He tightened his grip. Two of the Taiwanese men moved hesitatingly toward Dave.

"Why not just tell me, Song?"

"This will get you into trouble," Song warned.

"Is Wiley the target?" He looked around and saw several men in uniform approaching from the nearby street. He released her arm but stayed close. "Please!"

"Look, Mr. Blue, your friend threatened Dr. Diamond. He pushed him into the railing. Dr. Diamond almost went over …"

"That doesn't sound like Wiley."

"It's on video. And believe me, it doesn't look pretty."

Dave backed away. Wiley rarely made mistakes, but Dave believed Song. "So you brought in some backup men to handle him. And made sure I couldn't help him." The uniformed men had circled them and were asking Song something in Chinese. She pulled a badge and identification out of her pocket and waved them off. They looked surprised but backed away a few yards, watching carefully.

"That sounds like overreacting to me."

"No, I don't think so. Dr. Diamond is important to us. He's my responsibility. You and Mr. Stone are saying terrible things about him to me and others. Mr. Stone tried to kill him last night. Then you dismantled our surveillance so that you could meet together, laughing and drinking and plotting against him. That's a serious crime in my country. Can you blame me for calling in help? This is simply a show of force to get your attention. And prevent violence."

"You're completely misreading the situation, Song."

"You come to our cruise as tourists, and then you threaten a great scientist and our country's friend. You and Mr. Stone are huge, Mr. Blue. You are frightening."

"This is crazy."

"You and Mr. Stone were never tourists."

"So I'm here and Wiley's with your goons!" Dave shouted angrily, but he felt like a fool. "Nice planning, Song."

"They're not goons. They're highly trained professional policemen who will do their job with appropriate restraint. Besides, I didn't have

271

to persuade you to come on this outing, Mr. Blue," Song chided him. "I just let you know I was going along." She smiled and turned away.

Dave lowered his voice but kept talking. "Perhaps, just perhaps, you are honestly doing your job. But Song, you have no way of knowing how wrong you are about Joe. Dammit, you don't want to see or know anything that doesn't fit into the party line—like the pollution or coal dust or the desperation in this city." He watched through his monocular as people in uniforms and helmets descended from the helicopter.

"Go back home, Mr. Blue, and fix your own country. You and Mr. Stone have brought threats and subterfuge, while Dr. Diamond has been nothing but helpful and sensible. He's our benefactor. He certainly has earned our protection against vigilante Americans," Song said angrily. "You bring charm and nothing else."

The helicopter slowly rose into the sky. Dave looked through his glass and saw the uniformed men walking toward the ship.

"You're going after the wrong guy, and it's going to cost you, Song." She turned away with disdain. The threat sounded hollow. He knew that what was happening was his and Wiley's own fault. Sick at heart, he began the long run downhill.

CHAPTER 39

Gymnastics

Wiley woke to the sound of propeller blades cutting through the air. He heard the whoosh of a descending vehicle and the cacophony of a nearby landing. A soft hand shook him gently. He opened his eyes. Gloria was sitting up, holding a sheet to her naked chest. She looked unexpectedly vulnerable after a night of uncompromising lust. He fumbled for his watch on the table next to his pillow. It was almost noon.

"What is that sound?" Gloria asked.

"I think it's a helicopter landing nearby. Probably bringing supplies or personnel."

"Maybe they're going to arrest us for depraved unmarried sex." Gloria snuggled against his chest.

"Mmmm. Maybe, but it would be worth it. You feel so good."

She pulled the sheet more securely over her body and moved still closer. "We're forgetting that helicopter." He pushed her gently away and sat up. "Could they really be coming for us?" she said.

"Seems unlikely." Wiley grabbed at her sheet, leaving her breasts naked, her nipples erect. He gazed at her breasts. "You're perfect."

She tugged the sheet back under her neck. "Show's over. Time to check out that machine that's roaring in our ears."

Wiley rolled off the bed. "Just in case there's trouble, let's get dressed."

"Spoilsport," she laughed, but followed suit.

Wiley hastily pulled on briefs and jeans. He carefully opened the shades to the balcony and peered out while Gloria changed in the bathroom. A Bell 412 police helicopter stood on a narrow field just 100 yards away. Four men in loose dark attire climbed down and walked in line toward the ship. A fifth, wearing an elegant white linen summer suit, followed at a distance.

Gloria, now fully clothed, joined Wiley at the window. "What do you think is going on?"

"Somebody has brought an assault team to check out the *Viking*." He walked to the phone and dialed Dave's room. "No answer. He's probably still on the tour of the new city. Most of the passengers who took the gorge tour are probably gone as well."

She shivered inadvertently. "If we're the target, they picked a good time to come. When I was a child, the soldiers would wait until the men had gone. There's no resistance when only the old people, women, and children are left in the camp. Of course you make it all different." She trembled and Wiley put his arm around her. Their night together had left him completely open to her.

"Maybe I should go," Gloria said.

"Soon. Remember, we've done nothing wrong. If it's about one of us, we should be together. I'll make us a cup of coffee."

He filled the small coffee machine with beans and water, and flicked a switch that glowed red. Gloria stayed at the window. "They're definitely coming on board." There was a load roar of an engine firing up. "And the helicopter is leaving, which means the men are staying."

"I don't like this," Wiley said, tying his shoelaces.

"Guilty conscience," she said anxiously.

"More like fear."

"I'll bet Song's behind it." Gloria put her arms around Wiley and hugged him close.

Loud footsteps echoed in the corridor leading to their room. There was a knock on the door. "Please open."

"Not good," Wiley said softly, and finished pouring a cup of coffee for each of them. He moved toward the door. "Who is it?" he barked.

"It's a police officer. If you are Mr. Wiley Stone. I'd like to talk to you."

Wiley opened the door carefully. The man in the white suit stood in front of him. Two uniformed men were behind him. Two others were at attention several feet down the hall.

"My name is Chang Yung. Can I come in?" the man said.

"I'd rather you didn't. I have a guest."

Chang, followed by two of the men, pushed in. Wiley reached around them and closed the door.

"So now that you're in, what's this about?"

"I would be pleased if you called me Chang. It is easier for Americans." He took a badge from the inside pocket of his jacket and held it up to Wiley. He was stocky, about five-foot-four, and looked to be around 35 years old. He spoke English with a distinct Southern American accent. "I'm the head of Special Services and attached to the Shanghai police." He nodded to Gloria and then bowed slightly to Wiley. "My sincere apologies for interrupting your morning."

Gloria moved to Wiley's side.

"Why are you here?" Wiley asked.

"We were asked to come here by Ms. Song. She told us you had threatened one of our VIP passengers. Song will explain further when she gets back from the city tour."

He held out his hand to Gloria.

"Gloria Garcia."

Chang bowed slightly.

"We could use breakfast," Wiley said. "We would be happy if you would join us."

"I'd like to question you privately, Mr. Stone."

"Do you mean away from your men?" Wiley asked, glancing at the silent pair. "Or from Ms. Garcia?"

Chang nodded. "Both, for the moment. Perhaps out on the balcony." He glanced up at the ceiling. "We could talk more frankly with fewer cameras."

Gloria walked away from the two men. "If you don't mind, I will freshen up."

Chang watched her leave the room. "A beautiful woman, Mr. Stone." Wiley smiled benignly as Chang cleared the room of his soldiers.

"European breakfast, Mr. Stone?" he said when he returned.

"Wiley. Wait a moment," Wiley said. He conferred with Gloria through the closed bathroom door. Then he picked up the phone and ordered two American breakfasts with eggs, pancakes, bacon, muffins, orange juice, and coffee. Still holding the receiver, he turned to Chang.

"I've ordered for Gloria. And for you, Mr. Chang."

"I like what you ordered." He took the phone from Wiley and spoke in rapid Chinese. "I've also ordered something for my men. They will eat in an open room down the hall."

They moved to the balcony and pulled two chairs around a small glass table. Chang said, "This will give us some privacy." He sighed. "The river is so beautiful in the morning, don't you think?"

"What is this about, Mr. Chang?" Wiley asked.

"I've already told you. Song called for help and we responded. She was worried about Dr. Diamond's safety. Song believes that you and your friend Dave Blue are more than tourists, that your visit to China is related to Dr. Diamond. Those inferences and your attack, apparently caught on video, were enough to bring us here. More than enough, don't you think?"

"I'd like Ms. Garcia to hear this. Dr. Diamond hired her to help with his security."

Chang nodded.

Wiley walked back into the room and knocked on the bathroom door. Gloria appeared, looking ravishing in a tight yellow blouse, matching shorts, and high-heeled sandals emphasizing her long legs. He bent down and kissed her on the lips, and then took her hand as they both joined Chang, who held a chair for her.

"Mr. Chang is worried about Joe Diamond's safety," Wiley told Gloria. "Song says I attacked him. There is a video of the event."

"I have not been allowed access to the security tapes," Gloria said.

"I am not a violent man," Wiley said. "My size and strength gives me that responsibility. But there was an episode that could have looked like an attack. I would like to see the video."

"Song says you are aggressive. You will understand my concern."

"Films can be doctored," Wiley said, feeling anything but confident. "But first, Mr. Chang, it would help if I understood your relationship with Song."

"Song's authority should be obvious to you."

"Not at all," Wiley asserted. "I know little about police bureaucracies in my own country, let alone China. It's far from obvious how it is that Song can request help and a team of men, including an officer of your obvious abilities, hops on the next helicopter."

"You would understand if you understood China."

"Then explain."

"It is not a secret that Song is a Party member. I had no choice but to

276

agree to her request for assistance. Song's authority is also limited by my role. Dr. Diamond made an informal complaint against you, Mr. Stone. Whatever Song finds, I will make an independent report."

Wiley frowned. "If there is no formal complaint, then I have to ask again why you are here."

"This is not an investigation, Mr. Stone. It's a fact-finding exploration of the situation. I was in the United States for two years. In Washington, D.C., I was trained by an agency of your government in police methods, including appropriate limits. What I am doing would be similar in your country."

"Hardly reassuring."

Chang laughed. "We are not here to trouble you without reason. Frankly, I see this as a pleasant outing for my team. Shanghai is very hot at this time of year. The river is a nicer spot despite the pollution."

"Let's be honest, Mr. Chang. A helicopter and four armed men is hardly a pleasant outing."

"We are concerned about any risk to Dr. Diamond." He stood and walked around the table to Wiley's side. "Let me state the obvious. You are almost a foot and a half taller than me and far stronger. Your friend Mr. Blue is almost as tall, and I am told he is remarkably agile. Can you blame Song for being fearful? Even I, a professional, feel slightly anxious just standing next to you."

"That is your problem, Mr. Chang. And theirs. A professional should know how to deal with physical differences."

"Touché. I keep a gun in my pocket, which more than narrows our difference. There are also the men outside."

Gloria spoke angrily. "Come, come, Mr. Chang. Do you think Wiley will attempt to subdue you by force in your own country?"

"No." Chang smiled and walked toward the door. "I will send my men to the restaurant. We will have our breakfast here. Soon, we will all look at the video of the alleged attack. With any luck, it's just a misunderstanding. And my team will leave the *Viking* as soon as the helicopter returns."

As Chang opened the door, Dave's voice echoed loudly through the hall. There were shouts and sounds of a scuffle. Dave appeared, running full bore, followed by two security men, guns held in front of them, a few feet behind him. Suddenly Dave stopped, squatted, banked his body to the left side, and kicked his right foot low across the hall. His foot caught the lead man at his ankles. The man tried to roll as he took the blow but failed. His gun clattered on the floor as he crashed against the wall. The other man stopped and tried to aim at Dave, who balanced on one bent arm and dropped flat to the floor, leveraging his hands while whirling both legs in a fast, high kick, dislodging the gun. Another kick dropped the second man to the floor. Dave came up fast and caught the firearm on the fly.

Breathing hard, he stood, gun at his side, surveying both fallen men, and readied himself for two more, who were running down the hall toward him.

Chang shouted something at his men, which stopped them in their tracks. Then he slowly helped the downed officers from the floor.

"Did they hurt you, Dave?" Wiley asked.

"Do I look hurt?" Dave said through deep breaths. "But they tried. They ambushed me as I was walking down the corridor to this room. Tried to hit me with one of their sticks, no reasons given. I walked away, but they came after me."

Chang turned, shaking his head in frank admiration. "So much for our special teams. I've never seen moves like that before."

Dave turned to Chang. "You're the boss of these thugs. Are you responsible for their attack?"

Chang nodded wearily to himself and with a few terse words dismissed all his men. A waiter appeared, pushing a cart of food, and then, seeing the police, rapidly reversed direction.

In obvious frustration, Chang yelled at the waiter, who reversed again and wheeled the cart into the room.

"Set it up on the deck and then go. Don't come back until we call," he commanded.

Chang followed Dave and Wiley to the outside table, where the food was already set up. Chang signed the check, and the waiter left quickly with obvious relief.

"Mr. Chang is a policeman from Shanghai," Wiley said. "This is my esteemed partner, Dave Blue."

They shook hands and sat down at the table opposite Wiley and Gloria.

278

Wiley began, "I sincerely hope your men are not hurt, Mr. Chang. But judging by the way they just acted—without warning or provocation—perhaps there is need for consultation to your team. Dave has helped law enforcement before. He could be persuaded …"

Dave laughed. "I do not train people to become bullies."

Chang looked from one to the other and shook his head. "I see why Ms. Song asked for help."

"We're not looking for trouble," Wiley said. "Certainly not with the Chinese authorities."

"Your elite men didn't even try to question me before attacking. Perhaps their English is limited, but still …"

"Their English is excellent," Chang said.

"You really didn't provoke them, Dave?" Wiley asked. "You have a way, you know."

"I was just ambling down the hall toward this room. But I was worried about you, Wiley."

"And what exactly were you worried about, Mr. Blue?" Chang said.

Dave looked at Wiley, then Gloria. "On the tour to the new city, Song was being unusually nice, even flirtatious. Not exactly her style, so it made me suspicious. Then I saw the helicopter landing near our ship and uniformed men getting off. I put two and two together and came to the rescue." Dave looked at his friend, then more closely at Chang. "Perhaps I overestimated the threat. You both seem so relaxed. What's going on?"

"Dr. Diamond has lodged an informal complaint against me. There is a video. Song accepted his version," Wiley said. "She will be here soon."

"Mr. Blue," Chang said, "you are also under suspicion. Song has another video showing that you dismantled the surveillance system of this room. That is a criminal act, if we choose to prosecute."

"You would win. But please, Mr. Chang, this is supposed to be a tour ship. How would China's visitors feel knowing the whole ship is bugged?" Dave said. "You can't smile at a cleaning lady without being observed, let alone have sex with the waitress. We have a great deal to complain about."

"Dave," Wiley said, "we are here at the pleasure of the Chinese government, which may not react well to complaints. So calm down and eat your breakfast. Song will be here soon."

"All of this will go much faster if you tell me why you and Mr. Blue are here," Chang said.

"Fair enough. It's about Dr. Diamond, Mr. Chang," Wiley answered.

"Why is Dr. Diamond your concern, unless you are working for your government? Or mine?"

Wiley replied, "I'm sure you've already checked what we've told Song."

"Of course, and I found nothing. I still have excellent informal contacts in Washington, and no one's heard of you for years, but you are well remembered. Legends, actually. Two members of a championship team. Three times All-American. Undefeated teams. Very impressive." He paused. "Perhaps there are political dimensions that I am not privy to."

"Now we work for ourselves," Wiley said. "Not for any government."

"But doing what?"

"I assure you, that has nothing to do with you, Song, or your government. From your perspective, we are tourists."

"Why not just tell me? It's obvious there is more."

Wiley remained silent.

"When I was in the States, Don Shula, the ex–Baltimore Colts football coach, told me about you." He smiled at the memory. "Do you know him?"

"Before our time," Wiley answered. "But he showed up at award dinners. How did you know him?"

"I met him at a squash club when I trained in Washington. He was older, but we were well matched on the court. I remember him saying that you were the best quarterback since Unitas."

"He overestimated Unitas," Dave said with a chuckle. "Always did. But he said nothing about me, Mr. Chang? No comparisons with Jerry Rice? Dwight Clark?"

"Afraid not."

"He obviously didn't know much about good ends." Dave seemed genuinely hurt.

"Perhaps he mentioned you, Mr. Blue, and I have forgotten," Chang said.

Gloria interjected, "There's only so much boy talk I can take. Why not just ask your questions and show us the video?"

Wiley said, "Gloria is very direct, Mr. Chang. In everything she does."

"I can believe that." Chang looked at her and then the sumptuous fare with obvious delight. "After the drama in the hallway, I believe I will consider this an official interrogation, which makes this wonderful breakfast a courtesy of the Chinese government. We would like for all of you to see the tape I mentioned. But first we eat."

His cell phone rang, and he took the call inside the room. When he returned to the balcony, he sat at the table and grabbed a sweet roll. "Song will be here soon."

Gloria served Wiley eggs, pancakes, and coffee, taking a waffle for herself. "You, Dave?"

"What Wiley has, times two. I've been busy this morning."

"And you, Mr. Chang?"

"Half of Mr. Stone's portion. And thank you, Ms. Garcia."

"Perhaps you would be interested in my views," Gloria said warmly.

"Of course," Chang said, falling under her spell.

"Dr. Diamond's security was my concern as well as Song's. And yet Song never collaborated with me despite her initial promises to do just that. Perhaps it is because I am a woman or Latino."

"We are a xenophobic nation, Ms. Garcia. Song has probably never met anyone like you."

"Perhaps. On the personal side, she is interested in Dave."

"It's my fate wherever I go," Dave said, deadpan.

There was a knock at the door. "That'll be Song," Dave said.

"Try to be nice to her, Dave," Wiley said. "You too, Gloria. Mr. Chang is telling us she's a powerful lady."

Chang rose to answer the door. "Mr. Stone's advice is correct. She can put both of you in jail. So be careful. The tape, if it's what she claims it is, isn't going away. As for collaboration, Ms. Garcia, I doubt that was ever taken seriously. Again, I must remind you to be careful."

Song entered the room bathed in sweat. Chang greeted her formally, and they walked to the edge of the balcony and spoke quietly together while Wiley, Dave, and Gloria ate the rest of their food and sipped coffee.

When Song finally addressed them, Chang looked chastened.

"You must forgive my appearance. I've just returned from a tour of the New City, and listening to the report of Mr. Blue's assault on our police has taken up my time since I returned."

"With cause," Dave said quietly.

"Have a seat, Song," Gloria said. "Coffee? Food?"

Song remained standing and shrugged off the offer. "Chang believes we should all view the tapes together. I bow to his knowledge of police procedure."

Dave and Wiley remained silent.

"I just told Chang that I was not pleased with this friendly breakfast together."

"I'm glad you've come," Gloria said quickly. "We can use another woman here. The three of them have done too much talking about football for a woman's taste."

Song looked through her. "Ms. Garcia, I do not feel in a friendly mood, and I've had to watch far too much of your body on tape for my comfort."

"Voyeurism is your business, Song," Gloria said furiously.

"Finish breakfast. I will be in the video room." Song turned on her heel and left the room.

CHAPTER 40

The Mind of a Prodigy

J oe Diamond slept poorly, a sure sign that his depression was gaining momentum. An antidepressant would help, he thought absently. Perhaps a course of one of the newer SSRIs, like Effexor. Unfortunately, it took a week to kick in, and he was sure that the problem with Paul would be over by then. He thought of the prototype he had developed as a graduate student and how he had to watch helplessly as his boss and the drug companies took the patents and the fortune that went with them. Why did he still care? He had so many patents, such large royalties.

He awoke at 4 a.m. with no hope of more sleep, so he devoted himself to the mixed pleasure of masturbation and release. His fantasies were all variations on threesomes with Paul and Debra Jean, but afterward the brief orgasm devolved into compulsive worrying about his friend. He finally dragged himself out of bed, ordered a coffee from room service at 6 a.m., and once again watched the sun rise into the chemical sky from his deck.

He went back into his room but remained lost in his depressed obsessions until the helicopter's noisy arrival completely changed his mood. Now he felt like working. He placed a "Do not disturb" sign on his door, took out some oversized graph paper, and opened his computer to the secure website that housed his scientific projects. He worked well for a while, but the sense of dread returned when he thought of the pleasure of collaboration with Paul.

Joe was startled out of his trance by a knock on the door. Glancing at his watch, he saw that it was already early afternoon. What had he been thinking about all this time? Something about the magic inner space that he had discovered simultaneously with his first orgasm, a place he had called Splendor that he sculpted for the flights of creativity that inspired his youthful discoveries. He glanced at his work notes. Worthless babble. He thought again of Paul. Without him, Joe's work would indeed be meaningless.

He walked to the door and looked through the peephole. It was Song. She had coffee and sandwiches with her. He let her in, knowing it must be about the men who had arrived by helicopter.

"What is it?" he said with calm he didn't feel.

She walked into the room and placed the tray on a coffee table near the desk. "Sorry to bother you, but you've had that 'Do not disturb' sign up since 7 a.m., and the cook told me you'd only ordered coffee. I brought you some food. Part of my job."

"How nice of you," Joe said irritably, though he was glad for her presence. "I've been busy—got lost in my work. Your company is appreciated," he said, amazed at his own show of weakness.

She glanced at the messy piles of paper next to his computer. "Is this a time we can talk, or would you rather be left alone? I want to bring you up to date."

"Go ahead. Anything new?"

"I've been reviewing the tapes of Stone's attack, which I am about to show to the Shanghai security team. Its leader is a man named Chang. He strongly suggests reviewing them with Stone, Blue, and Garcia."

"Why with the Americans?"

"He wants to see their reactions."

"Not a bad idea," he said, picking at a piece of toast. "More subtle than I would have thought."

"China has grown up, Dr. Diamond. In fact, you are a part of those changes."

"And I believe in supporting your society's transformation," Joe said.

"Garcia's reaction to the tape should be particularly revealing. After all, she is also responsible for your security on board."

Joe's nod confirmed her comment. "We haven't used her. Romantic involvement with Stone makes her biased. But do not underestimate her loyalty to me. I am her benefactor."

"She was in Stone's room when the team arrived."

"It's likely that Stone is manipulating her, not the other way around," Joe said angrily.

"I think you're right," Song said. "Here are the verbal transcripts from the tapes."

Joe scanned the first page and frowned. "It is unintelligible." He scanned through the remaining papers. "This is very preliminary indeed."

"The sound of the engines overrode your conversation. Unfortunately, you were facing toward the camera. We have almost nothing of what Stone said to you."

"I should have realized … ," Joe mused.

"But we know you were talking about his father when he grabbed your shoulders."

"So what?"

"Did you know that subject would make him upset?"

"Do you mean, was I trying to provoke him? We have a childhood saying in America, 'Sticks and stones may break my bones, but words will never hurt me.'"

"In China, we take words more seriously, like weapons. After all, we made a world revolution around a little red book."

"Don't lecture me, Song. And yes, I did know that Stone would be upset by that topic. It was one of my strategies for getting information from him."

"It seems cruel. Our culture venerates our parents, our elders. We would never do that, Dr. Diamond."

He leaned closer, his face almost touching hers. "You're out of bounds, Song."

"I watched the film very closely," she said, holding her ground. "Stone grabbed your shoulders. Then your knees seemed to buckle under you, and you fell against the railing, dragging him onto you."

"Yes. It was very unpleasant. I almost went into the water."

"I looked at that part of the tape over and over again. I am unhappy with the body mechanics of your backward fall. You could have been pushed, or Stone could have been drawn off-balance by your sudden move. It's hard to tell from the tape. And of course, Stone pulled you back from the railing."

Joe pushed the tray away and leaned back into his chair. He pursed his hands under his chin. "I am confused, Song. Are you really suggesting that I tricked Stone into attacking me? He is a gifted athlete, a football player trained in feints and misdirection. He is also a foot taller than me. It is obvious that I was the victim, not he."

"Chang is an expert in such matters. He will also notice these details."

"We both know your Party membership will override Chang's opinion, so you must have your own doubts."

"The tape does not quite fit your story, Dr. Diamond. I can influence Chang but not my superiors."

"Your superiors. Be careful. A word from me, and you may not have a job."

"Dr. Diamond, the Party does not exist in a vacuum. The police are a powerful subgroup. If Chang does not believe the tape is sufficient evidence to arrest Stone, his report will be taken into consideration. The real problem continues to be Stone's motivation for his alleged attack. It would help if you could tell us what you know about it."

"That is not my job, Song."

"It would be best to learn more before we act," she insisted. "Motive is part of our legal code just as much as yours."

Joe watched her eyes. He saw no hint of subterfuge. "How will you proceed? The cruise is almost over."

"We have a video of Blue dismantling our surveillance system. That is an unambiguous violation of our law. We could arrest him and also hold Stone as an accessory. We could do that as we disembark tomorrow. It would cause far less disturbance and publicity. Once they were in custody, we could proceed with our investigation in a less cautious manner."

"I approve. And my safety until then?"

"Chang will see to that personally. What remains of his team will stay here as backup."

Joe looked at her inquiringly.

"Several were hurt by Blue in a skirmish near Stone's room. They will need medical help in a local clinic. The helicopter will take them back in the late afternoon and return tomorrow."

Joe was stunned. "You must realize how preposterous this sounds. Not only was I attacked, but the very professionals brought in to protect me were injured."

"Chang's men attacked Blue without any provocation. He fought back and proved superior."

Joe fought to control his temper. "How can I feel safe under these circumstances? They have assaulted me, and yet you do little. We both know you are tiptoeing around Stone, and I'll soon find out why, Song."

"I respectfully disagree with your conclusions," Song countered. "My caution is warranted because a full investigation would inevitably include you, Dr. Diamond. We choose not to pursue that course in order to protect you." She smiled and crossed her arms.

Joe carefully assessed her comment. Perhaps she had been told about the scene at the Empress. "I would rather they are arrested before I am attacked again, but I depend on you." Song's threat was a new factor.

She paused, examining his response for the weakness it revealed. "As you probably know, Dr. Stokes has changed his schedule for the trip to San Francisco. He asked me to arrange a trip for himself and Dr. Lieberman to visit Xian and view the Terracotta Warriors. Is that your wish as well, Dr. Diamond?"

"I'm not sure," Joe said as evenly as he could. More betrayal, he thought.

"Please let me know as soon as possible," Song said. "If you do not go to Xian, we will use the helicopter and return you to Beijing in the morning. I will travel with you. You are my first priority, Dr. Diamond."

He nodded. "I'd like to finish my work."

"Of course," Song said. She stood and walked rapidly to the door. "I am at your service if you need me." She closed it quietly behind her.

After she was gone, Joe rose from his chair and began pacing. He felt short of breath and his heart was pounding. With trembling, sweaty hands, he counted a pulse of 110. Breathing slowly, he tried to clear his mind of intrusive images of Debra Jean and Paul in Xian. His pulse gradually rose to 130, and his breathing became more difficult. He knew he was on the verge of a full-blown panic attack. He walked to the bathroom, popped half a milligram of Xanax, and lay down. When the drug finally kicked in, he rose, collected his working papers, and resumed pacing the floor.

Even through the filter of the Xanax, his mind was crowded with Song's revelations. She had pretended to be an unbiased professional.

In practice, that meant she was no longer on his side. Far worse was the unexpected independence of Paul. Despite sexual failure, he was planning a private trip with Debra Jean. Even more telling, Paul had said nothing about it to him.

Song would have suggested Xian, and he was sure that was aimed at him, which meant he had no one on his side. All her talk of the legalities of Chinese justice was a cover story. He knew she could do what she wanted with Wiley and Dave. A simple e-mail to her boss in Beijing would be enough to get them thrown into jail. Instead, she was protecting them at his expense.

Could Song have fallen in love? Dave? The new-city tour that he had joined must have been a rendezvous. The conversation with Wiley had been a brilliant success, but Song was trying to spin that in another direction. All this vulnerability because the basic problem was unsolved. She too was searching for a motive for the Americans' behavior.

Dammit. Why was Wiley here? The multiple scenarios circled aimlessly in the labyrinth of his brain. The Xanax had been a bad idea. His mind had always been his best weapon.

He plunged on obsessively with his analysis. He imagined Song and Dave as a couple. Hardly positive for her aspirations in the Party, but then sexual attraction could never be underestimated. Perhaps her apparent sophistication hid a constricted young woman with little actual experience. So many of the young successful Chinese men and women had been raised as pampered single children of the Cultural Revolution, carrying the scars of their humiliated parents. Their apparent conformity hid subtle seeds of revenge against a party that had been merciless and corrupt with the people they loved most.

Dave was a perfect fantasy to activate those seeds: tall, graceful, and probably sexy to her, he was also a magician representing the rebellion she obviously held within.

Joe stood and shook himself like a wet dog to clear his head. He felt as if his brain were in a constricting device. How he hated boats. Why had he agreed to this cruise? It was a prison with none of the special pleasures that illuminated his life. There was no guiding intent in his meanderings because he was still missing the key—their motive, Wiley's motive.

He walked out to the balcony and surveyed the Yangtze below. The river was gradually widening as the ship approached the great dam. A putrid miasma hung over the surface of the newly grown reservoir. Joe looked for evidence of pollution and saw hypodermics and bandages washing up on the shore. Mountains of garbage would be shipped here for dumping. The slag from the coal mines would find its way to the bottom. His own factory in the suburbs of Shanghai was one of countless projects that daily added to the pollution. The moguls of Beijing, their financiers in Shanghai, and international entrepreneurs like himself were the winners; the displaced peasants and their children with leukemia and toxic syndromes were the losers.

None of this had ever bothered him before. Why identify with the victims now? Because he was the victim! Joe kicked at the rug. Losing Paul was all that seemed to matter, Paul and only Paul. Their relationship had always been his Achilles' heel. Months ago, he and Paul had planned this business junket as an overdue vacation just for them. It was to be their appetizer to Stockholm and the coming Nobel Prize. They had laughed until they were giddy at the thought. But Paul had forgotten, replacing their pre-celebration with the company of an unremarkable woman and her mysterious friends.

He had the sudden image of Paul, a razor-sharp scalpel in hand, painfully dissecting the Achilles ligament free from his own heel as Wiley and Debra Jean looked on.

The frightening image brought him up short. He was spiraling too deeply, first into his childhood fantasies and now into fear. It was time for action. Joe picked up the phone and dialed Paul's room. There was no answer. He hung up quickly, hating to think of Debra Jean and Paul together in that room listening to his needy voice. Joe paced the room like a caged lion. He now saw his conversation with Wiley as just an early skirmish of a longer war in which Paul was a pawn. Wiley, a master strategist, so skilled in competitive games, would accept being a touchdown or two behind as he feinted toward the all-important end game.

He strode through the room and kicked the table hard, sending the tray of food to the floor. He watched a coffee stain spread across the rug. Conrad had said it all too well: boat trips could be dark passages for a creative man. He would ask Song to find all of Conrad's sea-voyage books to read in Beijing.

Right now, he had to concentrate on getting Paul back.

Joe left his room and walked to Paul's. He listened at the door, hearing nothing. He knocked. Silence. In anger, he kicked the door. Still no answer. Where was the man? He continued down the hall, fighting the accelerating drumbeat inside his chest. He ran down three flights to the main deck and the dining room. The room was wide and plain except for wall-to-wall windows overlooking the river on each side. It was crowded; the passengers had returned from their outings. The loud Taiwanese tourists occupied at least half of the dining room, but it was easy to spot Wiley and Dave at a large round table, their tall frames towering over the rest of the room.

He sat down in an empty chair in the corner, suddenly embarrassed to be there alone. They were all together: Wiley, Dave, Paul, Debra Jean, Gloria, even Song and a new Chinese man, who was probably Chang, the policeman from Shanghai. They must have finished looking at the tapes. Had Paul been there, too? He hoped not. Debra Jean and Paul were sitting next to one another but angled away, not talking. Gloria was leaning over Wiley, listening to Dave hold forth. Song and Chang were sitting slightly apart from the group, but Song's gaze was nonetheless fixed on the storyteller.

He knew there was a plot against him. He tried to calm himself by focusing on Paul, who was trying his best to be a bona fide member of the group. They were including him, but Joe could tell from his body language that he didn't quite include himself. Joe relaxed. His friend could still be rescued.

Just then, Gloria saw him in the corner and signaled something to the rest of the table. Dave stopped talking, and all eyes turned in Joe's direction. Reacting quickly, Joe stood and walked confidently toward them. Debra Jean placed her hand on Paul's knee as he moved to greet Joe.

Joe halted at Paul's chair. "Well, well, it's wonderful to see all of you together enjoying lunch," he began. "I've been missing a lot by sitting up in my cabin alone."

Song looked guilty. "Why not join us, Dr. Diamond?"

"No," Joe said sharply. "I can see you have a lot to say to each other. I'd just like a word with you, Paul."

"Sure, Joe," Paul said, brushing off Debra Jean's hand and pushing his chair away from the table.

Joe began walking toward the end of the room. He could hear Paul following him but sensed his hesitation. Joe turned, and they faced each other in the middle of the room. "I won't take you away for long. I hear you're going to Xian with Debra Jean. I thought that was to be our trip, a prelude to Stockholm."

"Things have changed, Joe. I tried to tell you in San Francisco."

"Paul," Joe said sternly, "I need to understand what's happening."

"I'm not sure I can explain."

"Look, I'm going to eat. Join me." He took Paul's elbow and began moving away. They walked a few steps together and then Paul stopped.

"No," he said, and impatiently shook off Joe's hand. "My place is there." He pointed to the group. "They are all waiting for me."

"I see." Joe looked away, amazed at his own welling tears. He turned back to Paul, deliberately showing him the pain in his face. "Then please, meet me on the observation sun deck by the back engines. Six o'clock, if that works for you. We should be going through the dam by then. Most of the people will be on the forward decks at parties, so we'll be relatively alone. It's important that we talk."

"Yes, Joe."

Joe pointed to an empty table. "You sure you don't want to sit with me?"

Paul faltered, then pulled himself together. "I can't just leave them now. Don't worry. I'll be on the sun deck. We'll figure it out." He turned away and made his way across the dining room toward the group. But there was indecision in each step. Joe knew the signs. He was on his way to getting Paul back.

* * *

"So how is Joe?" Wiley asked Paul, who stood behind his chair, poised between sitting and leaving.

"I can't talk about it, Wiley. To you, to anyone."

Debra Jean reached for his hand. "Paul. We all need to know, and Wiley can help you."

He shook her off roughly, his voice shaking. "No, nothing can be done. I'm OK. I'm sorry. I've got to be alone with this." He stared at each of them in turn and then at Joe still at his table across the room. He lifted his head until his neck was taut, and then grimaced and strode determinedly out of the dining room.

Wiley nodded to Chang and Song. "Can we have a few moments? This is very personal."

Chang stood.

"We have the right to stay," Song said.

Chang's face wrinkled in a smile. "But not the need. Besides, you and I have to talk."

After they left, Wiley turned to the group and spoke with urgency. "I am extremely worried about Paul. Obviously Joe still has an immense claim on his feelings." Debra Jean nodded in agreement.

Dave turned to her. "No. There's more, more than depression, isn't there? Something new is happening. It's as if all our questions have suddenly penetrated his defenses. He's understanding something terrible about himself, and that is transforming him." Dave thought for a moment. "I'm not sure he has the strength to handle it. We're losing him; he's losing himself."

Wiley looked across the table at his friend. "Joe's afraid and showing it. That's why we're here, Dave. That's got to be our focus. If Paul's caught in a maelstrom of his own making, we're not here to protect him from that. No one can."

Gloria said, "Too little compassion, Wiley. I'm with Dave. We're missing something important about what's happening to Paul. The strategy of using him to pressure Joe cuts both ways."

Dave sat bolt upright. "It's all happening too fast, Wiley. It's out of control."

Debra Jean glanced at Joe's table. "Look, I feel very sorry for Paul, but he's not my first concern." Her jaw clenched as she continued. "Right now, Joe is sitting alone 50 feet away from me. You told me from the very beginning that revenge is a wild card. A lot has happened between Joe and Paul because of what we began. But my focus is still on Joe. It's why I'm here, and after more than two years I'm ready to face him." She stood and turned her back to their table.

"Hold on, Debra Jean," Wiley said, reaching out a hand to restrain her.

"Why?" she flared, moving away from the table.

"If Dave and Gloria are right about Paul, he could be in serious trouble. We don't know how much, but you know him best. Perhaps you should try to help."

Her voice rose in pitch. "No. That's exactly what I shouldn't do. He's got to find a way out of Joe's spell all by himself." Her voice broke. "Trying to rescue him would be one more sacrifice to Joe's power."

Gloria grasped Debra Jean's hand. "There's a moment when you've got to make a move, no matter what the cost. And there usually is one." She turned to Wiley. "This is her time. Her show."

Their eyes met, and Wiley nodded to Debra Jean. "Your call."

Debra Jean walked to Wiley, bent down, and kissed him on the cheek.

"Break a leg," Dave whispered.

CHAPTER 41

Showtime

Debra Jean walked resolutely away from the table and toward Joe. Out of the corner of her eye, she saw the waiter approaching with his food. She stopped him and asked for coffee to be brought to Joe's table. "For me." The words sounded just right to her.

She took the few remaining steps to the table and then stood across from him, one hand on an empty chair, the other on her hip. "Like to talk, Joe?"

"I'm always in the mood for an attractive woman." He pointed to a chair but remained seated. "So you finally have the guts to face me. Admirable, my dear." He paused, chuckling to himself. "I guess it isn't easy to sit down next to the man who is supposed to have destroyed your life."

She sat. "You take too much credit."

"Quite right." Joe gave her a knowing smile. "I'm curious about what you've been plotting with that clever brain of yours. By the way, have I said how well you're looking? If I have, it deserves repeating. Perhaps I did you a favor. No longer the overcompensating mouse."

"No longer," she snapped, and leaned forward until their faces almost touched.

Joe slowly backed away and appraised her thoughtfully. "None of the worshipful poses you affected at the lab. Good. I like your new confident style. You must've found a good therapist."

"And learned how to recognize bullies." Her voice was cold and mocking.

"You're more frank now, and you've added a temper. Working in the suburbs has done wonders for you. It must have been tough being there with your brains."

"Don't patronize me."

"You couldn't have said that to me two years ago."

"You are quite a bit older than I remember you, Joe. Is it anxiety, guilt, or just bad living?"

His face grew red, and he rose slightly in his chair, then caught himself. "Let's not get this conversation off on the wrong foot, Debra Jean. I've known we've needed to talk." He sat back in his chair. "Where should we start?"

"If you were a decent man, you'd start with an apology. But you aren't, and for someone like you, apologies are words without feelings. I've been learning about you, Joe. Fingering an awestruck young woman in a fancy restaurant was just a pit stop. Child abuse is so much more your style."

"I honestly have no idea what you're talking about," Joe said blandly.

"The Empress!"

"That again," he said disgustedly. "Wiley is spreading a fantasy, Debra Jean. Have you ever wondered why he didn't go to the police with his suspicions?"

"There are reasons."

"Like not wanting to be caught in a lie. I was there, just like he was, and like him, I was there for reasons unrelated to those unfortunate children. He didn't go to the police because he was guessing. He told me what he thought he saw. If he really believed it, he should have reported it. Perhaps he didn't want to get involved. It doesn't matter. I wasn't in the room with those children, no matter what Wiley says. I was otherwise occupied. I smelled smoke, heard the alarm, and left as quickly as possible."

"Of course you'd say you're innocent," Debra Jean said with a smirk. "Beginning with Jardinière. You're full of lies, Joe. It's the sick world you inhabit—"

"Please," Joe cut in. "Spare me your judgments. Jardinière? Is that the trigger for your witch hunt? Wiley implied that, too. Well, I have nothing to hide. I was playing with your own sexual fantasies about Paul and me. It's those fantasies that bother you, not my behavior. Or else you would have reported me to the ethics committee at UCSF."

Debra Jean was silent.

Joe watched her thoughtfully. There was only one thing he wanted from this woman, he thought, and now was the time to get it. "Look, I thought you'd like what I did. I thought you were a player in one of the sexual games that make the world go 'round. Playing footsie, hand jobs under the table, fucking in elevators. Good stuff, but I obviously misjudged your tastes and lusts, and I am sorry for that."

He relaxed his voice. "I admired your work, Debra Jean. That's why I hired you. For an inexperienced postdoc, your science was brilliant and probably could be again. You attacked problems aggressively and creatively. But as it turned out, you were also in my way. You took bench space, and time, and most of all you were too independent to go along with my program—work or fun. Now you're saying I should have treated you with more respect in both." He leaned closer. "You were a coauthor on one of my papers. Jardinière should have been payback. I'd hoped for more than a wet finger."

Debra Jean stared back in disgust.

"Too crude for you? Well, face it. I am crude. I love risky games. It's why I make unexpected discoveries. It's the Wild West at Mission Bay, which means Joe Diamond territory. You wanted on my team, all right, but you wouldn't play by my rules. That's why I had to get rid of you."

"You're so fucking proud of your brains and your games. The Greeks called that hubris, Joe."

"Good word, hubris, an excess of pride or arrogance. And as any hubristic person would say, I have good reason for my pride."

"Hubris leads to one's downfall. It's why the gods kill us for their sport. People like you."

"Don't lecture me, Debra Jean. Being blessed with virtues that the gods envy entails risks I gladly take. Neither men nor gods have taken my measure yet."

"They will."

"Good. I love challenges. So far, no one has had the balls."

"Maybe someone already has."

"You're confident," Joe mused. "I wonder who you have in mind."

"Someone like Wiley, for example."

"Right now, I doubt if he'd agree with you. You're so smug, Debra Jean. I wonder why." Joe thought for a moment, then pushed a finger toward her face. "Well done, Debra Jean. I keep rejecting the possibility that Wiley is here working for you. He as much as told me that, but it doesn't stick in my brain. Wiley can't take me, Debra Jean. He's already tried."

"The game's not over," she blurted out, instantly regretting it.

Joe smiled victoriously. "Yes, you're right. There is always the end game. And that gets us into another set of gods—the tricksters: Loki, Coyote, Lucifer. They're my models. They arrive after heroes like Wiley are long gone." He smiled again.

Debra Jean flushed. She had a memory of bringing in pages of data to his office and watching that smile spread across his face. She'd learned to hate it. It meant her work was now his.

"It's not over," she repeated defensively.

Joe leaned back in his chair. He'd gotten what he needed from her, and now he was bored. Debra Jean was always boring.

"Debra Jean," he said in as conciliatory a tone as he could muster, "why be angry with me? In business, good people get fired all the time. And women get propositioned. It's the culture. OK, I apologize. That's what you wanted, right?"

He watched her turn toward the table at the other end of the dining room. Well, she wouldn't get any help there.

Then, suddenly, unexpectedly, he felt a rush of negative feeling, despair instead of triumph. Because of Paul. The way he had left their conversation, the way he had left the room. Debra Jean was part of turning him.

"I can be useful to you, Debra Jean. You think I'm unprincipled, and you may be right. But I also don't hold grudges. I really don't. I can get you back into science, if that's what you want."

"You sound worried, Joe," Debra Jean said coolly. "Why is that? What are you afraid of losing?"

"I'm just making amends," he said offhandedly. "Last chance, Debra Jean."

"No sale. You don't have anything I need." She licked her lips. "Maybe if you'd propositioned me like a man instead of a 13-year-old kid, then we could've gone back to your apartment, and I would have dressed in ways you liked—little-girl clothing or something even darker. I mean, what kind of man gets off on violence to little children?"

"Bitch."

"Your word for a woman you can't buy." She spat out the words and turned on her heel.

Joe didn't bother watching her go. She was dead to him.

He signaled for the check. He didn't have to look at the table across the room. He knew they were laughing at him. Stay cool and focus, he told himself as he settled the bill and prepared to leave. It was only Paul that mattered. Paul wasn't going to be hoodwinked by amateur Robin Hoods. He had to give Wiley credit, though. The man had invented a new twist on an old profession. But they didn't have the mental equipment or ruthlessness to go up against someone like him.

He strode to the main deck and looked out at the river. It was so much wider, now that they were near the Three Gorges Dam. He glanced at his watch. Just a few hours till they reached the giant structure. Soon the river would be a vast reservoir. The guests were already moving on deck, searching for the best spots to view the great spectacle.

He was just pumping himself up, he knew. He felt exhausted. The successful conversations with Wiley and Debra Jean had done nothing to reduce the burden of loneliness. He lay down on an unoccupied lounge chair at the front of the main deck. He set a mental alarm timer for a half-hour. A brief nap would help, and he needed inspiration for his coming talk with Paul. He looked up at the yellowed sky. Floating down this river in the early evening reminded him of being on the Charles River so many years earlier. Even then, as an undergraduate, he was sure that he would scale the heights of his field before the first arc of his life was over.

He had almost reached his goal. The Nobel Prize was just the beginning. He would soon stand in an ancient hall in Stockholm and give a speech that would catapult him to the upper echelons of global influence. He could almost see the great stage, the glitter of invited celebrity clapping appreciatively. The words were already in his mind. They had always been there, he thought dreamily. He was looking down at the audience, waiting for everyone to quiet. Only one group was still talking, and people were turning around, trying to silence them. They were standing far back near the exit doors watching him with a different expectation. They were familiar. Who were they? His parents? Someone else. He couldn't tell who, but he knew they didn't belong in the august throng. He felt a tinge of anxiety. He could overcome that, he thought, as he drifted back into the reverie. The words he had been waiting to say all his life were on his lips.

"Ladies and gentlemen, honored guests, I am here to change the world."

CHAPTER 42

Moment of Truth

Joe woke from his nap with a start. He lay back on the deck chair he had claimed, relishing the hypnagogic image of Stockholm and the Nobel Prize ceremony. Prophetic or just wish fulfillment, he wondered. He focused on the last image—the unruly group milling at the back of the hall as he began his acceptance speech. Who were they? The people he had left behind, like his parents, who had used his talents for their own profit? The professors who had taken away his discoveries? Wiley's group? The part of him that remained creative and free even as he accepted society's greatest reward?

Then suddenly it came to him: he was missing what really mattered. Paul wasn't anywhere at the prize ceremony. Paul wasn't with him on the podium. That he would be without Paul on such an occasion filled him with dread.

Joe checked his watch. Paul would be waiting. He got shakily to his feet, climbed the stairs to the observation sun deck, and threaded his way past the crowds jostling for space at the front of the sun deck. He headed toward the noise of the engines at the back of the ship. It was empty except for the lone figure of Paul standing at the railing and peering into the receding water. An immense wave of affection rolled over him. He needed Paul. The thought of his loss shook Joe to the core. He wouldn't survive without Paul.

Feeling momentarily dizzy, Joe pressed against the railing next to his friend. He closed his eyes and immediately found himself alone on the Stockholm podium beginning the salutation.

"Paul!" he cried out loud. "Where are you?"

"Right here, Joe," Paul answered.

Joe shook off the apparitions and hurried toward him. "Thanks for coming," Joe said and hugged his friend. It felt good to finally make contact.

"You knew I would." Paul pulled himself free and regained the rail. "I'm always with you in the end."

"In the end." Joe laughed, regaining his composure. "Wrong idea entirely. We're at the beginning, Paul. But something's up with you. It's why we need to talk. I just had a dream that we had gotten the Nobel Prize, but you weren't at the ceremony."

"And that's the way it will be, Joe. This is our last conversation together."

"What do you mean?" Joe said, taken aback. He grabbed the railing and faced his friend.

"Just what I said. It's our last meeting, and time for a review of our friendship. Take a good look at me. Who do you see, Joe?"

"That's easy. Somebody I like very much. Somebody whom I find very smart, whom I can count on. Somebody who's been part of my world and success."

"That's all about you, isn't it?"

"You're right. I can be selfish." Joe looked deeply into Paul's eyes, trying to understand what he needed. "I see someone in the prime of his life with the world at his feet. But I also see a sad man. A struggling man."

He waited for a response, but Paul remained silent. "There's a good reason for that. We both know what it is." Joe went on more slowly. "Rather, *who* she is. Her name is Debra Jean, and she's come between us."

Joe watched the lines between Paul's eyes constrict inward. His hands gripped the rail more tightly, his knuckles blanched.

"I know something's very wrong. That's why we're having this talk," Joe said. "I'm very concerned about you."

"No, Joe. You're concerned about yourself. You're concerned about losing your only friend."

Joe felt a trembling in his chest. "That's true. The thought drives me crazy. But believe me, I am also concerned about you."

Paul turned his head and peered into the water.

"We're together, Paul. That's always been true. Think of the Nobel!

301

That's been our goal, Paul. You've been my collaborator, my partner, my good right hand, the part of me that makes things happen in the very real worlds of laboratories and personnel. Maybe I haven't thanked you enough for my success. Our success. But beyond all that, it's your presence that matters to me."

Paul shuddered slightly. "Invaluable and necessary—to you. That's the key, isn't it? I'm there for you. The sad part is that I've forgotten how to be there for myself."

"We're interdependent. That's the beauty of our relationship."

"You're right." Paul grimaced, remembering how he had left Debra Jean and the others hanging at the table. "If you hadn't picked me for your friend in high school, I'd have had a very different life. I'd be more of an ordinary guy, a skilled engineer or a fairly successful business-man. I'd have a pleasant, loving wife and a family in a cozy suburban home."

"Nonsense."

"I'm not a prodigy like you. There is nothing of the infinite in my ideas, no grandeur in my visions. I'm clever, sure, but my job has been doing odd jobs for a genius."

"You always sell yourself short." Joe moved closer, so that their bodies were almost touching. "You're never ordinary to me, Paul. So what if it's our connection that makes you extraordinary?"

"I don't need your reassurances, Joe. Remember, I know my worth to you."

"Someone like me needs a partner like you."

"And I've done only what you need, Joe. I'm going to change that."

"And the Nobel?"

"Your dream got it just right. I won't be there."

"You're trampling on everything we worked for!"

"I want you to understand me, Joe. The prize will be empty for me. Everyone else in that room, in the scientific community, knows where the intellectual and creative power resides in our pair. I'm your hands, Joe, and you own them. I'm like those children tied up in the hotel room waiting for the cut of the knife at their wrists. Only you never cut mine. You made them into your slaves. And I let you."

Joe could feel his gorge rise. "Wiley again. You can't believe his lies."

"I wish I didn't. Wiley told me about the scene at the Empress, which, thank God, he and his friends averted. I don't believe he invented it, Joe. I recognized you in his description: the control, the cruelty, and the victims. I've known about the snuff films and the child abuse. I know about Sons of Mozart, who they are, what they do."

Joe gasped and steadied himself on the railing. The boat was slowing as it approached the dam. "I tried to keep it all from you. But now that you know, we can be even closer." He smiled. "You can be part of it."

"But I already am, Joe. I'm like those good Germans in World War II, pretending innocence while providing the psychological fuel for the Nazi evil. And like them, I've never said a word or tried to stop you. Like them, I've kept my mouth shut and watched it happen."

Joe said, "Remember how we started, Paul—all the sex with those girls? Fun, wasn't it? I won't let you spoil all the good things we've done together. C'mon, Paul, lighten up. You loved that stuff, and there's more to come."

"No, there isn't. I've never had your appetites, then or now. Do you know Scarpia in *Tosca*?"

"Of course. One of the great opera villains. For my money, the best character in Puccini."

"Yes, and also the character who represents evil and sadism. Like you, he had to torture helpless others to feel pleasure. But here's the thing: Only a part of this is about you. You're just a catalyst for decisions I've had to make, but blaming you is not why I'm here. It's my fault. I never tried to resist you." Paul felt a darkness descending as his words painted the lie that was his life. "I became dependent on your excitement for mine. When you went to Harvard, I thought I was free for a while. But you had different plans for me, and I couldn't resist. Without you, I couldn't feel excited by a woman's body or anything else. So I'm not blaming you. I didn't have to live my life through you. I just let it become my fate."

He took a long breath and let it out slowly. "But Joe, you made it hard. Your tastes ripened and rotted."

"Dammit, Paul! You've distorted everything. Yes, I go to the edge. Yes, I straddle boundaries. Yes, my games span heaven and hell. That capaciousness is why I'm so successful."

Paul turned away, but Joe pushed even closer. He was afraid to stop talking. "Do you hear that noise? That roar is the water flowing against the Three Gorges Dam, the biggest dam in the world, Paul. And we're part of it because we're part of China's development. Soon we'll be Nobel Prize winners, icons, and we'll ride that chariot to a heaven we create for ourselves."

"This conversation isn't going the way you want. Right, Joe?"

"No, it's not. You're accusing me of committing the worst possible crime, without a shred of understanding," Joe said angrily. "It's Wiley, isn't it? I feel his presence in you. He's persuasive and charismatic. He's the football player whose team would die for him—and, by the way, his father did just that. Some hero. I don't know why this man is so against me or why Debra Jean Lieberman and the rest of them believe all his lies. They're peons compared with the likes of you and me, Paul."

"Disparaging others—your standard ploy when things get hot. You divert by opening a new road in the conversation and finding someone to be the scapegoat!"

"More of their psychobabble, Paul. Look, the last few days have really brought home to me how important you are. And whatever I've done to you or to others, it is water under the bridge. Soon the Nobel will make it all worthwhile."

"For you, not for me."

"Paul, don't you see that Wiley and the others are after something? They want to destroy me and MI, and they're using you. They believe you're my weakness, and they're right—I am so terribly vulnerable to you."

Joe looked at Paul and saw that he was hardly listening, lost in his own thoughts. Then Paul's focus seemed to return. "I see myself in everything you do, Joe. I feel like I have no perceptions or feelings other than yours. When they talk about you, they're talking about me. I'm terrified by what they show me."

"More of their induced hysteria, Paul," Joe said, trying his best to sound dismissive. "They're exaggerating what would have happened at the Empress. It was all a show; the kids would have been released and given money they desperately needed. And about Jardinière, the problem is that she took it so seriously. Just now I talked to her about what happened. I apologized. I asked her back to MI. I think she finally understands that it was meant as a come-on rather than harassment. You know me. How could I resist all that ripeness?"

Paul leaned on the railing and carefully placed a foot on the lowest crossbar. "She was young and star-struck. You crushed her without a second's thought."

"A harsh word, 'crushed,' but even if I accept it, what's the real harm? She's changed, Paul, thanks to a large dose of reality, psychotherapy, you, and perhaps whatever Wiley and Dave have cooked up. I saw a spark in her today. She's going to be a powerful woman when this is over." Joe relaxed. Paul was engaged, arguing with him now. Soon his anger would resolve and they would move on. "I'm curious, Paul. What about Wiley and Dave? What's so compelling about two used-up jocks?" The moment he said it, he wanted to take it back.

As if signaling his mistake, a loud horn blast rent the air. Startled, they both turned to the front of the ship. Above the *Viking Century Sky*'s prow they could see a gigantic concrete monolith that spanned the river. The Three Gorges Dam loomed in front of them.

Paul spoke, urgency gripping his voice. "We're getting close, Joe. There's not much time, and I need you to stop explaining yourself. I want you to understand me. I want it clear—what I'm doing and why. Please. As a last present to me." His voice left no room for argument. "Dave and Wiley are special men."

"Paul—"

"Joe, try not to be jealous. Debra Jean is Wiley's client. It's about what you did to her. That's why we are all here, including Gloria."

"Wait a second. I invited Gloria. She's working for me."

Paul ignored him, pushing out the words with increasing speed. "We both know that Debra Jean came apart emotionally because of what we did to her at MI. What you did at Jardinière only precipitated her downward slide. She barely functioned for over a year. She blamed you and me for that, and rightfully so, though it wasn't the whole story. She didn't have the self-esteem to fight back. Not then. She became your victim just like me. You bring that out in people, but I won't blame you for her feelings. Or mine." Paul's eyes brightened. "And then she got lucky—real lucky."

"You mean the money she inherited when her father died?"

"Sure, the money he gave her provided some security and support, but his death was another blow. No, getting lucky was meeting someone who referred her to Revenge, Inc."

Joe absorbed Paul's description as their cruise ship moved slowly toward one of the giant apertures in the heart of the dam. "Revenge, Inc., huh?" he muttered. "Kind of catchy for a vigilante scheme. So Wiley and Dave gave Debra Jean a way to get to me. And they found others to help: Gloria, you, Chang, maybe even Song. All part of their strategy with her, no doubt. None of that matters to me now, Paul. All I care about is that you're my dear friend, and they turned you against me." Joe's voice hardened. "And they crippled and half-blinded Zvi as part of their fancy scheme. Is that OK with you, too? Doesn't that make you wonder about their real goals?"

"He was at the Empress, Joe. He escorted the children to the hotel room."

"So you've bought into all of it." Joe stepped away from Paul. "You're part of their cabal to destroy me." He took a deep breath and then eyed Paul shrewdly. "Wait a minute. There's something I'm not seeing. If you've made up your mind, why are you telling me all this?"

"Why? Because I love you, Joe, and I know you need an explanation for what's about to happen. Because I'm worried about how much suffering you can handle before you break."

"Why not just come back to me?" Joe pleaded. "Why can't you do that?"

Paul was silent, staring at the water.

Joe said, "I'm going to win. I always do."

"They are tough, Joe. Zvi was in the way, and Dave put him in the hospital. And they believe in what they're doing. They're committed. They follow through. Remember they're the football players whose team always won."

"We'll see about that."

Paul turned away, resigned. "Telling you about Revenge, Inc., is a present. It's my way of saying good-bye."

"Good-bye?" Joe stared blankly at Paul.

"Yes, Joe."

"For that motley group and a bitchy woman you can't even fuck? You're a fool. They'll drop you when they don't need you anymore. They're probably collecting a healthy part of Debra Jean's inheritance on the way."

"I'm not counting on them in my future, Joe."

"Listen to me." Joe began pacing back and forth. "Their game is pretty simple. Debra Jean is their route to you, and you, our friendship, is their route to me. That's been Wiley's plan from the beginning, and I wouldn't believe it. They are good, just as you say. They've found my vulnerability, my love for you, and figured out a way to use it."

He waited for this to sink in. "But you're missing the larger picture. They are not interested in Debra Jean's little grievance. I'll bet she doesn't even believe that's important anymore. Right? Wiley doesn't care about my sexual habits or what he believes happened at the Empress; otherwise, he would have gone to the San Francisco police long ago. No, all of it must have another motivation. I'm on their trail. I'll find out what's going on, and when I do—"

"You keep trying. I'll give you that, Joe."

"Of course I do, and so should you. We'll join forces. We'll counterattack together. We'll destroy them!" Joe exclaimed.

"No we won't," Paul replied quickly, peering over the railing at the looming dam. "It took me a while to believe what they kept saying to me, that our relationship is your only experience of love, that I'm what really matters to you. It's still hard for me to believe, even now when I see it in your eyes. When I see your fear. I was a malleable kid who became part of your grand plan for success and pleasure. How could I know how much of your emptiness I was meant to fill? All the sordid worlds you created with drugs, Sons of Mozart, the tortured children—they were mirrors of your empty soul. Our friendship has always been the only thing that stood against that emptiness."

He held Joe's eyes in his gaze. "Joe, have you ever thought about why you're so turned on by the helpless? Why you destroy the hands of little children? Why you're so intent on keeping me a victim?"

"No, I haven't." Joe cupped his ears and turned away. "It's a dumb question and a waste of time."

"Not to me. I am like those children. I am just another living sacrifice to the fear that runs you."

The ship had almost stopped moving. Ahead they could see another ship in one of the huge tunnels embedded in the dam just ahead.

"You may be a prodigy and a genius, but without me, Joe, you barely qualify as human. It's time for me to face that and atone."

Joe's chest trembled. "Wiley, Debra Jean, or is it Dave? You're mouthing their words."

Paul reached out and put his fingers on Joe's lips. "It's OK. No more. It's over. We're at the end of our journey."

Ahead of them the enormous concrete dam covered the entire horizon. A loud horn sounded, and the *Viking Century Sky* came to a complete stop in front of a 50-foot-high filigreed gate blocking the entrance to a colossal steel channel. Every element of the channel's infrastructure was visible: metal gratings, large pipes, and electronic devices. The enormous container ship, at least ten times their cruise ship's height, was approaching the gate from inside the channel. A red light started flashing, and the gate slowly rose, allowing the other ship to just clear the gate as it slowly edged out into the river.

Paul moved to the side railing to look, and Joe joined him there as their own ship began moving again. The *Viking Century Sky* entered a small channel delineated by a thin web of plastic, a subdivision of the larger tunnel, still occupied by the exiting container ship. It was a tight fit; they could almost touch the smooth steel lateral wall of the body of the cargo ship moving in the opposite direction.

Joe wondered what kept both ships on so precise a course. The navigation would have to be flawless, and he could see no tugboat. He looked up and spotted the fine steel wires with sensors at their tips—a guidance system embedded in the plastic. He had never seen anything like it and had to stop his mind from calculating the kind of technology that was behind it. There would be time for that later. Now he had to focus on getting Paul back. This spectacle had given him a brief respite, and he had to take advantage of it.

"Please. I'll come apart if you leave, Paul. People change."

Paul's voice was cold as ice. "It's too late."

"I can change."

"It's all Joe again. It's always about Joe. How many victims were there over the years, Joe—children, women, scientists? I knew about most of it and did nothing." Paul's voice lowered to a whisper. "We are a disgusting pair."

The enormous ship was almost upon them as it moved out of the darkness of the dam. From the other direction, the *Viking Century Sky* had slowed, waiting for it to clear completely. The two ships were almost touching.

Paul was now focused on the two ships. He leaned farther over the side railing and tentatively put out a hand. "It's too late to change what we've done. But I will do something about my responsibility for it."

Paul pointed at the tiny sliver of lights showing between the two ships. "Come closer, Joe, and watch what the Chinese engineers have built. It's quite something. The kind of mechanism that should interest you."

Joe breathed a sigh of relief as he edged closer. "And we'll figure it out together, Paul. Like old times."

They both stared in silence as the steel wires in the plastic mesh detached and descended until they were between the two ships, robotic electronic sensors to manage the passage. The engines of the container ship revved up with a mighty roar, and their own ship answered with a small growl of its own. Both were moving faster now in opposite directions.

Joe said, "The guidance system had better work or we'll collide. We're too close to that huge ship. Two or three feet at the most. Any error in those sensor wires …"

"It will be tight," Paul said. "But I'm sure they have it figured out. Remember the Chinese build everything for us these days. Even the medicines you created at MI."

"We created."

"I know you're scared, Joe, and not about the ships colliding. But here's the thing: Only a part of this is about you. You're just a catalyst for decisions I've had to make …" His voice was drowned out by the horn.

"What are you talking about, Paul?" Joe yelled.

"I'm surprised you haven't figured it out."

"I always do. Just give me a little time." But Joe's words were obliterated by the engine roars of both boats, which created a dissonance that made his flesh crawl.

Paul gestured for Joe to come close, and Joe obeyed. He whispered hoarsely into Joe's ear, "I'm not weak anymore. Right now I'm very angry. And I need a hug or a handshake, something from you."

Relief surged through Joe as he moved to comply. He felt Paul's body so warm against his chest. A shrill whistle sounded, and Paul began yelling incoherently, "No, don't! You have to stay away!" He turned his back to the rail, grasping Joe's shirt in his fist. "Don't come any closer!"

Joe tried to back away. "Have you gone crazy?"

"Don't, Joe! Don't hurt me!" The words came in frantic bursts as Paul pressed his left foot back against the vertical tubing of the railing. He continued to scream as if talking to an unseen audience. "I can't stand your manipulations anymore! Leave me alone!" He leveraged his body against Joe's and fell backward against the railing, his head sticking out over the water and almost touching the other ship. The toe of his shoe went straight into Joe's groin. Joe bent forward in pain, his head lurching into Paul's chest. There were simultaneous blasts from the two horns as the ships moved forward in opposite directions. For a moment, both men teetered against the railing. Then Paul pushed both knees against Joe's body for leverage and toppled backward into the tiny space between the two ships. There was no sound as he plummeted down into the darkness.

Joe forced himself upright and looked frantically down over the railing. He couldn't see Paul; the huge belly of the container ship obscured the water below. But as the boats drew apart, Joe screamed as threads of red filled the water. Horns continued to blare, drowning out his screams as the two ships slid past one another. Then he collapsed against the railing, and from nowhere Song rushed toward him.

CHAPTER 43

Revenge by Death

The late springtime was Wiley's favorite season in Sausalito. The fog that blanketed the coast in the summer was still a month off, and there was plenty of warming sun to lift a light steam from the deep blue waters of the San Francisco Bay. He stood on the upper deck of his barge surveying his dominion and waiting for Dave to arrive with their lattes and muffins from the nearby Bayside Café. To the west, the Marin Headlands and the coastal hills were still green from winter rains. Wildflowers and cultivated gardens on the lower slopes of the hillside town of Sausalito sparkled with color. To the north was the undulating silhouette of Mount Tamalpais that inspired the mountain's nickname, the Sleeping Lady.

Dave's and Wiley's return home from China had been marred by a two-day stay in a Shanghai prison, reasonably benign thanks to Chang's helpful expediting and vigilant protection. The physical odors of prison confinement and China's pollution still clung to Wiley's skin like a phantom limb. But the enduring horror of the trip was Paul's death, made even more poignant by the simultaneous announcement that he and Joe had won the Nobel Prize in Chemistry. Now he mourned the quiet, handsome presence of the man with a pragmatic intelligence so like his own father's. Looking out over the sparkling water, he relived the kayak ride they shared when he had supported Paul's nascent bid for independence from Joe. He remembered the look in Paul's eyes: excessive appreciation bordering on worship, a feeling that Dave believed was born of an ambivalent longing to find a replacement for Joe. That day kayaking on the water had tipped a fatal balance, inadvertently provoking Paul to a level of risk and courage that proved far beyond his emotional capacity to endure.

Wiley prowled the deck obsessing on the immediate events leading up to the bloody death. Dave and he had both thought of Paul when the alarms on the ship began blaring and the *Viking Century Sky* shuddered to a stop. They had instinctively raced for the observation sun deck, but it was already sealed off. Then they had tried to reach Paul's cabin, but the VIP area was completely secured. Within minutes, a shipwide curfew was imposed: all passengers were to stay in their rooms until further notice, which lasted most of the night. For the next several hours, Wiley had watched through his porthole as police and rescue teams arrived in steady streams by helicopter and boat. He had reached all of his group by phone except Paul. Curfew on the VIP deck was less confining; Gloria had told him of rumors that an American had gone overboard and later in the night confirmed that it was almost certainly Paul.

In the morning, the *Viking* finally was allowed to pass through the giant locks. While the passengers disembarked, he and Dave were kept separate from the other passengers and flown to Shanghai in a police helicopter in the custody of Chang and his team without seeing Debra Jean or Gloria. Chang had tersely confirmed Paul's death but would offer no more details, except that Song was in charge of the investigation.

Then when Dave and Wiley were released from prison, they were shown an American newspaper that headlined both the death of Paul Stokes and the simultaneous award of the Nobel Prize in Chemistry to him and Joe Diamond. The official Chinese government news agency reported that Paul had been killed in a fall from the ship's deck while his cruise ship passed through the shipping lanes of the newly opened Three Gorges Dam. A nearby container ship, navigating the dam in the opposite direction, had dragged Paul's body some distance in its wake, leaving a few shredded remains floating in the water before discharging the body into the lake behind the dam. Dredging the reservoir had proved fruitless; whatever was left probably mixed with the construction debris and settled in its depths.

On the flight to San Francisco, Dave and Wiley had gone over and over what they might have done differently in the last hours of Paul's life. Their last glimpse of him had been as he left the dining room after his talk with Joe and brief return to their table. Neither had gone after him; they had waited for Debra Jean to return. Then, on Dave's insistence, they tried to reach Paul's cabin to check on him but had been turned away from the VIP area, where it was located. A telephone call to his room went unanswered. Then they had walked down to the tourist deck to search further and found most of the tourists and ship's personnel watching as their ship navigated toward the entrance of the Three Gorges Dam. They had forgotten their search in the mesmerizing presence of the gargantuan concrete structure. But when the alarm bells rang and the ship shuddered to a stop, they both knew that something had happened to Paul.

So now, Wiley thought morosely, he had to live with a significant responsibility for yet another fatality of a man close to him. And with Paul, just as with his father, the official view was suicide.

Wiley knew in his heart that his father had been murdered, and Joe had more than confirmed that in their last conversation. But despite a myriad of hypotheses, Paul's death was still a mystery to him.

Wiley stopped pacing and thought of Dave's encounter with Song just before boarding the plane home. She had been with Chang when he escorted them to the airport for their nonstop flight from Shanghai to San Francisco, first class, courtesy of the Chinese government. She and Chang were silent during the drive, refusing to acknowledge even simple questions. But at the departure gate, Song drew Dave aside to say good-bye. She didn't pull away when Dave transformed her handshake into a hug.

"Where are the videos of the conversation between Paul and Joe before he died?"

"There were none," she answered quietly, remaining in his embrace.

"We need them, Song. I'll be waiting."

Looking up at him as they pulled apart, she nodded imperceptibly. Dave winked at her, she blushed, and he took advantage of her embarrassment to lean down and kiss her on the cheek near her lips. Dave later told Wiley that she had said something to him then that sounded like "soon." They walked to the plane, and both men waved to her. She looked tiny and vulnerable as she nervously waved back.

Wiley laughed out loud thinking how much Dave and he had parsed that sound. What did "soon" mean, or had Dave simply misheard Song's name? Without the tapes, they might never know the truth behind Paul's death. They would just have to wait and see.

"Goodbye, friend," Wiley said out loud to the water, closing his eyes, losing himself in the gentle sensations of the barge rocking on the flood tide. He could almost feel Paul paddling in the front of the Klepper, an echo of his father's arms around him when he was young and learning how to sail.

"Wiley, man," he heard Dave yell as he jogged down the ramp. Wiley looked up to see his partner holding a promised latte in one large hand and a brown bag in the other, and as so often happened when he saw Dave, Wiley's mood immediately changed. There was such light and litheness in the man—not a wasted move as he glided along the rough-hewn boards of the gangplank.

Watching him approach brought up another set of happier memories: the muscular grace with which Dave had eluded the grasp of defensive backs, moving in a private invulnerable space immune to the hostile intent of grappling hands and desperate blocks and tackles. Dave was the truly great All-American of their pair, but then, as now, he deliberately remained in Wiley's shadow. Of course, the sports cognoscenti knew his remarkable talents, and his pro offers were as big as Wiley's own. When Wiley's father died, Dave refused to consider the Rose Bowl without his friend, and even now, ten years later, he seemed comfortable in the role of trickster and sidekick. Wiley didn't fully understand Dave's motivation any more than Paul's. But since his father's death, Wiley rarely questioned his friend about his life decisions. He was simply glad Dave had stayed close, feeling that he never could have gotten through without him. Selfish, he thought, and a disturbing resonance with Joe's need for Paul. But he couldn't help that Dave held him as leader of their pair even though Wiley felt like a simpleton next to his friend's complexity. Someday soon, Dave would leave and go his own way, but for now, Wiley was always grateful for his presence.

"Sorry for the delay. Got waylaid by the damsel foaming our coffee brew!" Dave laughed, standing on the ramp to the barge. He took the steps to the upper deck three at a time and placed the food and drink on the circular table. "Damn, you look gloomy. Remember, it won't help

Paul." Dave looked thoughtfully at the calm water. "Time for a break before the women show up. The tide is high. What about a quick swim?"

"I guess," Wiley said, marveling at the man's energy. He had run ten miles from San Francisco and then volunteered to get their breakfast. "A shower would be more efficient."

In reply, Dave pulled off his sweat-soaked jogging clothes, lay them messily on the deck, and, naked, leaped onto the deck railing, balancing like a gymnast. "But there's more to life than efficiency. Come on!" he yelled, then dove into the water with only the tiniest splash. He stayed underwater for almost a minute and emerged 50 yards out, blowing water like a porpoise.

He shouted something inaudible and then dove below the surface again. Wiley disrobed quickly and followed with his own dive, skimming the muddy bottom before resurfacing next to his friend. Shivering, they headed back to the boat with strong crawls and stopped to tread water.

"Too cold for you, Wiley?"

"I'd call it bracing and delicious. I'd race you to Angel Island and win if we didn't have the social engagement pending. It wouldn't be seemly for us to be naked in the water when the women arrived."

"It might cheer them up."

"You're such a child, Dave." Wiley hoisted himself up onto the dock, and then grabbed a towel and threw one hard at Dave.

* * *

A few minutes later, the two men were sitting on the barge's deck with their coffees.

"From your Portuguese days?" Wiley asked with a smile as he handed a muffin to his friend. Dave's light blue T-shirt boldly announced that he was a graduate of the Universidade de Coimbra. "Celebrating life is the best way to honor him. He did too little of that for himself." Dave licked latte foam from his cup.

Wiley drank down the rest of his latte. A loud banging sound began on the deck below them. A female voice sounded next to the barge.

Dave and Wiley peered over the railing. Debra Jean was deftly maneuvering a kayak parallel to their dock. "Hey, give me a hand. I brought breakfast." She grabbed at a large shopping bag stowed in the front.

"That means she's still our client," Dave whispered to Wiley.

"Of course I am. But not for long. How I'm going to exist without the two of you I don't know. I was 50 yards north, paddling toward you guys, when I saw Dave standing naked on the railing. Quite a sight. More than enough manliness to make me stay around. Great dive too." She steadied the boat against the dock. "Oh, you're manly, too, Wiley," she teased. "It's just that you're not a showoff. Hey, isn't anyone going to give me a hand with this stuff?"

Dave vaulted back over the railing and landed lightly on the deck. "Great entrance, Debra Jean." He took the bag from her and helped her out of the kayak, and then the two of them hoisted it onto the deck.

Wiley shouted down to her. "How long have you been a kayaker, Debra Jean?"

"Since sunrise," she said gleefully, stowing the paddles. "I couldn't sleep, thinking about Paul. So I drove over here before dawn and persuaded the set-up guys at the rental place to let me rent one of those kayaks before they opened at eight. The nice man gave me half-price, called it a sunrise special. I paddled out to the east side of Angel Island and watched the sun come up. Then I paddled back here and left the kayak by the park near Mollie Stone's and bought bagels and lox for all of us. I put it in my kayak, paddled to your marina, and here I am, full of fun and rarin' to go."

She carried the bag up to the top deck. "Actually, I've been obsessing about Paul the entire time. The swells of the water, the depth, the sunrise, all of the beautiful life that he no longer can experience."

"Your friendship was a beautiful thing, Debra Jean."

"You're right, Wiley. Complex and troubled and still beautiful." She sighed, her eyes filling with tears. She looked away. "I was partly responsible for his death, wasn't I?"

"I think we all feel responsible for what happened," Dave said. He sipped his coffee. "Is it pointless to say that his death doesn't make this morning any less beautiful? Memorial services, requiems—they all invoke both sadness and beauty. Debra Jean, you created your own sacrament so naturally. An ecstatic sunrise in a kayak to balance the despair at losing a friend. Now there's a ritual, and a woman, I can appreciate."

"But it leaves out the moral problem: one consequence of my wanting revenge was that the bad guy won the Nobel Prize while the good guy died. Unless I'm missing something, that's a nightmare outcome," she said glumly.

"A nightmare that belongs to all of us," Wiley agreed. He motioned for Debra Jean and Dave to have a seat at the table. Debra Jean emptied her grocery bag and began setting out her purchases.

Dave nodded. "Enough food for all. It's the West Coast's version of the Jewish ritual of sitting shiva: Food. Friendship. Beauty. Reflection. Remembrance. Celebrating humanity while balancing the world of good and evil."

Debra Jean nodded. "Where's Gloria? I want her in on our conversation."

On cue, an old Toyota drew up at the marina, and Gloria emerged and walked quickly up the dock, carrying a large grocery bag. "A little something for breakfast," she said as she climbed up to the deck; then she broke out laughing when she saw the feast.

"Just like Catholic wakes in my childhood village."

"We all read from the same script around death," Dave said, watching Wiley take Gloria into his arms. Dave and Debra Jean added their bodies to make it a group hug.

They stood silently until Gloria could no longer contain her emotions. "It's been a little over a week since all of us were together on the *Viking*, and two weeks since we sat around this table with Paul for the first time," she said, eyes tearing. "Back then, I had lots of fantasies about our trip to China. But none of them included one of us dying."

"The stakes have been very high from the beginning," Dave said. "Remember the last meeting here—my fight with Zvi. By the way, I've located him in a rehabilitation hospital outside of San Francisco and got into his records. Blind in one eye and a permanently crippled leg."

"Right. Another casualty from this case. Well earned, I would say. But now we have to honor Paul." Wiley popped a bottle of champagne and filled glasses all around.

"And find a way to understand," Dave added.

"Paul did love good food and wine. And maybe the lab was his playpen."

"That was Paul," Debra Jean said with a smile, turning to Gloria. "I see that you have some extra goodies for us. Great stuff from the Mission?"

"Would you believe lox and bagels!" Gloria said as she unpacked her bags. "And yes, I did throw in some special pastries from Tartine." She sat down opposite Wiley and began to munch on a cream-filled tart. Dave and Debra Jean took the other chairs. Then Dave added an empty one next to Debra Jean.

"So, it's a breakfast communion," Wiley said, raising his glass. "For Paul." The group clicked glasses and drank.

"For Paul," Dave echoed, and then chanted the mourners' Kaddish in Hebrew. Wiley joined in and then sang "Dona Nobis Pacem" in his high clear tenor.

"Mozart's Requiem," Debra Jean said. "I wouldn't have guessed …"

"My dad loved classical music. I'd sit and listen with him. He particularly loved this part about finding peace after the turmoil of life and death."

They lapsed into silence, with only the wind on the water and an occasional revving motor from the freeway high above breaking the sad spell.

Wiley leaned back in his chair, hands behind his head. "So, my living friends, are we ready to try to make sense of what happened?" He turned to Debra Jean expectantly. "You're our client. It's your show. At least at the beginning."

"I'm back for a final go-round."

"I'm glad," Wiley said. "We all need some closure."

He told them about the two days in a Shanghai prison and Dave's encounter with Song at the airport. Then he turned to Debra Jean. "Fill us in, including anything you can add about the facts around Paul's death."

She sighed. "Gloria and I were immediately isolated and put on a plane to Beijing and then home."

"Were you questioned before leaving?" Dave asked. "If so, what you were asked could tell us something."

Debra Jean replied, "There was an interrogation of sorts. They asked about Paul's state of mind. There was no attempt to implicate me. Bottom line: I learned nothing about Paul's death."

"My 'interrogation' was equally uninformative," Gloria chimed in. "Nothing about my work relationship with Joe and Paul at MI."

"So no new information about Paul," Dave said, leaning back in the deck chair. "Wiley, do you mind if I speculate?"

"Do I have a choice?"

"Probably not, and I think we all could benefit. Some things are easy. We all agree that Paul was depressed. But it wasn't just Paul who was in trouble. We also saw Joe coming apart that last day on the ship."

"I agree," Debra Jean said. "When Joe and I spoke at lunch, he had less bravado. He was definitely anxious."

"You never told us what happened in that last conversation with Joe," Dave said. "At the time, you thought it could be important."

She reached for one of Gloria's pastries and described the facts of the conversation. "It felt good to confront him, but it was also unsatisfying. Mostly I think he was trying to get information from me, and he got something."

"What did he want?" Wiley asked.

"What did he get?" Dave interjected quickly.

"He wanted to know why you were there, Wiley. He said he couldn't put it all together. I inadvertently gave him the answer, at least part of it, by mentioning Revenge, Inc.—the concept, anyway. He relaxed more as he played with the information. By the end, he was far more conciliatory. That's when he apologized for what happened at Jardinière and offered to help me get back into science."

"And your guess about why he was acting nice?" Dave asked.

"All about Paul. I think he wanted to take away any influence I might have on his friend. That's what really mattered to him."

Wiley frowned. "But why was he so scared, given, well, the way the romantic part turned out?"

"Oh naive man," Gloria said.

"Meaning?" Wiley asked.

"Sexual humiliation can become an addiction. Joe knows about that stuff. Paul's repeated failures would have worried Joe as much as success."

"Gloria is right," Debra Jean said. "Paul was humiliated. It made him depressed and desperate, but it also made him want me in a different way, more like a woebegone child than an adult."

Gloria put her hand on Debra Jean's. "Men come in many forms, but they all need endless reassurance."

"You're right," Debra Jean said. "When I came back from lunch after speaking to Joe, Paul was waiting in my room. You know what he did? He came over, put his head on my lap, and cried. And after a bit, so did I. We were both very sad. And here's what I haven't told anybody till now. He said he was going to speak to Joe 'one last time.'"

"He said 'one last time.' Those words!" Dave exclaimed.

"I only thought about it after he was dead. Boy, I wish I had that to do over. I assumed that it meant he was planning on leaving Joe and MI, not suicide."

Dave rose, flipping his legs to sit cross-legged in his chair. "So he was saying good-bye to you, Debra Jean, a prelude to saying good-bye to Joe. It supports what we all feel, that Paul wasn't pushed and didn't fall by accident. He jumped from the boat, timing it just right so … he'd be crushed."

"But why?" Debra Jean asked, eyes wide. "It can't be just about me, can it?"

"Hardly," Dave said. "But I think his failure with you highlighted the perverse nature of his relationship with Joe. He hated what he had become. Once he saw himself in that way—and all of us, not just you, Debra Jean, had a lot to do with that—he wanted to obliterate himself and punish Joe. Paul was nothing but pragmatic. He found the answer to both desires in an ultimate revenge—his own death!"

A light wind came up from the water.

"That's a stretch, Dave," Gloria said. "You're saying that Paul killed himself to punish Joe?"

"Yes, but also to stop his own pain," Dave said. "Wiley, you kept telling us, 'The way to Joe is through Paul.' I thought it was a weak and naive plan, but you were right. You told Paul that he had the ultimate power over his friend, and he learned the lesson well. And being forced to watch Paul's suicide might be just the beginning of Joe's trials."

"But Paul's dead and Joe lives," Debra Jean said in despair. "What kind of power is that? Life is the great prize, isn't it? Don't—"

"OK," Wiley interrupted. "Let's get some confirmation to go along with the philosophy. What did the interrogators ask you, Debra Jean? They may have heard what Paul and Joe were saying. For starters, who was it that interrogated you?"

"Chang. As I told you, he asked me over and over whether I had thought Paul was suicidal. He was clearly upset. When Song came in, she apologized for Chang. She said he was desperate to get answers. I told her I didn't have any.

"She was as upset as Chang. She said that providing security for Paul was her job and she had failed. When they both left, I turned on the television. That's when I learned that Joe and Paul had gotten the Nobel Prize. It seemed so unfair, and I just fell apart. I couldn't stop shaking. Eventually I got hold of Chang and asked to make sure that I could go home on the same plane as Gloria. Chang agreed. Thank God for that." She turned to Gloria and smiled. "You were great." Gloria smiled back.

"Did you see Joe before you left?" Wiley asked.

"No. Only on TV."

Wiley got up from his chair, stretched, and walked to the railing. He looked down into the water, thinking that without a record, without the tape, they might never know what happened on the back deck of the *Viking Century Sky*. He felt weighed down by their decision to take on Debra Jean as a client, an act that had led to Paul's death. Yes, his strategy had worked, and a man had died as a result. Joe had prevailed.

Shadows from migrating ducks passed over the shallow water, looking like deep swimming fish. He had fulfilled his contract with Debra Jean. He had helped a pampered but talented woman to regain her life force. But in the process, Paul's life had been exposed. Suicide had provided a final solution.

It was the law of unintended consequences writ large. Wiley remembered his own disastrous efforts to cope with the threats on his father's life. He went home, planning to seek advice from his father about what to do. But looking at the man he loved and admired, he knew what his father would expect of him. He also knew that he had no right to ask his father what he should do. He had to handle it himself. So he kept the threat to himself and asked about a current architectural project that had gained notoriety by unexpectedly leading to racial violence. His father understood something of his son's anxiety, though not its real cause. "I try to design my projects as well as I can. I try to make them beautiful and functional. I try to be true to my work and my profession. The rest is up to fate. Even if you do your best, and you must, one never knows how it will turn out." Then he smiled and patted his son on the shoulder, and they wolfed down the harvest feast that Wiley's mother had prepared. Twenty-four hours later, Wiley's father was dead.

He continued to watch the migrating ducks headed north over the headlands until they were dots in the blue sky. Dave was standing at his side and slowly guided him back to the group.

Wiley accepted a glass of water from his friend. "Gloria, you haven't said much about what happened to you after … well, Paul's suicide. Like do you still have a job at MI?"

"Yes, but I won't keep it. Right now I'm here with you guys mourning Paul. But I did see Joe after Paul's death."

Wiley nodded for her to continue.

Dave said, "Please tell."

"I was in my cabin when the sirens went off. I went up on deck. A Taiwanese man who spoke English said that someone had fallen overboard and there was a search under way. I tried to go to your room, Wiley, but there was a security man stationed at the door. I tried to make contact with you all by phone, but I couldn't get through. A few hours later, both Song and Chang came in to question me. They said that one of the Americans had fallen overboard. You can imagine my relief when I learned that it wasn't any of you, and the horror when I discovered it was Paul. They wouldn't tell me anything more. They interrogated me about both of you.

"When they were finished with their questioning, they said that Joe wanted to speak to me. Song insisted on going with me; I was relieved not to face him alone. We went to his cabin. One of Chang's guards was there. The place was a mess, and Joe was incoherent. I'd never seen him like that before. He just kept repeating that Paul had gone overboard. As much as I hate the man and what he's done, I felt compassion for what he was going through. And I knew I was seeing the tip of the iceberg."

"Go on," Wiley said.

"He kept looking through me. I'm not even sure he saw me. Then he seemed to close down completely. He became absolutely still, as if he were frozen."

"Catatonia," Dave said. "Move and you destroy the world with rage and pain. So you don't."

"I guess. He stayed that way, so after a while we left the room. They wanted to know what I thought. I told them I didn't know, that I wasn't a psychiatrist. Song questioned me some more, but I was pretty shaken, what with Paul and seeing Joe that way and not knowing about you and ..." She looked around the table. "Not knowing about any of you. Eventually she told me that I was going to be sent home as soon as possible. Then I asked her if I could talk to Joe alone. He was my boss, after all, and I was responsible for his security. She said that Chang had asked her to keep all the Americans away from Joe. Then she did something funny. She asked me if I was really an American, because I looked so dark and different. I was quiet, but she seemed to get that it hurt me. So I pushed on her about her attitude and then asked again to see Joe alone. Amazingly, she said I could, as long as the guard stayed. She said he didn't speak English.

"I went back in there with Joe. He was still in that frozen state. So, hoping to focus on something neutral, I asked him if I still had a job. I think he recognized me, and he suddenly began to cry. I'd never seen anyone cry like that. Through the blubbering he said that he wanted me to stay at my job. He said he needed me now more than ever. Then he slowly turned to ice again, and was gone.

"Eventually I left. I told Song that I wanted to take him back with me. It seemed the right thing to do at the time. But she said no. Then her beeper went off and she left the room. I slipped back in and whispered to Joe that I would stay if he wanted. I know he didn't hear me; I don't think he even knew who I was by then. He was completely out of it."

"Could Joe have been acting?" Dave said.

"No way. No one could act that well," Gloria said. "Then Song burst into the room with a radio phone in her hand. She told Joe that he had a call from Sweden. That woke him up! He took the phone and listened for a while, and then asked a few questions about when and how much. He said something about Paul. Then he hung up. He whispered something to Song, and then sat back and just stared at the wall. Finally Song turned to me and said, 'Dr. Diamond and Dr. Stokes just won the Nobel Prize.'

"I congratulated him, but he kept mumbling about Paul. Song called for some guards and they escorted him out, and within a few minutes I heard a helicopter take off. You know the rest. Debra Jean and I left Beijing and flew home."

"Anything else, Gloria?" Wiley asked again.

"Besides needing to use the bathroom?"

"Ditto," Debra Jean said.

"Me too," Dave said. "And my cell phone is vibrating. Death and sex and madness are interesting, but the kidneys will have their way with us."

"Sounds serious," Wiley added. "Let's take 30 minutes."

CHAPTER 44

"All We Like Sheep"

D ave and Wiley took their break in the downstairs office. The space contained Wiley's bedroom, bathroom, and living room, and was dominated by large windows that ran from three feet above water level to the ceiling. The walls were shiny white, and the reflections from outside created the atmosphere of an Impressionist painting: rippling swaths of pale blues and greens from the water's surface, clear light from the sky and sun, and a collage of bright colors from painted boat hulls and many-hued sails. The mirrored light from the water's surface was the dominant influence and gave the room a green-blue cast, a muted underwater feel in contrast to the topside dazzle.

"I just spoke to Song," Dave said as he joined Wiley at the other end of the comfortable sofa. "From Beijing with love."

"What did she say?" Wiley said, and then added, "Song is hardly your type, Dave."

"I'm not so sure. Song is like a porcelain doll on the outside, but who knows what passions lie inside that perky little body? I'd bet there's more to her—"

Wiley cut him off. "I know your lover's poetry by heart."

"Don't let jealousy dim your appreciation of my troubadour skills," Dave retorted.

"There is always a yearning female lurking at the end of our Revenge, Inc., capers," Wiley said, more seriously than he had intended. Now we have a porcelain doll. ..."

"Some men are natural lovers. You remember Mozart's *Don Giovanni*—his servant catalogues every conquest of his boss. The numbers run up into the thousands!"

"You're both out of my league, Dave. I am a one-woman man with a constant heart."

"You mean one woman at a time!"

"OK, party's over," Wiley said wryly. "Can we get back to Song's conversation with you?"

"I wrote down exactly what she said: 'I'll be passing through San Francisco on my way to Stockholm to see Dr. Diamond receive his prize. And with what Dr. Stokes told us, collect ours.' Mysterious, huh? But get the last bit: 'You're all invited to the ceremony, courtesy of and paid for by the Chinese government.'"

"Wow to the last part!" Wiley exclaimed. "And very obscure in everything else." He appraised his friend. "I can already tell that you've psyched it all out."

"Of course."

"So what is the prize she's collecting?" Wiley asked thoughtfully.

"I think it's Joe himself."

"Hmmm. And what do you think she learned from Paul?"

"That's harder, but here's my speculation. Song and Chang had a chance to watch all the tapes. Remember how they couldn't make out your words when they monitored you and Joe on the observation sun deck? They had to have beefed up the audio surveillance after that debacle. 'Dr. Stokes told us' is saying that Song knows what was said between them and that Paul knew he'd have an audience."

Wiley caught Dave's eye. "Paul deliberately left a message for them before he went overboard?"

"It's logical when you think about it."

"His suicide note." Wiley stared at the bay's flickering pattern on the ceiling.

"I think Paul had been deciding whether to take his own life ever since we arrived on the scene," Dave said.

Wiley nodded unhappily.

Dave continued, "Apparently, Paul planned the whole thing. Talk about revenge. He wanted Joe to understand the damage he had done and pay for it. He wanted Joe to see him die and to live with that image all his life."

Wiley nodded in agreement.

"He also understood that revenge is about control and punishment *over time*. His suicidal jump was the biggest blow but not the last. He gave the Chinese control of Joe— and he knew they do control well. The tape gives Song and her Party buddies a hold on Joe that will last a very long time."

"It all fits together, Dave," Wiley acknowledged.

"We won't know what Song actually knows until we see her." Dave frowned. "I remember worrying about how he looked as he left our table, the last time we saw him. It was the determination in his stride, along with the grimace on his face. If Debra Jean hadn't been so determined to confront Joe. If only we had acted. … None of us are innocent in this one."

They were silent for a few moments, watching the play of light and color in the room. Then Wiley smiled broadly. "So we go to Stockholm. Better that Debra Jean springs for it than the Chinese government. Too many strings attached to that one. Do you think she will?"

"Probably." Dave rose from his perch on the sofa and began a series of increasingly rapid capoeira passes on the rug.

"What a case," Wiley mused.

Dave paused to catch his breath and then assumed a headstand, alternating right and left hands as support every 10 to 15 seconds. "It's Paul, not Joe, who really gets me." Dave lost his balance, but with an effort he righted himself before he fell. "'All we like sheep,' Isaiah says. It's brilliant. He defines humanity as a complicit species, and I know he's right. Joe is an evil leader, but he couldn't survive the likes of Paul. And I say, never again."

Wiley stared at his friend. "It's the Jewish thing, isn't it? That's always there when I can't follow your reasoning."

Dave somersaulted into a standing position and regained his seat. "And why should you, Wiley? We're alike in so many ways, but our deepest heritage still separates us."

"I guess."

"I'm convinced that Paul knew everything about his friend: sex with little children, snuff films, and God knows what else. But he never confronted Joe on any of it. Sure, his support of Joe's crimes was passive, but that's exactly what Joe required." Dave's voice broke with emotion.

"Without Paul regularly jerking off his friend, some children out there might still have had a chance. Joe made Paul his psychic puppet, his scapegoat, but Paul had a choice. Like 'all we sheep,' he lacked the courage to act on it."

"I thought he had more in him, and I was wrong," Wiley said regretfully. "But I always liked Paul, Dave. Always will. Out in the kayak that day, I felt he wanted to become someone different. When I used him to get at Joe, I never dreamed he would destroy himself in the process." Wiley leaned back and stared at the ceiling.

"We all misjudged him, Wiley. Paul wasn't a hero. Maybe suicide was the best he could do; that was obviously his conclusion."

For a while, both men stared in silence at the wavering light on the ceiling.

Dave spoke first. "Did you know his parents were Jesus freaks? The motto of their community was 'Who taketh away the sins of the world.' It's what he was raised to believe—that a living God would hold the bag for him."

"Such a waste of a life." Wiley roused himself and headed for the door. "It's hard to believe that Paul is dead. It makes me hate Joe even more."

"None of us need more excuses to hate Joe."

"Do you think Joe will bounce back? He's a survivor and is about to get a big boost from the Nobel Committee."

"Hard to know. What's your guess?"

Wiley took his time answering. When he spoke, his voice was somber. "I think Song is going to Sweden to deliver the final blow. That's if he doesn't self-destruct on his own." Wiley checked the time. "We need to get back to our friends."

Dave followed Wiley up to the kitchen and climbed the short flight of stairs to the deck. Debra Jean and Gloria lay on the deck in the sun, talking quietly. When Gloria saw Wiley, she stood and kissed him firmly on the mouth. Then she sat down at the table. Debra Jean and Dave followed suit.

"Sorry to keep you gals waiting," Wiley said, flushing with pleasure. There was a slight breeze now, but the sun was even brighter than before. The tide was coming in from the Gate and beginning to stir the waves. Strong afternoon winds would follow, he knew.

"We were having girl talk," Debra Jean said lazily, smiling at Gloria. "Chatting about fashion and guys. Letting you do the work."

"I'll bet. Just like we spent most of our time talking about football," Wiley said mockingly.

"Anything we should know?" Gloria asked.

"Lots of theory and retrospectives," Dave replied. "Main thing was getting a call from Song. She's coming to San Francisco, and she let us know that it will be a stopover on her way to Stockholm. Song and her government invited all of us to the ceremony."

"To watch Joe accept his Nobel," Debra Jean affirmed. "It's in December, in case you don't know."

"I didn't, actually," Dave said. "But why do you?"

"Every ambitious scientist knows that, Dave. It's like the Rose Bowl for college football teams."

"But why invite us?" Gloria questioned.

"Frankly, the contents of her message were obscure." Dave read the short message out loud and added a summary of his conversation with Wiley. "I think we won't know until we get there."

Gloria said, "Maybe we'll find out what happened the last few minutes of Paul's life. I like to think his final act redeemed him. It would help us all with our guilt."

Dave turned to Debra Jean. "Even Wiley's friendship wasn't enough to make up for Joe."

She said, "But you're not an easy model to follow, Wiley. I'm afraid that's how Paul must've felt—like he was always in danger of letting you down. I feel that way knowing you. You too, Dave. You're both amazing men."

Dave glanced at the fog forming as white curls coalesced on the surface of the bay. "That means a lot, Debra Jean."

"Ditto," Wiley added. "Are you saying you're satisfied with our work? I hope so. And will you be with us in Stockholm?"

"Yes to everything except going to Stockholm, although I will foot the bill. There's something else I've got to do, and it doesn't relate to Joe. At least not directly."

"No hints?" Dave said.

Debra Jean smiled enigmatically. "I'll tell you all when it's over." She stood and stretched. "Right now, I feel like a snake with a brand new skin. I have to move around in it a little to make it feel good. And I know exactly what kind of wiggling will make that happen."

CHAPTER 45

Nobel

Joe Diamond sat on the stage of the Stockholm Concert Hall waiting with the other laureates. The Nobel Committee's award ceremony was in full swing; the prize for chemistry was all but his.

And Paul was dead.

All feelings of glory or accomplishment eluded him. Before Paul's death, scientific achievement, financial success, and Sons of Mozart had served his vanity well enough. But now the truth of Ecclesiastes—"Vanity of vanities, all is vanity"—echoed obsessively in his mind like a mantra.

He had criticized the inflated pride of so many of his colleagues, but he had always known it was his credo as well. He thought back to the glib answer he had given the press when he left his tenured professorship at UC Medical Center to begin a start-up company in biogenetics. "Why leave the great medical center at the height of your remarkable career?" he had been asked by a local TV news reporter. His impromptu reply had received national attention: "Because I can," he had said, laughing loudly at his own answer. "Academic science is a childish world full of excessive devotion to silly vanities." And he had gone on to talk about his field's dirty secrets, detailing petty financial dealings and corrupt bureaucracies that discouraged creativity and productive alliances. It was not a pretty picture he had painted that day.

Of course, his comments had irritated nerves and earned him enemies; nobody, especially academics, liked to see their foibles aired in public. They all wanted to keep their perks: cash honoraria and consulting fees, summer professorships, paid vacations, and conferences in exotic places.

Joe had turned down the stream of vanity prizes that padded other scientists' bank accounts and egos. Instead, with Paul, he created MI and turned his discoveries into patents, royalties, stock equities, and lucrative and influential positions in the world of big and "little" Pharma.

The reporters who would interview him after the medal ceremony were bound to ask why, given his previous sentiment, he now accepted this pretentious and lucrative prize. 'Good question,' he had rehearsed for the post-Nobel interviews. First, as prizes go, the Nobel is the High Mass of modern rituals. Second was the integrity of the prize itself: nomination by esteemed colleagues and being voted on by a committee with a dollop of taste and learning. And third—and here he would pause for effect—"the Nobel is a scepter of power in the scientific kingdom, and I want a chance to use it."

That was the key. Like so many great scientists before him, he had struggled to transfer creativity in the lab to power in the world. Few had succeeded: Einstein, Teller, and Watson in modern times. But the list of casualties was far longer. Men like Oppenheimer and Galileo had paid dearly. Now it was his chance to test the limit of what was possible.

That was all before the death of his best and only friend, he thought. Now he felt no elation in winning. He was barely capable of greeting colleagues and listening to the invocations. All afternoon, he had watched distractedly as the new Nobel winners walked to center stage in the magnificent hall and bowed their heads as the king of Sweden placed a small gold medal around their necks and handed them their million-dollar checks. His turn was coming, but his mind was besotted with lurid images of the residue of Paul's body, bloody shreds of his flesh floating in the murky water of the Yangtze.

He tore his mind from the horrors and forced it to ponder the neurophysiology of acute emotional deadness. He imagined the molecular blocking mechanism affecting the chemical transmission of neural data, and the consequent deactivation of the hippocampus and thalamic emotion stations deep in primitive areas of his brain. With cool precision, he visualized how the blocking mechanism would look on a contrast-enhanced CAT scan. At another time, pondering this mechanism might have spun off some new avenue of research. Now all that mattered was holding intact the thin wall between his all-powerful intellect and the frozen inner wasteland that threatened his tenuous hold on sanity.

His gut churned and he tasted acid in his mouth. Not only was Paul dead, but his part in the prize had been expunged from the official record. The Nobel Prize rules stated that posthumous awards could occur only if the individual died between nomination and the decision of the awards committee, not after. He had begged to have them change that rule, as they had twice before, most notably for Dag Hammarskjöld. But he had been told that this was not the Nobel Peace Prize, and besides, Hammarskjöld was Swedish, one of their own.

Joe raged at the dismissal of the dead man's legitimate rights, but the committee's representative had not yielded, implying that Paul's suicide—after all, they had snidely suggested, if it had been murder, Joe would be in prison—was a very different business than a plane crash in the cause of peace. So the prize had been rewritten to make Joe its sole recipient. He would ensure that they regretted their prejudicial decision. The new power they provided would be leveraged. Sons of Mozart would rise against them.

Rage and revenge were comforting, compared with the ominous quality of the mental symptoms attacking him. He recognized the signs—a pre-psychotic infection of the kind that had almost overrun him in childhood, when he had been similarly visited.

His mind wandered unbidden to his mother's stories of how, when he was small, she cuddled him on her large lap at bedtime and read him books. He had always been an irritable child, she had said, never simple to hold and comfort. Desperate to soothe her high-strung child, she had used nightly storytelling as a way to make contact with him. Joe remembered one fateful night when she told him a story of a prince looking for the treasures to win the hand of the princess and gain a kingdom. The first two trials, killing the dragon and overcoming the wicked witch, had been easily accomplished by the young hero, but in the third and last trial, the prince had come upon a frozen kingdom whose inhabitants existed in perpetual hibernation. Something in that image filled him with an unbearable dread that far surpassed the more familiar dangers of dragons and witches. He could still remember his own screams of panic as he took the book from his mother's hands and threw it on the floor. She had continued reading, but his tantrum raged on no matter what she did. For days he refused all contact with her and his father; he even stopped eating.

It was the last time he allowed his mother to read to him, and it precipitated a headlong rush into willful self-reliance. He denied himself the comfort of his mother's lap. He pored over books explaining science, math, history, and philosophy, and worked out the meta-rules behind those operations. The more he explored his mental powers, the more he separated himself from his family and schoolmates.

At eight, after his first best-selling book, he allowed his mother to take him to a child therapist, secretly hoping that the doctor would be able to fathom and assuage his unendurable fear. The gray-haired lady took Joe to a playroom, where she placed a puppet on her right hand—a friend, she said, who cared but also knew a lot about him. His puppet friend did listen and seemed to understand. One afternoon, the puppet declared that he, Joe, was the prince in the frozen kingdom, and his escape was doomed unless he learned about love. He tore the puppet into shreds and dedicated himself to building a mind in which all feelings were instrumental, never fundamental.

Finding Paul had been his one and only compromise to that ruling principle.

None of this was complicated, Joe thought. Paul had been his single link to the warmth and love that was also his greatest threat. Without Paul, he was in grave danger of being forever imprisoned in the frozen world.

Joe's reverie was abruptly halted by the announcement of his name from the podium. The representative of the Prize Committee had begun the ritual that would make Dr. Joseph Diamond a Nobel laureate in Chemistry. He droned on about Joe's accomplishments as if they belonged to the committee, not him. Joe stopped listening and scanned the faces of the audience. He knew many of the guests: great scientists in his field or patrons of the sciences and arts, political notables, former Nobel winners, all invited to honor him and the other laureates of the day. As he made eye contact, there were occasional nods but none of the genuine affection and appreciation that had greeted earlier winners.

A brass fanfare summarized the award with a précis of his accomplishment: "Mankind has benefited from the work of Joseph Diamond, the scientist, whose advances in the basic science of biophotochemicals have opened up a new and wondrous field of study, and Joseph Diamond the physician, who has devoted his time to applying these findings to decreasing suffering and ameliorating disease. We are grateful to this multifaceted creator who has offered his contributions and service to the world. Dr. Diamond, will you kindly step to the podium and receive the Nobel Prize in Chemistry."

He willed his body to advance to the podium. The waiting dignitary introduced him to the Swedish king, who grasped his hand firmly and then held it aloft to the audience's applause. But inside, Joe remained frozen in an increasingly vast stillness punctuated by an emergent female voice, that of a psychiatrist at his medical school. She listed symptoms of psychotic depression: disassociation, loss of personal boundaries, acute anxiety paranoia, and hallucination. The reality of that voice, he knew, was the undeniable hallucinatory proof of impending dissolution.

Frightened, he looked to the audience for help. At the very back of the auditorium he saw a group of people who looked familiar. Song, Gloria, Wiley, and Dave were gesticulating wildly toward the stage. Song caught his look and elbowed Dave and Wiley with a gleeful smile and a condescending nod to him. Wiley and Gloria threw back their heads and roared with laughter. Surely an apparition, but what if they were actually here? And they weren't applauding him like the invited guests. They were catcalling and jeering, making fun of this great moment in his life.

It would be better if they were not delusions but flesh-and-blood enemies. And he suddenly recalled that there were other enemies out there. How could he have forgotten the vellum letter he found on a silver tray on the coffee table of his hotel suite last night, the flag of the Chinese government elegantly imprinted on envelope and message?

> Dear Dr. Diamond:
> Videotape surveillance that has been recovered from the ship clearly demonstrates that Dr. Paul Stokes's death was not

suicide but murder. Our investigation, including your participation in an organization known as Sons of Mozart, strongly suggests that you have been involved in child pornography, including extreme scenarios common in snuff films.

I'm sure you will understand our position, Dr. Diamond. China is willing to hold this material confidential and to accept your contributions to our country, but on very different terms than before, which we will discuss after you accept the Nobel Prize in Chemistry.

The note had been copied to the encrypted address of Sons of Mozart, warning about further collaboration.

The king had stopped talking, and the Swedish national anthem had begun signaling the presentation of the prize. With all the control he could muster, Joe walked to stand next to the king and readied himself to accept the medal. He felt a structure inside his brain alter as the loss of Paul, his inner demons, and real persecutors in China coalesced.

The music ended, and the king held up his right hand to the audience, who dutifully rose and greeted him with the rhythmic applause that was de rigueur at the presentation of the award. Joe bowed his head to receive the medal, and the ribbon with the gold medallion was slipped onto his shoulders.

With a sudden movement, Joe wrenched the medal from his neck and threw it on the floor. Then he jerked the microphone from the king's flabby hand and turned to face the audience. The speech he had prepared for this moment scrolled through his mind. It was good to know that even in the midst of chaos, his powerful mind still held sway, his uncanny memory still intact. With all his senses sharpened for survival and control, he readied himself to speak.

Both audience and presiding committee were shocked into passivity. He knew he was in direct violation of 100 years of protocol, for only the winner of the Nobel Peace Prize was allowed give a speech at the medal ceremony. Joe also was sure that no one would stand against him. They would listen as he modeled courage and risk taking with his own revolutionary action on this Stockholm stage. He could almost see the headline: "Guerrilla Theater at the Nobel." The truth in his words would prevail over protocol, and the creative rule breakers in the audience would inevitably back him. And so he would move to the next level in his career, demonstrating his own vision of what constituted the highest standard in leadership and ideas.

Joe steadied himself on the podium, clearing its contents with his elbow. He sensed that the words he prepared were insufficient and an entirely new rhetoric was emerging. He began as planned. "Ladies and gentlemen, honored guests. I'm here to change the world." Then he softened his voice to establish intimacy. "Dear friends," he began again, feeling a dam of emotions burst within him. "I have won this medal through my work in chemistry. I have worked hard to achieve this accolade. The theory I have founded is brilliant, the practical applications immense. Like many of my projects, it has succeeded in ways that even I could not imagine. And of course all of it has made me rich. But at what cost?

"I learned about the award at the end of a cruise on the Yangtze River, viewing the Three Gorges Dam, the great project of the Chinese government. And as I marveled at the engineering feat, I heard the immense roar of water as it crested against the dam and was held by the wall of concrete. I heard other sounds as well: whimpers and screams of children who could not and would not bear the pain of their lives." As he spoke, the memory of those sounds came unbidden to his throat, a long guttural moan that grew louder and higher until it became a shrill reverberating scream. He breathed in deeply and from the slow exhale fashioned a resonant sound of a birthing child. He breathed again and heard the cry of a baby in pain; another breath, a young man gasping for air; and a final breath, a man overwhelmed by his own tortured emotions. And he knew he was re-creating his own song from the agonies of his tortured and torturing life.

"That song, too long silent, is the sound of my sacrifice for you, dear audience. It is the sound of the personal cost of my gifts to you. It is the emotional narrative of a child who was used and abused by the world, the moans of a little boy so talented that he had to suffer at the pleasure of his parents until he turned on them and became their master, at further cost to himself and children like him. My song is the revenge of childhood genius forced into an unripe manhood, a scientist who healed and served mankind with deeds incubated in the steamy perversity of abuse, torture, and control.

337

"Dear audience, nobody knew or cared about my pain and sacrifice, except one man, my true friend, Paul Stokes, the man who has been denied his due here in this Nobel ceremony. Paul held me close with a love that made me believe that I was still made of flesh and blood, that I was still human.

"Paul's all-encompassing love was a promise of healing and a new life for both of us. Perhaps he died so that a new Joe Diamond would finally emerge and stand alone." Joe extended his arm straight ahead and pointed his finger to emphasize each phrase: "A new man, a Christ born out of pain and loss, a Christ who would remain on the earth. A messiah who would save the world through his reigning compassionate genius."

Below him, Joe saw that the audience was growing restless, moving in their seats, even shouting obscenities at him. A few were heading toward the exits at the back and sides of the hall. His prescient words, his revelations, were obviously too much for them, and he sought a more reassuring voice to continue.

"All this must be frightening to you, but do not worry. Great work is in the offing, and all of you will be the beneficiaries." He stepped forward then, teetering at the edge of the stage, holding out his hands to the audience.

"A new leader is born," he said with joyful laughter. "I bequeath to you my body and brain to improve your lot, my hand and heart to protect you from the world's evils. I am your ultimate gift." He bent down, retrieved the medal from the floor, and held it up. It glittered in the spotlights, and with one grand, magnanimous gesture, he flung it into the audience. It landed on the floor in their midst with a clatter. No one moved to pick it up.

Yes, he thought angrily, listening to the jeers around him, it is as it has been for so many prophets before me: Moses, Elijah, Jesus, Muhammad, so many others. Few could understand the great ones. The corrupted priests and the rabble hordes were standing in the aisles and at the back of the hall—a few listening; some laughing, taunting him; but all unsure. He resisted scolding them. Instead, he calmed his voice and spoke with soothing rhetoric.

"Study my work, for it contains clues that will unlock all our secrets and mysteries. Join me and my fellow prodigies in guiding the planet to another level of hope and joy."

338

He folded his hands on his chest in a humble gesture. "Forgive my sins and honor the memory of Paul Stokes. Remember his humanity and his gift of love. Remind yourself that this love made Joe Diamond—prodigy, genius, entrepreneur, Nobel laureate, and yes, pervert and miscreant too—the complete human being you see before you."

He paused again, smiling down at them. "If you do that, you will all share in my prize. If you do that, I will bequeath all my gifts to you."

Joe felt a presence and turned to see a group of men in black uniforms and riot gear moving up behind him. He felt strong fingers gripping his shoulders. He surged against the firm hands that bound him. He held on tightly to the microphone and said, "I tell you that science is not only about objective discoveries. For science to be true, it must be warmed in the fire of love from another being. This is what Paul brought into the world. That is my Paul. My love." He sobbed convulsively as strong arms wrapped themselves around his body.

In the background, he heard the Swedish band strike up a triumphant hymn. He stopped resisting. He had said all that could be said. He felt content. And besides, the Chinese were waiting.

As Joe was gently escorted offstage, his thoughts were only of Paul. Paul's flaw had always been a failure of courage. At the Three Gorges Dam, a path had opened for Paul to join him in a great quest. Instead, Paul had jumped from the ruin of his life to the crush of ship hulls and cold churning waters below. He had blamed himself instead of accepting Joe's gifts as his own.

As Joe was bound in folds of cloth and tied with wide cotton belts, he heard Paul's words in his brain: "But here's the thing: Only a part of this is about you. You're just a catalyst for decisions I've had to make"—what decisions? Joe wondered. Surely Paul was telling him what to do here and now, finding the greater purpose they had searched for all their life together. Perhaps, during that moment of free fall, Paul had finally seen who his friend really was and who they could have been together. It was something to think about, and he knew he would have a long time to do just that.

The officers held his arms while the king rushed forward and placed the Nobel medal around his neck. With a rush of emotion, he knew that Paul and all of them finally understood.

CHAPTER 46

The Final Revenge

AKRON, CHRISTMAS EVE

Debra Jean stands in her mother's living room watching her fourth replay of Joe Diamond's weird rant at the Nobel Prize ceremony, televised live from Stockholm. It is remarkable entertainment, a world-renowned scientist-celebrity in the midst of a florid psychotic break, spouting a chaotic mix of prophecy, polemics, and personal confession.

She marvels at the truth of Wiley and Dave's simple but prescient hypothesis: that Paul was the key to the man's sanity. Despite Joe's prodigious intelligence, despite his survival instincts and resilience, Paul's death has reduced the great Joe Diamond to a raving lovesick madman. Joe's relentless obsessive outpourings are barely disguised screams of agony over Paul's death. His damaged mind is lost in a perpetually iterating equation, a quest for a strategy of release that is forever doomed, for he cannot bring Paul back to life.

"All your brains won't help you this time!" Debra Jean shouts at the mute gesticulating figure and does an angry little dance on the plush cream rug directed at the woeful figure on the screen. "And get this, Joey boy: your naive postdoc victim was the instigator of the whole shebang, with a little help from her friends at Revenge, Inc." She switches to a flamboyant jig. "Crazy Joe, crazy Joe, don't you know, don't you know ..."

She knows enough about psychiatric illness to appreciate that Joe's frenzied behavior is just the beginning of a mental transformation from which he will not soon recover. The Chinese will have their prize carefully wrapped and immobilized until needed, just as Song signaled in her message.

Sated, Debra Jean presses the mute button and breaks into hysterical laughter. "Good riddance!" She affects a rich Irish brogue: "Ah, Joey boy, we knew you so little and too long."

She reluctantly breaks off her ridiculously satisfying antics and plops down on the sofa just in time to hear a key turning in the front door lock. "Mom and Carl back from Christmas shopping, and me still in my shortie breakfast bathrobe," she thinks delightedly, smoothing the clingy silk cloth to cover her upper thighs. Not exactly the most decorous outfit in which to greet her mother's boyfriend, but perfect for her plan. She wonders how it compares with the very brief tennis skirt and T-shirt that her mother wore when she greeted Debra Jean's new boyfriend all those years ago. Maybe she will ask her mother when this is over. Maybe not.

Debra Jean watches from the living room as her mother and Carl, looking like the queen and crown prince of Prussia, enter the foyer carrying their colorfully wrapped packages. Veronica is still beautiful, and she dresses to show it. There are no residual signs of mourning or loss, but then her mother was little affected by her father's death a little over a year ago. "Of course I loved him, but there's nothing to be gained by dwelling on the death," she said brightly soon after the funeral, and proceeded to sign up for a new facelift and some touch-up body work. The unexpected return of a former lover—"Wasn't he one of your old boyfriends first, dear?"—completed the transformation from widow to happy woman.

Debra Jean wonders how her mother's defenses will hold up against the little experiment her daughter has carefully planned.

She rises to greet them as they stamp snow from their shoes, hang up their wet coats, and organize their packages of Christmas presents on the hall table. They both look surprisingly young: Mother could easily pass for Debra Jean's older sister rather than a woman in her early 60s; Carl, with his still-handsome face and graying temples, exudes vitality augmented by the subtle accoutrements of a Harvard Business School education. In the last few evenings, Debra Jean has heard too many alcohol-tinged tales of brilliant investments laced with anecdotes of fleecing competitors and stealing secrets. Her mother listens, smiling enthusiastically when he falters. All in all, her old boyfriend's life path has been remarkably faithful to the youthful ambitions he voiced so confidently at their first tryst in Harvard Square over iced tea.

Debra Jean hopes that by the late hours of this Christmas Eve, all that will matter less. She has no second thoughts about what she will do, even though years have passed since her mother took her young boyfriends into her arms. She briefly wonders about her lack of compassion. Tomorrow may bring other feelings, but now revenge will have its way. That's what matters tonight; her mother is ripe for the picking.

Akron winters come early. Her mother hates the cold and would prefer to be comfortably ensconced in her second house in Jamaica. It was Debra Jean's moving plea for a family Christmas that put off the yearly Christmas migration to the Caribbean. Her mother agreed to stay, just as Debra Jean knew she would. "What's a little cold, compared with my estranged daughter's earnest appeal for holiday reconciliation?" she said, her tone emphasizing her own sacrifice. "Carl will love it. You know, he has no children of his own. Your presence will be a blessing for him."

Debra Jean is surprised at how much the two seem to love each other, which only makes her plan that much more delicious. She sees more affection and caring between them than she ever perceived in her father and mother's union when she was a child. Carl might be gold-digging a rich widow—she assumes that he pads his boastful estimates of net wealth—but he genuinely enjoys her company and shows no signs of upset over their almost-20-year age difference. "She's everything I want," Carl told Debra Jean one evening when they were alone in the living room while her mother made dinner. She nodded her approval. Why not? It all works so well with her plan. If her mother disliked this guy, well, she'd have to come up with something else.

They are holding hands when they enter the living room. Debra Jean hugs her mother and then kisses Carl primly on the cheek, carefully holding her lower body away from his.

"That's quite an outfit," Veronica says sarcastically, appraising her daughter's scanty robe with a worried glance.

"I never got dressed after breakfast," Debra Jean replies easily. "I decided on a real lazy day. I feel so at home here, Mom. It's like old times, playing teenager, getting up late, making myself breakfast, watching

342

TV, and just fooling around. The time got away from me, mostly because I was caught up watching my old boss make a fool of himself."

"Isn't Diamond something?" Carl says jauntily. "Your mother and I heard some of it on the radio coming back from our shopping trip."

"He's a disgrace to America," Carl continues with a touch of pomposity. "The big-shot Nobel Prize winner in chemistry turns out to be just another scientist making a fool of himself. I'd bet he doesn't know his ass from his elbow in the real world of boardrooms and stock options."

"He did make a few important discoveries to get the prize, dear," Veronica says, patting him lightly on the shoulder. "That counts for something."

"Just barely." Carl places his hand over hers and squeezes. "Anyway, the Nobel isn't everything. He could still be a fraud. Look at what he did to Debra Jean. Took her work and made it his. Maybe that's what it takes to be a success in academia. I knew plenty like him when I was at Harvard. He's like all those arrogant nerds who used their fathers' money to get ahead." He turns toward Debra Jean, his gaze lingering a moment more than needed. "I mean, you know him. Aren't I right?"

She smiles at Carl but says nothing.

"Well, that's what I think. This guy sure wins the prize for acting. I don't know anything about psychology, but it looks to me as if he's hiding something behind all that blather." He turns again to Debra Jean. "You're the doctor. Is he conning us or really crazy? You knew him pretty well before he fired you. Come to think of it, he must've already been crazy to do that!"

"Thanks for the vote of confidence, Carl." Debra Jean leans forward and kisses him lightly on the cheek. "When I worked in his lab, he was horrible to me in ways I can't even describe. He was worse than mean but never crazy." She looks down at the floor and then up into Carl's eyes. "But what I saw on TV today wasn't playacting. He's psychotic, and I don't feel a bit of compassion."

Veronica grabs at Carl's hand possessively, and he hugs her to him. She looks at Debra Jean over his shoulder and then shrugs. Her disinterest in Debra Jean's expert opinions and dislike of her effect on Carl are plain. "No more serious talk," she says, and walks toward the kitchen. "It's Christmas Eve, and for once we're all together enjoying each other.

I'll get the dinner started, and then we'll settle around the fire with some drinks and maybe watch movies together." She stops. "It's been a long time since we've done that, Debra Jean. Remember how it was, dear?"

"I do, Mommy." She involuntarily moves toward her, but Veronica is already through the kitchen door.

Carl watches her disappear and moves to follow. Then he stops, takes a long look at Debra Jean, and starts back toward her. "Do you really think Diamond is crazy?"

"Yep, but I also think Mom is right. It's not a pleasant subject for a holiday night." She saunters back to the sofa, her robe riding high on her thigh. She gives her hips a little shake to return the garment to a more decorous place and looks back at Carl. "Joe did some bad things, so I guess he got what was coming to him." She sits down on the sofa. Her robe parts slightly at the upper thighs, and she waits a moment before flicking the two edges of the cloth together with her hand.

She sees that Carl is having trouble keeping his eyes off her body. "Don't worry, Carl," she says, looking him in the eye. "I'll dress for dinner."

"Hey, I'm human," he says, barely hiding his embarrassment. "It's a pleasure to see such a beautiful woman who's on her way to being my daughter-in-law. Keep that under your hat, by the way. And we do have a history, Debra Jean. I mean, there are memories ..." He laughs nervously. "We haven't talked enough since you've arrived. We should catch up. A lot's happened since Harvard Square and the Parker House."

She leans back against the sofa cushions, stretches, and smiles up at him. "You're right. We must make time for that. There's been no time for us to talk. You and Mom are pretty tight."

He shrugs. "Yes, we are tight. It's good; I like making your mom happy." He catches himself staring again. "I should get into the kitchen to see how she's doing."

"I'm sure she can use the company. Anyway, I need to take a shower and dress for dinner. And then we can all watch movies," she adds, mimicking her mother's inflections. But she doesn't move, and neither does he. He takes a step toward her. "When ... uh, when can we talk?"

She wiggles a foot at him, revealing almost everything. "Soon. Now run along, Carl, and let me dress. Mom's waiting."

He turns and disappears into the kitchen. Yes, she thinks with pleasure, this is going to go just as planned, and tonight, Christmas Eve, is the perfect night for it all to fall in place. Smiling to herself, she climbs the wide spiraling staircase to the second floor and walks down the hall to what was her childhood room. Being here again has brought up so many memories: her dad putting her to bed when she was little, talking with her about his work and his friends, and, when she was older, talking about her boyfriends or college plans. Why did he have to be away so much? she thinks angrily. Her mother never cared about any of that. No matter how much her child needed her, she just couldn't help focusing on herself. And how was DJ to make sense of that, except to take it all in and blame herself? Debra Jean got a glimpse of what was wrong with her mother when she read descriptions of the narcissistic personality disorder in DSM-IV in her psychiatry clerkship: a grandiose sense of self-importance, unempathic, a sense of entitlement, interpersonally exploitative, envious of others.

That was Mom, all right.

She knows now that Joe, who precipitated so much, was never her primary target. That is why his dramatic downfall wasn't enough. The old wounds are still leaking, so she can't let it go, let bygones be bygones, and happily join the new family that her mother and Carl are creating out of their clinging love. It would be so much easier to savor the good parts of her family, past and present, and put away the bad. That's what her mother would probably like from her and what her therapist thinks she should do. Shouldn't reconciliation trump revenge in a 21st-century America already burdened by too many wars generated from settling scores?

Great idea, but it just doesn't feel right to Debra Jean and DJ. When she told Gloria her plan after the last meeting on Wiley's barge, she was surprised and pleased that without a moment's hesitation Gloria gave her an exuberant thumbs-up. That was the kick she needed to activate all she learned in the weeks with Revenge, Inc. She knows that Gloria will tell Wiley and Dave. She wonders if they will think it's petty and regressed, given the magnitude of what they've all been through with Joe and Paul. But a mother who steals every vestige of femininity from her young daughter and then signals her triumph by sleeping with her boyfriends is a worthy target for revenge, is she not? Debra Jean hopes her heroes will understand. And if they don't, too bad. She isn't doing this for anybody but herself.

She stands quietly and listens for the sound of voices downstairs. Long practice as a child tells her that Carl and her mother are still in the kitchen. She walks quickly to her mother's room and opens the door to the walk-in closet. There are plenty of clothes she doesn't recognize— it has been years, after all—but there are also skirts and dresses she knows well from childhood. She lingers uncomfortably at the grouping of white tennis skirts and tops and running shorts just like the ones she saw scattered on the floor when she came in from shopping so many Thanksgivings ago. She moves on to find what she wants for tonight: one of those sheer, off-the-shoulder, deep-cut sexy red dresses her mother saved for the men who visited when her father was gone. She riffles through the soft fabrics and chooses the most outrageous creation. She holds it against her body and looks hard in the mirror. Close enough, she thinks. It fits well. Her mother will be envious and Carl even more turned on.

She undresses in her old room and takes the red dress as her only covering down the long hall to the bathroom. She hopes Carl will inadvertently catch a glimpse of her from downstairs, just as she had hoped her father would do in her early teens. She hangs the dress on the door and showers leisurely in the hot water. The dress's wrinkles will dissolve in the steam. Drying herself with the luxurious towels and rubbing expensive creams into her skin, she hears Carl and her mother walk past the bathroom on the way to the master bedroom. She hears the door close and again walks naked to her own room, holding the dress in her arms. Her father is dead, but Carl is just a thin door away. A perfect revenge scenario for what she wants most: to turn the tables on her mother, past and present, in the only way that will forever change the balance between them.

She dresses carefully, trying to reproduce the woman who had so attracted her own father and all the other men who had come visiting when he was gone: lots of cleavage; eyeliner, mascara, powder; and blush on her cheeks, with just a touch on her upper chest. And perfume. Dabs of perfume on her wrists and neck and nipples. Showy jewelry that catches the light and jangles.

She checks herself in the full-length mirror in the bathroom. Her reflection, made alluring by the remaining wisps of steam, shows a stunning woman dressed to attract everyman. She softens her eyes and sees her mother dressed for sexual adventure, the adulterer who neglected her, the envious Queen of the Night who stole her boyfriends and her self-esteem.

Satisfied, she walks downstairs to the now-empty kitchen. She carefully prepares the drinks that Carl and Veronica have adopted as their romantic ritual before dinner.

Sometimes, she thinks, it is handy being a physician, having access to whatever drugs she wants. Her mother's favorite Burgundy, a decent Gevrey-Chambertin, is already opened to breathe, readying for the big holiday dinner. She pours a glass for her mother and adds 7.5 milligrams of Valium. She watches the white powder quickly disappear in the deep red liquid. Then she adds 50 milligrams of finely crushed Viagra to the glass that Carl uses for his single malt and pours an ample shot of the amber liquid over the powder with water and ice, just the way he likes it. Stirring both glasses dissolves all but a faint mist of her additives, but it won't matter. They will be staring into each other's eyes when they drink, toasting their love.

Not that Carl will need erectile enhancement tonight when her mother begins to fade. Her young body, her appearance, and the situation will be more than enough to arouse him. She remembers this man's body, the part that is so predictable. Viagra will make it more difficult for him to do the right thing and resist demonstrating his continuing potency. Besides, she could use a long, lustful evening; he was a wonderful lover such a long time ago, and she might as well use his talent for her own pleasure.

Soon they will be coming down the great staircase, hand in hand, lady and lord of their kingdom. She will greet them at the landing, drinks in hand, and they will glow under her approving glance. Yes, Santa, revenge is *the* gift she wants most for Christmas, and watching Joe fall apart on TV was the perfect appetizer to the main meal. She feels the absolute rightness of what she is doing. She knows without a doubt that her mother was and still is an enemy who cannot be forgiven, only superseded. Joe, in his dark, dirty wisdom, cracked the masculine armor she had crafted for DJ's protection, leaving her as helpless and vulnerable as DJ had been, finding her beautiful Harvard man naked in her mother's arms.

Debra Jean is now in full motion. She can hardly wait for this night's events to unfold and finally free her from the maternal curse. She pours a glass of the dark, fragrant Burgundy for herself, twirling the gorgeous scarlet liquid in the deep snifter and smelling its fruit-sweet aroma. She sips the wine, and it tastes of revenge. Right now, revenge tastes like victory, and forgiveness is definitely not on the menu for tonight's salacious meal. Debra Jean and Carl, Veronica's daughter and lover, will soon revisit and enjoy each other's bodies until their flesh is wrung dry. And she will watch—Debra Jean will force that upon her—and she will be consumed by jealousy and finally know herself as a pathetic old widow coming to the end of her romance with Carl. Debra Jean wants to see that knowledge in her mother's eyes as much as she wants anything, and when she does, she will rise from the lesser passions of sex and repeat the words she first heard that lazy November afternoon so many years ago:

"If you still want him, darling, he's all yours."

ACKNOWLEDGMENTS

Revenge of the Scapegoat, the second book in the Revenge, Inc.
series, relies heavily on an informed moral compass balancing issues
of revenge and forgiveness in the scientific community. I have worked
as a scientist and been fortunate to know some of the great ones,
including Nobel Prize winners (and their take on award ceremonies,
which enters this book). Some, but not all, have affirmed the substance
of Gandhi's quote at the beginning of this book, that "knowledge
without character" and "science without humanity" are indeed social
sins. The Joe Diamonds of the world are alive and well in our academic and commercial worlds. They do great science and are praised
and gain from it. Who can stand against them? Do we even try? Well,
Wiley and Dave at Revenge, Inc. do, and I'm glad I had them around
for this book about its dark, polluting villains.

Of course, real teachers helped the most. I especially want to
acknowledge David Rioch, former director of neuropsychiatry at
Walter Reed Army Institute of Research, who helped me to navigate
the treacherous waters of scientific research during the Vietnam
War. The values he taught me then have seen me through careers in
research, psychiatry, and later spinoffs in which incredible opportu-
nities might have turned my head (and made me famous and, later,
infamous) if his wisdom hadn't prevailed. My father, Jack Colman,
became another wise and moderating influence on hubris and unwise
ambition very late in his life. John Perry and Joseph Henderson,
sometimes wise analysts and often foolish men, helped me to respect
others and trust myself in making difficult ethical and moral decisions
in my work and personal life. Friends such as Don Sandner and Steve

Vincent also shared their wisdom with me. Seeing my adult children deal with their life choices, and helping patients and advisees to struggle with theirs, has been equally important. I sometimes imagine that they are all watching over me.

The people who helped me to think deeply about *Cloud of Terns* have continued to be more than generous with *Revenge of the Scapegoat*. I'm including Paul Thomason, Andrew Moss, Jonah Colman, Jannie Quinn, Jon Greenleaf, Jay Schaefer, Robert Colman, Eliane Ubalijoro, Ruth Geos, and Douglas Armstrong here, but there are many others.

Jon Greenleaf read the manuscript and created a terrific cover from his artistic perspective. His collaboration with me has been gracious, inspiring, and above all fun.

Karen Peterson, who helped me with related websites and publicity, has also become a welcome partner in many exciting exchanges of ideas around my dining room table and computer.

Elissa Rabellino, while nursing the editing and production of Revenge, has been a resource at every level of creation, as well as a crafty poker player (her high-low betting is legendary).

Most of all, I happily acknowledge Pilar Montero, my love and partner in all endeavors. She has been an unending source of inspiration and ideas. Her deep knowledge of character and her gifts as a plotter, quite unexpected and rare, have been a wellspring during every draft. Pilar, you are mind and heart and muse for me. Best ever.

Arthur D. Colman
Sausalito, California
April 1, 2013

Arthur D. Colman is a Harvard-educated physician, psychiatrist, and author. He is currently a Jungian analyst in Sausalito, California, and professor of psychiatry at UCSF School of Medicine. *Cloud of Terns*, the first book in the Revenge, Inc. series, and his nonfiction titles, including *Earth Father/Sky Father, Up from Scapegoating: Awakening Consciousness in Groups*, and *Group Relations Reader* and *Group Relations Reader 2*, have sold more than half a million copies worldwide and have been translated into many languages, including German, Spanish, French, Portuguese, and Chinese. He has consulted on issues of scapegoating, revenge, and reconciliation in South Africa, Israel, Brazil, Mexico, Canada, and the United States. He has three grown children and five grandchildren, and lives in the San Francisco Bay Area with Pilar Montero, a psychologist and Jungian analyst.

You can learn more about Arthur D. Colman's work with scapegoating on DrScapegoat.com and about the Revenge, Inc. series on RevengeIncThrillers.com. He is working on the third book in the series, which deals with revenge in the world of music.

www.ingramcontent.com/pod-product-compliance
Lightning Source LLC
Chambersburg PA
CBHW050913250626
47155CB00001B/222